THE BITTER TRADE

The Bitter Trade is Piers Alexander's debut novel. Piers is also a serial media entrepreneur, and he lives in London with the singer-songwriter and author Rebecca Promitzer.

This paperback edition was first serialised by The Pigeonhole, an exciting new publishing company that serialises all its titles just like a TV series. There is also an audiobook edition of *The Bitter Trade* available on their site.

As a reader of taste, you are eligible for a free Pigeonhole book – just visit www.thepigeonhole.com, subscribe to a title, enter the word POKEYROLL as the discount code and get involved in a reading revolution.

THE BITTER TRADE

Being The Life Of Calumny Spinks; Heretic; Smuggler; Rebel

PIERS ALEXANDER

Tenderfoot

Second edition published by Tenderfoot, 2015

www.piersalexander.com

A CIP catalogue record for this book is available from the British Library

ISBN: 978-0-9928645-4-5

Cover design by Jessica Bell

Text design and typesetting by The Curved House

Printed and bound in Great Britain by Clays Ltd, St Ives PLC

For Rebecca

And with huge thanks to Matthew Bates

England, 1688.

It is nearly forty years since Cromwell overthrew King Charles I. Though the monarchy was restored in 1660, the country is still in religious and political turmoil. Catholic and unpopular, the new King James II seeks an alliance with Nonconformist Protestants by issuing the Declaration of Indulgence, allowing Dissenters to worship freely after years of repression. Powerful aristocrats have begun to plot against the king, and now the Dutch ruler, William of Orange, threatens to invade and claim the throne.

I am Calumny Spinks.

Between me and the satin-blue sky hangs the hempen noose.

It has swung there in the faintest of breezes, waiting for me, all my life.

CHAPTER ONE

Salstead

In which Calumny Spinks
carelessly provokes Mistress Ramage

I was born to a raging Frenchy slugabed mother, sired by a sulking silk-weaver with a battered box of secrets under his floorboards. From her I got my flaming hair, so red that the scabfaced villagers of Salstead spoke of the Devil's seed, spitting in the dust for salvation when I walked past. From my father came my sharp tongue, the quick wit to talk above my station, and the shoulders to take the blows that followed.

I was the lowest fellow in Salstead. I had to greet men by "Master This" and "Mister That", thumbing my forelock. To them I was but "Boy", a long-limbed red-haired Frenchy gawk, spinning and twisting silk like a halfwit.

The goodwives laughed behind their tippets when they passed me at the wayside, where my father Peter made me sit outside to work. "The silk must be spun in the fresh air, but woven in the dry dark," he said. If he had his will, I would rot in that village like Squire Salstead, whose bones hung in the rusty gibbet at the crossroads.

I should have been in London, not in this Essex midden swirling with pigeon-chest men and their gossiping dry-venus wives. I was no fighter, could not read or write; but by Christ I had the smooth tongue to fool any man. And so I dreamed of becoming a city gentleman by the power of my own wit. But London was a forbidden, fading memory: of dazzling lights, the broad river bristling with sails, of laughter and scented wealth.

We once had land-title in the city, so my father was known as Mister Peter Spinks then. But he weakly let merchants cheat him from his property and his title, and now he was merely a craftsman.

My own apprenticeship had been delayed so long that in almost three months, on my seventeenth birthday, I would lose the right to learn my craft and be called "Master". And without a trade I would never have the coin to buy my own land-title, to rise up and become Mister Calumny Spinks.

The night before Peter denied me my craft, the rain crushed the slender grass-stems outside my window. For a short while, I watched the fierce dawn make steam swirl from the ground, then went down into the dim workshop. I was hungry, and I had not tasted meat since the spring.

Peter had been at work since before sunrise. Silk weaving paid less each year, and there had been no silver in our house for many a month, only copper coins, their edges jaggedly clipped by thieving merchants.

I stared at my father between the warp-threads: his long white hair split in the middle and curled inwards to his shoulders, its ends stained yellow from years of weaving-sweat. Though his neck was humbly bent, his back was pike-straight as he sat on a crossbar, his feet on the long slim treadles. He let his fingers see for him in the dark, always flitting back and forth along the weft to pull out flecks of dirt. At night the whole house was filled with his dingy smell, waking me as it rose up through my little coffin-room.

Peter was reaching the end of a fathom-bolt of silk. It crept across the frame and slid sullenly over the rolling-bar in front of my thighs. Like a man taking honey from a bees' nest, he reached up and slackened the nuts that held the warp. Then he ran his cutting blade along the trailing threads, a steel butterfly's wing clenched between scarred thumb and liver-spotted forefinger. Taking care to hold the finished silk as it was cut away, he swept the bolt into neat folds in the wicker trough.

Leaning my head against the low wormy joists, I cleared my throat.

"Shall we thread the headboards? Will you show me?"

"It is forbidden by the guild law," he snapped.

"Then let me be apprenticed!" The squeaking in my voice shamed me.

My father reached down into the round basket that held the silk. He pulled a thread out, running his thumb and forefinger along it, trying to fault my work. Cack-fingered potrillo, his weaving had more flaws even than my throwing.

"Calumny, you cannot be apprenticed until we have it written in the London guild-book. Should I carve the law on the eating-table?"

"And how would I read the words?" I mumbled, picking up my other work-basket and stalking out of the front door. How indeed, when he had denied me the learning?

I was too afraid of him to say it out loud: that by Saint Matthew's Day, the twenty-first of September, it would be too late. I'd be condemned to a life of servitude or thieving.

I sighed and put the silk-basket down next to my stool, sitting with my back against the ill-made house. Its clay daub was so watered-down that it would have fallen off if it were not held up by dark oily vines. Behind the house, marshy ground sucked the walls slowly backwards, making the windows gape in winter. It was much like my God-fool father: more than sixty years old, but too stubborn to die.

Combing and sorting the waste silk was the worst task of all.

My hands and forearms were patterned with scars from the sharp husks. I took a handful of silk waste and began plucking out twigs and cocoon-pieces, ignoring the sting of scabs opening up. Then I began to comb gently, twisting the loose ends into threads around my distaff.

I thought of Sarah, the field-girl of two summers before. I had plunged my fingers into her hair's feathery softness, soothing my skin as she bucked and panted to the beat of the harvest-fair drum, her lips brushing mine like a cloudburst. What I learned from her I had already shared with two village goodwives in the lee of the church. A married woman will not fear to be got with child, and so may be more easily bedded.

And then there was Agnes Perment in the chestnut-glade, kissing and teasing with her knees clamped tight against me. Sweat broke on my forehead.

*

Peter's ghostly voice crackled suddenly just behind me.

"I go to London today," he said, gazing at the diseased pear orchard behind the house. He had put on a knee-length overcoat and a pair of boots with empty spur-holes. The overcoat's ancient wool had faded to ash-grey except for a dusky line that ran crosswise from his left shoulder to his right hip. His brows looked fiercer and darker under his flat-brimmed Puritan's hat.

"Then my name can go in the guild-book!" I burst out. At last I could take the first step on the road to becoming Mister Calumny Spinks.

Peter ticked his tongue against his teeth.

"London is hell," he said. "In that city of thieves they will hang you for a drop of French blood or a prayer said wrong. And... Well, you know that the deeds to our home were taken from us by, godless merchants and money-men after the Plague and Fire. May the Devil take those who put coin before honest labour –"

"But how did they –"

"Hold your tongue, lad!" snapped my father. He never would let me ask how he, Mister Spinks, lost his property and became a penniless Salstead weaver.

"You cannot come with me, Calumny. That is my word. And your mother..."

His eyes drooped like a dotard dog's. I knew what he meant. *Your mother's chest is so weak – she has no joy in life but you...*

"But it is only for a day or two," I protested. "Since I am to be apprenticed, you could already teach me to read and write."

Peter snorted. "Reading and writing will do you nought but ill in a place like that."

As he squinted, the wrinkles on his pale face knitted closer together. Suspicious, I persisted.

"At least say that you will write my name in the book –"

"In God's name, boy, know your place!"

"My place is in London, but you lost it!"

Peter struck out, catching my nose so hard that it bled great gobs down my shirt. I did not cry out, but nor did I have the courage to speak back as he limped his way up the lane towards the London road, shaking his head. I knew that stubborn back better than his face, so often did he spurn my wants.

Jesus Satan, I thought, must I sit all my life on a stool spinning thread like a girl, and all because of my pig-headed father and crack-chested mother? London was not twenty miles from Salstead, but if I let him go without me this time, I would be stuck here for the rest of my days.

And I wanted more than my apprenticeship. I wanted to follow my father in his true craft. For Peter was no weaver. Despite his limp, his ashen wrinkled face and rounded shoulders, he stood like a soldier, and by God he could strike like one too. I wanted to know why he never spoke of that past, and so I followed him.

When I caught up with Peter, he had stopped at the flaky iron gibbet, drinking from a flask as he stared at the skeleton hanging in its rusty chains. The skull had been eaten away to the bone, save for a few mangy scraps of hair that clung to the crown. Its hollow sockets looked down at the dusty soil. A little dry circle of morning sky showed through the gaping jaw and the eyehole above it. I could not help but touch my own chin, my tongue, my eyelid, to be sure the flesh still clung there.

Three years dead now, Squire Salstead had been a Dissenter who joined the rebellion against the new Catholic king, James, but was captured and given to his village to be punished. It was a scolding, such as you might give a sharp-tongued goodwife or a thieving tinker; but instead of ducking the rebel in the pond, they chained him in the gibbet and pelted him with stones and knives and dung, all the while banging their pots and pans, shrieking to high heaven. The wilder fieldsmen took their pitch-forks and wrenched at his guts and hamstrings. Then the sheep farmer, a newcomer called Sand, turned his vicious eyes on my mother, Mirella, calling her a traitor for her Frenchy blood. Before the violence could turn to her, we fled into the woods, but the screaming kept pace with us all the way.

The squire was not dead when we came back past the gibbet at nightfall. He moaned through the night, thrashing about weakly, barely a stone's throw from my bed. When he at last died in the heat of the day, they left him to rot.

Pain beat out its rhythm in my bloody nose as I gathered up my courage to speak, desperate for him to give me my trade.

"Father –" I began.

"They put a popish whore on the throne," whispered Peter, sunlight glaring on his eyeballs, "after a hundred thousand died to keep this country free of Rome. And then when honest men took arms against him, they murdered them at the scaffold, every blessed one of them."

He lifted the flask to his lips again. Gin fumes stung the air, and I thought bitterly of how much mutton he could have bought for the cost of it. He jerked his head at the corpse.

"That man was an elder at my old meeting-house, know you that?"

"Father, you must not speak of that! Mother says –"

"If I wish to speak of my meeting-house, I will. My goodwife thinks I should pretend I never was a Dissenter. But –"

He paused to catch his breath.

"Half the cowards in Salstead went to my meeting-house before they turned it into a church! You were too young to remember it. They raised the preacher above the people, they put in a Communion rail, they raised a graven image to worship. The Church of England, so they call it. Some English Church, when its head is a Scottish Catholic whore!"

I tried to shush him, for his voice was rising loud enough to be heard from the nearest houses now. He raised his hand to strike me again, but he was too much in his cups. He swung wildly in the air and had to catch at the gibbet to break his fall, swinging just above the ground beneath the cage. The dead man's jaw fell open, dropping a fistful of bone-shards onto my father's head.

He brushed it off like it was barley flour.

"Stay where you are told. And trust no one," ordered Peter, getting to his feet. He tramped on alone for the London road, leaving me with the skeleton. Barely thirty years the squire had lived before they ripped the life from him.

Old fool, to risk his skin for his faith while his own wife and son starved. I swore then that I would never put another man's cause before my own. Coin, women, title: they would be my religion.

From the gibbet, the high-walled path looped towards the village, with the church spire glowering over the graveyard to my left.

The granite wall on my right was newer, barely four summers old. Pigs and sheep had once grazed in the fields behind it, the meat and milk fed the poorer craftsmen of Salstead, but the sexton Ramage had enclosed all the common lands. Now they were ploughed and reaped by hired men from Norfolk. Since then, many right-thinking Salsteaders had packed up their carts and handed over their cottages to sour-faced Church of England folk, with their miserable wives and monstrous boil-ridden brats.

Boots tittled their way up the lane: Mistress Ramage and Mistress Sand, the gossip-judges of Salstead. Quickly I stilled the squeaking gibbet.

"Boy, your father's drunken shouting shames the village. And you must not touch the blasphemer," hissed Mistress Ramage.

Her pale skin was drawn in tight ridges over her forehead and cheekbones, and beetle-leg hairs peeped out from under her plain snowy cuffs. She wore a fine Flemish lace scarf over her lank thundercloud hair. It was she who had condemned the squire to his vicious death, and I had not forgotten her shrieking face as she flung stones at him.

"...touch," echoed Mistress Sand, a soft-willed booby who followed Mistress Ramage everywhere. I liked her face well enough, her big eyes wide and childlike in her clear-skinned face, her gentle curving hair peeping out from a little teasing bonnet. She had a taste for frills and bows, but Mister Sand, her husband, was the villain who had called my mother a traitor at the scolding. I thought I might put the horns on him for revenge.

I kept my bony backside on the milestone, turned with what dignity I could hold, and looked them up and down. Ramage turned her bird-head away, but Sand looked down, and then up again, blushing a little. I draped my gaze around her like a sweaty arm.

"It is my Christian duty to pray for the dead," I announced in the marbly voice of Cowans the rector. Sand looked behind her, as if the preacher himself stood in the road.

This mimicking of mine had fetched me many a blow from my father. I could make the voice, the face, the walk, of any man alive. I could give a husband's command so well that his wife would throw a purse of coins out of her window at midnight.

But my father told me my mimicry was Satan's gift – and now, I had mocked Salstead's foremost wife with it. I cursed myself as Mistress Ramage clenched her fists, making her goatskin gloves squeak.

"This is no Christian carcass. This is a devil who raised a sword against the king."

"Raised sword," whispered Sand, pushing out her chest and making an eyelash-butterfly to hide how she stared at my lips. For though I wore the Devil's hair, I was taller and broader than most men in Salstead, and my Frenchy mouth bewitched their wives.

My father's rage filled me. I wanted to sting these women. I took a careless step towards them, wiping down the nose-blood that stained my shirt. Mistress Ramage had to back away to avoid my touch.

"It is my Christian duty," I said brazenly, "to gaze upon this poor wretch and consider what should be my path in this world. For we may all be tempted, may we not, Mistress Sand?"

She blushed violet-red and looked to Mistress Ramage.

"Even Mister Ramage, when he is not chipping away at a coffin lid, he may be tempted, and it is a sign of his Christian nature that he has not turned away from true marriage with you, Mistress Ramage."

Her eyes went in different directions as she searched for my insult. She did not find it.

"And so I am inspired by this man who did not believe the king was chosen by God…"

"Ahhhh," hissed Ramage, believing she had caught me.

"…for we must be humble in the knowledge that even our Saviour was tempted by the Devil."

This rubbish I remembered from Mister Cowans' sermon the Sunday before. Ramage pointed a finger at me.

"Insolence! Your father is a drunkard and your mother is a Sabbath-breaker. Remember you, Calumny Spinks, who is godly in this village and who is not. Or this devil here will not be the last heretic to hang in Salstead!"

"Mistress!"

It was my mother. Her voice was tinged with breathy fear as she hurried up the twitchell towards us. Mistress Ramage muttered a prayer but waited for Mirella to come closer.

"Your buttons, I have them, mistress…"

Ramage held out her hand. Careful not to touch flesh, my mother placed a few buttons in the palm, carefully wrapped in deep pink thread. They looked like rose-petals. I looked away, shamed by my family's lowness, and made a play of staring at the delicately engraved silver locket that sat pertly on Mistress Sand's flushed chest. Nervy, she twisted it in her fingers, and I watched the sweat-mist melt from its burnished skin.

"Penny-farthing, I pray you –" began my mother.

"Boy, tell this woman that I do not make commerce on the road like a beggar. Else punishment will fall on you both," said Ramage without meeting Mirella's eye. She closed her dry fingers on the button and turned away.

"God willing, I will see you in the church… yard," I teased Mistress Sand.

Not sure if she should tut at me or wiggle her apple backside, she did both as she followed Mistress Ramage to the village. Swishy tut, swooshy tut, like a robin's mating dance.

Turning my back to Mirella, I picked away at the rusty cage until I caught a sharp flake under my nail.

"Touch not, idiot," she buzzed, her Frenchy voice all scratched up from years of yelling at Peter.

I made a pinched face, pulling the rust from my bleeding thumb.

"Oh Calonnie, my little…"

At last she saw my puffed-up nose, and tried her best to clean my face, her fingertips flat and rough from holding the darning needle. She was so forengie, my mother. After twenty years, she still stood out in Salstead, like blood on lace. I pulled her hand off my face. Mistress Ramage's threat had stuck in my gut. Those women and their money-hungry husbands had murdered for land before, and they would think little of hurting an ancient Dissenter and his heretic wife.

"Why do you let Peter leave me in this shitpump place, to go to London without me?"

"You are to call him by 'Father', not that name." Her breath whistled like a dying man's.

"I will go to the city by myself," I said roughly.

"In London they will do this to you too!" she screeched, her eyes bulging wildly as she pointed at the gibbet.

"It would be a mercy," I said cruelly.

"Oh, you are an ignorant like your father."

"London is my place!" I shouted at her. "And we cannot go because we must stay here and look after you. We must sit and gather mould in Salstead!"

"I too want to be in London as it was promised me," she replied. "I want not to be in Salstead. But your father…"

I let my tears flow, for I knew it would sway her.

"Can you not give me leave to follow him? Must I stay here and have them spit when I pass?"

"Well. One day you shall go to London again, as you did when you had five years. He will write your name in the book," she said, walking weakly back towards our house. I ran after her and took her arm. I did not believe her fully, but she had given me a taste of hope.

Five years old. Now I remembered it a little. Climbing on Peter's horse behind him. The great houses, lanterns and candles and fires everywhere, and sails taller than churches rising up behind the streets. The floating petticoats, the hammering of craft and the tinkling of coin…

Mirella wheezed, and I clenched her arm to hide my fear of her sickness, hearing Mistress Ramage's voice again.

This devil here will not be the last heretic to hang in Salstead!

Did she mean my father?

I thought of the dying man rattling his chains. Of Peter in that cage.

CHAPTER TWO

The Mercer

In which Calumny's path is barred once more

It was many long days before Peter returned. I slept but raggedly in my little coffin-room, plagued by the buzzing of bluebottles. The third day was Sunday, and I went to church while Mirella prayed alone at home. The rector, Mister Cowans, seemed to her too Romish with his incense and chanting, and she would not go.

To tell true, it was a relief to go to worship without my troublemaking father. The year before, Peter had made a great nuisance of himself in the congregation, for he had heard that the king had made a Declaration that Dissenters and Catholics could worship freely again. Gin-foolish, my father had stood in the tavern on a Saturday night and boldly asked if any free-thinking men had heard the Declaration. Since that day, most of the villagers had been cold towards him: words were no protection against a landlord. And still Cowans had not read the Declaration in church.

Hours before the worship, I let myself quietly into the church, hoping to catch Rachel Cowans alone. Though her father the rector was a pudding-faced potrillo, he was a man of property, and his daughter's husband would be a Mister too. I did not mind that she had never given me a kind word. A kiss and a pokey-roll would be enough to force the wedding.

But the church was empty. I sat down in our craft-pew, far from the pulpit, which we shared with the stone-mason's family. The pews lining the sides of the church were each enclosed with waist-high wooden walls, while the lower people sat on the benches in the middle.

I scratched myself and listened for Rachel's voice, thinking of slipping off her lace cap and pressing my nose into the fair hair that gathered at her nape. Though she was cat-vicious in her words, I had felt her gaze at worship, and knew she was there to be taken. But the only sound was the murmuring of Cowans and Ramage, sitting above me in the counting-room. The sexton owned half of Salstead, and he paid the priest his wages, more than a pound a week.

Footsteps creaked as a man walked over my head to the steep wooden stairway in the vestry at the side of the church. Ramage spoke, his voice echoing clearly down towards me. From where he stood, he could not see that there was someone in the nave, so his words were unguarded.

"You cannot read the Declaration here," he said bluntly, as if he tried to put an end to a long argument between him and Cowans. "I will tell you how it is, *Mister* Cowans. If you allow this, then there are four-dozen heretics still in Salstead who will no longer come to the church or pay their tithes. They may even become bold enough to refuse their rents."

I held my breath in the chilly silence that followed: it would go ill if they knew I'd heard them. No rents would mean the end of Ramage, and of the priest's easy living too. When they began talking again, I dashed to the great doors and squeezed through, careful not to let them creak.

I ran straight into Douglas Perment, the stonemason's son, who had been my friend until he caught me lifting his sister Agnes' dress last Michaelmas. He opened his mouth to ask my business, but I seized him by the arm and led him quickly around the church. His father, gentle Jarvis, had the claw-finger and could barely hold a hammer, so Douglas had the running of his workshop now, though he was but a year or two older than me.

I dragged him behind the knight's tomb and sat on the low stone step on the far side, out of sight of the church and lane. I found that my chest was heaving.

"Put your face in your shirt, Cal," Douglas said as he sat beside me, his Scots accent softened by Essex living. "Slowly does it."

His father had left Scotland a few years before, hoping to find work in London, but the guilds took ill to Jarvis' Celtic race and would not let him work. A Dissenter like my father, he had found his way to Salstead, which in those days was a gathering place for right-thinking men.

"Put your face in your shirt…" I murmured, rolling the words around my mouth in the Scotch manner. Douglas began to chuckle, but frowned and squeezed my leg to make me stop, his hammer-headed fingertips bruising my unfed flesh.

"What d'you do there, Cal, running from the kirk?" he asked, and I told him what Ramage and Cowans had said.

At the end he nodded and looked down, picking at the dead skin on the heels of his palms.

"Ah, there's little enough they can do if your father takes care. That Mister Ramage might think to put up the rents, but he'll find no more tenants in this God-forsaken place," said Douglas, leaning back against the grave.

"God-forsaken it is," I blurted out. "Will you not lend me a shilling to follow my father to London?"

His face darkened. "You know full well I must husband my coin, since I am the one to feed my family. And I have not forgot that you have tainted Agnes –"

"I did not..." I protested. There is the taint that fills a womb, and the taint that does not.

Douglas stood, and flicked his dusty hands to bid me rise. "There is work in Salstead, Cal. Work is God's desire for us. And a shilling will do you no good. Even if you pass the pickets without apprentice-papers, it costs you four-pence but to breathe in that foul city."

He was right. I stood helplessly as he walked away. Douglas had been my only friend, now that many of the right-thinking families had left, and I had lost him to his duty. And to an afternoon's frolic with his lusty sister.

I left the churchyard and went to sit at the waymark until the bells rang. Mister Ramage was stood at the church door with his list.

"Calumny Spinks," he said, narrowing his eyes as he made a mark by my name. Behind me, a gaggle of youths sniggered, newcomers in smug lace collars who read books of law in their brick-built houses.

"Good churchwarden, will you mark by my father's name that he is in London and will worship there?"

"In what manner of place?" demanded Ramage harshly. "A heretical –"

He stopped ranting as Cowans appeared behind him and muttered in his ear. Grudgingly, the sexton made a little mark on his list and nodded at me to go inside.

The days ground on. When I was not working, I mooned around by the London road, dreaming that Peter had got our land-title back.

The next Saturday was stifling hot, but I still had half a basket of thread to throw. The late June sun beat down, my shoulders burned, and the sweat made angry pools in my tear-buds until I could barely see.

"*Calonnie, mon chou...*" said my mother, and I turned to look at her in the doorway, blinking her watery eyes in the harsh light. She struggled to breathe and sleep when the summer blossoms were out, but when she smiled at me, her worry lines smoothed out. Though her freckled face was not beautiful, there was craftsmanship in its shaping. Her grass-green eyes were set wide apart, and her teeth were almost white even though she neared forty years of age. Her red hair was long and rich behind, but chopped messily on the top where she had cut it with her own tailor-shears. Her ribbon-laced boots were now bound with twine.

To be called a cabbage is not a manly thing, but I let it pass, remembering that Mirella's brother had died as a boy. When Peter took them both from France, he hid her in the high crow's-nest of the sailing ship, but put my uncle Jean-Pierre in a barrel in the hold because the boy feared heights. Well, the popish vermin of the French army were hell-bent on stopping any Huguenots leaving France alive, and so they sealed up the hold while the ship was still in port. They blew smoke into it until the rats and stowaways had all choked to death. It filled the ship so thick that Mirella nearly died herself; her tongue was stained black for a year, and her chest ruined forever by the ashes that had settled in it.

"My father, while he lived…" she began, but fell silent. Though I could not wait to leave Salstead, I would miss her tales if I went. Peter would always grumble at them. I could not reckon how they chose each other, the silent stone and the flickering flame.

"While he lived…" I said after a while.

"He heard a Turk in Strasbourg speak of Persian silk, ported on camels across the deserts and mountains to Stamboul." She spoke quietly now, as if she told the secret of Christ's resurrection. "They bring it in *cocons.* And no man has managed to bring the cocoon-silk to Paris or London. Whoever can do it will be able to draw the silk thread at half the price. And there is a prophecy, that a red-headed man with the gift of tongues, born on the feast-day of Saint Matthew…"

Mirella looked at me with one eyebrow raised, and we both burst out laughing. That was how all her stories ended. A red-headed French mimic becoming the richest man in Europe. Though they were only tales, I held a secret dream that there was truth in them. That I might have my own coin. Land-title. The name of Mister.

But it was an empty hope. All the other young fellows in Salstead were properly apprenticed, and after three years they would be free to become journeymen, to travel around learning their craft. I was the only fool to be his father's slave.

I could not even read or write. Mirella often complained at Peter, and told him he should teach me the letters, but he would not have it, saying that there was too much work for me to do without being confused by learning. She would complain out in front of the house where the village could hear her shouting, and he hated to be shamed in that way. Though he would not strike her like the other men did their wives.

In a fury now, I began throwing the thread again, ignoring my mother. After a while, she said gently, "Calonnie, you will be *apprenti* –"

I spat on the ground and finished my throwing. After a while, Mirella began to wilt in the midday heat and went inside to sleep. So weak, my mother, and her sickness was a heavy chain that bound me to that house.

I coiled the last cords carefully onto the lace basket-covering, took the silk inside to stop it from fading in the sun, and made for the London road, grateful for the low-hanging beech branches that shaded the lane.

I walked to the clearing where carters camped overnight. I had found myself a perch on a bough above the roadway; there I would watch the world pass by from above. Each cart and coach, every trudging hawker, told me that I would never leave Salstead, never be called to London for my fortune. I curled myself into the hollow where my bough met the beech tree's trunk, and dozed as hooves and wheels and booted feet crackled over the stony road below.

I was woken by laughter – the first joyful noise I had heard in a long time. It came from a high-sided wagon a hundred paces away, drawn by a single horse and neatly stacked with cloth-covered baskets. Two men sat on the driving seat – one big and broad-headed, waving one arm about. The other had white hair and a neck that was bent with age, but his mouth was wide open with laughter. It was my father – a man who believed God should be worshipped with a frown – making merry with a stranger. Bile stirred unquietly in my empty guts.

The wagon drew closer, and now it was the big man's turn to laugh at something Peter said. The horse tossed his head and pranced, annoyed by the noise.

"*Pssh, Cucullan, mon garçon,*" the driver told the animal, who tossed his head again.

"*Bête de bon esprit,*" said my father, praising the horse in his grinding English accent. To hear him laugh and speak French in one day was too much.

The wagon drew closer to my branch. Peter's hat lay on the driving seat next to him, and he had tied his hair in a bunch at the back of his head so that he looked closer to forty years of age than sixty. His collar was open, he had one foot up on the driving-board, and he was cutting apple slices to share them with the driver.

The Frenchman was young enough to have been Peter's son, though still old enough to be my father. His broad head and neck were weathered, his nose and chin bullish, but his long-lashed eyes were soft as a doe's. Long wavy hair poured back from his high forehead, and I supposed that a woman might have thought him handsome, with his slow smile and tuneful voice.

His sleeveless waistcoat was the dim colour of ivy in winter, set with cream-trimmed frogging from neck to balls, and he wore bright bunches of ribbons at his shoulders. His forearms, hairy as a wolfhound's hide, did not pimple in the cool wind.

The wagon slowed in the clearing below me as the two men ate the fruit. Unseen, I peered at the baskets in the back. There were eight of them, their velvety black covers hinting at fine wares beneath. But did not Peter loathe merchants?

The Frenchman crunched on an apple. Well, I thought, I am too hungry to sit and watch these fools eat. Let us have some sport with the old man.

I slid off the branch and landed on one of the covered baskets.

"Excise!" I snapped, in the dry twiggy voice of the county tax-collector. "Reveal your wares!"

Quick as an adder, Peter turned, grabbed me by the shirt-front and pulled me across the seat, his knife at my throat. With a blink, he saw who it was, frowned and muttered, "*Mon fils*," to his companion. My son. My heart pumping, I wondered how close he'd come to cutting me open.

The Frenchman laughed and took away Peter's blade, still wet with apple juice. He wiped the knifelet on his arm and threw it in my father's lap, all the while keeping his other hand heavily on my chest so he could have a look at me.

"*Malin, le bonhomme*," the merchant chuckled, praising my wit.

"*Malin, le bonhomme*," I said in his own tuneful voice, and he gave me a look of surprise.

Peter, shamed by my mimicking, raised a hand to strike me. "Satan's work!"

"Say him again," commanded the merchant, staying my father's hand. Like all Frenchies, he could not make the English words march in line. They danced into each other like drunken fairies. "Say my words to me."

I said it again, in his voice, perfectly. I made my body a reflection of his, copying the way he tilted his neck, how he stuck his feet right out over the driving-board.

"How are you called, brother?" he asked. Well, to be called "Brother" instead of "Boy" was a gentle feeling for me. I waited for my father to answer, but he remained silent, so I gave the Frenchman my name.

"Your father has spoken many times of you." He nodded, his wavy fringe dropping into his eyes. "I am called Garric Pettit. And this beast is Cucullan." He pointed at the horse, now trudging slowly onwards.

Thoughts plashed in the muddy waters of my mind. Why had my father told this man about me? Why was he so friendly with a merchant, and what had they been doing in the city together? Peter's jaw was set and his eyes looked forward, ignoring me as he always did.

"*Puis-je?*" I asked Garric politely, pointing at his wares. He shrugged and raised an eyebrow. I leaned back and plucked the cover off the nearest basket to show a pile of folded silk sheets of different finishes.

Feeling each in turn, I murmured, "Damask... crepe... watered satin..."

"How tell you the names of the silks?" the merchant asked me, more quietly.

"My mother," I said shortly, and twitched away the cover of another basket. It was the richest piece I'd ever seen: a corseted gentlewoman's dress of burgundy brocade, decorated with lilies and dragonflies. The gold stitching flickered in the dappled light. I would have wagered that it was worth more than my father's house and loom, and the three of our lives too.

Peter's gnarly fingers clamped into the soft flesh above my elbow, making me let go of the brocade. Garric swiftly covered the basket back up, tucking the damask in so that not an inch of gold thread showed.

"Keep your hands to yourself," snapped my father, "and ask Master Pettit's pardon."

"Are you apprenticed, Calumny Spinks?" asked Garric quickly.

I bowed my head. "I serve my father."

"But learn you the craft, the weaving?"

I shrugged instead of saying no. I had no craft but to spin and gossip like a woman. I had no reading or writing. I was nothing.

"Yet you are seventeen...?"

"On Saint Matthew's Day."

Garric clapped his hands.

"Then we have little time, my brave! You should be in London, not in a field with the geese and cows. The good God knows there is trade enough for a tongue-adroit like you. I will apprentice you to myself if your father will agree it…"

Peter leaned across me, grabbed the reins and pulled until the horse pranced to a standstill.

"Enough of this, we have business to speak of. Calumny, you shall walk home," he said firmly.

"*Mais* –" protested Garric.

"Let him walk," insisted Peter, turning his face back to the road.

I had barely touched the ground before my father flicked the reins again. He drove the horse faster than Garric had, but the road went a long way round before going down the hill towards our house, and I knew I could get there before them if I took the other path. I needed to know why my father was being so pigheaded. He should have been pleased that Garric offered to apprentice me – it would save him the trouble of teaching and feeding me.

I ran to the wood's edge and scrambled down through the spiky gorse bushes to the graveyard, then stumbled through the tombs towards the crossroads and hid, waiting for the wagon to arrive.

The church walls loomed like a hanging-judge's shoulders over the graves behind me. Life was so short. Sixteen years of my time had passed in spinning and making foolish voices, and I doubted that I had much more than another twenty granted to me. I would make the Frenchman take me back with him.

The village looked like a toy dropped by a careless brat, the houses all higgle-piggle. Roofs were freshly thatched, and a stranger might have thought Salstead a pretty place. But it was filled with sharp-nosed, dead-eyed people, a suspicious wart on the old soft skin of the world.

When I was a boy, children ran through the houses, tumbling over roosters and piglets, laughing and crying to the skies. The enclosures had killed that old Salstead. No more grazing for the beasts, no windfall fruit for the hungry children, no more young mothers.

London was hell, Peter had said. Well, so too was Salstead. I would not wait uncomplaining like a sheep at feast-time, waiting for my throat to be cut by Mistress Ramage and her ilk. Garric Pettit the silk merchant would be my way to London, I was sure of it.

The wagon rattled down the narrow lane and halted before the gibbet. I hid and watched Peter climb down from the other side of the wagon. He turned and spoke, cold-eyed, to Garric.

"Take your wagon away from my house and stay on the London road. There is passing trade enough for you up there. I will give you my reply tomorrow, after the Sabbath worship. Speak to no man in Salstead."

"You must come," said Garric. "If we do not bring the English and Huguenot guildsmen together before winter, the Catholics will rule all. It must be you, Peter Spinks. You know why. Think on my offer."

My father took a step closer and whispered, "Calumny must stay here. The boy cannot read or write. He cannot count coin. He is no mercer's apprentice."

"Then why did you come to the House, if not to give him the craft?" asked the mercer. "The boy could learn much in the city, and it is plain that he desires it."

Peter reached up and seized Garric's arm. "If you use the boy against me, I shall refuse."

Garric's face was turned towards me, and I watched as rage banished the cheerful smile from his face. He took a breath, uncurled my father's fingers from his sleeve, and flicked the reins.

My father stared after the mercer as he drove towards the tavern, biting his lumpy nails to the quick.

I stayed behind the wall, watching him. Hating him.

After a while, Mirella came out of our house. She stood just before the doorway and stretched her arms up to the sky, embracing the cool clouds that made her breathe easily. Peter came to her, and she laid a hand gently on his shoulder, asking a question.

My father did not leave off his nail-biting. She stood before him, arms on hips, and asked it again. Peter mumbled that he had not found an apprenticeship for me, not looking my mother in the eye.

She fell into a fury, screeching at him in her mad-woman's English, pulling at her own hair and cursing him for a stubborn fool. He did not protest, but stood there looking at his gnarly hands while she ranted.

Shaking my head to shut out Mirella's shrieking, I crept back through the graves to the church, hoping to catch Garric Pettit. This was my last chance to be apprenticed, but Peter had refused the Frenchman's offer – had lied to Mirella about it. If I did not leave with Garric, I'd be my father's slave; but he would not take me without my father agreeing to come too. So what was this House he had spoken of; what offer had he made, and why did Peter refuse it?

Mister Cowans stood at the church door with his arms crossed, looking up at the sky as if he asked for rain. It was his habit to stand there every day, frowning, for what has a priest to do between Monday and Saturday but watch the sky and make trouble for his congregation? I touched my chest in greeting as I passed him.

Sexton Ramage came out of his house, the closest one to the church. He shuddered to see me, spat and went indoors again. *Mister* Ramage. He was no gentleman before he came to Salstead, only a ham-fisted carpenter from the Southwark marshes. But the Church gave him his lands cheaply, and now he could lord it above true craftsmen like my father.

I followed the lane as it wound left around the church wall, then curved the other way up to the brow of the hill. It skirted the pond where the drovers watered their sheep, a slippery-sided pit that was foul with the beasts' piss. Beyond it slumped the Salstead Arms, little more than a dark and smelly, horsehair-plastered room where spiteful men slurped weak ale.

Garric was not there. He must have taken the overgrown, rutted track that ran past the tavern to the London road. I stood on the green, unsure whether to defy my father and follow.

Shadows sharpened as the sun scalded its way through the clouds. It was not yet harvest-time, and the village sulked in silence, broken only by the sour murmurs of the thatcher, who worked alone on the tavern roof.

To live in London. To have property, a name. To be Mister.

I wanted it all so much that I could not bear to hear Peter deny it me. Not to be Garric's apprentice, but to spin and moulder here until I was crippled and bitter like my father.

I could run, I thought. Take the old lane and find Garric. Tell him Peter said that I could go.

But I knew enough of the Frenchman already to see that he would not let a lie fly past him so, nor would he take me without my father agreeing to his proposal. And he knew I could not read or write.

Three youths came out of the tavern. It was hardly noon, but they were in their drink already, and the fellow in the middle was being carried by the others. He was the son of Ramage's bailiff, a straw-haired clodpoll who never gave me good day. He pushed himself off the shoulders of his friends and spat at my feet, making a clumsy evil eye against me and my red hair.

I gave them my Satan-face, my tongue pushed out pointy and my eyes bulging big in their sockets. Every young man in the village had his hot eyes on Agnes Perment, but I was the only one to have touched her taut belly on a spring night.

"Son of a French whore," said Thomas Boulter, the bailiff's spawn, making a basket of his hands and thrusting his groin at it.

Well, I had not the skill to fight three lads. I stood with my hands on my hips, my face bright red, snorting like a spent horse but afraid to strike. They laughed and pushed me roughly away from the tavern, aiming kicks at my legs until I ran for home.

Sick mother or no, I would not spend another day in this place. If Peter refused Garric on Sunday, I'd follow the Frenchman to London.

CHAPTER THREE

Past Due

In which Calumny unearths a long-held secret

I dreamed I was lying naked on a muddy hillside, holding the thinnest thread of silk, just as it comes from the worm's carcass, floating so lightly that I could not hold it. Above me, I felt the gross lump of a mud-boulder drowning my clammy throat. I was alone, grasping at the fine thread while I waited to be crushed by the looming boulder.

I woke in a cold sweat, tears crusted on my lashes and my head aching as if I had wept for hours. The night had the strange warm glow of summer.

The coffin-room I slept in was once the landing at the top of the stairs, but Peter had boarded it up, making just enough space for my straw pallet. I had my own window at least, a clumsy hole where Peter had bashed out a couple of the old stones. In winter, the Devil's own icy breath would come in while my dreams mingled with the swish of the shuttle, as if Peter pinned me into the weave while I slept; but in summer, the hole was my salvation, letting in the sweet night breeze.

I lay on my too-short pallet, my head propped up at one end and my feet high on the wall at the other, and watched the stars float slowly through the dying branches of the pear tree. Some nights, I wished that tree would fall and crush me in my bed.

I dreamed of glory from time to time, as all man-boys do. When my father stood by the traitor's bones and spoke against the king, he'd planted a seed in me. To be my own man. To fight against the kings and Catholics and enclosures of the world.

It had always felt a foolish dream, but now I felt it rising in me again. This merchant Garric Pettit had spoken rebellious words. Had my father fought with Cromwell against the old king, Charles? Was that why Garric wanted him to go to London?

I could not believe it of the old ghost. No man who had defeated a king would spend his elder days tugging his forelock to the likes of Mistress Ramage.

Still, the Frenchman knew something of him, something still hidden to me. Last night, Peter and Mirella had carried on arguing in low voices. They had both wanted me to be apprenticed to another trade. Now Peter had changed his mind, and would not tell her why. Well, if he did not give me to Garric then I would leave anyway.

I could not sleep.

I watched the unclouded night sky, letting my eyes go soft until I could see plain through the gauze curtain of stars and into my own destiny. Garric Pettit bringing me among the rebels against the king. Calumny Spinks with uniform, gun and sword, giving orders to men who called me "Sir", not "Master" or "Boy". Fighting the bastard Catholics, who in my half-dream looked like Ramage and

Cowans and the spawn who had taunted me by the sheep pond. Varnished wood-panelled houses, fine paintings, a soft bed as big as a house. A woman… A rich girl, some Mister's daughter for me to marry…

A sound dragged me out of dreamless sleep.

"*Mehnrrrmrrrbrrn, nehbrrrnrrrmehhh,*" came a voice from below me. It was Peter, grumbling at something. I opened my eyes wide in surprise. I had never heard him speak more than a word in the mornings, not until he had done his day's work. He would shove his gruel between his thin lips as soon as he had risen, and then sit down at his loom. *Chumpa chumpa* it would be from then until dusk, only rising from his stool to take a sip of water at noon.

A whiny voice replied. Itching to know who this stranger was, I climbed out of my window. Tall though I was, I had climber's fingers, and I skittered lizard-like down the vines, then crept along the side of the house until I was under the window.

"You thould know that thith ith patht due now," said a man. He sounded like a rat chewing straw.

Silence.

"You have ethcaped thith debt for too long. Well, I know who you are."

"*Brrrehmehnrrr,*" growled my father.

"You may thay tho," lisped the rat, "but I know the truth. Four monthth."

For a breath, there was silence in the room, then the limping thud of Peter's heavy boots as he went to throw the door open. I scurried back around the corner. Hiding, I watched a man click-clacking down the path, clad in an ash-grey cloak that minced in at the waist. His shiny silk stockings were tied with leaf-green bows. The lisping rat did not look back, but threw himself onto a mare and trotted off towards Salstead.

Peter was stood in the doorway breathing coarsely, his face sandstone-pale. He wiped a muck-sweat off his balding head with both hands, the way a drover would wash himself after a hot day's riding. I dared not breathe lest he catch me watching.

"*Qu'est-ce qui se passe?*" hissed my mother, coming up behind him. What is it, she asked.

At first he did not answer. He left off his wiping and stood with his back to her, hands hanging uselessly at his sides, his gnarly shoulders rounded as if to hide his heart.

"*Menteur, lâche, réponds-moi!*" she cried, her freckles burning scarlet as she called him a coward and liar.

Peter spun around and lifted her fully in the air, his fingers digging deep into her elbows to pin them. She kicked his shins, but he did not even wince as he carried her across the threshold and back into the house. I crept under the window again, looking down the lane to be sure that no sharp-nosed busywife had heard her crying out in the still dawn air.

"What is that about the money?" she hissed at him in English. Perhaps she thought to whisper so that I would not wake. "Do not shrug at me, liar!"

"That man claims a debt is due," he said in a tomb-voice.

"How much? How much, Peter?"

"This is not for you to know," he growled. "Did you ask me what I owed when I took you from those dragoons, when I put you on that ship, when you demanded a child of me?"

And then the harsh biting sound of my mother slapping him. The blood pounded in my ears and my chest tightened. The truth was that *she* had demanded a child of Peter. He had not wanted me.

Now she spoke quietly, her words cudgelling my gut.

"This is from your own sin. You should have kept your secrets in your pig-hut and never gone to London, but you have brought this debt into our home, and you will pay it. I am not your wife."

Wheezing, weeping, she tumbled up the stairs to her bed. *Crack.* A mighty blow was struck on the chimney breast not a yard from where I held my ear to the other side. Jesus' blood, I thought, now he fights the house itself. I turned and ran, crushing daisy heads under my feet. I had a mind to look at that pigman's hut.

When I reached the hut, I saw that its wrought-iron lock and door-handle were smooth and new. No coin for mutton, but he'll waste a shilling or two on ironwork, I thought sourly.

I rattled the handle but Peter's voice seized me. "Cal!" he barked from the doorway of the house, a puff of steam showing against the dark roofs of Salstead behind him. He had found my bed empty, and the poker was still in his hand. The dawn glowed through his ragged hair.

I crouched behind the hut so he could not see me. Then came my mother's voice from behind him. I could not make out her words, but she was marching up the twitchell towards the village. He turned and followed her, arguing fiercely.

"This is not for you to meddle in – do as you are bid!" yelled Peter, grabbing Mirella and dragging her roughly back to the house as she struggled against him.

He pushed her inside, and came down through the grass towards the hut. I thought of fleeing, but this was my only chance to see the old man's secrets for myself. I lay on my belly, shivering as the cold dew burst onto my skin.

Peter unlocked the door, wrenched it open and stamped inside, one foot heavier than the other. Lying there, I could see into the gap between the walls and the hard-packed earth beneath the hut, just as he lifted up a hatch in the floor. My cheek pressed against the moist ground, I saw his hand reach down and lift a long box out of its hiding place. He went outside again, limping heavily.

I lifted my head as high as I dared and watched my father's hunched back through the dew-clad grass. He held something in his hands, waiting as if for a word from God. Then, with a sigh, he stood taller and raised the thing closer to look at it.

It was a pistol, its sleek hardwood body inlaid with flowing leaves of staghorn. Steel fittings bound it without screw or nail, and on its right flank were two grooved wheels, nestled into little coils of springs and levers. It hummed with the power of a violent angel.

Peter turned the pistol on its side, laying it on his outstretched left palm, and gently lifted up a little silvery hatch on its flank. With his teeth, he pulled out the stopper from a little vial, then carefully poured powder into the open hatch. He placed powder and a shot inside the muzzle. Kneeling, he took a little wrench from the box and turned a shaft on the side of the gun until I heard a click. Once he was done, he pointed the gun, still sidewise, at the church spire.

I dropped my head and quietly let out my breath into my chest. When I looked up again, he had taken two paces towards the house, the pistol at his side.

He will kill the rat-man, I thought, feeling a fierce pride I could not understand.

Then my father hesitated. He sighted the pistol again, shook his long white hair weakly, and scuttled back inside the hut. When he was finished, he locked the door and trudged heavily back through the orchard to the house.

Still lying on my belly, I reached under the hut and felt for the box, which was wrapped in oilskin. I had to dig away at the moist earth before I could free it from its shallow hole. My fingernails were filthy and my arms aching by the time I had dragged the box out from under the hut. I sat up and freed it from its wrapping. A scratched cherrywood box lay in my lap, its ancient varnish still clinging on in places. I let my palms rest on the rounded corners for a breath, then lifted the lid.

The finely crafted gun lay on a red velvet bed, starched and shaped to hold its treasure snugly. I knew it was loaded and ready to fire, and so I dared not touch it at first. I wiped my hands on the wet grass to clean them.

But I was Calumny Spinks, and my devil's blood drove me on. Staying in the hut, I lifted the gun out and held it cautiously in the light to admire the staghorn carvings. It was longer and heavier than I expected, death adding its weight to wood and steel.

For a moment, I was the Huguenot hero, *mon seigneur de Calonnie.* I tilted the pistol on its side as Peter had done, and pointed it at the trees hanging over the stream, longing to fire it. But I was too fearful. Peter had never really wanted me for his son, so why would he not beat me for stealing his property?

Now it was my turn to dither as I squeezed the oil-smooth handle. Dare I take the pistol; use it somehow to make my fortune in London? Blood sang in my ears until I could not bear it; cravenly, I went to put the gun back in its box.

This time, I noticed a scrap of sable cloth peeking out from under the red velvet. Carefully, I laid down the pistol, lifted up its bed and took out a little straight-sided sack of black silk, slashed here and there with holes, and with gold letters stamped on its hem. I looked close at the shapes of the letters. I could not read, but I could remember a picture and draw it well enough. First was the swell of a child-bearing belly. Then two church steeples side by side. Then the tines of a pitchfork lying on its side. "Belly, steeples, fork", I whispered to myself.

Under the sack was a purse. I pulled the strings apart and piled Peter's coins on my hand. The copper farthings and pennies I knew, and there were two silver shillings, but I had never touched the like of the small golden coins in there, their edges unclipped and perfect.

I did not have the courage to take his coin or his gun, but I tucked the black silk into my smock. Peter had his secrets and now I wanted them for myself.

I put the box back into its wrapping and pushed it back under the hut. I looked at the damp-mossed house in the low light. It had the look of a saggy-faced old man whose spirit had died but whose body still lay there in the bed, his husked-out heart rising and falling as slow as lake-tide.

The front door was open, and Peter was in the workshop, weaving. Well, I was not going to face the old ghost. I scrambled back up the ivy and tumbled into my bed.

I looked again at the old man's gold-lettered cloth, and wondered what glory he had known to be given such a thing. And why did he keep such a pistol when he could sell it for a month's meat? What did he fear from Salstead – boneyard village that it was?

Your own sin, my mother had said. But a pistol in a box is no sin.

The loom creaked and groaned as Peter kicked the treadles back and forth like a man possessed. Like a fighting man.

For sure, my father was old enough to have fought for Cromwell. He always spoke of kings as devil's worms, or popish whores. But why should a soldier become a weaver, and live shame-filled in Salstead?

I began to wonder about the rat-voiced man and this debt he spoke of, but it made me smile to think of a man in rich silk stockings going to the poorest old man in the village for money. The rising sun warmed my room, and my thoughts flew up and basked in the growing light.

CHAPTER FOUR

The Scolding

In which Death descends on Salstead

I woke to the sound of bells. Peter had not stirred me for church as he usually did, thinking that my bed was still empty, and now I was late for worship. The crow-voiced bells were nearly at the end of their song, and it was fiendish hard to creep into church once Cowans had started the rite.

I threw on my Sabbath linen shirt and waistcoat. Tucking the scrap of black silk into my breeches, I scuttled down the stairs and dashed out of the house. I ran fast, but the church doors were already closed. I wondered what to do.

Should I wait outside and sneak into the crowd of Salstead potrillos when they came out? Or gently push the door open, and risk being seen coming late? Either way, my name would not be marked on Ramage's list.

While I stood there, unsure, I heard the crunching of boots further along the lane, and the wheezing breath of my mother as she struggled up the hill towards the green.

What did she want with the tavern? On Sunday mornings Mirella would always sit at home and worship on her own, praying in her French tongue. But today she must have been waiting for the rest of the village to go into church before creeping past, secretly.

Should I follow my mother? I feared Peter's anger if I did not come to church, his gnarly arm wielding the cast-iron poker, and so I left the worm of doubt to sleep in my gut, and slipped between the church doors. I tippytoed to the last pew and sat, my breeches still damp from running through the long grass at dawn.

I was filled with shame at my own cowardice. All my life I had let my parents hide the truth from me, spinning and sleepwalking through my rotten days. Not once had I demanded to know why they did not go back to London and claim my father's property. I knew that the pistol and the black silk held some of the answers, but still I feared to follow my own mother and learn the rest.

My father, neat in his square lace collar, was sparring with Mister Cowans. The rector's hairless fingers clutched at the pulpit as he struggled to cover his anger with a pious smile. Behind him stood a bust of the Catholic king, and above it hung a simple wooden cross with a sheep-eyed Jesus nailed to it.

"Does this church not declare the king as its head, ordained by God?" Peter demanded, pointing at the ugly bust. All around the room were sighs and growls, and yet it was permitted to speak once the rector had made his sermon. Watery splashes of rosy light bathed the congregation, bored clouds of dust rising and falling as they breathed.

Cowans was careful how he replied, for Peter's Bible learning was far better than his.

"The king is ordained by God to defend the faith of the Church of England. Therefore the faith must be preserved above all other matters."

The busyfaced goodwives in the church nodded and clasped their hands together, as if Cowans was the archangel Michael himself, and not a fishmonger's brat from Ludlow.

"Yet if God has ordained the king, then God has ordained that *you*, Mister Cowans, should read the Declaration of Indulgence," said Peter, and sat down with a smile on his face. Always he did this, quarrelling with the priest, never wanting to see the frowns and shaking heads behind him.

I saw Mistress Ramage poke her husband in the ribs, her eyes sparking like blown embers.

"A man cannot be true to the Church and desire that heresy returns to Salstead – that is for good and sure. The Act of Uniformity is final!" snapped Mister Ramage, turning to speak to the higher folk in the pews around him. I looked hard at Mistress Ramage, but her head was turned. Her family box was right in the corner of the church, overlooking the whole nave like a watchman's tower. From her high seat she could also see clear out of the vestry window and into the lane.

Mistress Ramage's eyes narrowed, and I knew she had spied my mother walking towards the tavern. She whispered in her husband's ear and he nodded carefully, keeping his eyes on my father. Jarvis Perment tugged at the tail of his waistcoat, but Peter shook him off.

The gossip-wives and their potrillo goodmen on the right side of the church began to hiss and cry "Shame" at my father, while the lower folk, the true Salsteaders, mumbled fearfully that they should let him speak.

Peter, treading heavily towards the pulpit, cried out, "Read the Declaration and let each man worship his own way, Dissenter and Episcopalian alike!"

It was like throwing a fox into a farmyard. The whole village was on its feet, shouting. Cowans raised his arms to the heavens and called out to Ramage and his band, and for a breath it seemed as though blows would be struck. Through the turmoil, I saw Mistress Ramage slip out of the back of her box and into the vestry, closing the door behind her.

She was following my mother, and she meant trouble by it for sure. I wanted to catch my father's eye, but he was telling the right-thinkers around him not to raise their fists to Ramage and the others.

I jumped back over the pew and squeezed out of the church doors. Mistress Ramage was already out of sight around the bend. I ran after her, sweating in the parched air as she skirted the sheep pond, sliding on its muddy rim. She walked straight for the low lodging-house leaning at the tavern's side. I dared not follow her across the green, and so I went the long way around the back of the tavern, keeping unseen below the brow of the hill.

When at last I got to the lodging-rooms, Mistress Ramage was running full pelt back to the church, with no care for the mud that splashed on her white linen skirt.

"I will give you all," said my mother's voice from the far window, no longer trembling and wheezing, but from the pit of her belly, like a soldier facing death. I crept towards her voice and lifted my head above the cracked wooden sill. Through the dust-flecked window I saw a man's back. He was on his feet, moving like a dancer. Mirella was not there. I breathed out my relief. This was only some halfwit traveller.

Then she spoke again.

"I will give you all if you forget you have seen Peter Spinks."

He turned a little. I still could not see his face, but there, kneeling at his feet, was my mother, naked from head to toe. From his green stocking-ribbons, I knew that he was the same man who had come to our house that dawn.

He shoved his thumbs into the corners of my mother's mouth, forcing her jaw open, and I could not bear to watch more. My breath caught deep in my throat, and perhaps Mirella heard me wheeze, for the light caught her eyes as if she wept. Whirling stars filled the middle of my sight, blocking out her face, and then I was falling backwards into the muddy grass below the window.

Not my mother anymore. This was a Frenchy *putain* who dared to whore while all others prayed. Not my mother.

The rasp of his breath, and her choking sobs, and the sun burning through my eyelids, its bloody shape bursting into raging black.

Barely a moment passed before I woke, knowing she was damned for what she had done. Weeping, wheezing, I struggled to my feet. All I could think was to run to the church and pray, full of terror for her soul. When I reached the vestry door, I had to puke, a thin yellow soup pouring from my scalded throat. I stumbled into the church, where Mistress Ramage was stood next to the pulpit, whispering into Cowans' ear as she tapped a coil of bell-rope against her leg.

Mister Sand spied me and seized my shirt-front, pressing my face against his musty dun-coloured waistcoat to stop me warning my father. I tried to get away but his hands were ram-strong.

"We must save a soul today!" called Cowans. "Good-wives, will you oust the poor sinner for us?"

"We shall," cried Mistress Ramage, echoed by Mistress Sand. The close air of the church thickened with women's scent as they rushed past me: their unwashed venuses; the lemon smell of shawls washed and dried in the summer sun. Mister Sand dragged me out after them, through the vestry door, and on up the path towards the tavern. Behind us, I heard Cowans calling on the congregation to follow through the main doors.

I tugged at Sand's grip and looked for Peter, but he was in the middle of a lump of men, all still pushing and shouting at each other. Cowans was stood apart, one hand on his pulpit. Watching the running wives, his proud face showed how much he needed this one act of shame to be strong in the village, wielding the power of damnation. And Peter, the only threat to his power, silenced by cuckoldry.

They meant to scold her. Terror nailed me to the spot as I remembered how the squire had died.

"Peter! Father!"

Peter followed Mister Ramage into the vestry, still raving at Mister Ramage about Indulgence. Ahead of us, the women rushed up to the lodging-house, breaking like a wave over the ridge of the green. A scream rose above their vile shouting.

"Peter!" I yelled.

This time he saw me. His eyes opened wide at the sight of my puke-spattered face and muddy clothes. Sand had my neck in the crook of his elbow as he wrestled me up the hill.

"Try to put the horns on me, would you? God damn you to Hell, whoreson Frenchy!"

I butted my head against his chin. He grunted from the pain of biting his own tongue, and clamped my hands fast behind my back. Now we were in the middle of the mob of men and boys as it surged over the ridge.

"They are taking my mother!" I shouted at Peter, who was stumbling up the hill behind us.

Mirella, naked, was being pulled across the green by screeching women. Mistress Ramage first beat her with the coil of bell-rope, then wrapped it around her neck.

Peter ran towards her, but slipped. When he rose, Mister Ramage held a chisel to his throat.

"You do not master your whore wife," yelled Cowans, his voice high and trembling. "She screeches her foul French curses, she disobeys her husband, and now she fornicates on the Lord's Day. Let her be cleansed!"

The whole village was now gathered around the sheep pond, watching the shrieking women claw and scratch my mother, Rachel Cowans among them. From the other side of the pond, I could see the red marks on my mother's bare back where Mistress Ramage had beaten her. Clumps of her hair flew up, glistening with blood at their roots, and I closed my eyes in agony as I thought of her brushing it out, a hundred strokes each side before sleep.

Then the lower women of the village took their turn, roaring and foaming at the mouth as they threw dung at my mother. "Whore, whore, whore!" they yelled, as if she had bedded every husband in the village. Only Agnes Perment held back, her eyes fearful.

The men were silent, stood in a half-moon on the other side of the stinking pit. Peter had stopped struggling. He looked at my mother, chalk-faced, Ramage's chisel pressing at his neck. I could not tell if he cursed her, or asked her forgiveness. A shadow flitted behind the mob of women on the pond's muddy rim, and I knew it was the man who had touched my mother. Why was he unpunished for his lechery?

The women pushed Mirella out in front so that we could all see her across the pond. She tried to cover her nakedness but they pulled her arms apart. The skin of her body was pale next to her sun-marked face. It hung on her bones like wet paper. Peter choked, though still he spoke not. We knew she was to be ducked.

Cowans stepped forward as if to bless her punishment.

On the other side of the pond, Mirella shouted my name and stepped forward. Now, even though he was still hidden in the crowd, I felt the gaze of the silk-stockinged man on me, and my blood ran cold. He was watching to see who my mother called for in her fear.

Mistress Sand pushed my mother so that she slipped down the steep muddy sides of the sheep pond. She fell towards the water, but Mistress Ramage still held tight to the rope that bound her neck, jerking my mother's head back before she tumbled below the scummed surface. She did not raise her head when her body bobbed back up, and the crowd hissed at her shame.

"Thou shalt not…" cried Cowans. "Thou shalt…"

He fell silent. Mirella was still face down in the water, the taut rope running from her neck up to Mistress Ramage's shaking hands.

"Oh Jesus," I whispered. "Her neck –"

I wrenched free of Sand and hurled myself down the slippery pond-sides, wading through the stink, but Mistress Ramage got there before me. She turned my mother over slowly, and we all saw from the empty eyes that Mirella Spinks was gone. A bruise the colour of a magpie's tail-feathers stained the soft skin of her neck, and her breasts floated on the filthy surface, barrenly.

"The whore is dead," said Mistress Ramage into the silent air.

I reached my mother's body and kissed her face. I held her close but could not weep because my chest was too tight. So cold she was already. I pulled her gently towards the bank and laid her down, taking off my waistcoat to cover her.

Ramage touched my head. "It is not your sin," she murmured.

Her touch was like a knife-cut on my scalp. I sank my teeth into her wrist, pulling her down so I could push her sharp face into the mud. I punched her ribs until the other women pulled me off. They clasped my arms to my sides, swaddling me tight, and I could feel Mistress Sand's trembly fingers on my chest.

Mistress Ramage sat and wiped her muddy face, tears of pain falling on her bleeding wrist. She pointed her bony forefinger at my father.

"*You* brought this whore to Salstead. You let her naysay you, unwomanly and immodest. You let her free on the Lord's Day to tempt good men with her devil's eyes. Look how her child bears the red hair of Lucifer! You, Peter Spinks, *you* brought her here to die with your weak and ungodly ways."

Peter closed his eyes. Fat tears rolled down his cheeks and into his open weeping mouth. Douglas Perment tried to get closer to my father, but Mister Sand pushed him back.

"Let him be scolded too," screamed Mistress Sand in my ear, for once speaking unbidden.

The other women cried out, "Scold him too!"

They turned their backs on the dead woman, seized their girl-children and moved as one back down the lane towards the village, sweeping Peter and the menfolk up in their wake. Mistress Ramage got to her feet, spat on Mirella's face, and ran with them.

I was alone with my mother.

"Calonnie," she had called out before they snapped her neck.

I knew what calumny was. It was when the laws of the world were broken with savage lies. I wanted to close her eyelids, to clothe her, but I could not touch her body again. It was not my mother.

My legs lay in the foul water of the pond, my breeches clammy, but the sun was already drying my shirt into stiff armour. I looked up into the uncaring sky, and for a breath, all was still.

Baba clang baba clang. The air rang with the clashing of pots and pans.

Peter. They would kill him like the heretic in the gibbet. I sat up, breath trembling in and out, unsure. Would Garric Pettit help me? Or Douglas Perment, who had stood silent while they cursed my father?

The pistol was the only friend I could trust, but I would beg the Frenchman's help while there was still time. I looked at my mother one more time, painting her swollen sad face on the secret cave-wall inside my head, and then I was running like I had never run before.

The earth flew away below me, all the bones in my body thundering as I dashed towards the clearing. I knew that Peter had little time before the banging of pans became a beating.

"*Garric! Au secours!*" I cried as soon as I saw the mercer dozing on his driving seat. Cucullan reared and jerked forward in the traces.

"*Ils ont tué ma mère! Viens vite!*"

I pointed up the road, showing Garric that he should drive the wagon down the lane, but his knuckles whitened as he restrained the horse.

"Your father lives?" he asked calmly. "Peter Spinks, he lives still?"

"They scold him!" I yelled, running for the narrow path though the gorse bushes. "Help me!"

I hoped it was enough to tell him that my mother had been killed. If not, I would face the whole of Salstead alone, armed only with a single ancient pistol.

Spiny branches tore at me as I ran down the slope. I leapt over the church wall and ran through the rows of graves as the clashing of pots and pans grew louder over Peter's cries. They had scolded him the length of the village, and now they would finish him in front of his own home.

I hurled myself past the gibbet, hitting it so hard with my shoulder that the old skeleton broke into pieces and shattered on the flaking iron floor of the cage. Pushing through the weathered old gate, I stumbled down to the pigman's hut. I spied men running into our house, but I knew I could not stop them alone.

I ran at the door and burst it off its hinges. Kneeling, I lifted the cherrywood box through the hatch and took Peter's gun out, laying it down with care so I could take the purse as well.

Woodsmoke filled the air as I rushed back through the dying orchard. Flames burst out of our home as the loom popped, ripping apart the weary years of my father's labour.

Peter staggered down the lane, the youngsters who led the mob pelting him with dung and straw. Blood poured from his lip, and he held his left hand to his chest like it was broken. His best Sunday coat and woollen breeches were torn and stained with blood and dirt, but still he looked a better man than any of those who tormented him, banging their pots and pans like devils, the families at the back pushing and fighting to see the scolding better. All the children had come out to join the terror.

Peter saw the burning house, but not me, and he stopped where he was in despair. Raising the pistol, I ran carefully across the lumpy meadow towards him, careful not to fire off the gun. I would have one shot and no more, and for sure they would kill me afterwards. I slipped my fingertip inside the guard and felt two triggers. Two barrels, I thought. I must take care to fire one at a time.

The sons and daughters of Ramage's band had begun to pick up pebbles and small stones from the lane, hurling them from no more than an arm's length away. Agnes Perment tried to snatch at their cruel arms, but her brother, shamefaced, held her back. Peter cried out each time he was struck. He reached the gibbet and clung to it as if he would climb inside, rattling the broken bones.

The rector stood on the church wall, arms open wide like the Messiah.

I closed my eyes, held the pistol sidewise with both hands and pulled hard on the first trigger. I was aiming for Cowans, but the ball flew far from him, breaking splinters from a gravestone. The sound was huge, a crack of hellish lightning, and straightaway the banging and stone-throwing stopped. The villagers stared at me open-mouthed. The shot had jarred my shoulders back in their sockets so that I could scarce hold the handle of the gun, but still I came slowly forward, arms trembling, until I could stand between the mob and my wounded father.

I laid my finger on the second trigger, lifted the pistol to shoulder height and looked down the barrel at Cowans' wobbling face, making the crowd shrink away.

"You Satan whore!" I screamed at him. "If you do not call a halt to this villainy I will blow your poxy face open for the crows to pick at!"

I looked around. Shame had swallowed up the scolding party, and dry smoke from my burning home curled among them, stinging their eyes. Mistress Sand was weeping again, her hands a-tremble, and blood trickled from Mistress Ramage's nose. I hoped I had burst her heart with my blows.

Wheels ground on the roadway as Cucullan stepped boldly down the lane, the reins slack on his back, and stopped a few yards from the gibbet where I held my father. Garric stood upright in the driving seat with his legs braced against the slope. He held a cudgel as long and thick as one of his arms, its end studded with nails and flints, and he had rolled up his sleeves fully to the shoulder so that the village could see the strength in his broad body. Still pointing the pistol at Cowans' pocked face, I put my other arm around my father's shoulders and walked him two paces sidewise towards Garric's cart.

Cudgel in hand, the mercer climbed down and slowly led his horse in a circle around the gibbet. The mob drew back, but Garric was watching my father: his limp, the hurt hand he clutched against his chest, his eyes.

He lifted my father clean into the air, putting him gently on a pile of cloths in the bottom of the cart. Peter was no small man, and I heard a gasp or two in the crowd at the Frenchman's power. I had no time to wonder that he would have risked his life for us; I lifted myself awkwardly onto the tailboard, keeping the gun pointing at the mob.

"You will bury my mother in the churchyard. You will give the prayer," I told Cowans, loud enough for all to witness.

He was too terrified to shake his head. Mistress Ramage tutted at him, but blood rose in her throat and choked her off.

"You will swear to God, you cuntfaced potrillo."

"I… I swear… I swear to God I will."

The Salsteaders pressed their cowardly backs to the lane walls as Peter pulled at my hand to sit himself up. He would not look at the faces around him, but stared past the church spire at the rise where Mirella's body lay. For a breath he held my arm, squeezing the flesh above my elbow. That touch was the truest thing he had ever told me.

Garric flicked the reins and we rolled slowly away, looking back. Agnes stared at me sorrowfully, her back to the shaking rector Cowans. The goodwives were trying to douse the fire in our house, but I could see already that it was too late. The tools, the silk, the loom, everything we owned was burning. All we had now were Peter's coins. And the gun.

As we watched wordlessly, Douglas Perment took three others with him to fetch my mother. They walked up the lane with their arms around each other's shoulders in pairs, as if they already carried the weight of her coffin.

CHAPTER FIVE

Silk Street

In which Calumny is forbidden the coffeehouses of London

Peter lay on his back with his arms across his chest, eyes closed. I cleaned the stinking dung off him as best I could, ripped up my shirt-tails and spat on them to clean his left hand. He cried out loud; his fingers had been bruised when he'd warded off the flying stones.

I covered him with damask and climbed up next to the mercer. He let the reins lie limply on the horse's back as it trotted up towards the London road.

"He knows where he is going, this Cucullan," murmured Garric.

I watched the beast's tail twitch, muscles swimming like eels under his glossy chestnut hide. When this horse is killed, I thought, the hide will look the same, and yet the moving will have stopped. Though he enjoyed the slack reins, his life was truly no more than pulling loads, eating grain and drinking water, the master and not the horse choosing which road to travel upon.

Seeing me shiver in my still-wet clothes, Garric covered me with his coat. He left his arm around my shoulders, but I flinched and shrugged it off. I took the reins from him and bucked up the horse. Cucullan swung his head around, rolling his eyes as he broke into a trot. I had stolen his freedom.

The lane passed into the oak wood above Salstead and into the carters' clearing. I had to pull back sharply on the reins as a troop of horsemen cantered through the clearing, rabbly despite their soldierly uniforms and feathered hats. Red-eyed and unshaven, they jostled tiredly against each other. I remembered my friend Douglas' warning – I had no papers to give me wayleave. We were not safe yet.

"*Des Ecossais*," whispered Garric.

I was careful not to look the Scots soldiers in the face. Their grumbling sounded like a blackbird chewing on pebbles. Once most of the troop had ridden by, Garric whistled at the last straggler, a runty fellow with curly black hair and forget-me-not blue eyes.

"Who you wheeshing at, you English bastard?" he growled, pulling his horse's head around.

"Who call you English, halfwit Scotch?" Garric smiled, standing up on the driving-board and scratching at his groin. I looked at the soldier warily, wondering why the mercer had stopped him.

The Scotsman laughed and spurred his horse over to us. "Frenchy, is it? Lucky you are no Dutchman."

"Why so? Why does your troop ride all night like this?" asked Garric. "Your horses look half-dead."

"So they are."

The soldier leaned forward in his saddle.

"They say the Dutch are raising an army to invade England, and so the king has called for more Scotsmen to garrison London. Though but…" – he spat on the pitted roadway – "…I cannot see for why you would defend a shite country like this."

He sat back, hand on sword-pommel.

"And why fight you for a Catholic king," asked Garric softly, "since I see from your plain clothes that you are a good Protestant?"

"Better to serve a Scots devil than an English angel," laughed the soldier, turning his horse's head south for London. "Have a care, Frenchman. Do not ask your questions so freely in the city."

The wagon bounced and creaked as we crossed the rutted clearing, much slower than the cavalrymen had. Before we reached the other side I was asleep, chin on chest.

Warm rain struck my bent neck and trickled softly down my back, washing through the muddy leavings of the sheep pond. We were climbing a slope, and as I blinked the rain off my eyelashes I was sure I saw Mirella ahead of us, walking up the lane to the tavern. I reached out to stop her this time. Pain sank its clawed feet into my shoulder-flesh, and my hand began to tremble. The cold shaking spread up my arm and into my chest, and I bit my finger to keep from calling out for my mother. Twice I could have saved her: once from the rat-man, once from Mistress Ramage, and each time I chose to hide in the church.

To shut out those thoughts, I looked at the merchant, sleeping soundly on my left. The horse had trotted on unbidden through the warm afternoon, and now the sun spread crimson as it sank below the clouds.

We were going to London. I had not understood it before, only that it was safe to ride with Garric. God knew what Peter would do in the city. Perhaps I could leave him with Garric while I found work, for the coins in his purse would not last us so long there.

"Cal," said my father.

Again, I saw Mirella walking away towards the tavern. Had my father known that she was going to sacrifice herself for him? *Forget you have seen Peter Spinks*, she had said.

I looked around at my pale and shaking father. The raindrops fell in chilly clumps now, and my shirt was soaked through. Still I stared at Peter, and he back at me, wincing every few paces as the wagon bounced along the roadway. His eyes were red; he was as guilty as I. He spoke my name again, and I opened my mouth to curse him.

The falling rain woke Garric. Quickly, he saw what passed between us. He thrust the reins into my hand and climbed awkwardly into the back of the wagon, pulling cloths and covers from here and there to make a little tent over Peter. He squatted next to my father with a waterskin, letting little drops fall on his lips.

"You must keep him warm," he told me silently, making the shape of the words with his lips.

I shook my head so hard that rain flew off. I would not touch the old man.

Garric frowned at me, but I would not be shamed. He shrugged and lay himself down next to my father, letting his warmth flow into Peter's trembling body.

"Follow Cucullan," said the mercer.

I was glad to be alone. Again the terror of the day took hold of me, my teeth chattering so hard that my ribs ached. This time the tears came, but they were hard and reluctant. They brought no relief. Each racking sob came with a shameful memory: my mother kneeling; her hair catching the sun as the women ripped it out; her naked body floating on the pond.

The rain fell harder until we had climbed up into the low hills. At last, the sky cleared and I saw a long narrow glow, covering the horizon from side to side: London, light glimmering from countless houses.

Soon we had passed below the hillcrest, and I fell asleep again and again, each time jerking my head up when it touched my chest. Cucullan pounded on tirelessly while his master snored behind me, unafraid.

We came on a crossroads, lit by campfires. The Scots soldiers we had met earlier sat among their weathered tents playing cards and talking in low voices. Not one of them looked at us as I halted Cucullan, wondering which way to turn the horse.

"Take the Whitestone way," growled Garric, without raising his head.

The horse snorted and jerked the reins out of my hands, skipping over the crossroads impatiently. Garric pretended that he had spoken in his sleep, but I saw now that he had watched over me through the dusk.

Peter woke.

Very slowly, like the old man he was, my father got to his knees and pushed the little tent-cover to one side, keeping his left hand against his breast. White-faced, he joined me on the driving seat. Still I would not speak to him. I could not forgive him his quarrelling, and his blindness towards my dead mother. Yesterday she lived; now we waited emptily for death.

He held out his good hand for the reins, but I would not give them up. He looked back at the campsite.

"We will not be robbed, at least," he said quietly. "Not with those soldiers on the road."

The darkness drew close around the moon-sliver.

"Turn right here," whispered Peter.

I pulled on the rein. The cart slid down a muddy turning and onto a narrower track below the hedges. We could barely see our smoky breath in the night air now, and we shivered as Cucullan marched on towards the city.

Garric rooted around, lifting the cover from the brocade basket to make sure the treasures were still there. "These are more costly than one may believe," he murmured, not meeting my eye.

He delved into another basket and handed us more fine cloths against the cold. We were a pair of broken paupers, wrapped in satin against the callous Essex night.

I woke to the rattling of wheels on cobbles. Brass wall lanterns breathed firelight on the wet streets, and wisps of steam rose from the damask as I stirred.

"London," muttered Peter from the driving seat.

There was a strange sweet caress in his voice, as though he were coming home to a beloved mother who stirred rich rabbit stew and dumplings over a broad fire.

But Peter's mother stirred no stew this night. Long before I was born, she was struck sick with the plague. While she lay there helplessly in her little house in Holborn, the land and property that would have made me a Mister, a plague-watchman painted a white cross on her door. Peter was in France, and it was months before he heard how the Watch dragged her out of bed and threw her in a burial-pit, where they poured burning oil over her pustuled flesh while she yet breathed. And she might have lived, if that cross had not been drawn.

That is the calumny they named me for. And so I carried murder in my name.

We drove further into London. Though it was the deepest part of the night, the streets buzzed. Coaches rattled past us, their curtains closed against prying eyes. Bands of watchmen huddled around braziers, gossiping cheerfully as they smoked their Dutch tobacco pipes.

We passed a tall house, leaking yellow light through its elegant blinds. Garric slowed Cucullan as we passed, and we listened to the bubbling sound of men's voices. Above the bruise-coloured door was the carved and painted face of a blackamoor in a strange cloth hat.

"A coffeehouse," said Garric.

"Is it like a tavern?" I asked, glad to shed the memory of the sheep pond for a moment.

"A man goes to the tavern to waste his coin and hide from his goodwife. But he visits a coffeehouse to make the business and wealth of the world his own."

"Ale makes men foolish," snapped Peter, "but coffee makes them dangerous. Do not think on it. Where merchants gather, there is knavery in the air."

Cucullan's hooves clacked in reproach.

"I do not mean mercers, good guild brothers like you, Master Pettit," my father said grudgingly.

Always it was like this. My father would tell me enough about the world to make me hungry for it, and then he would tell me it was not for me. His secrets had killed my mother, I thought, and my blood began to boil when Peter spoke again, his eyes soft.

"I will make us another home, my buck. You shall have a warm place to sleep again, I promise you."

My dry tongue swelled and prickled. Potrillo that I was, I reached inside my pocket and took out the moneybag for my father. He did not thank me as he took the purse, and with it my liberty.

Though my rage had faded, I was not foolish enough to give him back his pistol. A man may choose more freely with fire in his fist.

The street grew so wide that four carts could have passed down it abreast. I had never seen such houses, so great that you could have fit the whole of Salstead church inside one of them. Music poured out through the open windows of a mansion, sweet melodies sung in a forengie tongue.

"Do they sing hymns in the night?" I whispered.

"My faith, no!" laughed Garric. "They sing of love and women and war, as we all do."

"But on Sunday night… Does their rector allow it? How can they work in the morning?"

"They have no rector," said Peter fiercely. "And they do not work. Not the way we work, and not in the mornings. It is such folk you will see in the coffeehouses."

He folded his arms, wincing as he clamped his damaged fingers under his armpit. Then he gave me a sharp look.

"Though you shall not see them, for you are forbidden such places."

Tired and grieving though I was, I knew one thing for good and sure. I had never tasted coffee, nor did I know ought of the world's business, but I was going to a coffeehouse the first chance I got.

We turned left, and the houses were of a sudden much newer than those we had passed before, and the roadway cleaner and brighter. The whole street seemed stitched to the older part by a strange blackened streak that ran straight down the side of the houses and across the street. Garric pointed at it.

"That is where the Great Fire stopped," he said. "The soldiers blew up all the houses in this row so that the burning could go no further."

"And then the land-plans were lost," growled Peter, "and the popish swine who friended the king claimed the deeds, and built their own houses on the site."

He fell silent, pressing his knuckles into his hip.

And if you had been a stronger man, I raged to myself, you would have kept your property safe. I would be Mister Spinks, and my mother would be alive.

From Peter's ashen face, I could tell he thought the same. He jerked his head up. "Turn back... We must go back –"

Garric hummed a tune loudly, and drove Cucullan on.

A night-wind blew up, sending torn and printed papers skittering under Cucullan's hooves. With them came a strange stink, like the Salstead sheep pond but worse, as if it carried not just piss and night-soil but the dirty cursing thoughts and memories of a thousand sinners.

"Breathe through your mouth, for we must cross the Fleet," chuckled Garric, pointing at a high-walled bridge ahead. Though I hated his laughter, I breathed in through my throat, still choked up with smoke from my burning home. Now I could not smell the foul river air, though it stung the back of my mouth like bile.

On the far side, I turned in my seat and looked back over the river at the last row of houses. One stood nobly above the rest, each of its windows white-edged to stand out from the sandy walls. Looking up at its slate roof sparkling weakly in the moonlight, I dreamed I heard a faint creaking.

The wheels were quieter now that they rolled over hard-packed earth. There was no music on this side of the river. Shop-awnings were unpainted and the windows showed not a flicker of light.

"Now *this* is London, at last. Here in the true city, men work at their craft, and sleep well at night," said Peter proudly, breaking the silence. "Back there, in Holborn and Westminster, wastrels who profit from others' labour must carouse to keep the Devil at bay."

Garric cleared his throat and caught my eye behind my father's back as he looked back longingly westwards. He mouthed the words "*pour les hommes de fortune*". For men of fortune.

Dawn was drawing close by the time Cucullan came to a halt. Untired, he tossed his head, the steam rolling off him like silk sliding from a woman's smooth shoulders.

We sat there for a breath. Low enough for us to see the new moon; two neat rows of houses bounded the silent street, awnings tied down over their shopfronts. Each workshop bore a painted sign, all written in the same looping hand; and though the roadway was rough and puddled, it was tidy compared to Holborn.

My ears were full with the memory of Cucullan's endless clip-clopping, my eyes still blinded by the strange lights and sights of the city. Then it all came on me again: aiming the pistol at Cowans and the villagers; waiting to die once I had fired; my father's beating; my mother – I could not think on it more.

Garric climbed down from the driving seat and offered me his hand. I shook my head and jumped down, but landed on my bad ankle and had to grab his coat to stop from falling.

"What have you brought to Silk Street, you French fool?" a woman asked from the doorway of the house on our right.

"Take the boy, Abigail, if you please," said Garric pleasantly, as if she had not insulted him at all.

Abigail stepped forward, broad-hipped and barefoot, pretty eyes in her smooth-skinned face. Each chubby finger was filled with her warm spirit. She cocked her head, then lifted me clear over her shoulder to take me inside.

She carried me upstairs, squeezing between the splintering wooden railings, and pushed open a battered door. The bedroom behind was still warm from the dying embers in the fireplace, and I saw that someone had been reading by oil-light in a small chair by the chimney. Abigail dropped me on the bed.

"Take off your clothes, sweetheart," she said gently.

I shivered as I pulled them off, the soaking cloth sticking to my skin. As I dropped each piece on the floor, she pulled it away with her foot. She rubbed me raw with cloths, and I put my shamed hands over the wrinkled acorn of my pimmy. She dried my hair and cleaned out my ears, as you do with an infant. At last, I lay on my back while she covered me with blankets, dry for the first time since I had run into the sheep pond to hold my mother's broken body.

She clattered back down the stairs, murmured something to Peter, then banged open the front door. I heard her grumbling at Garric about how clumsily he had tied the horse, but he laughed and sent her back inside to cook while he groomed Cucullan.

The sounds skated over shallow puddles and echoed upwards to the blind stars.

I strained my eyes to look around the room, too tired to lift my head. Little portraits hung in egg-shaped frames above the fireplace, and bound books were stacked in a neat tower in the corner of the room. Their faded gilt names reproached me for not being able to read them.

I closed my eyes.

Garric shut and bolted the door below me.

"*Hmmrrrrgrrrnn*," mumbled Peter, his voice half-mute through the floorboards.

"*Shmmnnngrrblnn*," said the woman Abigail.

"I will kill him!" yelled Peter. "I will kill them all!"

Garric's boots clacked fast across the stone floor. There were grunts from below, and then with a roar Peter threw down something made of metal. It skittered ratlike into a corner.

"There will be no more killing," said Garric firmly.

Silence.

"You will not serve the boy with a murder. There is a home for you both here," he went on, quieter now.

"She was always itchy to whore it with the city folk," snapped Peter.

"You must work," replied Garric after a silence. "Tomorrow we will find you a workshop and a loom, for a man cannot stay long in London without coin or craft."

"There is the empty place across the street," said Abigail.

After a long silence, Peter tramped up the stairs and into my room, now wearing some ill-fitting clothes of Garric's. He curled himself under a blanket by the dying fire. I breathed quietly, listening to his roaring thoughts. Feeling came back to my numbed fingers.

CHAPTER SIX

The Exiles

In which Calumny trades insults with the scrofulous Ty Pettit

Peter worked the loom without pause, his mouth sewn shut like a corpse's, the stinking tallow candles flickering to the *chumpa chumpa* of the dancing frame. If he thought of my mother, he did not speak of it; and nor did I. The pistol and the gilt-lettered silk were hidden in my room upstairs, untouched since we came to this house.

Abigail had found us a Silk Street workshop whose Flemish tenant had been taken to the debtors' prison. The bailiff's men came and prised the boards off the doors and windows for us while Peter watched, grimly fingering the few coins in his purse. It was bigger but lonelier than our Salstead home, and the Fleming's breath still filled the place with gloom.

I sat out under the awning, watching a scrawny raker pass along Silk Street, though there was little for him to scavenge from the careful goodwives. The July skies had broken, and the rain was streaky with soot, corrupt with the smells of soap-boiling and tanning. I had hardly left Spitalfields, but I could not forget the clean streets and fancy shopfronts of Holborn. The roots of my devil's hair twitched at the thought of them.

Bolts of woven silk lay on a wobbly counter beside me. Peter had told me again and again which roll I should sell for a shilling, and which for half a crown. Though it was only eight weeks to Saint Matthew's Day, my birthday, there was still no talk of Peter writing my name in the guild-book. I needed to make my own destiny now.

It was late July, we had been in London more than a month already, and we had nothing left. Peter's purse had held more than six pounds, but it was a guinea to rent the place and more than four pounds to buy the loom from the Fleming's creditors. Clothes we needed too, which left us but a few shillings for food. It took an age for Peter to turn out his first full bolt of silk on the strange Flemish loom, with its many different headboard patterns.

Weaver-wives brought us stew and soup, frowning and pushing away our thanks as if we were plaguey beggars. The shops around us all belonged to Huguenots, who had fled France when those popish whores raised sword and flame against them. English weavers did their trade nearer to the docks, and were little seen in Silk Street.

The Huguenots spoke English as well as Peter or me, and yet they laughed and ate and drank like forengies, slow and satinly, and when I closed my eyes and listened to the street-chatter, I felt like I was sitting in my mother's kitchen.

Weavers would nod and tap their chests when they walked past me at my counter, as if to say, *God be with you, orphan-monkey.* Garric himself stopped and greeted me each day with a little wink, but he did not speak of taking me on either. He was my last hope of joining a trade; I would have to show him that I was worth apprenticing as a mercer.

The filthy rain kept the custom away, and so I watched Abigail across the street, chewing on a dried sausage and joyfully insulting her grim-faced Frenchy neighbours from her workshop window. She let me run errands for her now and then, and it gave me more hope that her husband would apprentice me.

Her son, the goblin boy, came out of the house, mumbling a little song to himself, his bulging wet eyes turned away from my gaze. He was of middling height, midnight hair swatched across his smokefish-yellow face. His curious narrow breeches were cut long, laced tightly over a gooseberry-coloured shirt that hung limply over bony shoulders.

He carried some strange magic in his body. Walkers on the street moved unknowingly out of the way of his weak goblin limbs.

I saw my mother's face in a puddle. Its pallor was broken by the reflections of gentle ladies tippytoeing down the street under their riding hoods, dashing from canopy to canopy to keep their soft skins dry. A breeze brisked us with the smell of sea-salt.

"Walnuts… Crack 'em and try 'em," warbled an uneasy hawker at the far end of Silk Street, afraid to walk among the Frenchmen.

"English… Bite 'em and eat 'em," mocked Abigail, and the laughter whisked around the roadway until the nut-seller turned tail.

I wanted to show my skill at merchanting, but I had only a few bolts of silk on my counter. Most of the gentlefolk walked by my scant wares to the heavy-laden stalls up the street. But two sisters with soft eyes stepped nervily up, shivering under their stormcloud-blue dresses.

"*Ooh la la, les belles dames de l'Ongland,*" I called out, loud enough for half the street to hear me. "*Venez voir la soie la plus fine.*"

Which was to say, *Show me your clean little venus, for I vend the finest silk in the land.*

I had seen that look before: on a rabbit, drawn terrified into the glow of a night-lantern. These two ladies were barely past one and twenty, though I would have wagered they wore the shackles of marriage to old men.

Afraid of my height and red hair, they clutched hands – but they were dry under my awning. I took a step away to show I meant no harm, touching my hand to my forelock in the Londonish way. They drew closer, as weak-spirited folk will. *Chumpa chumpa*, came the sound of Peter's loom.

"*Pardong me, je ne speak pas bien l'Onglish...*"

I pulled a length of turquoise silk over my knuckles, fluttering it so clear water seemed to run down my hand. I knew well that any woman would turn her head for a magpie sparkle and a kind word.

"*Si belle, si belle...*"

So beautiful, I called the silk, but I made the words sing in such a way that they both blushed. The younger woman held out her hand to feel the silk, lowering her stubby lashes. I gently took off her ring so that she could not rip my fine cloth, and gave it to her sister. My fingertips delighted in the quick cold kiss of silver.

"Is this all you have?" asked the elder, rain rolling down her wide nose and onto my counter. I pulled my bolts away – one drop of tanner-stink rain would spoil a yard: two hours' work for Peter.

"*Mais non*, good madam," I whispered. I opened the workshop door but raised my hand, close to the bosom of the first lady, forbidding her to enter. I lowered my eyes to the ground.

"*Mon père*... my fazzer... he is very desolate, he cannot spick..."

"He cannot spick?"

"He cannot spick no words, my lady. Not since... my *maman*..."

It did not hurt to say the words in play.

They looked quickly at each other, like two birds holding the same worm, and tenderly pushed me inside.

The meaty smell of tallow hung in the grieving air, its black smoke swirling streakily as the loom blew it back and forth. It was dim but warm, and the ladies opened their mantuas at the throat.

Peter had tidied our little eating-table, the bread crusts hidden away in an earthen jar the Fleming had left behind. On one wall, we had nailed up hooks in neat rows to hold the finished bolts of silk. Opposite were stacked wicker baskets of spun silk thread. In London, there was no shortage of starving Portugee women who would throw a fathom of thread for a farthing. That was why I sat at the counter outside, hawking the cloth.

Peter scowled at the ladies and carried on without speaking a single word. He looked as miserable a Frenchy as I had ever seen, and now I knew they would believe my story.

"*Quelle couleur?*" I asked, meaning for them to choose their silk.

They were staring at Peter's left hand, still bruised from the stoning at Salstead. Abigail had bound up the fingers tight for a fortnight, and they had healed well enough for him to work. It was a blessing that the right was his shuttle-hand, though.

"Poor man," whispered one, pressing her lips together.

The other pulled at a little purse that dangled from her waist-ribbon, itching to throw my father a coin but fearing his angry face.

"Which colour?" I pressed them in English, pushing them towards a vile green crepe. Peter had woven it from badly dyed thread that he had bought one dark night when he was too far gone with gin.

They hesitated, crinkling their noses against the stink, but I stood between them and the door. They knew that they must choose, or else stay longer in this little Satan-hole. The younger pointed blindly at the crepe, and I had rolled out and cut three yards before the other could say no.

"*Deux* shillings, lady gracious," I murmured, looking down sadly as I doubled the price.

Quickly she counted out the coins, and another twopence for my trouble. I let her brush by me as she left. Her lusty gaze had near scalded me, and when I squeezed her rump she made no sound at all. In that moment, Salstead seemed no more than a bad dream.

I looked back at Peter. He waved me away angrily. Going outside, I nearly bumped heads with the goblin boy. He had been stood by my counter, listening to my foolish play.

"To hear you speak French is to watch a cow dance on its hind legs," he said, measuring the thickness of a roll of silk between his thumb and little finger to guess its length. "One and sixpence ha'penny."

"To see you walk the street is to find a rotting mushroom growing on a pimmy," I shot back loudly, snatching the roll away.

Behind him, the two ladies heard my words, looked back in horror, and splashed away up the street. Other shopkeepers had come out to watch my duel with the goblin boy.

"You sell silk the way a pig shits in his own sleeping-straw. Two shillings eleven pence one farthing," said the goblin, and again he thumbed my wares.

"You spy at my door the way a crow feeds on its mother's puke," I said loudly, and there was laughter around the street as the weavers rattled their mugs and shears on their window-frames. Abigail stood with folded arms in her doorway, grinning like a hungry bear.

"Do you know the price of any of these rolls? For your empty counter speaks of an empty mind," he asked sharply.

He sought to shame me before his mother. Well, I would not let him stand between me and his father's good favour.

"Do you know the smell of a woman's venus? For your tight breeches speak of a beast well tethered!"

His mother shrieked with laughter and strode across the road, the rain bouncing off her white cap. The weavers rattled their metalware louder, just like the banging of pots and pans, and the sound brought Peter out from the workshop. He stood next to me with his face drawn, a hand on his weaker hip. He flinched as Abigail ran up our steps and shook the rain off.

"Enough, enough, you whip-tongued shrews!" she cried, plucking a thick rag from her belt to whack each of us across the head. The watching weavers pulled their heads back inside, still chuckling.

"Peter Spinks," said Mistress Pettit firmly, holding us by the napes, "your Calumny cannot count. And my Ty Pettit is too shy to sell fine cloth to pretty ladies. Let us put them together. Your sweet-faced devil can speak to the custom, while my mathematical monster counts the coin and measures the silk. What do you say?"

My father scowled at his feet and went back inside, leaving me red-faced at his ill manners. The loom started up again, *chumpa chumpa*.

"Garric!" yelled Abigail, quick-witted enough to see that my father would not speak to a woman.

Out Garric rolled, smiling and scratching his backside. He plashed across the street and kissed his wife, sticking his fat tongue in her mouth. Goblin boy shied away from the sight.

Abigail muttered a few words in Garric's ear, and he pushed her gently back over the street. Then he went inside the workshop. I pressed my ear against the shutter, but could not hear any voice over the sulking chatter of the loom.

"Wait," I whispered to Ty, and darted inside. Garric sat on the stool next to my father's, watching Peter plucking tiny flakes of dust and feather from the weft to keep it clean.

"Master Pettit, will you not apprentice –" I began.

Garric shook his head to dismiss me, so I gathered up half a dozen finished bolts and took them out to Ty. He brushed each roll with the hairless back of his goblin hand, clamped it from middle to edge to feel the weight, and told me the price. He could tell the quality and length from touch alone.

Ty and I began to sell silk together. We gave the Pettits half of the profit, though it was less than they deserved. Still, they thanked me kindly every day, and said that I was a good friend to them.

Abigail nagged Garric to apprentice me as a mercer alongside Ty. At first he grumbled and said I should follow my father in weaving, but after some weeks he relented. He would write my name in the mercers' guild-book at the next meeting, the third Wednesday in September – barely six days before it would be too late. In just a few weeks, I would be on the road to becoming Master Spinks.

The ladies came to Spitalfields to pet Ty, the thin yellow-faced mechanical, marvelling at his quick spirit. And they came to blush at my Frenchy outrages. At the end of each day Ty counted out the coin as quick as lightning, never keeping any back for himself or me, but making an honest split between our fathers. The first Saturday night, I watched Peter count out the week's coin, hoping I could begin to keep my own share.

He put a shilling into a little rusted lockbox, took a couple more for ale and food, and then he threw me twopence for my own spendings. And so it was every week after all that work.

Twopence.

The third Sunday in August, I was sat in the front window of Ty's house, resting my back against the frame. Dust fluttered lazily in the sunlight that slanted low through the half-open shutters. I had no duty to worship now, for each Huguenot man is trusted to pray in his own way.

Peter was gone from Silk Street, leaving my chest feeling light. Every Sunday he limped his way to the French church of Threadneedle Street. Perhaps he held on to my mother with the French words they spoke there.

Abigail was boiling bones in the back kitchen. The more rotten the stock, the better the soup, she said, and hers was as rich and spicy as a woman's summer-sweat. Ty worked at the eating-table, scrawling pictures and mathematic on the back of a pamphlet he had found on the street. He always carried a slim ash-board quiver of charcoal sticks.

Garric sat on a stool outside, humming a sad tune as he carved a coiled serpent from soft alder-wood. Each tiny knot in the wood became part of the scaly pattern. A little breeze lifted and dropped the fine hairs on his knobbly arms.

A shadow fell over him.

"*Pas mal le couteau*," growled a brutal voice. I like your knife, it said, coming from a giant with a scratchy black beard, hollow eyes and sprawling hands that twitched at his sides.

"Welcome, Bouleau," said Garric peacefully. "What think you of my serpent?"

"*Parle pas comme un chien*," spat the brute. Speak not like a dog, which is to say, an Englishman.

"There are no dogs here," replied Garric, resting his knife on his knee. "There are only beautiful creatures of God, with blood English and French all brewed together."

The Bouleau beast hawked deep in his throat. "*Les bestioles irlos vendent leur soie le dimanche*." The Irish animals sell their silk on a Sunday.

Garric shrugged. "Then let the good God judge their sin. And what are the silk guild's rules to a saddler?"

Floop.

Bouleau spat over his shoulder; a sweating glob veined with blood and yellow phlegm thudded into the dusty street. Garric spoke in a lower voice now.

"*T'as vu l'autre?*" Did you see the other fellow, he asked, and I wondered why he spoke in French now. To hide his words from Abigail?

The big saddler pulled his mouth down, as if to say, *I did*. And then he winked at Garric and clenched his fist, miming the smashing of a window. He caught my eye and stopped his play.

"*Dieu vous sauve*," he grunted.

"And you and yours," replied Garric.

Bouleau passed on, baring his splintered teeth at me in a snarl that might once have been a smile.

"The Bouleau brute…" I said quietly, hoping Garric would tell me the true story of Bouleau and what they did together. Who was the "other fellow"?

"That man, he is a brute indeed," said Ty, coming to the door with his mother. I sighed, knowing I could not ask Garric the truth now.

"Pssh," answered Garric, carefully carving a snake's eye with the tip of his knife.

"Ty has it right," argued Abigail. "He has brought horrors on Catholics that would make you piss your bed at night."

I could not hold my shudder in.

Ty, in a ghostly voice, moaned, "He has carried a severed head around the streets to terrify the world."

Abigail slapped him lightly on the crown.

"And so he hates the Irish because they are Catholic," I said.

"No," growled Garric fiercely, turning to me with a harsh look. "We all hate them."

At the mention of the Irish, Abigail joined in angrily. "They hawk their coarse popish rags in our streets at a price that would beggar a monk. We hate them because they break Sabbath and kiss their rosaries for forgiveness."

"But we are not all killers like this Gorton Bouleau," said Garric calmly, showing me the hissing face of his wood-snake. "I will finish this Sunday next. Where is my soup?"

CHAPTER SEVEN

The Making of Tyburn Tree Pettit

In which France makes joyous union with England

Ty never used his full and glorious name, which was Tyburn Tree Pettit. If it had been mine, I would have told the story of my birth all over town. But Ty, the maggot, was shy and secret with it, and I found out why the next Saturday evening.

Garric had invited the English master weavers to his home, together with Peter and the Silk Street weavers.

The money-purse had begun to fill up again, and the old man had gone to Draper Street to buy himself a new broadcloth waistcoat. He did not come back until dusk, grumbling that no tailor understood the correct fashions anymore. Which was to say that he dressed like an ancient.

He looked fine enough, even if he did insist on wearing his faded old coat on top of the new costume. He took a little pot of blacking from his coat pocket.

"A man cannot fight in poor boots," he murmured as he carefully smeared it into the cracked leather. I watched him from the doorway, listening to the boastful laughter of the French weavers in Garric's house. Outside, a little band of men walked slowly up the middle of Silk Street, staying suspiciously out of the lengthening dusk-shadows. Peter pushed past me and planted himself in the middle of the roadway.

"Guild brothers," he called out boldly.

"An English voice is a welcome sound," replied a little frowning fellow.

"A brother is welcome," said Peter quietly, "no matter what his nation."

The little fellow grimaced, but one of his companions stepped forward, a lanky man whose knobbled head shone in the dusklight.

"He has the right of it, Trosly," said the bald man to the little fellow. "I give you my hand, brother. Call me Alfred Middlem."

He clasped my father by the hand, squeezing his elbow with the other. Through his window across the street, Garric watched Peter greet the Englishmen.

"Middlem, is it?" asked Peter. "I knew a Robert Middlem once. Though he had a full head of hair, if you will pardon it."

"Killed at Edgehill when I was a boy," said Middlem with a friendly nod, ushering his companions into Garric's house.

"I was at Edgehill…" my father began, then saw that I had followed him half across the street to listen. Irritated, he waved me back, but it was too late. I knew for sure he had fought for Parliament.

I waited until they had gone inside before darting around the house. Ty was waiting for me in the alley, as we had agreed, and we stood on a pair of upturned baskets to watch the gathering through the shutter-slats.

The Englishmen were huddled in one corner of the room, with most of the Huguenots seated at the eating-table. Abigail had lit a dozen candles, giving wavering shadows to the neat piles of cloth that were stored on shelves around the room. Peter gave Middlem's name to Garric, and the mercer threw his arms around the Englishman and kissed him on both cheeks. Trosly tutted, but his companions laughed and stepped forward to greet the Silk Street men. Abigail fussed around, moving men from here to there until Englishmen and Huguenots were mixed with each other. My father sat apart, by the hearth. Ty and I shivered a little in the growing dark.

"About the Irish and the guild price –" blurted the little frowner.

"Will you not take ale, Master Trosly?" Abigail asked sweetly, handing out tankards.

"William, Mistress Pettit means to tell us that it is not the custom to talk of business without first drinking and conversing," chided Middlem.

"Comrade before woman," grumbled Peter into his cup. It was what he said when Mirella made him angry.

"Well," said Middlem, leaning back so that Abigail could fill his mug, "since you are the host, should you not begin the conversing?"

Auchan, a silver-haired weaver from Silk Street, rapped his knuckles on the table, the corners of his mouth wrinkling up. From making bed-smiles, Abigail had told me, and it was true that he was seen each month with a different woman.

"*Dis-leur comment* –" he began.

"In English, brother, if you please," called out Peter, raising a little murmur of thanks from the Englishmen.

"Pardon me," replied Auchan, who spoke English with very little accent, since he had spent so many hours in the beds of London girls. "I mean that we should tell the story of how an ignorant Frenchy like Garric Pettit came to be a master mercer and marry with the most glorious woman in the city –"

He broke off as Abigail twisted his ear.

"His stories are all lies," she said calmly, and kissed Auchan's crown. Garric groaned as she went into the kitchen.

"How would the mercer-guild let in a man without papers?" demanded Trosly sharply.

"They were losted!" called out Garric, mangling the word to raise a laugh. "The guildmaster believed my story…"

"…when you married his daughter," finished Abigail from the kitchen.

Auchan began his tale: of how, in 1671, Garric had come over from France in a leaky boat with nothing but a sack of lace, and was wandering the Hyde woods. He spoke no English.

"He had not eaten or drunk all day, and now he had a thirst on him."

"A thirst on him!" called out Trosly, holding up his tankard, and three or four others joined in, calling out "A thirst!" until Abigail came running in with the jug. Auchan carried on.

"Garric had heard a hellish noise through the trees, and thought it would be a fine idea to have a look. He came across a huge gantry, packed with people, all yelling and waving their arms like madmen. Before them was a cart under a wide gibbet, on which half a dozen players stood with rope tied around their necks. And then the horses were whipped, the cart moved, and the place burst into a hellish uproar. Women ran forward to pull at the hanged men's feet–"

"It was an execution at the Tyburn Tree!" Trosly broke in. "Do they have no hangings in France?"

"In France, an execution is no sport," replied my father quietly from behind him. He took another swig from his goblet, pulling his lips back as if the drink had stung him. "In France, many a man is hanged for the crime of being a Protestant, and a craftsman. And so the crowds do not drink or cheer."

The English weavers looked into their beer.

Peter broke the silence. "Let us not speak of France or the Catholics, nor of those Irish weavers who steal our living. Here we are all free men, all Protestants, all guild brothers."

"Brothers!" called out Middlem, raising his tankard to the room. Every man joined the toast, and drank deeply. Abigail, her arms across her chest, looked from Garric to Peter and back again, frowning. Peter drained his cup and filled it from a small jug. Gin, as I had thought.

Auchan stood up. The candlelight made his pointed chin cast eerie shadows on his face.

"A woman –"

"Ooohhhh," teased the Huguenots, glancing at Abigail.

"A woman was drinking from a tankard not five yards from him, and she too had her glassy eye fixed to the murderous scene."

Abigail could not help but laugh at Auchan's poetry.

"She supped deeply, stretching her spine back and back until he feared she would fall."

Auchan mimed the girl's drinking.

"In one strike of lightning, I knew this was the woman for me –" started Garric.

"Liar!" growled Abigail, her eyes warm. Auchan clapped his hands for silence.

"Garric stared at the girl thirstily. '*Frongsay*?' she asked, seeing the womanish cut of his jerkin."

Trosly and the others laughed out loud to hear such mockery of the French. Auchan came to the story's lusty summit.

"'*Erhhh, erhhh,*' burbled Garric, too thirsty to hide his true race. He pointed at her hip, where she was balancing the quart pot, and made a mime of lifting it to his lips and drinking deep. The girl made a face like a hawk looking at a rabbit and came over to look inside Garric's sack. Clamping the beer pot between her thighs, she stroked the raw silk with the back of her hand. You can feel the roughness that way."

The English weavers nodded.

"The girl made a sign with her fingers to show that she wanted an armful of the silk for her trouble. He looked at the pot she had clamped between her thighs, licked his lips again and nodded. So she put the pot behind her, far out of his reach, and pushed Garric down onto his knees."

Garric looked proud, but Ty turned away from the window, shame darkening his eyes.

"He put his sack behind him in the same way, and before he knew it her skirt was up over his head, her strong fingers were clamping his French face hard into her sweaty English –"

Abigail reached around Auchan and grabbed his crotch before he could talk of her venus. He groaned and pushed her off. All of the weavers drank down their beer, red-faced, staring hotly at Garric's wife as if they were in the story with him.

"'*J'ai soif,*' moaned Garric, I am thirsty, but her understanding had stopped with 'kes ker say', and she started to dance like a gypsy around his long nose –"

Auchan danced out of Abigail's reach.

"Garric forgot his thirst, he decided to eat instead, while above them the crowd were screaming at the next victim, louder even than Abigail's yelling. But she was full of ale and past holding her piss. It poured down Garric's face – and thirsty as he was, he gulped it down. His first taste of English beer, and believe me it tasted better for having been through an English woman's guts than not."

Trosly screeched with laughter and collapsed in his chair as the Frenchmen gathered around Garric to punch him on the arms and praise him for his lust.

"By now," whispered Auchan, drawing everyone close to him, "he was fit to burst. He parted the curtain of her skirt, and he spilled his garlic cargo in her beery hold before they could even kiss."

"Urrggghh," said Middlem in disgust, but Auchan finished with a flourish.

"The trapdoor dropped for the last time and the crowd booed wearily," he said.

Trosly and the Englishmen got to their feet to praise Auchan's story. I watched my father as he got unsteadily to his feet to join the cheering. "It is well," murmured Garric, watching Peter. And now I understood it all. Why Garric had come to Salstead. Why he had offered me an apprenticeship; why he had risked his life for Peter's. A weaver, a soldier, an Englishman with a French family: he could unite the guilds. For what, I did not know; but for a moment I was proud to be his son.

When they had all sat down at the table, there was a long silence, no man wanting to speak first. Only once all the weavers were looking at Peter did he speak, his voice powerful but slurred by gin.

"The Irishmen, brothers. The guild price…"

Ty had quietly stepped down from the basket at my side, shamed by the story of his parents' lust, so I took him over to our workshop for a crust of bread. We sat and watched the flickering shapes of the weavers in his house, and I told him the long story of how my uncle had died.

The talking and drinking carried on after Ty had gone home. Peter was among the first to leave, stamping out onto the roadway with his new waistcoat unbuttoned. He looked over at his workshop, swaying from drink, while

I hid behind the shutters. To my relief, he turned and limped up Silk Street towards the Clerkenwell.

More gin, I thought, and took myself to bed. Well, perhaps we may hear more truths before the night is out.

The Englishmen woke me, spilling noisily from Garric's house later that night. Peter had still not returned, and worry climbed the ladder of my spine.

I went downstairs and stood in the workshop, unsure what to do. It was the first time I had had the place to myself since we arrived in London. When we were not working, Peter and I would sit together under the awning waiting for custom, or else we would eat at Abigail's table while she and Garric laughed and quarrelled. Now the silence weighed on me.

A mouse pattered across the floorboards of Peter's room above me, a sound like the shuffling of Mirella's feet in the morning as she drifted back and forth, brushing her hair. On a Sunday, Peter and I would eat in silence below her, listening to her skirts swishing, and the little ouches as she pulled apart her tangles.

I had tried to forget what she had done, but now it came on me: the memory of her face through the greasy window, her arms clutching at the lisping man in white stockings, the dull yielding of her flesh when her spirit had left it.

The sight of her with that man filled my mind.

I sat up, my heart throwing itself like a madman against the bony bars of its cage. It was the same man who had threatened Peter. *Past due*, he had said, that same morning.

What was past due? Why would my mother whore herself with him? In all the terror and fury of that day, I had never asked it of myself.

Of a sudden, I wanted to rush out of the house, out of Silk Street, and hunt the great roads of London until I found that man and killed him. But I needed to know what it meant, and so I stayed on the floor, trembling with anger.

The door banged open and Peter staggered in, stinking of gin. I saw in the moonlight that the knuckles on his good hand were red raw, as if he had scraped them on a wall. Or struck someone.

"Cal!" he called, but my name stuck in his throat. I stayed where I was, breathing lightly.

Peter looked around him, his eyes narrowing. He closed the door, took a crust out of the bread-jar and munched, a rill of drool slipping down his chin. He struck a match and lit a candle.

"Who was that man?" I demanded.

Peter jumped, spitting the bread back out of his mouth. His eyes widened, as if he knew what I talked of, then dulled again as he sat at the table.

"Why did my mother whore herself to that man?" I shouted, pushing his shoulder.

Without standing, he hit me backhanded with his good fist, the one with the bleeding knuckles. I gasped at the pain as my lip split but did not step back.

"She was no whore," he said quietly.

"Then she did it for your sake," I persisted in a trembling voice, my head ringing from his blow. "You knew that man!"

"I did not," he said, staring at me like a farmer at a fattened calf.

"Then –"

"Hold your tongue, boy," he ordered.

Peter covered his raw knuckles with his other hand, puffy and bruised. I shook my head and balled my fists, not knowing if I had the courage to strike back at my father. Cripple though he was, I was no fighter, and I could not have borne to be bested by him.

The old man dug a wrinkled little waterskin out of his breeches pocket, flicked out the stopper and raised it to his lips.

When he had sucked it dry, he threw it onto the table.

The door opened and Garric burst in, his eyes afire. He looked at Peter's hands, then at my face.

"Come in," said Peter, as if nought was wrong with the world.

I made way for Garric to sit down. Peter offered him the maggoty bread, and he accepted, even though I knew he would already have eaten a pailful of Abigail's sweet rabbit stew. They chewed. Garric tilted his head towards me, and Peter shrugged as if to say, *Say what you will in front of Cal.*

The mercer leaned forward, his hands pressed down on the table.

"There is work for us, Peter. Work for men who hate the Pope."

My father sighed and crossed his arms.

"The man I spoke of… well, there is good money to be made, and it will spite the king."

"Money?" asked Peter, rubbing his fingertip on the middle of his forehead.

"Oh, that is the least of it!" cried Garric. "Do you not tire of weaving, weaving, weaving?"

He laid his hands on the table, pink palms upwards.

"Silk is dying," he whispered. "The Irishmen sell at half the guild price, then the Netherlandish bring their calico from the Indies... We cannot live on silk alone, Peter!"

"Then the guild must stop the Irish and the Dutch," replied my father, shrugging. "Guild price is the fair law. It is God's law."

"So you will not come to the coffeehouses with me on Monday?"

Peter shook his head. Garric slapped the table in frustration and turned to look at me. My father seized Garric's arm with his damaged left hand, wincing.

"You shall not talk to the boy!" he snapped.

"I can go to the coffeehouses!" I cried. "I can sell –"

Peter stood quickly, his chair falling away behind him with a bang. He took the bread-jar and flung it at the wall close to my head, spattering me with clay shards and weevils.

"You shall not leave Silk Street without my word!" he roared. "Men who seek money are the greatest whores of all – if you so much as cross the Fleet, there'll be no apprenticeship for you. No weaving, no mercering!"

Garric rose and stood between Peter and me until the moment had passed, then went over to the door.

"I will not speak of it again, not to you and not to Calumny. I swear it you."

My father kept his mouth clamped, a vein in his forehead

standing out like a bruise on his pale skin. I caught Garric's parting wink as he closed the door.

I knelt to pick up the pieces of the bread-jar, not looking at the old ghost. He sat down to work the loom, his back to me, and the shuttle bumped up and down in its path like a bird with a broken wing. I watched him until my feet ached, wondering how a man could stand so cruelly in his own son's way.

I went upstairs to my room. Peter never came through my door, and so he did not know that I still kept his pistol under my pallet, wrapped in the black cloth with gold lettering. I took them out. Belly, steeples, fork, said the letters. Who could tell me what they meant?

I thought about Garric. For a merchant, he did precious little merchanting. And his brocades were too rich for his little mercer-shop, which meant that he had money somehow. It was Abigail who bought the workings of the weavers, and Ty and I who sold the wares, so what did he do? Where did he go all day long while we worked for his profit?

He had some secret business in the coffeehouses, and I knew from his wink that it could mean coin for me. Coin of my own, not twopence a week from my squeezepurse father. Well, if Peter would not answer Garric's call, I would.

A man goes to a coffeehouse to make the business and wealth of the world his own. So Garric had said. Well, Peter be damned. He had stood too long between me and my trade. Apprenticeship be damned. With my wit, I would be Mister before long, and without breaking my back at a bankrupt's loom.

I held the pistol up in the moonglow. The perfect silver cogwheels flickered, and I felt its power running through my veins.

I had to cross the Fleet, whatever the old ghost said. It was more than coin and title I wanted. Somewhere in the great city, beyond the corrupt river, was a lisping villain who had ruined our lives. If Garric would take me into that world, I would find the man who had whored my mother.

I had been a coward in Salstead, trembling and dithering until it was too late, but no longer. I lay on my pallet long into the night, listening to the beat of Peter's sleepless loom.

CHAPTER EIGHT

Rebellion

In which Calumny defies his father's wishes

I was determined to defy my father and discover Garric's secret that next Monday, but the mercer seemed content not to go anywhere. Ignoring the damp heat, he spent the day arguing with Abigail, moving shawls and waist-coats from one pile to another until she shrieked at him in fury. At last he settled down to carve his snake under the awning. Sweat gathered around his hairline, but he did not brush it away, intent on shaping each serpent tooth perfectly.

Peter stayed in his workshop. We had not spoken for two days, and fury sang out in the waspish humming of the warp.

I carried the pistol in my waistband all that day, hidden under my shirt, the trigger wrapped in the black silk to keep it from firing unbidden. The steel warmed my skin until a little trickle of sweat ran down it, and the barrel poked my thigh painfully whenever I sat.

The fierce August sun burned away the muggy clouds, and the custom wilted like picked daisies. Ty and I stayed at our counter until we were blinking from the glare. Abigail bustled over to pack up the wares.

"Come to the shady side of the street," she ordered, rolling down Ty's high collar and touching the side of his throat tenderly. For the first time I saw the knobbled violet bulge that stretched from his Adam's apple to his right ear. A little sister-lump nestled under it, skin raw from rubbing against the linen collar.

"It is the King's Evil," Abigail told me softly.

Ty sniffed and lifted her hand off his neck. Grief clutched at my guts as I remembered Mirella's last touch, ruffling my hair with a sad smile.

"It has nought to do with the king. It is a mound of unwanted flesh to be cut off, is all. Here, touch it," he ordered.

"Do you want Cal to catch it from you?" demanded Abigail, yanking her son across Silk Street.

"Why is it called the King's Evil?" I asked her as I followed.

"It can only be cured with the king's touch –" she began solemnly.

"And then he will give you an angel," Ty finished.

"An angel?"

"He means a coin, an old coin," said Abigail wearily. "It is worth ten shillings –"

"Half a pound!" said Ty angrily. "But I may not ask the king's touch, or win my ten shillings, only because he is a –"

"A Catholic," I said in a dead voice.

So there was no hope of a cure for Ty. His own father had fled France because of his faith, and we all knew the papists to be our enemies. He was shaking from the heat, so his mother shooed him upstairs to lie down. I followed her indoors and took a ladle of water from the bucket by the door. While I sipped, I saw Garric put down his carving and look quickly indoors. He could not see me through the crack between door and jamb, so he took out a black bundle that had been tucked under his stool, slipped off the porch and disappeared down the side alley.

I followed, poking my head around the corner. Garric squatted next to the black bundle, took out a pile of clothes and slipped off his smock. Carefully, he put on a deep-russet pair of knee-length breeches, tied them with lilac ribbons, and donned two silver-buckled shoes. Then came the gaudy frogged coat I had first seen him in, and a pair of embroidered calfskin riding gloves. Last, he lifted up a black hooded cloak as if he would put it on, but squinted at the sun. It was too hot to wear coat and cloak that day.

Garric bent over the bundle again and took out a curly silver *perruque*, wrestling to pull it over his big head. I had to stuff my fist into my mouth to keep from laughing. Garric smoothed down the wig, tenderly put his other clothes in the bundle and slipped it under the raised side of his house where the rats lived. He walked swiftly down the alley, without a backwards look.

Now my heart began to pound. There was coin in Garric's business, he had said it to my father, and coin meant freedom from Peter.

I knelt down and tugged at the bundle. I left Garric's clothes but took the black cloak he had left behind. I turned it inside out to show the hemp lining, bent my back under the hood and tucked my hands into my sleeves, the way a leper hides his stubby swollen fingers. If Garric did look back, I thought he would see no more than a diseased beggar. I followed him, hiding behind the broken carts and jutting corners of the alleyway.

The alley soon ran into a narrow street. It had survived the Great Fire, and its houses still leaned lustily over towards one another, sealing in the stink of the open pissway that ran down its middle. Children played, sword-fighting with rotten splintered timbers, or singing strange songs. I could not make out their tongue, though many were red-headed like me, freckles splashing across their pale skin. Ahead of me, Garric skated his way through the crowd. I had not been this way before. Peter and I only ever took the path from Spitalfields over to the Clerkenwell to buy food at the market.

Mothers dragged their children away from the hooded hunchback. One woman I brushed against, and she shrieked and scrubbed at her bare arm with a handful of piss from the runnel, as if it would save her from the leprosy.

I followed Garric this way and that through the dead streets. Worn-out paint crosses still clung faintly to boarded-up doors, telling where the plague had struck more than twenty years before. The plague-watchmen had sealed the diseased inside to die of thirst and hunger. I fell further behind Garric, afraid that he would hear my following step in the graveyard silence.

At last the street opened out onto a grubby little market. Hawkers squatted behind upturned baskets. Here were battered pewter mugs and plates; here another fellow sat sharpening his one knife at his chipped whetstone, waiting for custom; there stood a hat-man, a dozen hats piled on top of each other on his wispy grey head, and dozens of ribbons tied one above the other on his stork-legs.

Then I saw a dozen silk-sellers, sitting in a circle. Each man's basket bore a single pile of a different colour or quality. Stubble-faced, with bristling eyebrows that met above their noses, they talked without cease out of the corners of their mouths. Within the circle stood a couple of bright-eyed women who spoke to the custom in accented English. Irish, I thought. *Les bestioles irlos*: the animals that Bouleau had cursed.

Garric walked slowly around the circle, nodding to the women in a lordly way.

"Virgin white for the fine sir," one called to him, holding out a cloth for Garric's touch. I moved closer, sitting myself between a tinkerman and a gypsy-woman repairing his wicker basket. They were too busy haggling over the work-price to notice me.

Garric took off his riding gloves and ran the back of his hand over the silk. His hand twitched away, as if the wiry hairs had scraped on a rough weave. He shrugged and put his glove back on.

"Will you not buy, sir?" asked the Irishwoman.

He rolled his hand left and right to say, *Perhaps, perhaps not*. He did not speak, as though French tones would go ill for him in this place.

"Tomorrow, then, mister fine gentleman," she cooed. Garric smiled back and walked on, as if he had no real care for silk one way or the other.

"Away with you, leper-man," hissed the gypsy-woman, kicking at my crossed legs. I spat in the dust at her feet, making her shrink away so that I could stand without showing my face, and followed Garric out of the market. We soon arrived at the Fleet Bridge.

I remembered the night we arrived in London, the music slipping out of the fine houses. Peter had not let me back over the river since, though we had smelled it well enough from the Clerkenwell market. I rushed over the bridge and down a paved side street. It made me smile to tread the smooth flags in my thin-soled boots instead of struggling through the sticky mud of Spitalfields. Such a sweet feeling, like a frog walking on lily pads.

Round a bend, the road was lined with shops, their awnings freshly painted in bull's-blood red and grass-hopper green. Lace and silver braid were stacked high on new-carpented tables next to mounds of pears, the big-bellied shopkeepers shouting for custom. The middle of the street was thronged with hawkers. Afraid of the shopmen, they barely whispered their wares. Garric stopped from time to time to speak to a hawker and feel the quality of their leather and tin. All the while I drew closer to him, until I was keeping pace on the other side of the street.

I felt like singing aloud. Though I played the leper and it was Garric who wore the gentleman's clothes, I felt his wild joy at being in the noise and business of London. We had crossed the Fleet, and here, no one knew that I had no title. Put on a wig and a pair of silver-buckled shoes, and I could be Mister Spinks for a day.

On Garric's side of the street were the saddlers' workshops. Each craftsman stood at a wooden frame, pushing the fat leather-needle through a binding, or scratching a pattern into the pommel for the journeymen to stitch.

On my side of the street were the chandlers, a long row of braziers keeping their tallow-basins melting hot. The white-haired halfwit who owned the first workshop had mixed up a vile soup of tallow, spotted with rat-fat and filled with flakes of soot. He had to dip his twine wicks into it three or four times to get the tallow to hold on, and even then his candles were lumpy and weak when he was finished. Another chandler was better at his trade, dipping his hemp wicks into the basin slowly – once, twice, thrice – each time dropping the candle into water to let the layer set, then swiftly cutting off the lumps with a razor.

I lifted my hood to watch Garric. He was leaning against the doorway of one of the saddlers' workshops, talking to someone inside. I moved on to look at the last chandler in the row, perched on a high chair over a porcelain basin, his leather apron spattered lightly here and there with candle grease. His shop bore a different guild-badge, for he was a wax chandler.

The candlemaker reached into his apron-front and took out a roll of wicking, carefully measuring two lengths from the tip of his thumb to the tail of his little finger. He cut it cleanly with a pair of scissors and held the thread up to the afternoon sunlight as if he searched for flaws. Then he pinched a tiny ball of clay around the end of the wick to weight it. My tongue was dry with envy. Such skill this man had, safe in his craft, and I did not even know where to start my own journey.

His slow pantomime drew in the crowds, and I glanced around again to make sure Garric was still there. It was Bouleau speaking fiercely to him. The beast punched his leather-needle through the saddle on its frame, then back through, again and again like a soldier stabbing an enemy. "*Bestioles*," I heard him snarl, and this time Garric's face was almost as angry.

Was he only here to curse the Irish with Bouleau? I had come here to join Garric's secret world of commerce, not watch him gossip with the saddler. Frustrated, I turned away. Next to me stood an incense-laden priest with puffy red cheeks, his Catholic cross worn shamelessly over his chest. I had never seen one of these villains before, and I clenched my fists inside my sleeves. I knew well enough that he was a servant of Satan, though the crowd did not seem to mind a popish rat in their midst.

Unhurried, the chandler dipped the wick in his bubbling basin, which gave off a faint smell of mead. I saw from his shop window that he made church candles of pure yellow beeswax. A Dissenting preacher looked on, clutching a threadbare Bible, rubbing shoulders with wide-eyed goodwives, all staring at the holy candle-making as if buying a blob of bee-shit could save their poxy souls.

Again the chandler dipped the wick, twisting it slowly as he ducked it in the basin. He bathed the thickening candle in the water bowl, then held it up to the light, turning it to make sure that the steam fell evenly. By God, he had more magic in him than any priest.

He dipped again, bathed again, until the candle was as thick as my wrist and as tall as my head. At last he set it on his little table with a sigh. With a flick of his head, he allowed the customers into his shop to buy from his two boys, still not meeting any man's eye, as if to descend to our level would be to lose his powers.

I shook my head as I pushed past the popish priest, who Hail-Maryed in horror at my leprous touch. By Satan, that was how to mint your own coin, I thought. Hold back, hold back, do not promise, until the custom are wild for your wares.

But what could I make? How would I buy myself such a glorious workshop?

Heaviness and shame filled my chest. The best I could hope for was to be one of those boys, jingling the pennies and saying "Yes, Master" to the craftsman. Still bent over, I trudged along the street and almost bumped into Garric. He was standing stock-still in the middle of the roadway, looking up at a sundial high up on the wall.

I slipped past him and waited under the low awning of a tobacco-man's place. I sniffed at the smoke that drifted under the awning, feeling light in the head, and noticed how women shied away from the strong smell. A man will pay handsomely, I thought, for a pipeful of dirty air, if only it can be puffed in peace, away from skirt-tails and gossip.

After a while, the shadow on the dial touched one of the marks around its rim, and Garric ducked under a low archway and through a door with a brass Moor's head for a knocker.

A coffeehouse.

No place for a leper, that was for sure, but nor was it a place for Calumny Spinks, spinner-boy, who at that very moment was thought to be in Spitalfields. I dithered, hunched in the low entryway.

I heard Garric's voice from inside.

A man may make the business of the world his own, I thought, pushing through the door.

CHAPTER NINE

Wig-thief

In which Calumny plays the gentleman, but for all too brief a time

I made my way up a narrow staircase. I thought this coffeehouse would be full of laughter, noisy with bargaining merchants, but it was low-ceilinged, quiet and dim, with billowing pipe smoke. Crop-headed gentlemen were huddled in packs at long varnished tables, murmuring confidences and reading papers together. Soldiers in uniforms of white-trimmed scarlet played cards, next to seven or eight gentlemen in powdered grey periwigs, making marks on a map. There was no sign of Garric.

I was hidden by a curtain half-drawn across the entryway. Behind the counter opposite was a handsome walnut-skinned fellow, perhaps a Turk. He clasped his hands behind his back, a little smile on his lips, slowly gazing back and forth across the room. From time to time his lips would move, as if he repeated what was said at a particular table.

One of the soldiers quit his game and clacked his way to the counter. The coffee-man asked the soldier his name and shuffled through the papers that were stacked behind him, at last handing over a letter. Well, I had not heard of such a thing; how strange, to leave letters with a Turkish stranger! He waited for the soldier to reach the middle of the room, and then said loudly, "I pray that you may come to me again soon, for my husband..."

The soldier blushed purple and spun on his heel, his hand clasping at his waist where his sword should have been. The Turk burst out laughing, and the other soldiers joined in, pulling their comrade back down to his seat. The lover-soldier muttered angrily and shuffled the pack, forcing the two halves into each other until the cards' edges frayed.

During the uproar, I decided I would play the gentleman and find Garric. Hats and wigs were hung on pegs in the entryway next to me. Keeping hidden, I seized a plain white periwig and tucked my red hair under it. Abigail had stitched me a pigeon-grey waistcoat when I began selling her wares, and I looked enough like a modern gentleman in its long sleeves and floppy buttoned cuffs. I turned Garric's black cloak the right way out again, throwing it across my shoulders like a cape.

The best way to hide is to walk in plain view, I thought, and so I strolled slowly down between the tables, looking on with lordly curiosity but never stopping to meet a man's eye.

Two men called out,"What news, sir?" as I passed, but I ignored them.

The room was shaped like a haunch of mutton, and I decided to tuck myself away around the corner. Next to a cold fireplace was a table with one empty chair, the other filled by a sleeping flat-faced fellow in a Puritan's black costume and old spurred riding boots. What remained of his hair was cropped short. Before him were a near-empty patterned dish and a brass spit-jug, its rim stained with grainy black. I sat down and feigned sleep, gazing at the coffeehouse through my almost-closed eyelids.

It was the finest room I had ever been in. The varnished floor glowed like dripping honey under the tables' clawed feet. The loamy brown walls bore delicate white rails at waist height, dressing the room as prettily as ribbons. Two maids tippytoed around the room, faces hidden under their billowy white caps.

Finest of all was the sight of all the gentlemen and soldiers nodding gravely and murmuring with tiny wise smiles. Not one of them feared to lose an hour here instead of working at their craft. I settled into my chair as a maid approached. Coinless, I hoped she would believe I was asleep.

"If you please, sir?"

I opened one eye. She was bent over the other sleeping man, insolently jiggling the buttons of his coat.

"Desist, girl," I snapped in Mister Ramage's dry voice, my eyes still half-closed. "Can you not see that this gentleman has travelled far to visit your…" – I flicked my hand at the room as if it were a sewer – "…rather *poor* establishment?"

"Gentleman is as gentleman pays, Master Wig-thief," she shot at me. She had a snubby nose and a chin that fell away too quickly, but her spirit shone out through her flickering hazel eyes.

The sleeping fellow grabbed her by the waist, making her gasp as his fingers pinched inwards.

"We will be served, then," he said wearily, his voice as thick as cheese, making "served" come out as "sherffed". "Bring me a pot of coffee, and another dish for my friend here."

He let her go, and she made a sullen curtsey before stalking off to the kitchens. My companion stretched his legs, shaking the sleep out of his head. His nose was curved like a falcon's, his sunken eyes pale-blue with age.

"Wig-thief?" he whispered, an eyebrow raised. Tobacco stained his front teeth.

I shrugged. "All things belong to all men."

"Only in a republic, young friend," he said sternly, still shushing through his words. "And this is no republic."

"Forgive me, sir," I replied, "but you are not of the English race, are you?"

"Dutch."

"Is that a kind of German, sir?"

"It is not. I am a Hollander, and there is no other nation on earth like us."

He took out a long thin pipe and began to stuff it with tobacco from a goatskin pouch. He smoked as we looked silently around the room. I saw his gaze linger on the soldiers, who had stood to take their leave of one another.

"Are not the Dutch at war with England?" I asked quietly.

"We have been, many years ago," he said without excitement, "but not so now."

I knew full well that war was threatened with Holland, and he spoke too calmly for a gentleman travelling in an enemy country. Well, Calumny, I thought, let us take this pretence where it wishes to go.

"If your king invades this country, will he give us another Catholic ruler?"

The Dutchman sucked deeply on his pipe. Its smell was soft and sleepy, like tree-blossoms on a summer night.

"You have the French blood, do you not?"

Surprised, I nodded. The three men on the next table had stopped talking for a moment and were reading pamphlets. The Dutchman waited for them to start speaking again before he carried on.

"Huguenot?"

I nodded again.

"And did you know that the ruler of my country is also a Huguenot? Hmmm? Our William the Stadhouder, his grandmother was from your race."

I shook my head. I did not know what to think now.

The pert serving-girl returned to lay down two cups filled with steaming black juice for us.

"Two shillings," she demanded.

I opened my mouth to protest, but the Dutchman put down his pipe, pried open a purse and gave two silver coins to the maid. She mouthed "wig-thief" at me as she went away again.

The Dutchman lifted the coffee to his lips and drew in a greedy sniff, closing his eyes.

"I see you think that a shilling a cup is an outrage," he whispered, "but this drink is so precious that only kings may decide who sells it. In Turkey, the Grand Vizier has a troop of soldiers with big… how do you say in French… *narines…*"

"Nostrils?" I left my cup on the table. I had but tuppence a week, and here was a shilling's worth of drink.

My companion took a sip from his dish of coffee, pursing his lips as if it contained sour milk. "With big nostrils. They sniff at every door in Stamboul… and if they find a merchant who is selling coffee…"

He cracked his knuckles loudly.

"You are not a very good spy, redhair."

I raised my eyebrows, but I could not help touching the wig, to see if any hairs had strayed out.

"You stumble in here not two breaths after that Frenchman, and steal a disguise. You stare wild-faced at those soldiers with a pistol hidden under your shirt. You pretend to sleep so you do not have to pay for coffee. And then your eyes become as big as a cow's when you hear I am a Dutchman."

He leaned close. I had quite forgotten that I carried the pistol.

"Do you think to rob someone?" he hissed. "Or do you have a quarrel with the army, perhaps?"

I stared at him, tongue-tied. Was this a trap? Did he mock me? He smiled at my confusion and held out a hand for me to clasp.

"I am called Martin van Stijn, and I greet you."

"I am Peter… Peter Ramage," I burbled, wriggling in my seat and blushing brightly. Van Stijn gripped my hand tightly, pressing his forefinger into my wrist, where the blue vessels thudded rapidly. Yellow and red flecks floated in his pale gaze like falling autumn leaves. I saw now the countless tiny wrinkles at the corners of his eyes and mouth, and the leathery folds where his chin sank into his neck.

"You are not Peter and you are no Ramage," he replied calmly, "but I will allow your deceit for now. It is wise to withhold one's name from strangers."

I began to wheeze. My stolen wig was worth more than a shilling, which meant the gallows for me if the Dutchman did not let go soon.

"Tisick!" he exclaimed, and released my wrist.

"Your health," I said. He snorted.

"I do not sneeze, Monsieur Huguenot. I say that you have the tisick… which is a breathing sickness."

I shook my head. "My mother, not I. It hardly comes to me. Only when…"

"It is the tisick," said van Stijn firmly. "My master… that is to say my king, William, Prince of Orange, he has it too. It is a terrible thing, when a strong man cannot draw breath."

His voice grew warmer. I liked him well now, this strange forengie who spoke to me like an equal, of kings and spies and Turkish coffee-sniffers.

"Gold," he said at last. "It is gold you came for, though I think not for your own greed. I have seen that look before. Well."

Van Stijn lifted his cup again and drained it slowly. I looked away from him, trying to hide the truth in my eyes.

"You know the Frenchman, that is clear. But I do not think you know my old friend, who is also here today. I think it would be a… kindness to introduce you. Can you read, citizen?" he asked sharply. I shook my head.

He pointed at the rows of boxes on the counter. "Do you know what that is for?"

"I do not," I said, looking over at the counter-man.

"It is the mail. A man may send or receive letters here, but he must beware that the counter-man may also read them, as you have seen with that unfortunate adultering soldier." So he too had been pretending to sleep.

I nodded seriously, my thoughts dancing with excitement, and put my fingers around my cup. Now, I would taste coffee. I would make the business of the world my own, with this wise Hollander my companion.

There was a muffled crash, and the Turk looked up and darted through the door behind him. Then came a shout or two, another crash, and then silence. All the while, the gentlemen carried on with their chatter and commerce.

I turned to van Stijn, eager to hear who his friend was. I felt myself on the edge of destiny.

Suddenly the door opened again. A grim-faced gentleman slipped out holding a paper, its wet ink glistening in the candlelight.

"Here he is," murmured van Stijn as the Turk came out cradling an arm across his chest, one eye badly bruised. Holding him by the scruff of his neck was a ruffian in gaudy clothes. Garric.

The mercer pushed the brown-faced man against the counter and turned to follow the grim gentleman, who had moved swiftly through the coffeehouse and out of a back door. Over his shoulder, Garric spied me, and roared out my name.

I dropped my coffee untasted, threw off my borrowed periwig and darted for the front door, nearly bowling over the serving-maid. Garric could not get between the gentleman and the counter, and so I was out of the coffeehouse and back down into the street before he could catch me.

A cluster of gentlewomen was gathering outside the coffeehouse, listening to a short woman wrapped in a giant shawl whose back was turned to me.

"Men enter the Moor's Head to waste their time and lose their potency," she cried, not noticing me slip past. Garric's boots thundered down the stairs, and over my shoulder I saw the gentlewomen surround him, shouting and gesturing.

I ran faster, back the way I came, Garric shouting my name behind me all along the street of chandlers. I was not stopping for him. The saddlers stared at me pelting along the street, but no one lifted a hand to stay me. What kind of business was this, breaking a man's arm to make him sign a paper?

The Fleet Bridge was crammed with cattle, carts and hawkers. I leapt up onto the narrow wall to cross the bridge, wobbling as I tried to keep my balance. Below me, the stinking river bristled with broken wheels and old ironware, warning me not to fall. Again Garric yelled, but he was stuck behind the mob on the Holborn side and could not follow.

I raced through the poor-man's market, taking care to run the long way around the circle of Irish silk-sellers. In the dead streets beyond, the fading paint crosses mocked me. The Watch had taken my grandmother, and now they would come for me. Wig-thief, liar, promise-breaker.

Soon I was in the alley by Garric's house, panting and sweating, the pistol swinging around loose in my waistband. Though I was sure he would beat me anyway, I took care to put the black cloak around the bundle of Garric's clothes and slip it back under his house.

As I crossed Silk Street, Ty called out at me from an open window above.

"Bring your father over here for dinner, Cal."

I shrugged and did not look back.

Garric had not yet returned when Peter and I went across. Abigail had made an oniony fish stew, filled with potatoes and herbs. She and Ty chattered like squirrels, but for once I would not join in. My father, who had not even mentioned my mother since we came to London, could hardly speak to Abigail. Though he said pretty words to Ty about her stew.

Garric walked in. He had not bothered to change back into his smock, but stood there wearily in the doorway dressed in all his finery. Abigail looked at him flinty-eyed but did not ask why he wore such clothes, nor why he had been out so long. He shook his hand out, the knuckles pink.

"All well with the guild, Father?" asked Ty.

Garric grunted and sat at his place while Abigail filled a bowl for him.

Peter looked at Garric, then back at his soup, and then he grunted too.

Would the mercer-brute tell Peter I had crossed the Fleet? Garric gave me a little shrug. He had no call to give Peter my secret, and I had no call to tell Abigail what I had seen either. I felt like a man at last.

Peter cleared his throat.

"I saw those Irishmen today. Not ten paces from Silk Street, hawking their rough threads in the middle of the roadway."

Garric stopped chewing and looked back at my father. Peter put down his spoon.

"They break the guild price under our noses," he said, in a voice barely louder than a whisper.

"We will speak of it with the brothers," said Garric, his French accent strong in the quiet room, and Abigail put her hand on his thigh under the table. For the first time, we ate in silence.

I could not sleep that night. I had been foolish to flee the coffeehouse instead of meeting the Dutchman's sombre friend. Though the beating of the Turk had made me unquiet, I was sure it was for a right-thinking cause; that van Stijn was an honest man.

But I had shown them that I was a foolish boy, and now Garric would make sure I did not follow him about his business again. I would never be a man of title. The best I could hope for was to be offered an apprenticeship, and then spend my days worrying about the guild price.

"Boy," I whispered to myself. I was nothing.

CHAPTER TEN

A Vicious Day

In which Calumny encounters Mister de Corvis

My black mood did not even last till morning. I worked and bantered and teased the custom, while my thoughts hopped from foot to foot like a naughty girl.

What Garric was, I had little doubt now. When a man breaks another's arm for a piece of paper, then that paper means money to him. *I cannot live on silk alone*, he had told Peter. So he had got me to take his place at the counter on the promise of an apprenticeship. Well, I would hold him to that promise, and once I had my trade, I had no need to obey my father. I could cross the Fleet and chase coin with Garric.

Who was Garric's sombre companion? Van Stijn had called him a friend. And the Dutchman himself? Well, I had heard about his countrymen, as tight-holed as the Scotch and as vicious as the Moors. Though this one had some calm authority about him, a quiet wit behind the eyes.

I knew I had found a secret that would pay me well in times to come.

I fell into my labour, and did not think of crossing the Fleet for all the weary rest of August. I had no coin of my own; and besides, I was afraid Peter would find out and deny me the apprenticeship again.

I saw how the King's Evil made Ty weak in the body. After two or three hours of work on the stall with me, he would become pale and disappear upstairs for a while, closing the shutters of his little room. He slept twice or more during the day to keep his strength.

Ty would not speak to me about his sickness, though usually he talked freely and cleanly of his feelings. How he worried for Garric, because the Irishmen were bringing in more and more of their cheap silk. His memories of living in a little shack as a boy, while the new streets were being so slowly built, ten years after the Great Fire. How he dreamed of a proper schooling, to learn the mathematic and the natural science. But his body was a secret from the world.

Well, I was always the black to Ty's white. My body was no secret. I wore my red hair scruffy and big and high, spoke loudly in my rough Essex voice, strode up and down the street with my chest out. But my feelings were locked deep in my belly.

And so it was that we became friends.

We played a good game with the custom, Ty and I. If a quiet gentleman of breeding came along, I would be the dumb boy to Ty's soft-spoken scholar. If it was a lady with a swing in her hips and a spark in her eye, then I brought a blush to her cheek while he added a twelfth to the price of the cloth. And if a squeeze-price bully came along, Ty would dash inside for Abigail, whose big forearms and smiling glare would snuff out the spark of any nonsense.

Garric changed as September birthed in showers of rain and blusters of cool wind. He did not laugh so much, nor carve his serpents, nor tell me stories of France and the old times. Peter had not forgiven Garric for his proposal, and I often saw the mercer looking over at my father's closed workshop door as if he could command it to open and release his friend.

Where there had been five of us sharing every meal, now there were usually three. Peter worked on, his *chumpa chumpa* echoing over the street whenever our chatter faded. And Garric stayed out longer and longer. He left all the merchanting to Abigail, on top of her long hours of tailoring. He put on his finery in the house now, and strode away without pretence to bully his way in the city. He always brought back some little gift for his goodwife – a bag of coins, a bead necklace, even one time a pigeon with an ivory ring on its leg. As soon as that pigeon was set down on the windowsill, it flew away south in a straight line. Abigail laughed, seeing that it had been trained to return to its master, but Garric did not join in.

From time to time, I would feel his gaze on me. It was not the pitying, cheerful look he used to wear when we first came to Silk Street, but a narrow-eyed hawker's stare that asked, "What commerce can I make with this boy?"

Once a week, the pamphlet-boy would come down Silk Street calling out his news, though it was little more than tittle-tattle of who tupped who, and who had been made bankrupt. Of the war with Holland, we heard nothing, and my thoughts began to turn to Martin van Stijn and his grim-faced friend again.

I was due to be presented to the mercers' guild on the third Wednesday in September. That Monday, Garric had said he would take me to the guild-house and help me prepare my oaths. And this time, Peter had not stopped him.

I put on a white Sabbath shirt and grey costume, and scrubbed my boots. When I came back down the ladder from my room, Ty was leaning on the doorpost, watching my father weave. His goblin kneeknobs bulged under pea-green breeches.

"Where do you go, Cal?" he asked breathlessly, toying with the book in his hand. Ty was always reading, his black brows twisted into a knotty frown.

Peter stopped weaving for a breath and pointed at Ty's book.

"What do you fill your mind with? What is this latest nonsense?"

He had never interrupted his work for me.

"It is the algebra, Master Spinks. Cal, do you know what that is?"

I shook my head and took a step away, towards the door, trying to show him that I had other coneys to catch that night, but he followed me, babbling away.

"It is how the Moors make numbers into letters. It is a way to make the mathematic without seeing the thing you measure. You can move this letter – so – and then this letter changes too."

I groaned at him. "Ty, you live in a forest of dreams. What need have I to change numbers to letters when I cannot read either? You are too womanish –"

Peter spoke over me. "Has not Master Pettit taken you to the College Secular? There is many a work on the mathematic there."

I knew nothing of this college. Secrets leaked from my father like pus.

"Mother will not allow it," said Ty, picking at his collar where it lay over his great boil. "Not while I am sick."

I poked his bony chest to make him move out of my way. Goblin potrillo that he was, he stood between me and the Dutchman.

"Where do you go, Cal?" he asked again, sulkily.

Peter stood. "Let us see what ails you, my boy. Come here."

Hot envy sank its teeth into my scalp, and I went to the window to avoid watching my father roll down Ty's collar. Garric was standing in the street in his finery, the long cudgel badly hidden under a travelling-cloak, staring at me. He winked without smiling, turned and walked towards the Clerkenwell.

My guts bubbled. This time, he intended for me to join him at the coffeehouses, but I had to get away from Silk Street unseen.

Peter was looking at the horrid lumpish mess on Ty's neck. Though I felt sick, he pressed his gnarly fingers on the boil to see if it leaked, and put his face close to sniff it.

"The King's Evil, is it?" asked Peter. Ty shrugged. I pretended to be disgusted, and slipped out into the fine rain to follow Garric.

"No popish villain will cure a thing like this," said my father, his voice booming pompously through the door. "But a philosopher of science and nature, a learned man... Well, your mother has told you 'No', and a mother must have her way on such things. Until she does not."

No doubt there was more of the same, but I was out of earshot, fifty paces behind Garric. He had avoided the Irishmen this time, and was striding through the craftsmen's streets. The air buzzed with the thoughts of tailors and moneylenders. Smug guild flags hung mockingly down from poles, their emblems speaking of brotherhood and belonging.

Too busy looking up, I tripped over the cobbles and landed painfully on my palms and knees. When I looked up, Garric had disappeared, and Ty was running towards me, calling my name.

How could I follow the mercer now? I got to my feet, brushed down my breeches and waited for Ty to catch up. He too was looking up at the guilds' emblems, chewing away at his lower lip.

"You will have your own trade soon," I said, not wanting to be envious of my friend. "Your mathematic makes you better for the mercering."

"I care not," he replied violently, his sallow skin tinged with pink. I looked at him, amazed, as he carried on.

"This commerce is empty vanity. People buy their clothes, they wear them out, and so it goes forever. And times always get harder. I am no fool, I can count well enough to see that trouble has already come to my father. He has some secret debts, else he would not have to… to have a second trade."

I held out my hand, pretending to test the rain.

"But the mathematic…" – he punched his fists together in rhythm with his words – "…is beauty. It is never the same shape twice."

He sighed and shook his head. We waited for a band of soldiers to march past us towards the Tower, their leather heels dinning on the cobbled street.

"You do not want to be a guild brother?" I whispered, forgetting about Garric now.

"There are other brotherhoods," said Ty, looking down at his boots. "Other livings to make. Universities. But –"

I nodded. I had seen the pride on Garric's face when he taught Ty his trade.

"Why do you not learn at the same time as you serve your apprenticeship?" I asked.

Still he looked down, his head wobbling heavily on his thin neck.

"My mother will not let me have the schooling. She says it leads to atheism and sin, and she will not listen to my father. She threw him out on the street for a month or two last time he crossed her."

I put my arm around his shoulders and led him away to the Clerkenwell. I thought I could lift his gloom by mocking the ranters there.

"Well, I will be your brother then. You can practise your learnings on me, and we will make our mercering apprenticeship together –"

"Cal –" he blurted out, stopping in the roadway. I had to pull him away from the heavy wheels of a hay-cart, so at first I did not see the troubled look on his face.

We had reached the Clerkenwell. Two Dissenting preachers strode through the crowd, handing out pamphlets and calling for repentance.

"Cal," he said again, mournfully, looking into the well's depths.

"What is it, Ty?"

Still he looked down at the slimy walls, smoothing his hair away from his sallow skin. The worm of doubt coiled itself weightily in my belly, and I sat down on the well's edge.

"The apprenticeship," I said in a deathly voice. He nodded.

"My father says he will not apprentice you now. He says he has other work for you..."

I closed my eyes and let despair drop its gentle blindfold over them. The fine rain patted my face tenderly. No trade. No title.

Ty touched me on the wrist and whispered, "Your father has followed us here, Cal. Should we hide?"

I had lost my chance to find van Stijn. It was plain as a Flemish whore that Peter would not let me cross the Fleet again. Everywhere I turned, my little flickering hopes were snuffed out: by Peter, by Garric, by my rotten birth.

I stood and waved at my father. For a breath, his face brightened, and I near forgave him for slaving me in the Silk Street prison. Then he frowned, shaking his long stained locks as he limped over towards us.

Peter could tell that something dark had passed between us. He sat with us to watch the red-faced preachers stamp around the green, yelling Bible-words while the passers-by clutched their purses, as if the ranters could make them poor with words alone.

The Fleet Bridge rattled and groaned from the pacing of numberless feet.

That Wednesday, the third in September, the weavers and mercers went to their guild-houses, as they were bound to. The women went with them too, for there were rooms set aside for the wives to chatter while the men smoked tobacco and talked of deep things. Even Peter left his loom, and went to join them as they walked up Silk Street with the sun at their backs.

I clutched at his elbow.

"Father, can you not take me to our guild-house? There are still a few days until my birthday..."

"*You*, master merchant?" he asked bitingly. "You are too good for weaving now, and yet not skilled enough. I know you crossed the Fleet against my will – well, I cannot help you now."

He limped off, his shoulders rounded. I struggled to draw breath.

Ty and Abigail came out of their house.

"Where do you go, Ty?" I asked, but seeing his mother's proud face, and the neat lace collar he wore, I already knew the answer. Garric was to present him to the guild as an apprentice mercer. I did not let him reply, but embraced him warmly to hide my hurt. Abigail kissed me on the cheek and led Ty away up Silk Street, tucking her hand under his arm.

As I watched them leave, Garric came up lightly behind me.

"*Tu restes là, Calonnie?*" he breathed, asking if I stayed. "To be *apprenti*… I promised it you, but if you stay here, then a sweeter trade awaits…"

I would not stay to hear his false promises. I ran back over the street and slammed the workshop door behind me before climbing the ladder to my room.

Even Ty, the sickly maggot, was to be apprenticed. He too could call me "Boy" one day, and I would have to name him "Master" in reply. My gut churned to think of it.

I knelt, lifted the corner of my pallet, and looked at the pistol and the black slitted scrap of cloth. I could not read the gilt letters on the silk, could not revenge myself on the man who rutted on my mother, had even missed Cowans when I fired at him.

Silk Street was empty, for the children had been taken to the guild-house, and I was left alone with my thoughts.

"Damn them all," I whispered fiercely. I was Calumny Spinks, Satan take them, and I would have no man between me and my desires. I could make a woman open her legs with a Frenchy wink, I could play the gentleman, and by God I would have my way.

I would learn to read. Ty must teach me.

Tucking the sable patch of silk into my waistcoat pocket, I swore I would find the meaning of the belly, steeples and fork. I would find the adultering rat-man and rip out his guts with my shears.

But first I would make my father give me my craft. Not skilled enough, Peter had said. Hell take him! There were still six days until the feast of Saint Matthew – I would show him that I was as good a weaver as any. Make him apprentice me himself.

Then I would call myself Master Spinks. Have my own coin. Marry a gentleman's daughter and become a Mister myself. And forget I was ever slaved in Silk Street.

Head stormy with my great plan, I hid away the rest of my treasures, went back down the ladder and sat myself at the weaving-stool.

"Master Spinks," I declared to the warp, in the booming godly voice of a Clerkenwell ranter.

Peter was halfway through a costly damask weave of forest-green silk. With great care, he had whittled out holes in a new headboard for weaving with: it was a long piece of wood that stretched across the top of the loom. He had to tie the silk threads in a clever pattern around the headboard that would form the weave below, here pulling more of the warp over the weft, and here less. That would give the damask its rich sheen. It was hard work for the old man, setting up the headboard with his stubby bruised fingers, but he would not let me touch it.

"You are for other crafts than this one," he had said to me, meaning the easy trade of selling and mercering. I can learn this weaving business as well as any miserable old cripple, I thought.

I nestled the willow shuttle tenderly in my palm. Tear-drop-shaped, it was stained almost black with sweat and finger-dirt. I ran my other hand over the strands of the warp, taut and ready to clamp the weft between its wings. I had never touched the silk in the loom before, as strong as iron and supple as sinew. It was a beautiful engine. I closed my eyes and breathed.

I settled my feet on the treadles and sat with my body tilted forwards, as Peter did. Shooting the shuttle between the warps, I kicked the treadles past each other, and looked at my work. A hair-thin line of weave was clamped into the cloth, here hidden below the warp and there glistening above it. I had made a row of damask.

I ran my finger along my new row and shot the shuttle back, working the treadles again, then faster, learning how to make my feet work in time with my hands, weaving faster and faster still until the cloth seemed to grow unbidden before my eyes. I paused for a moment to wipe the sweat from my brow, careful not to spill a drop on the perfect damask, and rolled up the finished bolt a little so that it did not bunch or crease. I checked behind the loom to see that the thread-spool was full and clean to run, looked up at the marvellous spider's web of threads coming through the patterned headboard, and began again.

I had never felt such peace before. The shuttle leapt from hand to hand as it journeyed swiftly through the pounding threads. I rocked back and forth with the rhythm of the treadles, and all of my weaving felt like an ancient chant. I was part of the soft song, not a plug-eared listener, and it was joy.

I was not watching the threads above me. The spinner had sold Peter a spoilt spool, and the line split as it entered the weft, snapping back and tangling with the next thread.

The headboard bucked, pulling the warp sharply towards the ceiling, and all of a sudden the shuttle was caught in flight, ripping its way out through the threads. The treadles jerked below me.

If I had stopped pedalling then, it would not have been so bad. Peter could have strung the loom again in an hour or two. But I lost my calm and forced the treadles against their will, and the tough sinews of the twisted silk threads dragged down at the new headboard. It broke in two, making the loom buck under my feet and pull the nails out of the wall-brace. The warp and headboard collapsed over the half-finished bolt as the engine sagged sadly towards me.

"Jesus forgive me," I whispered, half-standing. Our livelihood, the beautiful work, all undone. I shook my head hard, trying to make the world change before my eyes, but the destruction remained. I could not unbreak it.

I must run, I thought.

I must work every night for a year to pay Peter back, I thought.

I wanted to die.

The door was still open, letting in the muggy evening air. I walked slowly out and sat down heavily on the porch steps. The awning did not reach out so far, and I turned my head upwards to catch the raindrops on my closed eyelids.

After a good long time, I opened my eyes again to watch the drizzle. I watched the slow boiling of the clouds passing over London.

Click clack.

A well-dressed cocky tippytoed his way down the street. I watched him hopelessly, knowing I would never have trade or coin, never wear fine clothes like his. He lifted his beribboned shoes high over the puddles, afraid to scratch them on the roadway, holding his balance with a brass-handled walking stick. His mole-grey breeches were drawn so high above his waist that his baubles went their separate ways around the tight seam. Dense curls were oiled back from his square face.

For a moment I thought I knew him, but then it seemed that perhaps this fellow had taken the wrong path. He was too well-dressed a cocky to be a servant looking for cloths for his master, yet he was no gentleman either. There was a purpose to his walking. He looked at a shop on one side, then looked across at the sign opposite, repeating the craftsmen's names soundlessly to himself.

Then the cocky saw me and stopped, as if he knew my face. He drew a little lacy kerchief from his sleeve and waved it to me, as though he were at sea and I on shore – though in truth we were but ten paces apart, with no more than a half-inch of water lying between us.

"Thpinkth?"

I knew that rat-voice. I had only briefly seen this man's face, but his rattling lisp had scuttled around my nightmares for months now. Sick rage clutched at my guts as I thought of the pistol under my bed, barely a man's length from where I sat, yet hopelessly out of reach. If I am to revenge myself, I thought, I must taunt this devil and catch him unawares.

"Columby Thpinkth?"

"Yeth," I replied, making a lisp so gentle he could not be sure I meant it.

"I am Anthony," he announced.

"Anthony of which family?"

"Anthony," he said proudly.

"Of which family?" I asked him again, knowing it would prick his pride.

"I am named Anthony Anthony!" cried the cocky.

His rage told me that he had to repeat his name like this a dozen times a day.

"You thould not have left Thalthtead, for I have had to thpend many dayth finding you," he said furiously, planting his walking stick on the roadway. Though I had thought him a girlish sort, there was menace in the way he stared at me.

I stood up in a gentlemanly way. I cannot reach the gun, I thought, but just inside the door are my father's shears. I must not let him suspect I know him.

"I have not had the honour of making your acquaintance…"

"Eighty poundth ith patht due," said the cocky, all quiet, looking down at his walking stick, which looked more like a cudgel to me now.

"We have no such debt," I said, fury rising in my gorge as I stepped down from the porch onto the crunching pebbles of the roadway. Still half-mad from breaking the loom, I forgot about the shears.

"You are only alive because of my mathter, and yet you thpend money that ith due to him."

Anthony Anthony lifted his cudgel clear of the ground,

pointing its base through the open workshop door at the loom.

"Indeed we are not," I mocked, as if the street were full of listening gentlefolk. "My father paid for this loom with gold, for I saw him do so. Perhapth your mathter ith ath hard to underthtand as you, and tho you have come to the wrong houth."

Pretending I was insulted, I turned and stalked away from him, pulling myself up with one hand on the porch upright. I was sure he could not run as fast as I.

Swift as a striking snake, he flung the cudgel at my arm, cracking my elbow so hard that my fingers lost their power to hold. I fell hard into a puddle, banging my head on the harsh roadway beneath, and my eyes filled with muddy water. Before I could move, Anthony was upon me. He had seized the cudgel again, and he hit me with it hard and sharp in the shoulder, in the neck, upon the elbow, the knee; and then so powerfully in my back that I could not breathe. He took a slow breath between each blow, considering my flesh like a butcher making ready to carve a joint, and I was helpless to move in my pain.

"Eighty."

Whack.

"Poundth."

Whack.

He stepped around me, careful still not to muddy his lavender-coloured shoes. Now he struck me upon the head, cracking my knuckles where they cradled my scalp, not hitting me so hard now, but still it was a vicious torment to me.

"Twelve yearth."

Whack.

"Patht due."

Whack.

Anthony rolled me onto my back with his foot, pushing his weight down upon my ribs, and pressed the tip of the cudgel hard between my eyes. I stared at his features through a scarlet mist, marking them down for vengeance. At his waist he carried a little snuff-pouch, gold-stitched with a lordly badge: a snake, biting its own tail, circling a harp and a sword.

Still leaning on the club, he spoke very quietly, and his furry tongue seemed cured of its lisp.

"Tell your father that he has but eight weeks to pay the eighty pounds."

He took his weight off, and straightaway I pulled at his foot so that he fell beside me in the puddle. Wheels rattled down the street towards us. Now I feared that he had brought more men with him, and so I scrambled to my feet to run. He snatched at my leg and I fell again, cutting my left knee open. Then he was upon me, hitting and kicking faster and harder than before, and I curled myself up like a baby, waiting helplessly for death.

Of a sudden, his blows stopped, and there was a new sound in the air: the *whoosh* of a Chinese firecracker soaring upwards, then the snap of its explosion. Then another sound: a little cry like the whimper of a kicked dog.

Slowly I looked up, sick with the pain in my head and body.

Anthony Anthony clung to the upright of my porch, trying to shield his head as a gentleman dressed all in black struck him with the flat of a straight sword. After each blow, the gentleman twisted the blade to draw it back, leaving the very finest of cuts through the bruise he had just made. A little way up the street, a magpie-black carriage sat waiting, its uniformed coachman watching us from his high seat.

Whoosh. Crack.

The cocky fell to the ground. The gentleman stopped hitting and sheathed his sword. He booted Anthony below the ribs to be sure he was finished, then rolled him into the puddle until the pale breeches were brown with blood and mud.

He turned to me. Cold blue cat's eyes under cropped black hair, a narrow-bridged long nose rising from his sallow face, the dark shadow of a beard that would not be kept at bay, and an Adam's apple that stuck sharp out as if it would stab the air. I knew this man. It was Garric's grim companion from the coffeehouse. How did he come to be here?

The gentleman in black crouched next to me, breathing out a smell of spices and mint. I was too tired and bruised to speak, but there was no pity in his face.

"Frazier," he called.

Behind him, the coachman climbed down.

"Yes, Mister de Corvis."

"Take the young man inside."

CHAPTER ELEVEN

A Different World

In which Calumny meets Emilia de Corvis, a most unusual young woman

Frazier lifted me like a slain stag, his bristly hair brushing my chin.

"You'll be needing to hold round my neck, begging your pardon, young fellow."

The bruises on my arms grieved silently.

"Thanking you," he said.

He sloshed through the street to the coach. Over his shoulder, I watched Mister de Corvis stalking his way across Silk Street towards Garric's house. He did not glance back at Anthony, who was lying like a carcass on the muddy ground.

"Hup hup," grunted Frazier, awkwardly turning the carriage's door handle. He swung his body and thrust me onto the cushioned seat inside. Gasping in pain, I had not the wit to wonder why they made me sit in this coach, when my own bed was but a pace or two away.

The door closed with a soft click. The curtains were drawn on both sides, and it was as black as a popist's gusset. A strange spicy smell, half blossom and half musk. The sound of a woman breathing.

"Have you been captured by Mister Frazier?" she asked laughingly, in a bold voice that could have been heard across the Salstead Arms of a raucous Saturday night. In the dark, I blushed to think that she was making a jest of me.

Very painfully, I sat myself up straight.

"Mayhap you are a highwayman, intent on larceny?"

Her words were old-fashioned, as if she had been asleep since Cromwell's time. I could not make out her face in the dimness, but I felt sure she had seen me clearly: muddy-clothed, devil-haired, and beaten to mush by a lisping cocky. I made my hands fly about like birds, ignoring the sharp pains in my shoulders.

"I am Colonna di Spinco. I am from Italy."

"So you are indeed a thief?"

"Good lady, it is fortunate that you are not a man. Else you would be already dead for such an insult to my mother country."

There was a rough silence and I feared that my play had gone too deep, but then she seized the curtains and let light inside.

"You have not the look of a Latin."

She stared, her crisp ochre eyes a hand's breadth from mine. Her lashes were long yet thick, and her skin had an acorn sheen. Capless, her wiry black hair crowded her face, rising up into two curling heaps. She was not beautiful, although in that moment I would have sworn on Mirella's grave that she was.

"I say, you have not the look of a Latin," she said again, as if she were the judge and I the murderer.

"And you do not address me like a lady. In my country we would drown you for your words."

Now she laughed out loud, a fiery roar full in my face. She had eaten some kind of fish that day for sure, though her breath was not truly foul. As she rocked back in her seat, I quickly slid my gaze down her pale throat to admire the tight cut of her dragonfly-blue riding coat. She sat vulgar with her legs crossed on the seat, buried under the folds and billows of her white skirt, the point of a leather boot poking out from under like a bird's tongue.

I laughed with her, but my mouth was dry and my wounds gripped me like a vice.

"Forgive me, Signor di Spinco," she murmured, touching my elbow – though I knew she only pretended concern. I made myself as tall as I could, wincing inside, and she could not help but glance at my broad but bony shoulders, my winter-sky eyes.

"May I know your name, lady? For in my country I may not speak to an unknown virgin without that they cut off my finger."

She raised her trimmed eyebrow. I had put too many eggs in this Italian pudding, but I could not hold back now.

"I am Emilia de Corvis. And my virginity is my affair," she snapped. "Who was that man who set upon you?"

Emilia glanced out of the window at Anthony, who was clutching his ribs as he stood up. Mister de Corvis spoke a word or two to the cocky, who flinched and dragged himself away down Silk Street. I cleared my throat.

"I do not know him, nor in truth where in London I have found myself."

"Had you no business here?" she asked, her tongue delicious with cunning.

"Indeed no, my lady, but I have a passion to see the working people of all lands. But the street was empty of craftsmen."

"You tell a pretty story, sir," she replied. "Or at least you tell a story, pretty sir."

While Mister de Corvis climbed up on the cab with Frazier, she quickly reached over to squeeze my thigh, not a thumb's width from my pimmy. It gave me a mighty twitch, and I jerked my leg away from her in shock.

"Forgive me," she whispered wickedly. "Are you wounded... down there?"

"If I am," I gasped, "it wants but the touch of a woman to cure it."

"Then I have just such a woman for you..."

"Hup hup," called Frazier, and we jolted slowly forwards.

Emilia gently closed the curtain. In the darkness, I watched her for a while, but I could not keep my eyes open. With each beat of my heart, the aches that lined my body squeezed and let go, singing their lullaby of pain. I breathed in Emilia's spicy scent. What kind of woman was this, to tease me while her husband sat above us?

The carking of a gull woke me. The curtains were open again, but I had slid down onto my side so that all I could see was the sky and the bird's flying body rising and falling in pace with the coach.

Emilia was looking out of the window. I pulled myself up carefully. The pain had entered my bones, rattling and shrieking with the movement of the coach.

We rolled along the flank of the moody Thames. It was filled with boats clashing and watermen shouting, grey-white sails flapping around mast-poles. Idlers dangled their feet over the quay's edge, pointing and laughing. Below them, Chinese scavengers waded through black sticky mud with little spades, searching for coins dropped from ferryboats. Though I had lived in London for several weeks now, this was the first time I had seen the great river. For once I had nothing to say, struck dumb by the floating city outside.

Emilia still had her face to the window, but she watched my reflection, not the water-life.

"What is Dee Em Ee?" she asked me.

"Is it a song of your country?"

"No. It is the word you carry in your pocket." She showed me the scrap of black silk I stole from Peter's hut in Salstead.

"You bastard thief," I shouted, grabbing at her hand. I had forgotten that I was Colonna di Spinco, noble of Italy. Shamed, I let go, and she threw the silk at me.

"I said you were no Latin," she said tartly, smoothing down her skirts with her gloved hands.

"You said I was a thief, but you spoke of yourself." I tucked the silk roughly back into my muddy coat.

"It was a good play you made, to be Colonna di Spinco," she said thoughtfully.

"Are you so vulgar with your husband?"

I pointed at the roof of the cab, where Mister de Corvis sat with Frazier. She laughed again, not so loud this time.

"God save you, little actor, I have no husband. He is my father."

"But you are old to be a virgin," I babbled. Foolish hope filled my thoughts. If this Emilia was unmarried, then... It was too moony to think on.

Emilia reached over to slap me in the face, not so very hard. She left her hand there for a while, warm through the calfskin glove.

"I am but one and twenty. I will marry when and whom I please, and my virginity is my affair alone."

The coach swung away from the Thames, running now alongside a smaller stream whose stench soon filled the cab. I knew that reek of the Fleet, pisshole to the mob. Its twisting mudbanks were lumpy with broken chairs and piles of night-soil. Looking back, I saw how its filth stained the mother-river black where they met.

This Emilia liked to have the last word. I had never met such a woman, unafraid to touch a man. I had to stop myself from staring at her, drinking her in; though whether it was her charms that enchanted me, or the rich brocade on her gloves, or the curled letters of the emblem on the plush cushions, I could not say. A wealthy gentleman's daughter, fluttering her lashes at tradeless, penniless Calumny Spinks.

We clattered along for a while, crossed the Clerkenwell Bridge and turned left, heading down towards the Thames again.

"Bear Street," murmured Emilia.

"Hoooooo," called Frazier, and the horse clopped to a stop.

Mister de Corvis dropped lightly to the cobbles, and Frazier thumped down the ladder to open the door for Emilia. She stepped down all ladylike, and I tumbled out behind her. Frazier caught me just in time, for I had no strength, and would have been flat on my face without his help.

Looking skywards, I recognised the house. At the end of our flight from Salstead, this was the building I had most admired. It was made from large flat blocks of stone, neatly pointed with lime. It had a wakeful air, like a cat pretending to sleep so that the blackbird will hop closer to its clutching claws.

Mister de Corvis walked swiftly up a steep flight of steps to a tall door. He lifted a sculptured knocker, but the door was already opening. A capless, mannish woman greeted Mister de Corvis with a curtsey and a quiet word. Her lanky grey hair fell short of her shoulders, framing a jutting jaw and dagger-pointed brows.

"That is the woman who will tend to your… thigh," breathed Emilia laughingly in my ear.

The master turned and looked at me, lying foal-like in Frazier's arms.

"Frazier, take this fellow to the servants' quarters. Emilia, I have not yet seen your accounts for the week. Bring them to my study within the hour."

He went inside. Emilia followed him, while Frazier carried me around the side of the house to a simple wooden door. His face was pockmarked and weathered, one side of his mouth twisted upwards, with a tiny scar that gave him a kindly look. The housekeeper was there already.

"This is Mistress Frazier," he grumbled deep in his chest, not looking at his goodwife as he stood awkwardly on the threshold. From his wrinkled neck he must have been near to sixty years in this world, but his mistress was perhaps not yet forty. His old arms must have ached from carrying my long forengie bones.

"Put him on our bed," she ordered. Her accent was powerful, like a London tanner's, though her husband spoke soft and countryish.

He carried me down a passageway and into a little room. Daylight shone on the whitewashed walls, which were bare save for a little shelf by the door with a Bible on it. Frazier grunted as he put me on the bed. Mistress Frazier took the woollen shawl from her shoulders, wrapped it around me and then pulled off my filthy boots.

"Pardon the dirt, mistress–"

"Sssh, boy," she said firmly, tucking my bare feet under the shawl. "Frazier, heat me some water."

Without a word he stamped away, ducking his head under the door lintel. I wondered at this city, where the women had no fear of their men. In Salstead my mother had chided Peter in our house often enough, but in company she would always be the goodwife, meek and silent. Though it had not stopped them hating her. For speaking her mind, for smelling the air with a smile on her face, for touching my father's hand or face.

I turned my face into the thin little bolster.

"Where does it pain you?" asked Mistress Frazier, her hand warm on my side.

I was silent.

She did not ask me again, but set herself to poking me in the legs, the side, the chest, until I was squealing like a hog to show her where it hurt. Her touch was clumsy, as if she had never raised a child.

Frazier stamped back in bearing a basin of water and a sheaf of cloths. He sat with his hands folded prayer-like, watching his wife work. When he leaned over to help, she slapped his hands away.

Mistress Frazier rolled up my breeches and washed away the mud, then pulled the shawl back over my legs. Next, she bared my shoulders to clean the grazes on my skin. She told me to stay awake while she made soup.

Frazier kept me company, content to watch me silently from under his whiskery brows. His was the look of a man who had seen many wounds, and who had neither pity nor admiration for them.

"I am Calumny Spinks," I said at last.

He gave a little cough to say, *So be it.*

"Why does Mister de Corvis bring me here?" I asked.

A little shrug.

"My father..." I moaned.

"Aye. Peter Spinks. I will see that he is told," Frazier said, frowning, and stood up.

Soon Peter would be home from the guild meeting, and I dreaded to think of his fear when he found me gone. And his rage when he found the wreckage of the loom.

I heard the coachman grumbling at his mistress as they passed in the doorway. She held up a spoonful of soup, but it burned my lips. She waited, blowing upon the broth, slick with chicken fat, until I could stomach it. It was good.

When the soup was finished, Mistress Frazier left. I lay on my side again and closed my eyes. I was flushed from the soup, and sweat sat harsh upon my cheeks.

My dream was as hot and close as midsummer, dizzy with people moving in and out of my room. Mister de Corvis floated by, giving orders to Mistress Frazier. Emilia's spice filled the air, but she was not there. It was nothing, it was a dream; I was already dead. Lips kissed my burning eyelids, but were they Mistress Frazier or Emilia – oh Jesus, if it was Emilia.

"Calumny Spinks," she whispered in my dream. "Mister Calumny Spinks."

CHAPTER TWELVE

A Position is Offered

In which Calumny presses the limits of Mister de Corvis' benevolence

The red song of dawn woke me. Head pounding, I pushed myself up to sit. I leaned over to the windowsill and pressed my face to the cool window to see where I was. Below me, the filthy Fleet bustled with boatmen poling their way upstream between forsaken islands of shit, and broken wood, and discarded clothes. I thought that if I opened the window, the smell would kill me for sure.

I turned away and found that I could get up without crying out in pain. Anthony had bruised me badly, but he had not managed to break a single bone. I clenched my fists, thinking of how he had bested me, and became so restless that I wanted to leave the room. Its only decoration was a rusty ring hanging on the door, some kind of leg-iron. Perhaps Frazier had been a Watchman in the elder days.

Mistress Frazier had cleaned my clothes and piled them neatly at the foot of the bed. She had even mended the rips in the shirt-linen where I had rolled on the rough roadway. Under my clothes was the black silk with its Dee Em Ee, the gold letters peeling now. I tucked it away, wondering what the house-mistress had made of it.

Once dressed, I was bold again, filled with a strange feeling. I was now in the home of Martin van Stijn's companion. Now was my chance to find out what the Dutchman and Mister de Corvis did together, and to become a part of it. And if not, why then I might still find my way to Emilia's bed. One way or another, there was coin to be had.

I opened the door and walked carefully through the silent house. The kitchen was so cold in the early morning that I could see my breath before me. Copper pans hung in a pretty row high on the wall, from smallest to biggest. The fire was unlit, but the logs and kindling were stacked with care. I had never seen a home made so tidy. When I am rich, I thought, I will have a gaggle of Fraziers to stack my logs and chop my food.

I stole a small bitter apple as I tippytoed through the kitchen, my head light and trembly now. Another passage-way led to stairs, at their top a solid brass-bound door, and I knew I had found the way to the master's quarters.

Eighty pounds, I thought, that villain demanded of me. Well, there might be more than a hundred pounds' worth of gold and jewellery in a house like this. I paused, reckon-ing it for myself, before I remembered that Frazier knew my name and where I lived. For such a thief, the noose would be waiting.

But there was no harm in looking. Wincing, I climbed the stairs and tried the door handle. I rattled away but it was locked shut.

Of a sudden, it opened from the other side. Frazier stood there, pretending not to see me standing polite on the step below. Then he made a little surprised face as he dropped his gaze to my sweaty face, as pale as a three-day carcass.

"Important business. For the master. I will wait," I said, stabbing the words into the cool air with the iron sureness of Mister de Corvis' speech, keeping the half-eaten apple behind my back.

Before Frazier could slam the door on me, I was under his armpit and into the huge hallway, scuttling over the black and white checked tiles. Marble stairs rose away to my left, mighty varnished banisters swooping down their length, and the ceiling was so high that it made me giddy. A gentle breeze flowed through the hall, whisking away the traces of sewer-smell with lye and lemon-water.

I felt tiny among the patterned columns and the dark nightmare paintings in their heavy gold frames. Carved eagles and serpents leered down at me, clutching bunched stone vines. It all spoke of money and secret knowledge.

Frazier took hold of my shoulder and looked me hard in the face. My flesh ached under his firm grip.

"You'll be waiting in the study. The master will not be back for a good while yet."

He marched me through a side door and sat me down, servant-like, on a small stool in the room beyond.

The walls, gnarled with books, loomed over a massive desk of polished hardwood. Behind it was a portrait of a younger Emilia in a merchant boy's costume, hands on hips.

It was a glorious room. Though I could not read or write, I would have sat behind the desk all day, admiring my carpets and books and paintings. Even the ceiling bore a painting, of blushing bare-titted angels around an over-flowing cup of misty water. A wolfskin was stretched out before the unlit fire, its fur flickering in the candlelight.

Frazier shook his head wearily, looked carefully around the room to count the possessions in case I was minded to steal, and locked me in.

"Knock if you are thirsty," he said through the keyhole, his accent cosseting the words.

I finished the apple, waiting for his footsteps to die away. I got up and tried the drawers of the desk, but they were locked tight, so I looked again at Emilia's picture. She stared out of the lumpy colours, her eyes bright as winter snow, and I tried to follow the line of her gaze. It led me to the top of a closed beechwood cupboard, where I could see the corner of a paper sticking out. I reached up and tugged at it.

Down came a sheaf of papers, and I had to clutch at their charcoal-smudged faces to stop them falling on the floor. Drawings and paintings covered them: the likeness of a woman's hand, marked by the faintest of blue veins; a windy sea, the wavelets rearing up like cats' ears, a solitary ship bent low under the looming clouds.

Was this Emilia's work? I had never known a woman to do such things.

I took up a picture that vied against nature. Newt-green bushes bore unnatural berries, some of corrupt scarlet and some celery-green. The soil was the hue of dried blood. Blue mountains lay in the background, jagged and heavy, like words of warning in a strange tongue, and storm clouds choked the violet sky.

The drawing drew me in like the spice on Emilia's skin. Putting the other papers back, I folded up the picture of the bushes and slipped it into my pocket. I wanted my little part of this glorious house, and swore to myself that I would live in such a place one day.

I started, hearing footsteps in the hall. I barely had time to dart inside the cupboard and close it behind me before the door swung open, and then I was trapped. Oh Satan, what an ingrate I was, to spy around the house when they had fed and bathed me! I froze, not knowing if I should confess my hiding place, or stay hidden and hope to steal back to my bed when I could.

Two men clack-clacked their way across the shiny floor. The chair behind the desk creaked as one of them sat.

"You are behind in your work," said Mister de Corvis coldly.

"*D'abord on s'occupe des bestioles*," replied the other. First we deal with the beasts.

It was Gorton Bouleau, killer of children. I prayed to Jesus Christ that he did not hear me settle in the cupboard. It was completely empty, as if no man had ever used it.

"I will say what is first and what is last," said Mister de Corvis in a voice of death, and now I was more afraid of him than I had ever been of the saddler.

"*Ouais, ouais.*" Bouleau's words chimed with obedience.

"Remember, it must not seem as though you have chosen these coffeehouses in particular. Let your destruction seem like the rage of ignorant men."

I lifted my head to watch through the keyhole. Now the threads of the story began to fall into a single weave.

Garric talking to Bouleau in his saddler's workshop. Garric with Mister de Corvis, making the Turkish coffee-man sign a contract. Now Bouleau was in de Corvis' study.

The grim gentleman was reaching into a desk drawer while Bouleau loomed awkwardly near the door. These men were brutes who menaced shopmen for profit. It was clear as day that if the coffee-men did not sign their contract, then Garric or Bouleau would beat them and burn their houses to the ground. It was vicious crime, nothing more.

It was just as Peter had said. Only the worst kind of man will put money before his beliefs.

Bouleau laughed as a bag of coins flew through the air towards him. Catching it easily with his left hand, he touched a thumb to his oily forelock and turned to go.

When the door had closed behind him, Mister de Corvis stood.

"You may come out now, Calumny Spinks."

My right hand was filthy with charcoal. I rubbed it against my coat, leaving a little on my fingers. Quickly, I smudged the black dust under my eyes. Perhaps he would pity me more if he thought I was still in my fever.

I climbed out of the cupboard, stumbling as I put my feet down. He caught me by the arm.

"You look like death, boy," he said. "I wonder that Frazier let you get out of bed and go wandering in this way. It may be that we should tie you down next time."

"No sir," I babbled, "I must return home to my f-f-father before he is afraid for me."

Mister Corvis was very quiet. I was sure he saw the charcoal on my face.

"Before he is afraid for me," I said again in a baby-voice.

"Why do you hide in my private study?" he demanded. In the waxlight, his face looked darker than before, the brows heavier. He was fully dressed in riding coat and jackboots, a midnight-blue kerchief at his throat. A faint scent clung to him, like the burning of stubbled fields in the fall.

"I had important business…"

"I am not Frazier, boy." He clamped my arm harder. "I will decide what is important, and who may hear my private business."

"*D'abord les bestioles,*" I growled in the voice of Bouleau.

Mister de Corvis let me go, his eyes crinkling briefly.

"Say it again!" he commanded.

I hesitated, remembering the beatings Peter had given me for my mimicry. Mister de Corvis clicked his fingers impatiently.

"*Pas mal le couteau,*" I snarled, and even to me it was as though Bouleau was in the room, his rough shadow staining the neat lines of books.

"Do you have the French, boy?"

"My mother is… my mother was…"

He looked at me hard. "Did you hope to find money in this room?"

"No, sir," I lied, whispering.

"Did you hope to take my desk away, my books, my door handles? For there is no treasure in that cupboard, as you have seen."

"No, sir."

He let me go and pushed me to the stool in the middle of the room. He leaned against the desk with his arms folded, looking down at me.

"So you are no thief. And yet I am sure that you are not content to be a Silk Street apprentice."

Mister de Corvis turned to his desk and took a silver-coated pen from his pocket. Leaning over, he wrote fast on a sheet of paper. His letters were tall and sharp, so different to Peter's even little brick-shapes. He scratched up and down like a butcher scoring meat.

"Read this," he ordered, waving the paper at me.

I did not reach for it.

"Do you play the fool again, boy?"

I shook my head.

"You cannot read, is that it? Very well, I will read for you. 'I, Calumny Spinks, in recognition of my recent crime against Mister Benjamin de Corvis which I committed in full spite of his kindness, etcetera etcetera, do engage myself in his service for a shilling a week.'"

He gave me the paper again, and this time I took it.

"Now make your mark… here."

"But I do not–"

"You have no need to write, you must only make your mark; a cross if you will."

"But I do not engage myself to you, sir."

"Does your father give you a shilling a week?"

"No, sir, not tuppence hardly."

"Why then, we are agreed."

"No, sir."

He took the paper back from me and walked around his desk. With a faint sigh, he settled down, slid the paper onto the desktop and rested his elbows on the arms of the chair. I sat still and looked at my hands.

"Calumny Spinks, there are few men who will dare say no to me."

Even the wolfskin seemed to reproach me.

"And so I must respect your voice in such a matter. But are you so rich that you can afford to refuse my shilling?"

I shook my head.

"Or are you afraid of me? Or of Master Bouleau, mayhap?"

I shrugged. I tried to keep my face still, even though he had hit on the truth easily enough. I was terrified of the pair of them. And, besides, I had seen how he valued my gift of mimicry, and I thought he should pay more than a shilling for it.

"Yet your father… Peter Spinks, is it? It seems he owes a good deal of money to that ruffian I struck down today. It is strange indeed that you do not seek to help pay it."

Mister de Corvis was looking up at the half-naked angel on the ceiling above us. As he mentioned my father's name, the corners of his eyes drew tight. I wondered how he and Frazier knew Peter's name already, since I had not spoken it out loud.

"Well," he said, meeting my gaze, "I have warned that money-collector not to come back unless he seeks another beating. Though I do not know how long he will stay away if you do not have a protector…"

I could feel the blood rising to my neck. I knew it then, that the debt was real, that my father had hidden it from me. Mister de Corvis watched me for a moment longer, and then clapped his hands..

"Frazier," he shouted.

Stamp stamp stamp. Frazier opened the door and his master rose to take me towards him.

"Take this fellow home in the trap," he said, pushing me towards the servants' quarters, and he was back inside his study before I could draw breath.

Frazier whisked me out of the house. No curtained coach for me this time. We rattled along in the open trap, shivering in the early morning air. The horse snorted and tossed his head, and I saw that it was Cucullan. So Garric had sold the animal to the master of the tall house. It ran deep between them.

I wondered how I had dared refuse a man like Benjamin de Corvis.

CHAPTER THIRTEEN

Heavy Chains to Bear

In which Peter unveils his bloody legacy

The burnt-onion smell of work seeped out of the workshop door. Most days, it was like the cage of a dying moth, with the loom's flailing wings fluttering against the sagging old walls. But now it was still.

Guilt filled my chest as I listened to the trap roll away up Silk Street.

Peter lay by the fire with his head on a rolled-up cloak, his long greasy hair straggling over the flagstones. He clutched a scrap of paper to his chest. The cracked loom slumped in the dying firelight behind him. I did not know if he knew I had broken the engine, or if he thought the man who beat me had done it. What had Frazier told him?

My father jerked in his sleep, letting go of the paper. I knelt to take it with gentle thieving fingers, breathing in quietly. He smelled like the churchyard weeds, green and slow, and the damp scent churned my gut. My own skin was dusty and tangy, forengie like my mother's.

He'd been holding a letter: a greeting, a few words, a flounce of a signature. I folded it in my fist and curled up on the hemp mat by the hearth. I slept.

*

When I woke, Peter was sat at the loom with his shoulders hunched. He did not mend it, but held the shuttle in his hands, staring at the threads hanging loose on the broken frame. The sun pushed through the narrow shutter slits, burning little fiery paths on the stone flags.

I rustled the paper in my hand, waking Peter from his daydream. He rolled his eyes over towards me without moving his head an inch.

"Oh, God," he said, his eyes glossy. "Are you badly hurt? That Frazier told me about the man who beat you."

"I am well enough," I lied in the hollow silence. I opened the paper I had taken from him and stared at the letters blindly. He does not think I broke the loom, I thought, thanking God for my good fortune. I must play this well.

"Jesus help me," he muttered, rubbing his head with both hands.

"Why do you pray, father?"

He turned the shuttle over and over, tracing the scratches along it with his thumbs. It took him a good long while to reply.

"Calumny… I knew he would come," he whispered.

"Frazier?"

He closed his eyes.

"No. Anthony's master. He knows me."

I could not speak at first. If Peter knew Anthony, then those vicious blows were meant for my father. And what of the eighty pounds?

"How do you know Anthony was here?" I demanded.

He opened his eyes a little and pointed at the folded paper.

"This is from him?" I shouted, throwing it at the fire. It struck the hearth and fell to the mat unburned. "We owe no money, father! I saw you clear, you paid for all this with our own coin!"

"We are forever in debt, Cal," mumbled Peter.

"I am not! If you have thrown away *your* money it is *your* debt!"

I was screaming at him now, close enough to spittle on his unshaven face. My ribs groaned with each word I yelled.

He shook his head, clenching his bruised fingers around the shuttle.

"It is your debt too," he said in a hollow voice.

Furious, I rushed up to my room. I laid the pistol, the drawing, and a bundle of clothes out on my ragged blanket, and gathered it together at the edges to make a sack.

Peter was at the door.

"Cal, wait. Stay, my buck."

I could not see his face through the red stars in my eyes. He stayed there in the doorway while I laid the blanket down again.

"Cal, when you fired that pistol in Salstead, you took it from my box, did you not?"

I gave a tiny shrug.

"And did you find the… the cloth that was hidden there?"

I touched my breast where it was tucked away, wondering why he asked for a scrap of silk and not his precious gun.

"Bring it here."

I did not move, but let him limp closer and take my piece of silk. He held the cloth towards me and showed me the spiky gold letters that were stitched at the nape.

"Dee. Em. Ee. It means, *deus me exculpit.* God forgives me."

"But why do you bear such letters?"

Peter leaned back against the wall, rubbing his face the way he did when my mother died.

"I killed a man, Cal. In Cromwell's days, long before you were born."

I shook my head, confused. "But you were a soldier –"

"Soldier I was, a captain," he interrupted me. "But this was not in battle. It was… it was an execution."

Still I did not understand. "You were commanded to…"

I stopped as he shook his head. "I volunteered," he said hoarsely.

Silence spread in the air between us like a disease. Peter's eyes were empty, as if he had left his body, and I did not want to hear more. I knew that I would hate him for good and ever, once the story was out.

"This is a nonsense," I spat at him. "Some potrillo comes to us with a tale of debt and now you talk of –"

"The king," burst out Peter, banging his fist on the wall to quiet me. "I killed the king."

Nervy again, I laughed out loud.

Peter sighed, dragging the unwilling air out of his throat. He sat on my bed, pulled me down beside him, and held me tightly by the elbows to make me listen.

"It is no jest, Calumny. It is the truth."

Though his voice was sad, there was a spark of mad pride in his eyes as he showed me the hood again. "After the Lord Protector... after Cromwell and his men passed sentence of death on King Charles, they asked for volunteers to carry the axe, for the royal executioner could not be trusted. No man wanted to do it. You must remember, Cal, that most men still believed King Charles to have been ordained by God."

He looked me in the eyes. I was frozen in horror at his story.

"In the end, only two men were bold enough to do it, one to lead the king to the block and one to make the killing blow. Me. They gave us each a headman's mask inscribed with '*deus me exculpit*', so that we should know we were safe from Hell. In those days, I was so full of fire and reform..."

I pulled my father's hands off my arms and rose to my feet. Still he had not spoken of the debt, but I could feel its choking rope around my neck.

"Cromwell died," Peter went on, still sitting on my bed. "The new king came, and they passed sentence on his father's executioner, even though they did not know who it was. Death to the executioner. Death to his male heirs. The forfeit of all property. Forever.

"Death to me, Cal, death to you, no matter that you had no hand in it," he whispered.

I could not bear it any longer. Sobbing, I threw myself at him, trying to cover his mouth with one hand while I punched at his ribs with the other, wanting to burst his pride and his madness. Peter was too strong for me.

Dropping the silk scrap on the floor, he wrapped his arms around my chest, trapping me.

"And so I hid," he whispered, when I had stopped struggling. His breath was fast and scratchy. "And changed my name, and told no one but your mother. But still he found me. In London, long after we came back from France. I wrote your name in the guild-book, then went to claim our family house."

He spoke more freely now, not like the tight-lipped Peter I knew, but like a sick man coming back to health.

"There was a letter there, naming my crime. Though none but Cromwell himself knew who wielded the axe, someone had found me out. All it asked for was two pounds, but it called me by my true name, Peter Cole. So I fled London for good."

Peter let me sit up. Cold sweat clung to my temples.

"Now this man, Anthony's master, asks me for eighty pounds. He knows I have had a son, and so the price of freedom is forty-fold greater. All our money has been spent to buy the loom and rent the workshop, but I thought perhaps this man would give me time to pay."

"He will not," I whispered. "We have but eight weeks."

Hearing the first sounds of Friday labour, I turned towards the window. "How did he find you in Salstead?"

"I broke my promise to myself, so that you could become an apprentice mercer," said Peter gently, "but first I had to show Garric, and Abigail's father that it was your true name in the guild-book. My enemy had written 'D. M. E.' next to it, to show me that he knew of you. I came home without delay, but Anthony must already have spied me talking to Garric, and later followed him to our home."

My bruises cried out. Apprentice? Why had he never told me he had relented?

"Is there no other way to escape this? Can they prove that it was you?"

Peter took my hand and pressed it against his hip. The hidden bone jagged in and out like a crow's beak. "An axe-blow that near killed me at Edgehill," he said, his voice as dull as stone. "Anthony's master has it written that the king's executioner bore such a wound – and it is a mark that I cannot hide. Without a royal pardon, we are trapped."

Ghostly hemp tickled my throat. "Then what shall we do?"

"I have thought I might sell the loom and borrow what I can. Perhaps I can find twenty or thirty pounds, and perhaps this devil will let me work a while to find the rest. For sure, we are worth less to him dead."

"And stay in his power and in his debt forever?" I shouted.

I pushed Peter back, raising my hand to strike him again, but he was quick and his weaver's hands were strong despite his injury. He twisted my wrist hard until I had to kneel before him. But I was still hot with fury.

"We must find this man and kill him," I cried. "Or take a ship and leave England!"

Peter pushed me away.

"You are as stupid as your father. Change the world, kill the king, run away from your home and your duties, is it? And be like me, an old man with nothing in the world but a condemned son?"

Condemned. He had said it out loud now.

"Besides," my father went on, "I have already looked for Anthony's master. And that is what drew him to us here."

I thought of the night when he came back in a sour rage with bruised knuckles.

"And so you have given us away twice now," I muttered bitterly. "Well, I will be revenged on this man, even if you will not."

Peter rose to his feet furiously. "This crime is yours too now, Calumny Spinks. You were born to it, and you must work to bear it through your life as I have. You are not to seek this man. I forbid it. We work, and we serve, and good things will come in time."

He limped out of my room.

In time, I thought, picking up the headsman's hood. In eight weeks' time we die.

CHAPTER FOURTEEN

Employment

In which Calumny accepts Mister de Corvis' offer, and gets both more and less than he bargained for

I lay in bed listening to my father sawing and hammering. I wondered how much silk he hoped to weave and sell in eight weeks, even if he could mend the loom. Not eighty pounds' worth, for sure. The old ghost had condemned me to death, and now he thought to spin his way out of it.

Ty will know how to add it, I thought.

I tucked Emilia's drawing under my pallet with the pistol and went downstairs, striding across the workshop without glancing at my father. He did not speak.

I crossed the street. I did not wish to face Abigail's questions, so I clambered up the outside of her house to Ty's small window.

Tap tap.

"Ty, let me in."

"*Grrmmm.*"

He slept yet, the maggot.

"Open the window, goblin boy."

"*Grrrrrrrrrrrmmmmmmmmmmmm.*"

I rattled the glass in its casing until Ty let me in. I

tumbled over the sill and landed on his bed, groaning at the bruises given to me by Anthony.

"Is it true you were beat by an Irishman?" whispered Ty.

"What Irishman?"

"They say that an Irish weaver set upon you in the street."

I snorted and shook my head.

"Ty, how much money do you think Peter profits each week?"

He looked at me oddly, as if he thought I meant to rob my own father.

"Well, since I worked with you first, he has sold eight shillings in a week, then a pound, then twelve shillings, then ten. For that he must have paid sixteen shillings for the raw silk and the rest, which means that he profits more than eight shillings a week."

"Eight shillings? Then how much will he earn in eight weeks?"

"Three pounds four shillings," said Ty proudly.

"And in a year?"

"Twenty pounds."

"Only twenty pounds? Are you sure?"

He rubbed his eyes haughtily. He did not like to have his learning questioned.

"Ty, I cannot work with you today," I snapped.

"Cal, what troubles you? Why were you beaten by that fellow?"

"We owe the man who beat me eighty pounds. It is an old debt but we could not pay this year because of moving here, and now we must pay quickly."

I told him the story of Mister de Corvis and Bouleau, taking care not to say what Garric had done at the coffee-house. I wanted Ty to think first of me and my troubles.

"And what is to happen if you do not pay the debt?"

I shrugged my shoulders. Trust him I did, but not with my life.

"Listen to me," said Ty. "I do not like this thing with Bouleau, but you must go to see that Mister de Corvis. It may be that he can help you with money when the time comes. And, for sure, he wants something from you."

"But I must serve at the counter –"

"I will work for both of us," said Ty, clasping my arm. "I know you would do as much for me. In any case, I am now an apprentice mercer, the youngest such in the guild. My mother is so proud; I know she will forgive you."

I had quite forgot that my friend had been presented to his guild the day before. I hugged him proudly but gently, mindful of my bruises. All my jealousy had been forgotten, and for a moment my terrors too.

I was glad of what he said. Though I still thought of revenge, I knew that I wanted to go to Mister de Corvis' house again, to run away from Peter and his grim debt.

"I thank you, Ty," I whispered, and scrambled out of his window and back down to the street. I would cross the Fleet if it pleased me. I owed my father nothing now.

The house on Bear Street stood proudly clear of its neighbours. Wisps of stable-straw floated out of the side passage in the fresh September breeze. Frazier's murmurs rose and fell with the wind, sweet-talking Cucullan. Every man is most content to work when his goodwife is too busy with her own chores to nag him.

This time I did not go meekly down to the servants' entrance, but strode up to the main door, its fresh paint wetly reflecting the sunlight. The passing gentlefolk did not give me a second look, though in Salstead I would have been whipped for standing at the squire's front porch.

The bronze knocker, shaped like a ship's anchor, boomed when I struck it. I stood back with my hands clasped behind my back. A moment or two later, Mistress Frazier pulled the door open, one grey eyebrow raised. I waited for her to speak, to say, *Calumny Spinks! Why did you leave us so sudden? Let me make you some soup…*

But she did not look at me so fondly now. I peered round her folded arms at the statues on their little columns, beckoning my eye through the patterned marble hallway and up the swooping banisters to the high landing.

"Feast your eyes," snapped Mistress Frazier, "for there is no soup for you today, thief-boy."

I smiled at her in the false manner of the poxy villain Cowans.

"The house is well enough appointed, mistress," I replied in his sheeny voice. "It is what one might call an honest meal for my eyes. But the feast… well… she stands in the porch. In front of me."

Mistress Frazier cuffed me over the head.

"What is it you want?"

"My answer is for Mister de Corvis' ears alone."

"Well," she grumbled, "you cannot wait in the study

again. Come with me to the kitchen, but keep your magpie hands to yourself."

She swept me through the servants' door and down into the kitchen.

"Wait on this bench – but, mark you, I have counted my loaves and cheeses."

Mistress Frazier tapped her cheek. She was as tough as harness and as sharp as a carrion-crow's beak.

"I'll know if you cross me, thief-boy. I'll know it and I'll skin you with my cleaver."

She went through to the scullery. I listened for a while, but there was no sound of kitchen work, no peeling or clanging.

I breathed deeply, drinking in the faint taste of Emilia in the air. Mistress Frazier went out into the side yard, and I wondered if I dared go upstairs to find her mistress before Mister de Corvis returned.

It filled me with bile, the idea of begging for work so that I could make gold for the bastard Anthony – who had taken my mother, who had beaten me in broad daylight in my own street. Well, I thought, I will find a way to give him some coin, and then I will follow him and find who he serves. And I will kill them both.

I sat up as my bold plan announced itself. Emilia, who had sneaked in behind me, stuck her finger in my ear and snatched it away quickly. At first, I was too meek to stand and chase her, staying where I had been bid. But she teased me, circling the table until I was dizzy with her smell. Then she slowly climbed the back stairs, throwing me glances from under her tumbling hair as I followed.

Mistress Frazier growled at her goodman out in the yard. I got quickly to my feet and followed Emilia's laughing tread up the spiralling stairs. She raced all the way up to the top floor and slammed a door shut behind her. I ran up and peeked through the keyhole. A strange breathing kind of darkness and a rich smell seized me – it was her venus, I knew it. The blood left my head and I opened her door roughly, forgetting that I was the pauper and she the lady.

Emilia stood in the middle of a light-blue room, her dress pulled down neatly, challenging me with her stare. Behind her, shelves were piled high with cloth dolls; others were scattered on her bed and on the window seat. Slender books had been tossed onto the floor, mingling with piles of undergarments. This was the room of a little girl, not a woman deep into marrying age.

I was full of fury. The hangman waited for me, and I needed Mister de Corvis' gold, not to be teased by this spoilt girl. I wanted to dash back downstairs and wait for her father, but the smell of her had seized me like a charm.

"Sit," commanded Emilia, pointing at the bed.

I looked down at the street-dirt on my breeches.

"Obey me!" she spat, stamping her foot, and I sat on the soft covers. She turned and rummaged in the drawer of a dressing table by the window.

I took her pillow up gently and held it to my nose. Tendrils of Emilia slid into my gut, and my blood ran swiftly south. I leaned back on one elbow to seem as worldly as I could, watching the rich girl's rump twitch from side to side, thinking how close I was to becoming a Mister at last.

She turned and pointed a small dagger at me, prancing across the room towards the bed.

"You reek of ordure," she said in a deadly voice.

I tried to laugh but it came out like a slaughtered piglet's squawking, and my pimmy had taken so much blood that my face must have been as white as a baker's arse. She knelt between my legs and pressed the dagger against my throat, and the edge was so sharp that I could feel no pain, only the warmth of blood running down my neck. I lay back slowly, and she settled her weight on my lap. She was naked under the skirt, so that there was only the worn-out old cloth of my breeches between our secret parts.

Keeping the blade on my neck, the blood trickling round my jaw and up towards my ears, she gently opened my shirt. Breathing heavily, her heart pulsed through her warm weight on my groin. She touched me with her free hand, running it over my chest and shoulders, pushing my shirt apart.

"In that freckled face," she whispered in a sleeptalking voice, "lie eyes as turquoise-clear as the Caribbean sea… Shall I take the knife away now?"

I shook my head to show my courage, though I was sore tempted to say yes. I clamped my trembling hand to her chilly thigh. She drew the blade slowly down my throat towards my collarbone, and I pushed my palm up her thigh until I was tickling the edge of her secrecy. She pinched my nipple, and of a sudden my pimmy burst out from the top of my breeches. I moved my thumb across until she twisted it back sharply with her left hand.

Emilia leaned down, the crinkled tendrils of her coal-black hair tickling my nose, and made me blink with a puff of her lavendered breath. "If my father finds out..." she whispered, making the blue-tongued, goggle-eyed face of a hanged man.

I lay stock-still, my thumb twisted painfully, the waist-band vicious tight over my pimmy, and my right ear blocked with blood. She planted her venus on top of me for half a breath, just so I could feel what I was not to have, then whisked herself off the bed and back into the middle of the room.

"What do you want of me?" I asked desperately, and in that moment I was hers.

"Not to be slaved by carrying your brat," she shrugged, and threw the dagger carelessly among her hairbrushes. I lay back, my heartbeats shrinking back down with my lust. Eyes closed, the pillow blocking out all noise, I let myself dream that this was my house, my woman, my soft comforts. I did not think of how she had used me. Instead, I opened up my memory to keep safe the touch of soap-sweet hands, and the smell of hair that had been washed in the pure essence of flowers.

Mistress Frazier coughed loudly outside the door.

Now it struck me. I had come here to bargain with Mister de Corvis, to throw back his shilling a week and demand a way to make the eighty pounds, yet here I was, lying lustily on his only daughter's bed.

"Miss de Corvis! I must go downstairs!" I hissed, lifting my head.

Emilia was fiddling with the little bottles on her dressing table. She looked at me oddly, a dozen colours swimming drunkenly in her eyes, and held out her hand.

"Call on me again. Soon," she said lightly, rising to lead me out of the room and point me back down the maids' staircase. Mistress Frazier was tut-tutting back and forth on the stairs. She shook her head at her mistress, and took me down to the scullery to clean up my face and neck before ushering me through to the master's hall.

Mister de Corvis was waiting for me, gazing up at the high window, his blue eyes so pale under his jet-black brows. I prayed that he could not smell his daughter on my skin.

"Sir –" I began, thinking to haggle with him over my wage.

He spoke over me. "This man Anthony is a money-lender, is he not?"

I met his eye but did not reply.

"Does your father owe a great deal, then?"

I bit my lip, for such questions could lead to the scaffold. Beyond Ty, I had not a soul in the world I could trust with our secret. And never a man like this, who would beat a coffee merchant for a piece of paper.

He brushed his coal-black sleeves. Fine dust glittered as it fell to the chequered floor.

"Calumny Spinks, I will pay you ten shillings a week to conduct such business as may suit me, is that understood?"

I did not move. Why did he offer me the very thing I wanted, without me asking?

"If I am exceedingly pleased with you, I may pay you more. If I am displeased, you shall pay me back."

"Mister de Corvis –"

"Do you reject my offer again, even at ten times the wage?" His face was calm, but his toe tapped angrily in his sleek black boot.

"Sir, I cannot make the mathematic. Ten shillings a week for, say, eight weeks; how many pounds is that?"

"Four pounds, Calumny Spinks. More than a young fellow like you should gain in a year, do you hear me?"

"Yes, Mister de Corvis."

"And you will tell your father of our compact without delay. You will tell Peter Spinks. Do you accept?"

I had no choice. Four pounds was better than nothing, even though anything less than eighty would see me hang, and my father too. But I was a bold devil, and I felt in my bones that with a little silver in my pockets, I could make a fortune faster than any man.

Mister de Corvis led me into his study, went behind his desk and pushed a paper across its shiny top, showing me where I should make a cross. He dipped a quill for me, and its inky tip trembled and squeaked as I drew it over the rough parchment. I offered him my hand to seal the bargain. He did not touch me, but took out a purse from the desk drawer and dropped a rill of silver shillings into my palm.

"Here is your first week's wages. This is till Saturday next, which is more than a week, but those are my terms."

I spread the silver buttons into a little flower, two coins below each finger, the way Ty had shown me. Ten shillings – enough to eat meat for a month.

Mister de Corvis leaned over and took three of the coins back.

"Now you have repaid Mistress Frazier for her troubles, that day you ate her soup and slept in her bed."

He took two more coins, and my heart sank. The closer I came to salvation, the further it drew away from me.

"And that is my fee for the trouble of beating that foul fop. I have given you a great bargain there, Calumny Spinks, for I would not usually strike a fellow for less than two hundred pounds, let alone two shillings!"

He smiled thinly and folded my fist over the other coins.

"I will send for you when the time comes. I do not wish to see you in between times. And you are not to seek out this Anthony, do you hear me? You are bound to me in law by this contract-paper..." – the ink glistened as he whisked the parchment away from me – "...and you will do my bidding now. Frazier!"

He waved me out of the study and shut the door.

I looked up at the landing where Emilia stood watching, pulling a strand of her curly hair through her clenched teeth. I did not know whether to look away or chase back up and seize her. A passionate woman is never far from moony madness.

Frazier stamped heavily in through the servants' door, saving me from a rash act. He craned his neck to see what I gawped at.

Emilia had quickly brushed her hair back to look more mistress-like. She turned her back on us haughtily, and Frazier sighed. He seemed about to speak, but shook his head. He wrapped his pink fist around the handle of the front door and pushed me onto the top step.

I was out of the world of money again.

CHAPTER FIFTEEN

At the Threshold

In which Calumny seeks out Martin van Stijn

The thought of Emilia tortured me day and night. I had smelled, felt, wrestled, all but had her; and now I could not rest. If ever a woman wanted to slave a man, that was the way to do it.

I stole off to the Fleet-banks when my Saturday work was done, hoping to spy Emilia across the river. Her room was on the highest floor, lace curtains drawn, and I thought I saw her shadow once or twice, but no more than that. To tell true, I was content to sit there without a glimpse of her face, for my skin still tingled with the memory of her eyes, her crinkling hair, the touch of her skin on mine.

But I was drawn there by more than lust. If I could bed the rich man's daughter, it was but a step from there to the wedding-church, and to becoming Mister Calumny Spinks. To Emilia, eighty pounds was nothing, I knew it. No blackmailer would dare to cross me with Mister de Corvis as my adopted father. And then terror came on me: my father's ashen face as he told me of his crime.

I fixed my eyes on Emilia's window. She would be my salvation, I told myself.

A barge piled high with sacks was mooring against the sheer wall that bounded the Fleet, close to Mister de Corvis' house. The bargeman called out, a stocky silver-haired fellow with a guild-badge tattooed across his bare shoulders, and a gate opened in the wall above. I realised that it was in the back of my master's stables, at the end of the side passage.

My master… What kind of work did he have in store for me?

Mistress Frazier popped her head through the river-gate and began talking to the bargeman below her. He scuttled up the iron rungs, threw one arm around her neck and kissed her firmly on the cheek. The housekeeper ruffled the man's hair and touched his face tenderly. Then Frazier came up behind her, and she let the bargeman go. The two men greeted each other without warmth as Frazier threaded a rope through a pulley.

They began to haul sacks up from the barge, and I knew I should leave before I was seen. I looked at Emilia's window one last time, defeated by her lace curtains.

By Monday night, I had become impatient. I would not sit and wait to be called by Mister de Corvis; I would demand for my work to start at once. I climbed down from my window so as not to wake Peter, walking through the Clerkenwell while the moon danced in and out of the September clouds.

Though the river's foul stench swamped me as I walked down Bear Street, I could still smell the soft soapy warmth of Emilia's sheets. Not daring to knock on the front door again, I peered around the corner of the side passage.

Mister de Corvis and Frazier were talking to each other next to a low hatchway, standing so close that no one could have heard their words. After a while, the master put a finger to his lips to silence his coachman. He touched Frazier gently on the arm, and ducked inside the hatchway.

The bulky coachman sighed and leaned against the cold stone wall.

My breath spilled out in a little cloud.

"Who goes there?" demanded Frazier.

I stepped out of hiding.

"What d'you do here, eh?" he snapped, his bubbling countryman's accent thick with anger. "Dare you to spy, to listen at your master's gate?"

I shrugged.

"Mister de Corvis will be sending for you when he wants you, young fellow," Frazier said in a more kindly voice, seeing my confusion. He glanced at the closed hatchway, and then led me a few paces back up Bear Street.

"But I must work," I protested. "I need coin –"

"Coin is promised on Saturday, Calumny Spinks, and so it will be given. But not if you disobey, hear you?"

I patted Frazier on the arm, as our master had done, and left him shaking his head.

That week passed as slow as sap from the Salstead witching-pine. Every morning I waited for Frazier to bring me word from my new master, but he did not come. Each night, I lay sleepless on my pallet, the splintered beams making the shape of Emilia's face above me.

I had not told Peter of my employment, in spite of Mister de Corvis' order. I knew he would forbid me to take the work. He would rather stumble safely to death than risk everything to live.

He had fixed the loom by Tuesday morning, but it galled me to see him sat there working away for a few pennies, when the price of our lives was eighty pounds. I had to bear our burden, to pledge myself to the violent schemes of Mister de Corvis so that we might both live.

Nor did my father talk to me, though he did watch me closely when I crossed the street. He feared that I would try to find that Anthony bastard. Well, I had no need to hunt, for he would seek me out in less than eight weeks.

Garric began Ty's apprenticeship, letting me join lessons too. Since I had signed Mister de Corvis' contract-paper, the mercer was his old self again, teaching me the bawdy songs of Lyon, laughing at Ty's embarrassment as Abigail toiled away at her mending.

In the evenings, Ty taught me to read and count. At first I could not grasp the secret of the tens and the hundreds, but then one day I saw it. I held up all my fingers bar the thumbs, and whispered "Ten" to each of them. Eighty pounds seemed within my compass at last.

Later, when Ty was not looking, I whispered "A thousand" to each finger and thumb, kissing them in turn. A man is as great as the dreams he gives voice to.

*

Saturday afternoon came, and now Mister de Corvis was late to pay me another ten shillings. Seven weeks to live, and still I knew nothing of what he desired me to do.

Fearing that he would not keep his word, I thought again of the Dutchman, Martin van Stijn, who had spoken so kindly to me. I knew he was part of Mister de Corvis' schemes, and decided that I would seek him out. At the least, I would find out more about my master. I would not wait meekly for the butcher's knife. I would cross the Fleet and go to the Moor's Head every day until I met van Stijn again.

Peter had gone to the market, so I slipped across the street, taking the shortcut through the streets where the Irish lived. I felt like a plague-watchman walking among the infected buildings.

I came to the market, nearly empty now. One of the Irish weavers was still there, talking angrily to an old man in a long black cloak. I saw with surprise that it was Peter. I could not hear his words, but he shook his fist in the Irishman's face. I hid behind a fishmonger taking down his stall.

"Guild price!" shouted Peter. He spat on the ground and left, shaking his head. On his way back out of the market he kicked an abandoned pile of broken wicker baskets, scattering them high into the air. The *bestiole* laughed, but Peter did not turn back again.

I was glad to be out of his way. When that mood came on Peter, the belt was never far behind.

I crossed the Fleet Bridge. As I passed down the street of chandlers and saddlers, the craftsmen were tidying away their wares and closing their awnings.

At the sign of the Moor's Head, I stopped. I was not in a gentleman's clothes, so how could I hope to go inside? I stepped from one leg to the other, unsure, then decided to knock. A frowning face came to the little porthole in the coffeehouse's door.

"Away with you, wig-thief," said a pert voice as the door swung open. It was the serving-girl from before, pretty in a leaf-green bodice with ruffled linen cuffs, her hair sheening like kestrel feathers. She narrowed her eyes against the glare, keeping a cautious freckled hand on the door handle.

"I am no thief, miss. I am Calumny Spinks," I declared, leaning against the doorpost.

"And I am Lottie," she replied with a mocking curtsey.

"Of which family?" I asked.

"Lottie will do for you," she said, putting her hands on her waist to look up at me. "Now, do you hope to come in? In those clothes?"

I bit my lip.

"Well then, what do you mean by it? Why do you bar our doorway?"

"I am looking for my friend. The forengie… the foreign gentleman."

"Do you not know his name?"

It was trouble enough that I had given her my own true name.

"Is he inside?" I demanded. "Has he returned since –?"

"Since you ran away from that French ruffian?"

I had to laugh at her insolence.

"No, he has not been here again," she said, smiling. She touched me swiftly on the arm, and a tiny prickling flare passed between her fingertips and the sun-glowing hairs of my arm.

I sighed. As I had feared, the Dutchman was gone forever.

Lottie closed the door and leaned towards me, her breath fragrant with pear-fumes.

"Go to John Hollow's coffeehouse for a warmer welcome. There you have no need for wigs or silk stockings."

I could not understand why she would make trade for a rival coffeehouse, but before I could ask her more, she had slipped back inside the Moor's Head.

I turned and walked away quickly; I had no wish to run into the beast Bouleau.

Eighty pounds, I thought, wandering thoughtlessly into Holborn. Seven weeks to find eighty pounds, and I could not trust my employer even to pay me. Could not trust my own father.

Drunkards and whores smeared into side alleys as a dozen churches chimed the hour, their tones clashing horridly. The rich colours of shop-pennants shouted vulgar nonsense into the even-light, jostling with the smells of baking and perfumes in the mobbed air.

"Broadside a penny!" called out a running news-boy, waving an armful of printed sheets. "Dutch devils have embarked on their warships! Penny broadside!"

I came to a wide street, thronged with carters and market-goers, butting and grumbling at one another. Merchants scuttled along like dogs fleeing a beating, heads down and fists clamped around purse-belts. Chickens flurried through the mob, the uproar louder than the scolding-pans of Essex. Rival hawkers called out, "Orange, orange cloth, for farseeing men!"

Doxies were lined up on the other side of the road, plucking at the sleeves of passing men, idly showing a breast or a knee. It brought back my hunger for Emilia.

"What place is this?" I asked a fellow leaning against the bakery wall, his eyes half-closed against the setting sun.

"The Strand," he said bluntly, and pushed a finger in my chest. "Do not look a man in the face, freckle-frog, unless you be bully or bailiff."

"Why do they sell orange bands?" I demanded, brushing his hand away.

"Christ's name, but you are a country fool! Orange is the Dutch colour, do you see?"

He folded his arms and rudely closed his eyes against me. I sat on a windowsill to watch the world sway back and forth. Despair nailed me to that shady sill, but I kept my head high and watched men slip the orange bands into their pockets. There would be profit for me from the Dutch war, if I could but reckon it.

CHAPTER SIXTEEN

The Cutting-Party

In which the weavers show their strength

I did not come home till near dark. Peter was testing the loom's strength with his good hand, frowning. His pale scowl and hunched shoulders lent him the manner of a man who waited for something. He gave me an unseeing nod as I sat down at the stained eating-table.

The room grew darker. The last of the summer's mosquitoes whined its way across the floor, its wings so weary that it had to drag its body to a dying-place under the ladder.

The Spitalfields church bells rang. I counted the chimes, just as Ty had shown me. All of the fingers, one thumb: nine o'clock. From outside came the sound of men assembling on Silk Street, murmuring greetings. My father sighed and went to take a heavy pair of tailor's shears from a hook beside the door.

"It is a cutting-party, Cal," he said. "You are to stay and guard the house. Keep a watch on Abigail too."

He pulled the door open. Gorton Bouleau stuck his foul head into the room and pointed at me.

"Get your shears!"

Peter pushed the giant back, unafraid.

"Keep a watch," he told me again as they left. Garric, Ty and a dozen weavers and mercers were waiting in the roadway, holding staves and shears. Trosly, Middlem and a couple more English weavers joined them, clasping hands with the Huguenots.

This was the cutting-party the street had been whispering about. It was how the guilds punished any man who undercut their price. The weavers planned to chase the Irish *bestioles* out of the city.

Garric had his hand on Ty's shoulder, a lost look on both their faces. Ty had no place in such a battle, but as an apprentice he was bound to uphold the guild price. Though I was no fighter, I stared bitterly at Peter. I wanted to prove him wrong for leaving me behind. I wanted him to take me too.

I had a vision of the Irishman with the sour face cutting Ty's throat, blood staining his blue linen shirt, and I could not stop myself from stepping out onto the street. I could feel Peter's eyes on me, but I dodged his gaze, rolled up my sleeves, and trotted over to stand between Bouleau and Ty.

I swallowed my spit and threw my chest out, looking Bouleau in his close-set eyes. There was no colour in them, no warmth, just a deep sucking hole.

"I will go in Ty Pettit's place," I declared loudly.

Peter kept his mouth shut and his arms folded, disowning me with his silence. Auchan the storyteller poked Garric in the back and whispered in his ear. Grudgingly, the mercer spoke up.

"You are not a guildsman, Calonnie. My son... He must go."

I opened my arms wide to embrace their workshops and houses and spoke out in Mister de Corvis' voice of granite will.

"And you would leave this place guarded by a boy like me, one who is not even an apprentice? No, I tell you, a guild brother should stay behind. I will take Ty's place so you are not short of numbers."

Without waiting for the weavers to agree, Bouleau nodded at me, like a farmer to his fattest pig on feast-day. Peter cleared his throat.

"Ty, you must mind my loom for me. Keep my sheets rolling, or this party will be wasted. Cal cannot do it as well as you."

Though it hurt me to hear him say it, I knew it was the right way to save Ty's pride and keep him out of the fighting. He dashed into our workshop, and Garric blinked his thanks.

"We have all sworn the oath of brotherhood," said my father. "We stand and fight together, we defend the guild price. Let no man shirk his duty tonight."

The men stamped their feet and growled bravely as Peter split them into three bands, each man with a brother to guard his back. I was put into the second band with Garric. Inside the workshop, Ty began to work the loom, *clampa clampa*, like a war drum. Peter called out sharply, and we were off, rolling down towards the river like a bulldog with forty legs.

Auchan had followed the *bestioles* to an old plague-house near the Blackfriars, churning out their rotten farthing-a-yard silk. As we passed the streets of tailors and coopers, the cutting-party banged on doors.

"Guild price! Guild price! Guild price!" we chanted, and from the upstairs windows our guild brothers called the words back at us. Peter bobbed up and down at the head of our mob, panting open-mouthed like a wolf.

My anger flared into fierce pride, that these men looked to my father to lead them. In that moment, I wanted him to be proud of me too… to fight like a man for him.

"These are hard bastards we attack tonight," warned Auchan. "They paddle tiny Cork-boats across the stormy sea. They fight dock-men and sailors to keep all their wares for themselves. Keep your wits in your fists!"

Half a dozen hammer-wielding saddlers joined Bouleau, smelling of sawdust and fire. They nodded at Bouleau and helped him to kick down a flimsy workshop door. Quick as a whore's kiss, they ran inside; there was the tearing crack of a loom breaking, the rip of silk, and they each came out pulling one end of a bolt of cloth. Silk spilled on to the street like white blood.

"*Soie de merde*," they yelled. Silk of shit. Wild-faced boys ran down the narrow streets before us, counting our heads, pelting ahead to raise the alarm.

Garric was in front when we reached the Irishmen's plague-house, and he stopped and turned to face us. He alone had no snarl on his face: he breathed as easily as a sleeper, yet there was melancholy in his eyes.

"Break looms and rip cloth," he said. "No blood, no bone, unless we are set upon. We are here for guild price alone. If a man chooses to fight, break his leg so he cannot follow. And when all is done, let every thirsty man who has taste for fire and blood come with me."

"Guild price!" yelled Peter.

With Bouleau at his back, he ran past Garric and smashed through the plague-house door, two of our bands close behind. The workshop was packed tightly with a dozen looms, their heddles scraping on the low ceiling. Dusty air whistled fearfully in my throat.

The *bestioles* had heard us come too late. They were on the far side trying to break up a loom for staves. Between us and them, the women were still trying to pack up their cloth.

"Guild price," roared Peter, slicing through the nearest loom, his shears barely a nail's breadth from an Irishwoman's face. She screamed, and now a dozen men burst towards us, and Bouleau and Peter and the saddlers were among them, swinging their clubs and hammers.

We of the second band sliced and ripped as fast as we could. Seeing us destroy their living, the women fell upon us, biting and scratching at our faces and arms. The weavers could not cut these women, for the guild-oath forbade it, so they had to throw them off again and again until they were too bruised to carry on. But me, I was no guildsman. I saw Mistress Ramage and Mistress Sand in the Irishwomen's faces, and I screamed and punched and burst a girl's soft nose, weeping with shame and rage as I fought.

The third band burst in through the back of the room, surrounding the knot of fighting Irishmen, and I could see that it would soon be over.

Still we sliced and still they tore at us, the banshees. A proud-faced woman spat in my face while I held her off, and then her mouth was crushed from the side by a blow from Bouleau's cudgel. He laughed horridly, for he did not see there was an Irishman's club lifted above him. I cried out a warning, and swiftly the saddler bent over and pushed his long knife back through his belt and into the *bestiole*'s gut.

"A feckin' blade!" screeched the Irishman.

It gave his countrymen the rage to fight on. One was butting his head at Peter's mouth, but the old man laughed, for his tough yellow teeth had pierced the fellow's forehead. Bouleau drew his blade back out of the roaring Irishman's belly.

Now the *bestioles* and their women fled out of a side door, leaving us with the wounded man crying out in pain. Garric and the second band finished breaking the looms; Bouleau and his saddlers chased the Irishmen, but Peter stood in their way.

"We are here for the guild price only, brothers," he said, and shook his head.

The room was quiet.

"Finish," said Garric softly.

He grabbed an oil lamp from a shelf and dashed it against the nearest engine, and the plague-house creaked and snapped as the flames took hold. Peter and Garric dragged the dying man out with us onto the street.

The Irish were a stone's throw away, staring at us with tired despair: men who thought they'd finished a long journey, when in truth it had hardly begun.

"We're sorry for your man," said Peter, pointing to the bleeding man at his feet. "Guild price."

A little grumble of victory ran through our mob, and they all touched Bouleau and Peter on the shoulders as we marched back up to the marketplace, singing songs of Pope-killing and ale.

My chest ached from the pounding of my heart, and my mouth was dry as I struggled to get air into my lungs. I fell behind the cutting-party, drinking in the cool air.

A hooded man appeared out of a shadowed doorway and walked in step alongside me. A thin-stemmed pipe poked out of his hood, seeping with the scent of tree-blossoms.

It was the Dutchman – Martin van Stijn.

CHAPTER SEVENTEEN

The Thoughts of Ty Pettit

In which two friends devise an ambitious plan

"You fight as poorly as you spy," murmured van Stijn, his lips spilling smoke around the pipe-stem.

"You smoke as forengie as you talk," I hissed back at him, my pride bruised by his words. I knew that I had not shown courage in the fight, that I had even struck at the women, but I had hoped that no one had seen my cowardliness – least of all a man I thought could lead me to my freedom and fortune.

"Sometimes foreign blood may serve a purpose, citizen," he replied.

I stopped and frowned at him. "You did not happen on these empty streets at this time of night. What purpose do *you* serve, Hollander?"

He did not answer, but gazed ahead of us at the little mob, his bulbous blood-webbed nose poking out from his hood. I felt his challenge as he waited for me to answer my own question.

"You have been told of the cutting-party," I went on slowly. "I have seen you and Garric together before, and so I must guess that it is he who gave you the time of our attack."

Van Stijn sucked deep on his pipe. Tendrils of smoke drifted out of his nostrils, yellow-blue in the shifting moonlight. I carried on.

"What would it profit a Dutch gentleman to watch some ragged papists beaten about by the guilds? It is not for sport, you are too dry for that."

I thought I heard him snort.

"No, you came to see how strong the guild brothers were in a fight…"

He looked at me keenly. A hundred paces ahead of us, Garric was gathering the cutting-party in the market-place, and I knew I had little time to prise van Stijn's secret from him.

"It must mean that you need fighting men, who hate Rome enough to throw off a Catholic king. And this was their test, though only you and Garric knew it. This was their test!" I whispered.

I looked again at the guildsmen, among them my father, clasping arms and slapping backs with a wild look on his face. Furiously, I shook my staff at the Dutchman.

"How do you think to use my father and his good brothers, eh?"

Van Stijn folded back his cloak to show me his naked sword-blade. "Do not be rash, Citizen Spinks. No one will ask anything of your father that he would not willingly give."

"You think you can use honest Englishmen to make war on the streets of London? You think they will fight for a Dutchman? You have not seen what war can do –"

I stopped as I heard myself speak Peter's words. Van Stijn silently pulled up his black shirt to show a lumpish scar running around the side of his belly.

"I know enough of war," he said. "I took this blow from one of your 'honest' Englishmen in New Amsterdam, long before you were born. My only intent is to save both our countries from the vicious French king and his whoremaster pope in Rome. Believe me, I know as well as you what wounds they can leave."

I nodded my head, shamed by his right-thinking words.

"And may a Dutch king pardon an English crime?" I blurted out.

"What crime is this?" demanded van Stijn, dropping his shirt down over his marked body. The cloth had been cross-stitched with silver thread in a perfect copy of the scar.

I did not answer.

"Well, citizen. If you strike a blow for my king, he is the kind to wield a quill for you in return."

"Then I am your man," I whispered. Van Stijn turned over his pipe and tapped out the glowing embers.

"Keep a cool head. That is my counsel. It is four-and-twenty years since James of York – who is now that Antichrist on your throne – hanged half my company when he stole New Amsterdam from us. Though it was the other side of the world, and a lifetime ago, I have waited with patience to venge myself. This silver thread reminds me of the wounds I bear from him."

He smoothed his shirt.

"We will call for you, Calumny Spinks. And think on this – war is good business, for weavers and tailors."

He turned and disappeared swiftly round a corner, leaving me to rejoin the cutting-party with a sour taste in my mouth. I knew full well why he spoke of good business: Mister de Corvis had told him of Peter's debt, and I had strengthened their hold over us with my talk of crime and pardons.

Garric was squinting at a paper.

"Well, Brother Spinks, you have made a good account of yourself this night."

There was a mumble of agreement from the party. Peter did not join the praise, and I wondered if he too had seen me shirk the fighting. Garric turned to talk to the band of men, who were passing leather flasks from hand to hand.

"If you have the stomach for it, there is more work," he declared. "I have here a list of coffeehouses where the traitors Catholic meet. Let us write our message in fire and blood!"

Bouleau and a few others shouted wordlessly into the sky. The reek of gin bound the mob together.

"Is there pay?"

Peter spoke quietly into the silence, his eyes fixed calmly on Garric. The Frenchman smiled and roared out, "Five men to come with me, five shillings a head. And then we drink it, every penny, in the Covent Garden!"

One by one, saddlers and mercers stepped forward until there were a dozen men in front of Garric, though only two Spitalfields weavers joined them. The rest held back, looking to Peter. Garric only picked five saddlers to join him, Bouleau among them. They snorted like bulls as he clasped their hands in turn.

"And who is to pay the five shillings a head?" pressed my father.

Bouleau muttered a French curse, but Garric answered calmly, restraining the giant by his forearm.

"A good Protestant brother, that is who will benefact us. Now may the good God speed you."

Peter nodded and walked away from Garric and his band of saddlers. The rest of us followed him back to Silk Street.

Behind us, the six yelled wolf-like in the crisp air as they ran towards the Fleet Bridge.

The weavers walked home, Englishman and Huguenot arm in arm, speaking quietly from time to time. My father walked next to me, his shoulders hunched and his limp heavy now that the fighting was done.

The clouds pressed lower and lower until we were bathed in their fine mist. We were passing out of the alley next to Garric's house when my father seized my arm, his strong thumb digging into my flesh. He pointed at his workshop over the street. The dim light of a tallow candle shone through an unshuttered window, and there was a soft threshing noise, like the swooping of summer's last swifts. Anthony, I thought, and from the grim frown on Peter's face I knew he thought the same.

We stalked across the roadway holding our weapons before us. I did not want my father to think me any more of a coward, so with shaking knees I climbed the steps ahead of him. I peered through the open shutters and laughed with relief, beckoning Peter over to see.

There at the loom was Ty, his head tilted back in rapture. He wove, moving the treadles so gently that they swung voiceless through the air. The only sounds were the brushing of the upper and lower warps as they changed places, and the whispering song of the shuttle as it flew from one hand to the other.

"No weaver can afford to work so finely," grumbled my father. "It will take this fool all night to make up a single yard of cloth."

Peter's eyes gave the lie to his words, admiring how my friend worked the loom by feel alone. A harsh tang of envy burned my throat as I pulled open the door to break Ty's spell. He stopped weaving and turned on the stool, but his smile faded quickly once he saw we were alone.

"Your father will return presently," said Peter gently. "Now, let us see what you have made here."

My father lifted out a fold of sheeny white satin for me to try. I wiped the back of my hand on my breeches and ran it over the cloth's skin. It was as cool and flawless as mountain water.

"It stretches," I said to Peter, puzzled.

"Stockings," he murmured, tilting a handful of the satin back and forth to see how the candlelight flowed over it. "He has made satin fit for a duke's stockings. Or a general's."

He fell silently into memory. Ty coughed.

"Master Spinks, I must pay you for your silk skein. Pray you forgive me."

Peter looked up in surprise. "It is I who must pay you, Ty. This will sell in a heartbeat. And I am grateful that you did not explode my loom like Calumny here."

So he had known all along that I had broken his loom, not Anthony, but he'd waited to shame me in front of Ty. The old man fumbled at his belt, his lumpen fingers still stained with smoke and blood, and took out a coin for my friend. Then he pointed to the door.

"Now go tell your mother that Garric will be home in another hour or two."

I did not want to be alone with him.

"You may bolt the doors and windows, Father. I will stay in Ty's room tonight."

Peter ignored me, running his hands over the satin.

As we crossed Silk Street, I prised the coin out of Ty's hand. Threepence – more than my father had ever given me for a week's work. I shook my head as I gave it back. Ty was not to blame for my father's injustice.

Abigail had gone to bed. Ty cut open the shrivelled potatoes she had left to bake in the dying coals, and spread lard thinly across their puffed flesh.

We took them upstairs, where Abigail's door was ajar. She was in bed reading, wisps of fringe caught up in the frame of her spectacles. Her wide-set eyes were crimson-sore, though I could not tell if it was from reading in the flickering lantern light, or from worry.

"Father –" began Ty.

"He will not be home for a good while yet. I know it."

Ty took a bite of potato and went to his room. She lifted her book to the light again, her mouth delicately making shapes of the longer words. Still reading, she beckoned me closer.

"You do not stay in your own house tonight?" she asked, closing her book.

I looked down, pressing my left thumb into my right palm.

Abigail reached out, pulled my head down and kissed my forehead.

"Do not think on what you have seen," she whispered. "All will be well."

"But… Garric, how do you know –"

"An honest man tells his woman all," she said, letting me go. "And a clever woman knows what to say and what to keep close."

She winked. Though she was fat and motherly in her frilly nightcap, her eyes were as cunning as any shopman in London.

"Now sleep, Calumny."

Ty was already lying on his bed when I got to his room. I lay myself fully clad on a pile of clothes on the floor. We both stared up at the roof, listening to a mouse scurry along a rafter, out of sight.

I cleared my throat.

"Well," I said bitterly, "it seems that my father gives you what he holds back from me."

Ty chuckled. "That threepence? He did not give it to me. I tricked him!"

We laughed together falsely. We both knew it was no trick, that Peter had followed his own way in paying my friend.

After a silence, Ty turned on his side to look down at me, his eyes gleaming.

"Were you afraid?"

I puffed out my cheeks.

"I shat my breeches," I whispered, knowing that Ty was shamed that he had not come with us.

"My father?" he asked.

"Brave as a bear, and mad as a thirsty cat."

He lay back on his straw-filled bolster. "I do not like him this way," he said. "I am afraid someone will hurt him soon."

"What do you mean?" I asked.

"Oh, come now, Cal. You know full well that he has not been mercering these last weeks –"

I shook my head, but I could not hide the truth. As Ty stared down at me, his limp black hair cast his eyes into shadow.

"What do you hide from me, Cal?"

Ty was the only person in the world I could not lie to. I grunted.

"Well?" he demanded.

At last I told him the story of how Garric and Mister de Corvis had menaced the coffee-man, and how he had paid those saddlers to rush off into the night to beat and burn. But I did not tell him that his mother knew all, for I knew Ty would not forgive Abigail in a hurry.

And so our secrets pile up, like bodies in a plague-pit.

"I was not sure," he murmured, "but I have seen my mother's ledgers, and I know my father must have some debt. I cannot fathom what it is… And this is why you did not want to work for Mister de Corvis?"

"Yes," I whispered. "But there is more."

I looked at my hands. My fingers had become like my father's: raw-knuckled, spade-tipped, restless. I told Ty what Peter's hands had done, all those years before.

He swallowed and closed his eyes. Far off, cartwheels rumbled.

"Forgive me, Ty. Forget what I have said –"

"But why did you not tell me before?" he asked, leaning towards me. He put his hand on my shoulder and pressed warmly. "Why keep this burden to yourself?"

Now it was my turn to fall silent.

At last, I muttered, "We have the same enemy – money. If I do not find my eighty pounds, I will die. And if you do not find coin enough, then your father will keep risking himself too. We cannot sit here like fools and wait for disaster. And I cannot trust that Mister de Corvis. He has not called me back, not paid my wages..."

We sat with our eyes cast down. How could a weakling and a foreign fool make so much coin in this vast horrid city? Despair leaked from the pitch-black corners of the room.

And then the mouse moved again. It ran down the wall, squeezed through a hole, and pattered across the outside windowsill. Even a mouse, I thought, can find a way out into the free air and prosper.

I sat up and told Ty what van Stijn had said to me.

"What did he mean, that weavers prosper in times like this?" I asked.

Ty's eyes widened. "That satin I made tonight... Fit for a general's stockings, your father said."

"Well?" I demanded.

The clouds frayed, letting the moon through. From far off came the faint sound of the boatmen calling warnings on the darkened river. Ty tucked the limp black forelock out of his eyes.

"Cal, there has not been war on English soil for so long that there has been no money for new arms, new uniforms. But now, since the king fears invasion, he must fit out his armies–"

I spoke over him. "I saw new Scotch soldiers... coming down to London –"

"They will need to be equipped," finished Ty.

"But why should it profit a weaver that a soldier has a new pistol?"

It was not arms that he thought of. It was silk shirts, stockings and sashes for the officer gentlemen, and banners for the ranks: the army's seamstresses would be buying and stitching silk day and night, until the war began.

Ty told me how the army's quartermasters bought silk from the Genoese, his skin darkened with excitement.

"But... their guild price is the double of ours! How do they afford it?"

"It is not their money," said Ty quietly. "Men do not think twice about opening another's purse. And besides, the Genoese bribe the quartermasters."

"So do you think that we should ask the quartermasters to take our silk?" I asked.

Ty rubbed his shrunken chin. "I do not know," he said. "For sure, it would be dangerous to sell it straight to the seamstresses. But if we ask the quartermaster and he does not break his contract with the Genoese, then we will have trouble with the dock-guild. Let me think on it."

He held out his hand, his narrow fingers pressed together like feathers on a hawk's wing, and I held it in mine. We held our breaths, afraid to let them go lest our bold plan vanish with them in the air. I squeezed my eyes shut to keep my lies hidden from Ty's sharp gaze.

Outside, a booted man trod on the roadway. We knelt on Ty's bed and peered down. Garric was walking heavily down Silk Street, his face blackened with fire-smudges, his shirt open to the waist. One arm was wrapped around his chest as if his ribs were bruised, sweat plastering the curls to his great skull. As he drew closer, his steps slowed and his eyes flicked upwards towards Abigail's window, though he did not see us peeking. He shuffled his feet and coughed loudly, like a thief whose apprentice is cutting a lady's purse.

Abigail's bed creaked, and we listened as she went downstairs. Garric's eyes lit up when he saw her in the doorway beneath us. He opened his arms wide as if to call her to him, but she did not obey at once. Finally, one slow step at a time, Abigail went to him.

The mercer threw himself to his knees and wrapped his arms around his wife's waist, pressing his soaking hair to her belly. But she did not hug him back, standing with her hands limp at her sides and her face turned up to the starless sky.

After a while, she tugged at Garric's head to pull it away from her. Wincing, he let go of her, but not in time to stop her striking him hard across the face.

"No more, I told you," she said in a clear voice, and struck him again with the back of her hand. Garric made a soft groan.

Ty closed the shutters, and we lay down again, listening as the two of them came back inside. Abigail's steady step climbed the stairs alone while Garric shuffled around downstairs, and then she drew the bolt on the bedroom door. Her husband groaned again and made a fuss of lying down on the eating-table to sleep.

At last, Ty spoke.

"We cannot live like this any more, Cal. I am with you, no matter what."

Close by, Abigail wept softly as the moon took flight.

CHAPTER EIGHTEEN

The House of Three Mysteries

In which Benjamin de Corvis takes the measure of Calumny's wits

Curled up on the cold floorboards, I dreamed I was running through the city, knocking on closed awnings. Gold sovereigns were strung across the streets high above my head. I jumped to snatch at the coins, but they swung out of my reach, the empty shops echoing to the sound of Emilia's laughter. I leapt again, but the cobbles disappeared under me and I dropped into a deep pit. Kicking and flailing as I fell towards the bottom, I shouted, "No! No!" – and then I was awake, my shirt clammy.

I looked over at Ty, still sleeping, and wondered if our plan could truly bring eighty pounds in less than seven weeks.

Run, said a deep voice inside me. *Run, and it may be that they will not find you.*

Garric tippytoed up from the kitchen. I smiled to think that Ty and I would begin work when the sun rose. He had the body of a maggot, but his spirit was huge.

The door handle turned softly.

"Calumny," whispered the mercer, his eyes red-rimmed. The big man put a finger to his lips and gestured that I should dress myself.

Garric picked up my boots and led me downstairs, shivering. He sat and laid his forearm heavily on the table. It was patterned like a Moorish carpet, with scratches and bruises.

"Mister de Corvis wishes to speak with you," he said in French.

"But –"

I stopped myself, not wanting to confess that I had plans for the next day.

"You will return by morning, Calonnie," continued Garric. "No need to tell your father about it."

He saw me looking at his bruised fists, his smoke-stained cuffs, and shook his head. I had feared that my apprenticeship would start with fire and fist.

"Let us go, then," I said, briskly putting on my boots.

He rose and pushed me out onto the wet street, glistening with moonrays. The Irish quarter was still shedding sable ash into the night air, and we walked the other way to the Fleet Bridge to avoid it. Garric's clothes bore the fishy tang of woodsmoke, and though he must have been as tired as I, his pace was steady and purposeful.

I wanted to put all my troubles on his broad shoulders. Yet he too was desperate for coin, had stirred himself into the city's violences.

Garric halted on Bear Street, and spoke again in French.

"Sometimes it may seem as if the darkness will drown you," he said. "You cannot believe it will ever end. But the light always comes."

He poked me lightly in the chest and whispered in English, "The light she comes always, little apprentice."

"I am no apprentice," I mumbled.

"I say you are an apprentice good and well," replied Garric, raising his eyebrows. "And this night your master will teach you a new craft."

My master. It gave me a chill, to hear it said aloud. I glanced at him suspiciously.

"Garric, why did Mister de Corvis happen to come to your house that day I was beaten? Did he not know you were at the guild meeting?"

Roof shingles glinted high above us. I persisted.

"Then he knew I was alone. He came for me..."

He sucked in his cheeks.

"What would such a fine gentleman want with an ignorant boy? Why would you tell him of me?"

Garric put his arm around my shoulders and pointed past Bear Wharf at the Thames, swelling and shrinking like a sea-beast's miry chest.

"You have gifts, Calonnie," he said kindly. "Courage, the beautiful French tongue, the mimicking..."

Though his words soothed, I knew he lied. I only had the courage to fight women, and French-speakers were two a penny in London.

Garric had known that apprenticing me to Mister de Corvis would bind Peter in too; he'd let me follow him to the Moor's Head that first time; he had not told my father of it. I wondered how much my new master knew of our true debts; if Mistress Frazier had shown him the black silk scarf; if he knew what the letters meant.

Garric's voice cut through my thoughts. "*Elle m'a renvoyé*," he said mournfully. .

As Garric lifted the bronze door-knocker, I held my back straight, bracing myself. What villainy would the grim gentleman lead me into? And would I do it? Peter would not, that was for sure, but I knew my mother would have told me to do Mister de Corvis' bidding, if it meant I could live. She had sacrificed her body and risked her very soul by giving herself to Anthony that day, only to keep Peter's secret. To keep me alive.

Frazier opened the door, unshaven, his cropped grey hair sweat-matted and his waistcoat smeared with coarse dust. Wondering if he had been out a-burning with Garric, I took a sniff, but he smelled of earth and spice, not woodsmoke.

Garric and Frazier nodded at each other familiarly. The coachman led us into Mister de Corvis' study and knelt down at the small fireplace opposite the bookcases, taking kindling from a copper kettle. The only light in the room flickered from a fat candle on the master's writing-desk. Behind it sat Emilia, her legs folded up under her coppery dress, her hair bound up neatly. It made me unquiet to see her. All the days of watching and waiting across the river, walking around stiff-legged with the memories of her flesh; and now there she was, her eyes as fresh as midday.

Emilia watched Frazier closely, nailing her gaze to his head as if I were not there. The kindling flared, and he rocked back onto his heels to keep his furry eyebrows away from the heat. Unstockinged, I felt the chill in my booted feet.

"Frazier, you may take Master Pettit to the lower quarters," said Emilia in a hard voice.

"Miss," he replied, standing.

He and Garric trotted out and clicked the door shut, but I knew they had stayed just outside. Emilia gave me a look to say, *Speak nothing of what has happened. Others listen.*

I went to the fire, took off my boots and warmed my feet.

"Forgive me, miss," I said in a respectful voice, loud enough for Frazier to hear, "for I have not worn my finest dancing boots to your ballroom today. Master Pettit's invitation was somewhat brief."

"You may forget your japes, Calumny Spinks," she replied crisply. "You are here to earn your pay. In Ja… in my mother's house, I would have a servant whipped for such words."

I wiggled my bare toes at the grate. "Yes, miss. It would please me to serve *under* you."

She frowned and stalked over towards me, flushing. I had gone too far.

"I… Mister de Corvis instructs you to go with Garric Pettit to a certain place, this night."

"Yes, miss."

I wanted to ask her which coffeehouse we were to attack, but she seized my hands and thrust them under her skirt. Out of balance, I scalded my toes on the grate, but did not resist, greedily pressing my fingers on her tenderness. She dug her nails into my other hand, forcing it around her body and into the back place. Breathless, I wanted to resist now, but she was still talking.

"You must play a cloth-merchant's son from Devonshire…"

I gave in, letting her imprison my hands in her writhing groin, and now it was her turn to invade my breeches, scratching and squeezing, daring me with her eyes to stay silent despite the pains she inflicted on me.

"And it would be well if the men there take you for a fool, which is a part I believe you will excel in playing," she finished.

Now it was my turn to be red-faced, but I had lost the will to speak. She darted her tongue at the scar her dagger had left on my neck, twisted herself painfully on my fingers and then let me go, leaving me aching for more. As she went back to her chair, I turned and looked into the fire, muttering that I did not know the Devonish accent.

"Most certainly you do. Master Frazier is from that county, and I have seen how easily you make mockery of a man's voice. You must speak little, for your task is to listen to the converse of the men I will show you... Here!"

She rapped on the desk, where she had laid out some papers, and I came over to look.

"I cannot read, miss," I said. Both sweet and foul, the scent of Emilia's hidden places wreathed us.

"But you can see, Master Spinks..." – like a schoolmistress to the stupidest boy in the lesson, though she called me by "Master" for the first time – "...you can see, can you not?"

She turned the papers round for me, our sin-scented fingers almost touching. The first was a neat charcoal sketch of a dense-haired man with doe eyes and a small chin. I now knew from the hand that it was her drawing I had stolen from on top of the bookcase.

"This is Monsieur Coste," said Emilia, "a spice trader out of Madagascar. It is important to my f–, to Mister de Corvis, to know whom he is dealing with."

"Monsieur Coste," I whispered, shutting my eyes tightly to swallow his features down.

Next she showed me a sketch of a thin-faced fellow, long hair falling straight around his jug-ears. She had drawn it so well that I could feel his greasy blemished skin on my fingertips. His bony hand clasped his chin like a lying man does, a sore at the corner of his mouth.

"This is Lieutenant Collignon, of the French navy," she said, turning the page over and wiping her hands on her lap. "He is a vile man."

Though her body was still, it shimmered with unwept tears and untapped rage. I wet my lips as I watched her tautly crooked fingers worry at her hair, making it sheen in the firelight.

"What is it, Master Spinks?" she asked coldly, but her eyes caressed my face. I touched my soiled fingertips to my lips, then to my heart. The blood pulsed faster at her collarbone.

"Well, miss..." I gathered my wits. "Well, you should not call me Master, for I am master of no craft at all. And I do not know what I am to do now. It will not be daylight for a good while yet."

She looked at the door.

"This place you go to – it opens its doors after dark and bolts them before dawn. Frazier!"

Click, stamp, stamp.

"Miss?"

"Fetch the coach. Calumny Spinks, you are to go with Master Pettit tonight. Those gentlemen I have spoken of – mark what they say, and to whom. Mark it!"

Garric sauntered in, puffing as if he had come a long way. Emilia ignored him.

"Should my father be disappointed, *Master* Spinks, you shall not set foot in this house again, nor be paid another farthing."

"Well, miss, since I am most keen to come *inside* again…" – speaking now in Frazier's burbling Devonish tongue, I blew her a hidden kiss – "…why then, I must succeed."

"Three of the clock," said Frazier, bustling us out of the study. "Away now."

As I picked up my boots, I saw how small Emilia was in that lonely room: a girl weighed down with her father's plans and affairs of money. She watched me secretly through her lashes.

If her father's employment does not pay me well enough, I thought, his daughter's dowry might serve instead.

We followed Frazier around the house to the stables, where the black coach awaited us. Garric stretched and yawned, letting the ripe flavour of his armpits fill the chilly night air as the coachman rattled open the stall.

The horse's chestnut head tossed against the bridle as it skittered across the cobbled yard. It gave a haughty sigh I knew well: it was Cucullan. Of a sudden, I was that grieving fearful boy again, weeping through the long night's ride to London.

Garric and I sat on top with Frazier, our breath clouding as he coaxed the horse out of the yard. Rattling up Bear Street, I watched the mudlarks: scavengers wading through the Fleet's shallows with lanterns and hooked poles, looking for metal and wood. The stench sat in our laps like a drunken companion.

Cucullan snorted as he took us over the high-backed bridge, racing away down the other side until Frazier whoahed him back. I smiled at this horse that thought himself the master of men.

Garric watched me, his face empty of its usual merriness as we rolled past the ancient well. Sleepers huddled round it.

"Why do they lie out here in the open?" I asked.

Garric answered me in French. "These people think the spirits will speak to them, and so they make a camp. And every morning they will find their purses stolen. The Englishes are full of sentiment and superstition, and they would rather talk and starve than lift a hand to change their destiny."

"Like me, do you mean?" I asked with anger.

He replied in English. "Not like you, brother. But your father…"

I opened my mouth to defend Peter, but no words came. I knew Garric was right.

"I am desolate… I am sorry, Calonnie. It is not for me to say," he murmured. I looked away as we turned up a narrow side street, passing the dull square block of the parish meeting house. I shuddered. It was such a place that had spawned my father and his creed of despair.

The coach stopped.

"Be about it now," said Frazier gently.

"Be about it," I murmured, trying to make my tongue burr like the coachman's as we climbed down. Frazier nodded at us and turned the coach for home. I followed Garric up an alley that twisted its way round the back of the church into a dead end, its bricks dark with the mildew of age. Garric pointed out a low passageway in the corner.

"When all is done, come back out and wait at the end of that passage. You understand?"

He looked back to make sure the alley was empty, then lifted up a cellar door in a sidewall. He ducked his big head inside and pulled me through, closing the hatch behind us. We descended stairs that were as narrow as a man's shoulders, lit only dimly from beneath.

The light came from a long hot room edged by slatted benches. Clothes lay on them in piles, men's boots kicked away underneath. The roof was curved, barrel-fashion, with barely enough room to stand under the highest part. We had to walk past a shirtsleeved clerk at a counter. He looked at me askance but waved us through when he saw Garric.

Two naked men talked in low voices as they went through a curtain in the far corner. From beyond the doorway came a dull groaning noise. Above it was a badge: a bronze hourglass flanked by a great gold coin and silver cup.

"This is the House of Three Mysteries," muttered Garric. "Stand tall like a man now, and keep open your ears. Here is where the heads of the guilds make commerce with the gentlefolk and the natural philosophers of London."

I choked back a laugh. What nonsense was this?

"Why do they make commerce at this time? It is not yet dawn on a Sunday, have they no sense?" I asked.

"This is no market, Calonnie, nor coffeehouse not either. This is a place of serious intent," he snapped. "Guild men come in this door, and gentlemen and scholars through the other side. These men are not supposed to be seen in one house, you understand? Not since Cromwell has it been permitted: the king likes the Mysteries to be kept apart. This is where I met your father..."

I nodded solemnly, breaking sweat in the heat. A tanner had come in, stench wafting from his stained fingers as he pointed to his name in the clerk's ledger. Garric took off his shirt and breeches and rolled his clothes into a ball, then looked at me to show that I should do the same. I did it slowly. My pits stank like a newt's cunt as I pulled my shirt over my head, and I knew how young my chest looked next to Garric's broad hairy body and his big, scarred forearms.

Naked, I followed Garric through the sackcloth curtain, and suddenly steam boiled around us. The second room was lit by oil lamps. Men sat in rows on tiled steps facing each other under the arching roof. Horrid puce pimmies lay limp on the wet stone, tucked away under pasty fat bellies; it was like an ant-heap, with men crossing from side to side to be introduced to one another.

The cow-groaning noise I had heard before was the sound of gossip. Fretful, their fingers grubby from handling copper coins but free of calluses, I knew them to be merchants. They spoke of the price of tallow this, and the court circular that. I looked carefully from face to face, making sure not to meet any man's eye; neither of the Frenchmen were there.

Garric sat next to a round-faced pigdog near the doorway and whispered in his ear. The man looked at me and nodded. They shook hands, and Garric beckoned me over.

"Well, Mister Frantor, you are welcome as a brother in this House," he said. I had never been called Mister in my whole life, and in my amazement I barely felt the sting as he slapped me on the shoulder.

"Do you not stay, Master Pettit?"

"Why, I must send a message to your father in Exeter to say you have safely arrived, Mister Frantor," he said, giving me a polite bow as he pushed back through the curtain. A wall-eyed fellow, whose ears and nostrils sprouted hair, said loudly, "I'll not pay a war levy!" Immediately, his two companions shushed him, but it was too late. A bustling slender fellow with pale eyebrows darted into the first room to fetch the clerk, and the hairy man was made to leave to whispers of "Shame!"

In the uproar, the pigdog leaned close towards me and whispered, "It is not permitted to speak of war or taxes in this House."

I looked to the spot where the dissenter had sat, feeling altogether alone in this place.

"I am Varley," said my strange companion, his snub nose wrinkling as he pronounced his name.

Pale hair sat in tufts above his forehead and behind his ears, and the bald places in between were raw from wearing a wig. He rubbed his chest unquietly, making loops from nipple to nipple. Little flecks of his sweat landed on my belly.

I'd seen no man naked before but my father; yet these men gave their hands to strangers. I asked Varley if there was a cooler place to sit, for my head pounded with the heat, and my balls prickled. He raised a neat eyebrow and waved me through a second doorway. I slipped and slid on the sweaty stone floor as we went through to another room, the pigdog strutting ahead of me with sweat coursing down between his hairy shoulder-blades. The second chamber was cooler and darker, with just three men huddled in a shallow pool at the back. I squinted in the dimness, going closer to them.

"We might stay a while," said the pigdog; and now I saw that one of the men, a fair-headed lad with slender fingers, nuzzled another's neck. The third, a sinewy fellow whose lips could not meet around his buckteeth, was pressed backwards against him, his eyes shut. The rippling waters spilled out at my feet. The middle man was silver-haired and handsome, soldierly, eyes bright and strong in a weathered face. He made me a wordless invitation, filled with cautious lust. I shook my head and turned to touch the pigdog's arm, pointing to another curtain on the far side of the room. It had shaken me, to see men mollying with each other, but I would not show it.

The last room was twice the height of a man and broader than my master's hall, with four large steps running the length of each wall. The steam that filled the air was lighter than before, scented with lavender. Lantern-light shone warmly on the little groups of gentlemen and merchants. Here they did not slouch around shouting of trade and money. With blank faces and straight backs, they murmured to each other, eyes looking around the room and not at their companions. Three men wearing russet caps sat together at the far side, watching who spoke to whom.

There was another doorway, this time covered with an oilskin drape and guarded by a curly-haired Jew. A clothed servant stepped through it, bearing glass goblets of water.

"For nobles and gentlemen only," murmured the pigdog, his hairy belly brushing my buttocks.

I saw Coste the spice trader. His bushy hair marked him out from the Englishmen; his little chin and soft eyes were as Emilia had drawn them. He was talking to a tall pale gentleman. I pointed at a spot three steps behind them both, letting Varley lead so that I could stay out of sight. Seeing that we had come through the merchants' door, a pair of russet-capped gentlemen moved a dozen paces away, frowning. One of them, his spectacles misted, came over to breathe a soft word in their ears.

"Do not these gentlemen come here for commerce?" I asked, confused.

"There is more than one way to meet and exchange," replied Varley, an earnest frown making his face look honest for the first time. I thought he meant the molly-pool; but he nodded to the bespectacled man. "The College Secular... that is what the russet bespeaks... well, merchant and gentry alike, some of us are passioned by science. Knowledge has a greater value than trade... or flesh."

I noticed a thin man sitting mute on the step below mine, a few paces to the side. It was Collignon, scratching at the sore on his lips, his chin jutting towards Coste and the gentleman. Though I wanted to hear more of the College,

I gave Varley a stupid smile and leaned back so that the Frenchman could not see my features, pretending to gaze at the room while I listened to the men below.

"*Alors, votre épice spécial vient du Madagascar –*" began the gentleman. His voice was dry, faintly tainted with Scottishness.

"*Je ne peux rien vous dire de son provenance, Monseigneur,*" replied Coste sharply, making the other frown. I cannot tell you where my special spice has come from. "Monseigneur" meant that the gentleman was a lord. My spirits sank. What business had I fallen into now?

"Mister Varley, I am honoured by your kind attention," I said, watching Collignon's shoulders lift in irritation below us. He was trying to listen to the others, and it was hard to hear above the murmuring that filled the room. Now and then gentlemen would finish, clasp hands and move on to another group, the way ants swarm on rotten fruit.

"Ssssh," said Varley, planting his paw on my knee. Below us, the Scots nobleman turned to Coste so that I could see his face. Now I noticed that many men in the room watched him, drawn to his power. He was near as old as my father, his white fringe cropped short, and his light-green eyes glassy in the lantern rays. His cheeks and jowls drooped, but his features were firm, determined; and the stare he gave the Frenchman could have skinned a cat.

"*Il vous faudra des licences, quand même.*" You will need licences.

"*On vous donnera une exclusivité, milord,*" hissed Collignon from behind them, startling the lord.

What is an exclusivity? I wondered, trying to remember what Ty had told me.

"And when will you make the first delivery?" demanded the other in English.

"It will be in three months, sir," said Coste hastily.

"And not a day more," said the lord, standing with his back to me. Though he was wiry, flesh drooping off the bone, he held himself together with great force. His arms were knotted with veins and sinews, his neck and shoulders rough with ancient faded scars. This was a man to be reckoned with, I thought, glancing down at his signet ring.

A sword guarding a harp within a circled snake. Anthony's snuff-pouch had borne the same device. Had I found a path to my enemy's door?

The lord strode to the gentlemen's doorway, throwing a guinea at the Jew as he passed through. The guardian tucked it under his leg. Though my thoughts dashed around wildly, I marked the place. Now, should I stay and listen as I was commanded? Or follow the lord and hope to find Anthony Anthony and his master?

"*Putain*," hissed Collignon at Coste, "*impossible d'achever cela en trois mois.*" We cannot do this in three months, he said, and there was a world of rage and ambition bottled tightly in his voice. I knew that it would please Mister de Corvis to hear of it; I would follow the lord shortly.

Coste shrugged. "*A vous de trouver le moyen.*"

You find a way.

There was a harsh pause, as if they had suddenly remembered this was no time to be a Frenchman in England.

Afraid they would realise I was spying on them, I leaned forward to hail Collignon.

"Are you a German gentleman, sir? Are you of the Hamburg?"

"No, sir, I am not," he growled, trying to hide his strong accent in a rasping voice. He tugged at one broad ear.

"Well, Mister Varley," I said to the pigdog, "that is truly a shame. I have longed to meet the Hamburgish people, for I have heard they are masters of commerce, and I must confess myself a little ignorant in such matters. So be it. I must return to my lodgings and write a letter to my father..."

For a moment, I even believed I could write such a letter.

I sauntered down towards the fine oilskin curtain, hoping to pass for a gentleman. The warm tiled floor soothed my bare feet.

The Jew clutched my arm as I reached for the curtain.

"Sir, you may not."

"Sir, I am a merchant of Devonshire. Is it a London custom to separate a gentleman from his clothing?"

"But, sir..."

I pushed a hand through, and he was forced to rise and pull me back into the steam room.

"But, sir, your clothes are *that* way. You came through the door of... *commerce*."

"Well, I am most dismayed, I must tell you..."

I put a hand to my forehead as if I were as dizzy as a spring lamb, and sat myself in the Jew's place.

"Do you truly say so? That my clothes are that way?"

"*I* will show you to them, Mister Frantor," said Varley, pale despite the heat. He bowed an apology to the room and bundled me away.

"Oh, I thank you, Varley… All this Londonish steam and sweat has quite boozled me. Thank you, good Jew."

The guardian bared his gappy teeth as Varley led me back into the dark chamber. Over his head, I caught a glimpse of the two Frenchmen arguing in whispers. Not a soul had seen me lift the guinea from the doorman's seat. It would serve well towards the eighty pounds.

"Do you care to stay… in this chamber?" whispered Varley as we passed through the first curtain, flicking his fingers at the men who fondled each other in the darkness. They looked up, the soldierly fellow throwing me a look that pleaded and commanded in equal measure. The fair-headed fop under his arm gave a sigh that reminded me of Frazier's, that night I saw him in the alley on Bear Street. Behind them, a hidden doorway opened a little. Naked men passed back and forth in whispering oil-light.

"Good Varley, I am too hot to be squashed by you and these fellows," I said cheerily, pushing towards them. "Let you be so entertained, though."

I darted straight through the first chamber to the entry-room. There were now a dozen men in there: the hairy-eared merchant who'd complained of taxes, arguing loudly with the clerk and his friends; and seven or eight fellows gathered around a seated lawyer, who passed around papers and a quill for signature. Men clutched purses, reluctantly digging out gold sovereigns to seal each bargain. I had to brush aside a pile of papers to get to my clothes.

Varley, who'd followed me, whistled loudly through his teeth at the hairy-eared man. The chatter died down; all turned to look at the pigdog.

"The cousin himself was here tonight, Salter," he said dryly, plucking his balls away from his leg. I saw that he was swollen a little after seeing the molly-pool, but no other man seemed to care. They'd fallen silent when he spoke, and now I wished I had been more respectful to him.

"Then we must take more care," said the clerk, glaring at Salter. "Some *talk* must be saved for the water room."

He meant the chamber behind the molly-pool. Well, it was too late for me to be admitted there; Salter and his friends were staring at me now, a stranger. I bowed to the room and ran half-naked up the dark stairs. I opened the coal-door and darted to the low passageway opposite to put my shirt, stockings and boots over my steaming body.

I was the greatest spy in England.

CHAPTER NINETEEN

The Golden Guineas

In which, for the first time, salvation seems possible

Music and talking, faint as wormsong, echoed down the passageway. I followed it to its end, at the edge of a fine square. Crisp grass nestled round a ring of saplings. The pretty houses were made of broad stone bricks laid side by side with barely a hair's breadth between them. To my right was a neat half-timbered mansion, as old as any I had seen in London. The music came from this house, a strange soup of broken, unquiet tunes, and I wondered who would be so bold as to make music and commerce on the Sabbath. And so close to a church – by Satan, but London was a free place!

Coaches were driving up to the House under a covered way that hid them from the square. They greeted each other in whispers, and never by name, walking up the stairs in pairs and threes.

I started as the horse Cucullan stomped to a halt in front of me. I stepped back into the shadows, even though I was cold-pimpled and dog-tired. Mister de Corvis called to me through the open window, his face in shadow.

"No need to hide, Calumny."

He had not called me by my given name before.

"No, Mister de Corvis," I replied from the darkness.

"Have you earned your pay, boy?"

"As God is my judge, Mister de Corvis."

"God will not judge you, Calumny Spinks. *I* will judge you. Get in."

Mister de Corvis rapped the roof of the cab with his cane.

"Spitalfields, Frazier," he ordered.

I sat facing backwards on an old cloak, which must have been put there to stop me staining the fine cushions. My master sat opposite, his legs stretched out, and I had to tuck mine ladylike to the side so we did not touch. He wove his fingers together over his belly and gazed at me.

"*Crrrm, crrrm,*" I choked as I tried to clear my dry throat. "Well, sir, I have listened to the two Frenchies, and I can say that they will find their licences in three months."

I spoke boldly, as if I had understood all that took place between the two popish rats and the Scots lord.

"Do you say so?" he asked, mild as spring.

"Yes, sir, and I played my part to perfection. Like a Devon fool, I asked them if they were Germans," I carried on, sweet pride in my breast.

He rapped his cane angrily on the floor of the carriage.

"And so I have promised you half a pound to bring their attention to you, have I?"

"Oh, there is much more, sir," I babbled.

He laid the cane on the seat next to him. His voice grew lower, as if it climbed down deep into some cold grave.

"Then tell it me. Not what you think has been, but only and precisely what you have seen and heard. Word for word and twitch for twitch."

Mister de Corvis pulled the curtains against the first strains of dawn so that we were sat in darkness. A wild fear gripped me, that he would stab me when my story was done.

"Close your eyes, Calumny Spinks, and speak."

I breathed deep. I closed my eyes as I was commanded, and I told him where I had been, the words I had heard, each in its place, each speech in the voice of the man who spoke it. Everyone, from the round-faced beast Varley to the unknown lord and the guardian Jew.

When I was done, he tugged back the curtains and tapped me on the boot with his cane.

"It is well to practise remembering, to use the darkness so."

"Sir… who was that Scottish lord? I felt sure I knew of him," I lied.

Mister de Corvis narrowed his eyes as he answered me.

"The Duke of Firth, Calumny. The king's cousin and most trusted general. And it would be little surprise if you knew him. He owns half London, and now commands the Tower's troops as well as his own regiment in the Hyde woods. No other lord is trusted to station soldiers in the city.

"Now, show me that guinea you stole."

I remembered how he had taken back half my coins before, and I stuck my defiant hand in my pocket to keep the guinea in there. *Firth*, I said to myself.

"Now, Calumny, you may have no fear that I will steal from you," he chided. "For I have a guinea of my own."

He took the coin from his waistcoat pocket and held it out to me. The face of the new king bulged out, his fat

Catholic nose bumping up against the letters of his name. He showed me the other side. Between two crossed spears were four great shields, bearing gravings of the lion, the harp, the dragon and the thistle.

"Mister Corvis, how many shillings is a guinea?" I asked, thinking of the eighty pounds again.

"A guinea is as many shillings as a man will pay for it. When I was your age, a guinea was a pound, but now this coin grows dearer by the day. Today it buys you twenty-two shillings, but tomorrow – who knows?"

He placed his coin in my fingers.

"You cannot read, you say?"

"No, sir. But I can reckon a shilling or a pound as well as any man," I lied.

"Very well then. Let us read what is said, and then let us talk about what is truly meant. Next to the king's face, it says 'By the grace of God', in Latin. Do you see?"

I saw now that he intended to let me have the guinea, and it made me skittish.

"Well, Apprentice Spinks, let us say honestly to each other that the king does not rule by grace of God."

Mister de Corvis spoke too loud in his passion. Frazier gave a warning hiccup from his seat above us. It was treason to speak so, and all three of us knew it.

"Do you see, Calumny?" asked my master. "If this fellow is a king by the grace of God, did God then behead his father? If he is king by the grace of God, but men then put another king in his place, is that too by the grace of God?"

Christ's blood, was it not enough that my father should kill a king, without that my master be a traitor too?

Well, a dead man has nothing to lose. I closed my eyes and spoke to Mister de Corvis in the voice of my father Peter, the way he used to speak before Squire Salstead was gibbeted.

"We do not draw our grace from the popish villain on the head of the coin, but from the four great powers on its tail. The lion is the earth from which we are made. The harp signifies the songs we make from the wind that blows through us. The thistle is the water, the secret truths we carry. And the dragon is the fire of the sun that lights and gives birth to all. And let no man come between you and God, my buck, or between you and your fate."

Tears were in my eyes. Frazier stopped singing and the wheels fell silent. Looking out, I saw that we were outside Peter's workshop on Silk Street. Amber light squeezed out under the closed door, flickering to the loom's faint beat.

"Those are strong words for a young fellow of no name," murmured Mister de Corvis gently. He closed my hands over the coin and rapped on the roof for Frazier to hop down.

"Men who believe as your father once did, and who speak of it in the open street, most often die before their time. So beware, Calumny Spinks."

The door opened. I looked at Mister de Corvis, longing to be so sure of myself, to know so much of the world, but he looked away from me and I climbed down without another word. My father again – that was all they thought of, he and Garric. Old Peter Spinks, the crippled traitor. Well, I would show them all which Spinks was the man to follow.

Frazier cleared his throat. I looked up, and he threw down a little packet. He clicked his tongue. Cucullan tossed his head and gave me a backwards look as the coach rattled away.

Alone in the street, wrung out by my sleepless night, I clenched the coins tight in my fists and peeked in the package Frazier had given me. I closed my eyes to send a silent prayer of thanks for the dry-meat pie he'd given me.

I went slowly up the steps and pushed at the door.

Peter stopped weaving and turned to gaze at me. I wondered if I should give him the gold, if I should tell him that Anthony served the Duke of Firth, but he spoke first.

"That was a fine carriage you came in, Calumny Spinks."

"Did Garric tell you I was gone?"

"He did, but not where you went."

Peter fell silent, and I went to the eating-table to put down Frazier's pie.

"I care where you have been or what you do. Though you have abandoned me and your true trade, still I will warn you. When you do the bidding of rich men, it seems at first a fair exchange, your work for their coin. And then one day they will come to you with a new contract, promising you ten times as much gold if only this and if only that. And you will lose your soul."

He turned away. The injured loom beat its wings, flinging demonic shadows around the room.

Unbidden, Mister de Corvis' voice came into my mind. "God will not judge you. *I* will judge you."

"Father," I said, breaking off a piece of the pie for myself.

Chumpa chumpa.

"Ty and I have a plan to sell more silk today."

Today, I thought. It is nearly day already, and I have hardly slept since Friday.

Chumpa flish. His gnarly hand swooped in and out to catch a cobweb floating down towards the weft. Leaving most of the pie for my father, I climbed the ladder to my room.

My mouth filled with grateful spit as I swallowed the dried beef, pastry and blackened onions. I laid out my treasures on my bed. Two golden guineas, five silver shillings, a noble pistol and a traitor's silken hood.

And Emilia's drawing – my little piece of her father's world.

As I looked down at the strange bushes and blue mountains, I took off my damp clothes and used my shirt to scrape away the sweat and stink from my armpits.

CHAPTER TWENTY

The Seamstresses

In which two apprentices boldly seek a profit from impending war

The last hours of night were dreamless, a blessed wink of nothing that left Saturday's bitterness behind, and I woke with a cheerful flutter of hope.

The goblin boy's chatter buzzed in my ear, rising muffled from the workshop. Peter replied clearly.

"He is abed, Tyburn. He has learned his sleeping from his mother… Well, you may go up. I am for the church."

Ty scuffled up the ladder, burst into my room and threw a new dove-grey waistcoat over my head.

"Bastard beetle, maggot wretch!"

Laughing, I wiggled free and shook my fist at him, then opened it up to show him the two buttery-gold guineas.

"Cal, how did you…?" he asked, staring at the coins.

"Look close, goblin boy. I am the master here."

"Master in name you are not. But master in dress you may now be, thanks to my mother." He held up the waistcoat for me to admire. The lavender frogging was fine but not fancy; the long sleeves were puffed above the elbow, and it came down to the thigh in the modern fashion.

My white shirt was still damp from the House's steamy rooms, but I had no other, and I needed to dress my best if we were to succeed that day. The waistcoat fitted me like a general's uniform, and I felt so tall I feared I would strike my crown on the rafters. The broadcloth alone must have cost a shilling, I thought to myself, marvelling at Abigail.

"Now, we should begin with the Tower, since it is the closest barracks to Silk Street," said Ty, spreading out a paper on the bed. It bore a messy pattern, as if a child had scratched out a spiderweb in the dust.

"What is this?"

"It is a map, and here is the Tower," he whispered proudly, pointing to a tiny picture of a castle. "It is a way to show the city, how the streets go into each other, so you can find your way."

"I know what a map is," I said, and cuffed him for such condescension. My mother had told me a hundred stories of treasure and adventure, but this wriggling mass of lines and squares was far from what I had imagined then.

"See, this is Silk Street," he babbled on, jabbing his thumb at a grimy spot. "Here is where we are now."

"But I know that we are in Silk Street –"

"No, no, Cal. If you are at the Clerkenwell, say –"

"Well, I know the Clerkenwell too. I have been there."

"But if you are in a street that you do not know, then the map will show you how to find your way from there."

"If I am on a street that I do not know," I said slowly, "then how do I know what street that is?"

"Why then, you ask a stranger!" he replied in triumph.

"If I must ask a stranger, what need have I of a map?" I laughed. "Now where are the Hyde woods and the Duke of Firth's barracks?"

Ty pored over the map, found the Hyde woods, and squinted at me suspiciously. "This is the other side of Westminster. Too far for us. Why should you ask?"

Without giving him the story of the House of Three Mysteries, I told him that I'd heard Firth now controlled the Tower as well as his own regiment. I spoke nothing of seeing the duke himself, or his signet ring, or Anthony Anthony.

"You mean that the Duke of Firth's quartermaster holds the purse-strings for the Tower as well as his own barracks? Twice the journey, but twice the profit..."

Ty pressed his fingertips together, his nostrils twitching.

"Very well," he said. "I can walk there if you can. Let us go down and choose our wares. My mother will lend us ten yards for the day."

The mercery was quiet, for Garric had been banished to Auchan's house. Abigail helped us to pick out the two best bolts of silk, and then we carefully pulled them into a pair of linen sacks to cover them against the filth of the city. As we hoicked them onto our shoulders, she filled a waterskin for us from the wooden pail.

Not two steps out into the gentle sunshine, she called out to Ty, "The Tower, you told me. You aren't to take those into Holborn."

"No trade with Holborn," replied Ty loudly, without looking back. Once she had waved and gone inside, he whispered to me, "It is true that we will not trade with Holborn – since our goal is past Westminster!"

I laughed uneasily. It felt unlucky to turn our backs on a mother's words of protection.

It was a God-damned long walk to Westminster. At first I was full of sap and stride, clasping the long roll over my shoulder as I told Ty about my secret deeds of the night – though I left out Garric's part in it all. By the time we reached the Strand, my shoulders burned from shifting the silk back and forth, and we were bumped back and forth by the Sunday strollers. The looming houses shouldered each other, as if vying to bully the roadway with their gaudy signs. The middle of the road was noisy with traps and coaches, their drivers swearing at the slow plod of the pious. Though the shops were shut, the hawkers and whores broke Sabbath with raucous cries. We held our wares awkwardly against our chests now, fearing to be robbed, and we were both pink from tiredness when we reached the end of the surging crowds.

"This is where they put the Charing Cross pillory," muttered Ty unquietly, nodding at a monument of a nobleman on a prancing horse. "Next to the statue of old King Charles."

"There will be no punishment for us, Ty," I told him with a cheeriness I did not feel. "We are honest mercers serving the king's armies."

He bobbed his head and walked on. I could not help but look up at the melancholy features of the man my father had killed. His face was as narrow as Ty's, boyish under the pointed beard, and his eyebrows were raised in eternal surprise. *Deus me exculpit*, I thought emptily, and hurried on after Ty. Ahead of us, a shadowy line of trees loomed behind the noble houses that faced the Charing Cross. Admiring them, I did not see the soldier blocking the way to the woods until his pike-point was pressed against my belly, pricking at the new broadcloth.

"No commoners," he said coldly, pushing me a sliding yard backwards.

"*Lex collegiorum,*" answered Ty, with a bold hand on the pike-shaft.

"Not a noble name, Lex," insisted the soldier, jerking the weapon down to take it away from Ty's touch. Though his tones were full Londonish, his skin was the colour of a Turk's, and his beaked nose was the twin of his drooping pikehead. It poked out through the long black hair that he allowed to fall from under the rim of his steel cap. "Nor is Colijorum. Get you back into the midden you sprang from. This way is not for you."

Ty stepped closer, showing the guild-badge on his oilskin. "It means that we are of the mercer-guild, precedent of all guild companies, and that the ancient *lex collegiorum*, which is a common law above Parliament law, gives us passage to and through the king's parks."

"Mercer or lawyer?" demanded the sentry, grudgingly putting up his pike so we could pass by. "Lex colijorum, by Jesus' holy guts!"

I held my peace until we reached the sandy wheel-tracked road that led into the dense wood.

"What did you say?" I hissed at Ty.

"It is an old law," said Ty. "I learned it at the guild-house. It means that we may walk freely in these woods of a Sunday, even though they are the king's own hunting grounds."

I tutted, marvelling at his knowledge. "Such a head as yours, Ty… it will be the crown or the axe!"

We laughed a little as we walked into the woods, but I wished I had not spoken of axes. We had no business with the army, and we knew it. After a while we came to a rushing stream, half as wide as the Fleet and overhung by the spreading trees.

"The Tyburn," said my friend. "Time to leave the road."

We crossed over a wooden bridge, wide enough for a cart to pass, then turned down a muddy path to the left. The dismal trees were clumped together, their cracked dusky bark overrun with bustling burrs, like old men with the pox. Their leaves were turning already, but only a few had fallen, lonely wisps of summer rotting on the fernless claggy soil. The path was little more than a remembered dream, a streak of trodden earth that came and went with the sun.

The mud clung to our boots, splashed at the tails of our oilskin coats, pulled our hopes into its fallow depths. Because we only had eyes for the path, we did not at first see the long sheer wall stretching out silently along the forest's flank ahead of us.

It was a polished stone sheet, grey and ghostly in the mist, its flawless skin marked only by a narrow gate. The door's hard planks were bolted with cross-struts, and it hung open by a fist's breadth. At waist-height, a strip of pea-green cloth was stretched across the gap.

We shifted the bolts of silk to rest on our feet. No sound came from the other side, no smell of food or horse dung, no shouting orders. Now I felt daunted. Were we simply to stride in and demand to see the quartermaster?

Shouts rang out from within. Keeping our wares off the muddy ground, Ty and I went to look through the gap at the door's edge. A troop of horsemen cantered into a courtyard flanked by running pikemen, sunlight glinting off their acorn-domed helmets.

These were not the kind of rabbly men I had seen on the road from Salstead. They wore new leather armour embossed with their regiment's emblem, a pistol at every man's belt. At their rear was a coach flanked by two gentlemen-officers wearing gleaming breastplates, long feathers in their wide-brimmed hats. Spurs sparkled at their heels, and the horses carried their plumed heads high.

One of the officers called a command, and the troop halted. The riders dismounted as a wispy-haired soldier, his uniform faded and stained, led a pair of stable boys out from a row of horse-stalls on our right.

Ahead of us was a stone building with a big iron-bound door, a horsehair-and-plaster shed leaning against it. The pikemen stowed their weapons in a pine frame nearby, the wood joined so shabbily that it would have shamed the meanest loom-maker. I pushed open the door another inch to see beyond the stone house. There was a small street lined on both sides with long low houses, which I took to be the soldiers' sleeping quarters. A gang of dogs tussled and growled in the dust, rolling and chasing from side to side until the riders passed through, kicking left and right to separate the beasts.

We waited quietly until all the horses had been stabled, and the soldiers had returned to their barracks. Ty hesitated.

"Well," I said boldly, "if this castle is empty then I am the next king, by God's grace."

I pushed hard at the gate, ripping apart the green ribbon that had tethered it. I had not thought it would swing so easily, and so I stumbled over the smooth stone threshold and into the yard.

"You have broken the lock," laughed a woman's voice.

It was not high and girly as most women's were. This voice sparked with knowing, as loud as a man bantering in the open street.

I looked around the yard, but I could not see the woman. I put on Peter's voice and mimicked his wounded hip, putting on a play.

"And so it was in sixty-five, my boy, when I fled London. Beggars' children playing in the street, chasing and hiding among the plague carcasses, dogs chewing at the rotting flesh until they dropped down themselves and coughed their lungs out on the ground. And the horrid spider-pickers, stealing from the pockets of the dead with long poles, hiding their evil faces under black hoods. It was hell!"

I turned round suddenly and roared hoarsely in Ty's face to make him jump. The unseen woman laughed.

"Come up and tell me your stories, redhead! Taking the whores' gate will earn you a beating if you are found, so be quick about it!"

Now I saw her, up on my left, sitting in the upstairs window of a tall timbered house. She was a long-faced woman of Abigail's age, though much thinner, her raven hair cropped almost as short as a man's. Her sharp wit was written across her forehead in lines of laughter and concern. She sewed as she looked down, a dark-blue cloth piled up in her lap. Behind her stood another woman, hidden in the shadows.

"Here," commanded the woman, pointing, "here, come this way." Her room overhung a cloister, and a ladder led to a hatchway in its floor. In the lower part of the building came the sounds of men talking, and the clanking of knives and goblets. The barracks only seemed empty because it was the eating-hour. Suddenly afraid, we ran into the cloister.

Ty tidied away a lock of hair that straggled over his forehead, pushed past me, and tried to climb the ladder while still holding the silk. He had not climbed two rungs before he toppled backwards with the weight of the cloth, and I had to catch him. Laughter rang out again, this time a girl's voice joining the woman's.

I took the silk from him and stood holding the bolts upright, one on each foot so that the cloth would not touch the dirt. Ty climbed again, this time taking one step at a time like an old man. His body hid the faces of the two women from me. They were kneeling at the hatch's edges, and all I could see were their clean hands and slender fingers. Their nails were cut down short except on the smallest fingers, where they were long, and sharp as shears. When Ty had climbed through, I handed him up the silk, one bolt at a time, while he leaned back down through the hole.

Ty and the woman disappeared, leaving me to stare at a face that calmed the storm between my ears. Her brown eyes, flecked with dancing blue, were warm and steady in the dimness, sheltering under fierce brows whose ends curved like Araby swords. Hair parted softly over her temple so that one ear peeked out, pink and fresh as an oyster, while the other one played hide-me under the waterfall of chestnut strands. Her nose and chin were crisp and rounded like perfect eggtops, and in between was a kissing mouth, a thinner lip above that curled and twisted with strength and purpose, protecting its soft full sister below. Her neck glowed like moonlight as it slid into a simple dress that hid her body's secrets, and yet sang their promise.

She moved away, and I climbed up. The other woman gave me her hand to help me into the room.

Ty's eyes were huge in the murky daylight as he laid the two wrapped bolts of silk carefully on a work-table. I watched the younger girl as she walked around the long room with a taper, lighting tall candles in brackets on the whitewashed walls. The elder sniffed at her.

"Violet, why do you fuss so?"

"I will be done soon enough, Mother," she replied, doing a little dance as she crossed the room. *Step step swish, hold, step step step step.*

Lead-mullioned windows kept out the best part of the cloudy daylight, but the room felt warm even before Violet brought light to its dark corners. Sheets of scarlet kersey were draped from every beam. Finished soldiers' uniforms, white-trimmed, were pegged to lines high above our heads, and breeches were strewn across the sturdy work-table in the middle. The bed in the far corner was walled with beige sheets laid over high frames so that it seemed like the postered den of a duchess. Though the room was swathed with cloth and colour, it spoke of tidy order, and I saw how not a table or chair had a lick of dust on it.

Violet crawled across the wide bed to light the last candle. I swallowed and looked away, and her mother gave me a hard glance.

"We are..." coughed Ty, who was still sat cross-legged by the hatch.

"What are you, indeed?" asked the older woman, smiling.

"We are looking for the quarter... the quartermaster of the barracks, Mistress."

"Well, in this room there is no quartermaster, only Seamstress Fintry and her daughter-apprentice, and I dare say you need some tailoring, indeed. Come here."

Ty went to Mistress Fintry's work-table. She looked him up and down, then spun him around so she could run her finger down the seams of his waistcoat.

"Off with it," she commanded.

Quick sharp, he obeyed.

"There is enough cloth in this piece to cut it better for you," murmured the seamstress, running her hands down his arms. "There is more to you than you show. But first, I will hear your business."

Ty looked at me. I was to be the speaker.

"Dear seamstresses, dear Mistress Seamstress and Miss Apprentice-seamstress, do not dismiss us, for so would you distress us. We carry silk, the softest smoothest skeins and sheets, to cover the brave bones and bold brains of England's proud protectors. Glory to them, glory to you if you buy our silk, by the grace of God, so let it be."

Violet covered her mouth at such foolishness. Mistress Fintry folded her arms and put her head to one side.

"By which you mean that you sell cloth?"

"Calumny Spinks does not sell cloth, mistress. But in the good company of Master Ty Pettit here present, he will from time to time make trade in the finest silks, for deserving buyers only, mistress."

"And can you supply me eighty-five yards of pure white, triple strand, ninety point? And for how much? And if I take fifty-five yards, how much?"

I made the face of a gasping fish, but Ty was quick to rescue me.

"I can spin you a shilling-sixpence yard into a sixteenpence-ha'penny yard if your eighty-five become ninety-five."

He took one bolt of silk out of its case and unrolled it a little for her to feel.

"Are you of the weavers' guild, masters?" asked Violet, who was darning a piece of red cloth.

I gave the girl a little bow to say that we were indeed weavers, taking care to fix her boldly with my eye. She looked up and cocked her head.

"Well, Master Pettit, it seems that you and I should speak of business," said Mistress Fintry, a little smile tugging at her lip. "Violet, take Master Spinks upstairs while I am busy."

"You may knock on my hatch when all is done," replied her daughter, face as blank as snow.

She did not wait for her mother's permission but, still holding the taper, she led me to the far corner, straight past where her mother was already smoothing her hands over the silk. A rope ladder dangled down from a hatchway, and I climbed up first, into a colder room lit by a window in the roof above. In the middle was a small pallet bed, covered over with a doubled woollen blanket the colour of clotted cream. A chimney breast rose at the head of the pallet, its plaster skin leaking the faintest air of soup and woodsmoke.

She had painted the chimney pale green, decorating it with dark-yellow stars rising towards the roof timbers above. In fine black strokes, she had made out wheels and snowflakes, round patterns that spun and pulled me in. Though I could still but barely read, I understood better than any man of letters could. There was magic here.

While I leaned over the bed to see her work, Violet lit the candles, humming a slow tune deep in her chest. Then she settled herself on the bed, swirling her skirts around her, and showed me that I should sit on a cushion an arm's length away.

Moved not, spoke not. The room turned around her. I did not understand this girl, why she should bring me in her room. Not for coin, not to use me like a beast the way Emilia had, not even to converse. She gazed at me, and I was still.

From far below us, in their eating-room, came the rumble of men's voices and the banging of cooking-pots. The chimney groaned and cracked.

"The eating-room is below our workshop," said Violet. "It keeps us warm. Better than any man could."

"I do not … I do not know –"

"Away with you," she said, blushing, "I do not mean in such a way. I mean that a fire is a fire, and it burns as long as there is fuel. It is not like a man, here one moment and gone the next."

I poured myself a cup of water from a clay jug that sat under the eaves. I looked up at her gabled window, darkening as clouds knit across the sun.

"Why d'you come trading of a Sunday?" she demanded as I drank, resting her chin in her hands, so that her cheeks were close enough for me to stroke if I had courage enough – which I did not.

"Why d'you let a trader in of a Sunday?" I sparred.

She rubbed at her eyes with her little fingers. "Mother does not fuss over such a thing. As long as we may go to our church of the evening, she says we are good enough for Heaven."

"A strange church, to meet in the evening," I said, but she frowned, and I cursed myself for my rudeness. I sipped at the water again and pointed at her painted chimney.

"I have never seen such a pattern in my life. What do they signify, the snowflakes and the wheels?"

Her eyes smiled and she opened her mouth to reply, but shut it quickly and crossed her arms.

"A pretty word will not get you into this bed, Master Merchant."

"Nor will a beautiful picture get me there, Miss Temptress," I shot back quickly. I had not yet decided to make the pokey with this sharp-tongued girl, and I had sins enough without a judgement on the evils I had not yet committed. "Is it the custom of army-women to give their virtue to every passing jackanapes?"

Violet did not ask forgiveness, nor did she accuse me again. Unfolding her arms, she gazed at me, the daylight behind her shading her mood.

"The pair of you seem young to have your own trades, to be married..." she began, but flinched as the sound of voices grew into shouts below us. They became suddenly clear, as a group of soldiers burst out into the courtyard. I stood and went to the window to peer down at them, and Violet joined me, sighing. We could see little past the edge of the roof, only a few heads bobbing back and forth, and the noise soon finished.

"It is the London men," she said bitterly, looking out at the woods. I waited for her to go on, and with the lightest of touches on my arm she sat me down next to her on the bed, close enough to hold her hand if I wanted. The world became as small as the air between our faces.

"His Grace – the commander – his company has been together for many years. In Ireland, in the north... They are good men, do you know? They do not harm women. Do not... take..."

I coughed.

"But the regiment is twice as big now. London men from the Tower, as used to be in the Duke of Monmouth's company. They have been sent here to be commanded by our captains."

"Scotsmen," I said, understanding now.

"And an Englishman likes little better than to pick a fight with a Scot."

She dug under her thumbnail, cleaning out a tiny speck of dirt. I wondered what troubled her.

"A soldier will fight," I said gently. "It is his trade."

Violet leaned away from me, pressing her shoulder to the chimney breast as she wound her hair around and tied it in a bunch atop her crown. Gossamer strands floated witchily in the warm air behind her neck.

"The air is safe for the innocent," cackled Mistress Fintry, banging on the hatch.

I looked at Violet, waiting for her to speak. There was now a heaviness in her shoulders and in her eyelids, and the spell between us had faded.

"Master Spinks," called Ty, "it would be well to return to our premises, for we have a *very large order* we must attend to."

I threw on my waistcoat, raised the hatch and swung my legs down. One more look at Violet, and I went.

Ty was on the other side of the great table from Mistress Fintry. He stood pixy-like with his weight on his widder-leg, his pigeon-chest puffed up, while the seamstress rolled the bolt of coarser silk up. There was a strange tightness in the dim room, and of a sudden I remembered what we had come here for. I hoped that the goblin boy had made good business, for if there was no money to be made here, how would I find a way to come back and see Violet?

I had clean forgotten what I needed the money for.

"Mistress Fintry, we make you a gift of that one," said Ty boldly, pointing at the cloth.

She raised a brow at him.

"For you... for your daughter..."

"And for the king himself, mayhap?" she asked with mischief.

Ty blushed. Watching him, I saw what the seamstress had done. She had cut his jacket wider at the shoulders and chest, opened it up around his neck, making him look stronger. He was a changed boy. A man.

"Ty... Master Pettit... You are a handsome fellow!" I exclaimed.

"And handsome fellows are better paid than brutish ones," finished Violet, tartly. She had come down her ladder and was stood by a window, hands on hips, giving me her witch's stare again. The hairs on my arms stood up on end.

"Well, let us thank Mistress Fintry for her kind custom. We must pass by Mistress Landman's home before it is too late," I said, thinking of Landman's tavern. Satan, but this confusion made me thirsty.

"Thanking you, mistress," announced Ty, making marks on a little parchment he had brought in his pocket. "Seven pounds it is, and I thank you for these fifteen shillings of deposit," he started to babble, "and I leave this silk with you, and I bid you good night, and I thank you –"

"He thanks you, mistress," I interrupted with a grin. I led Ty over to the main hatch.

"Finish your story for me next time, redhead," called Mistress Fintry, tidying up her bed. "Violet will take you to the gate. Be swift, for the eating-hour is near finished and you have no permission to be in these barracks.

Master Pettit, stay for one word more of commerce, if it please you."

Violet let me down the ladder. The yard was still empty, but the noise of soldiers crackled across it: the ordinary men taking their food in the eating-room behind us; the dry hawing of officers from somewhere the other side of the blockhouse; the pawing of hooves inside the horse-stalls opposite, their doors now firmly bolted.

She held onto my arm as we crossed the yard to the little gate, looking around to make sure we had not been seen. Finger-warmth pressed through my coat and tingled on my skin.

"There are men here who see me as a kind of daughter," she murmured, "and would take unkindly to seeing you with me."

She fell silent until we had gone through the gate, the ribbon I had ripped drooping at the lock.

"Why does this scrapping of soldiers sadden you?" I asked.

"I have lost one father," she snapped, "and I will not lose another."

I knew that I should tell her I had lost a parent too, that it would open the way to her bed, but I did not. Not for the memory of Mirella, but because I could not conscience it.

We waited for Ty on the edge of the woods, wordless. Violet clenched my arm a little harder, and I felt her looking at me from the corner of her eye. I could not stand to be tongue-tied, and so I dragged a thought from my cloudy mind.

"You did ask to know more of our trade," I said. "Would it please you if I told you about Spitalfields?"

"Is that where you have your workshop?" she asked, looking up at me. Her face was softer from above, like a wood-sprite from an Essex tale.

"Well, to tell true, I have no workshop of my own," I said, without a care that I had broken Ty's story. This girl would sniff out a lie, I knew it sure. "My father is master weaver, and Ty's a mercer, but I am neither. And Spitalfields –"

"It is enough that you have told me the truth," she told me. "It is good."

Swiftly, Violet reached up on tiptoes and kissed my chin, drawing her lips across the tickly stubble. She pressed my hand between both of hers, turned, and was gone before I could draw breath to speak.

The door swung timidly back and forth, the torn cloth peeking from the latch in a glimmer of green. I looked at it, hollowness filling my guts as the sound of the seamstress's steps faded.

Suddenly I remembered my true purpose: it had been half a day since we set out for the barracks, yet I had not even looked for a trace of Anthony, the devil I had come here to trap. I started back for the gate, but bumped into Ty coming through the other way, his sallow face flushed with pride.

"What is it, Cal?" he asked.

I could not tell him the truth: that I had brought him here on a false word. My first lie was too big to confess.

"I… well… when will we come back?"

I blushed crimson. Manly now, he slapped me on the back.

"We shall have to come here every day for a fortnight if we are to deliver all the silk Mistress Fintry has ordered," he said with joy. "Every day for a fortnight!"

I gave him a brotherly hug and we set off. Just inside the woods, we turned and looked back over the wall at the Fintrys' windows, but they were shrouded, no smiling faces to bid us well on our way.

"If your stilt legs were longer still, you could put your paws on the wall and your cold nose against Miss Violet's window," teased Ty, quickly running away from me, out into the dark wood.

"If you had an ounce of meat on you I would feed you to the dogs myself," I shouted, chasing after him.

It was heaven to run, our shoulders free from the weight of cloth, drinking the sweet mist as we chased. I followed the jingling of the fifteen shillings in Ty's pockets, and for a while I could forget about Anthony Anthony, and how I had failed to find him, and how there was one day less between me and the gallows. We slithered about like fools in the mud but never fell, and the air kissed our bare faces, over and over again.

CHAPTER TWENTY-ONE

Impatience

In which Calumny pulls against the leaden yoke of commerce

At the Tyburn bridge, we had to stand back to let a cannon-troop cross over towards the barracks. Behind ponies pulling brass-barrelled guns marched musket-soldiers, their tired faces glowing in the lowering sun. I realised of a sudden that almost a whole day had passed. The crossbarred wooden railings of the bridge shook as the cannons' iron-rimmed wheels clattered over.

After they were gone, Ty led me off the road and down the other bank of the Tyburn.

"It will be dark by the time we are in Westminster," he said. "We have too much coin to risk losing it to a cutpurse on the Strand. Safest to follow the rivers home, for the Thames is ruled by our guild brothers, the lightermen."

Free of our wares, homeward bound and downhill, our journey along the swift-flowing Tyburn was fast. The sun was smearing great streaks of bloody light across the Thames, low on its banks. Not a single boat moved, and a gull shrilly mourned the passing of the day as it settled on a rotten piling.

We climbed down to the riverbank, clinging carefully to tree roots, and wandered slowly along the drying pebbles, draining the last drops in the waterskin.

At dusk, the river was filled with forengies. Quiet Chinese crewmen stacked brass-bound boxes on barges, clapping their hands to keep them warm. Sad-faced bearded heathens from the Indies, their heads bound high with white cloths, gossiped as they rowed an empty boat hard against the flowing tide, and gypsies stalked along the shore, wading out to the tethered boats with baskets full of tin tankards and knives, singing to each other.

At last, my senses came back to me, and I began to think on the commerce of the day.

"Ty, do we have seven pounds' worth of the best white? How will we deliver so much?"

"Well, Cal," he declared, all pompous, his chest still filling out his wide jacket, "two merchants such as we must buy as well as sell if we are to prosper."

"Ty, what have you done, you maggot? You have sold cloth we do not have!"

I aimed a clip at his head but he was too quick and sly for me, darting away around a pair of gypsy women. They clucked at him and rattled their wares, but I dropped a wink and a bow to quiet them. Behind us, a slim fellow drew his cloak and hood about him against the evening chill. The gypsies bore down on him, but he shook his head and turned away from them, trudging in our wake.

"Ty, what have you done?" I demanded again.

"I have sold one hundred and five yards of finest white silk to the Duke of Firth's own regiment."

"Is it so? And how many bolts of silk is that?"

"Twenty-one!"

"And how many do we have in the workshop?"

"We had three before we set out today. And so if Peter has not sold more, we will need to buy eighteen from our friends on Silk Street, which is to say one pound nineteen shillings and tuppence's worth."

"Two pounds! And you have only brought back fifteen shillings! How are we to pay then?"

"Let us drink this gin in celebration, Cal." He showed me a flask, marked with the Duke of Firth's device. "Mistress Fintry made me a gift of it."

"You bastard maggot, you mean for me to pay with my fine gold guineas. How am I to find eighty pounds when I must spend all on your mad promises?"

Ty grinned.

"Perhaps you do not wish to see Miss Violet again…?"

We laughed out loud. The brown-skinned men on their skiff sang a hymn from their far country to us in reply, their white teeth flashing in the dusk, and we clumsily joined their melody. Red-eyed gulls swooped and snapped in time with the song, and in that moment we were kings.

The shore appeared to lengthen with our shadows. The Tower appeared, a tiny sharp-sided shape seeming to cling to the London-bridge like a fraying cuff to a beggar-man's sleeve, never drawing closer no matter how long we walked. For a good long while, the hooded man followed us, but just when I had begun to suspect him he left the beach. The tide turned, and I began to fret that it would catch us, but Ty uncorked the flask. The reek of gin stung our nostrils.

"We'll drown," I whispered to Ty as he drank.

He gasped from the gin and shook his head. We picked our wobbly way along the darkening shore, sliding and stumbling over the slime-laden pebbles as we passed the flask from hand to hand. Coughing at the fiery taste of gin, I wondered how my father could swig a whole mug of the stuff.

The last dregs of day drained away behind us, the beach narrowed, and we had to walk in single file. Drunk as I was, I still noticed that it was the first time ever that Ty had walked before me; taking the moonlight on his face, taking the first breath of the foul air, glancing around watchfully.

After a good while longer, the pebbled shore became mud, and then silty sand, and then it stopped, so sudden and dark that Ty nearly fell into the river that ran into the Thames from the side. From the unholy stink, I knew it to be the Fleet. I looked up, squinting to make out the shape of a wharf above us. Ahead, the way we had been walking, the sewer-river loomed, running too swift and too wide for us to swim across, even if we had the skill and will.

Ty pointed shakingly above his head, then turned to one side and puked, a spattering stream like a wolf pissing.

"Bear Wharf, this is," he said happily.

I pointed at him.

"Bear Wharf it may be, Monsieur Pettit, but we have nowhere to go now. How do we cross this river?"

"We climb," sighed Ty, pointing upwards again. "Up, up, up, and then along the Fleet, and then over the bridge, and thence to Silk Street."

We wearily climbed black weedy rungs to reach the wharf, our arms aching from the weight of the silk we had lugged across London. A hard thirst came down on me now, the cold night clamping my head in a vice of pain.

The wharf was worn smooth, its balustrades scratched and bent from countless barrels and crates that were stacked and taken away, again and again. There was no Watchman there, thanks be to the angels, and we climbed over the locked gate and into the street.

Now it struck me. Our way home would take us past Mister de Corvis' house on Bear Street.

I had not promised my labour to Mister de Corvis alone, yet I knew he would believe I had, that I had betrayed him too.

This was not a family to cross, I thought, guilt giving way to fear as I strode ahead of Ty. Though I had spent the night nursing tender feelings towards Violet, and though I still remembered the peace and love she had laid on me with her kiss, my thoughts began to wander. Emilia's spice seemed to fill the empty street. I felt her watching me, teasing me, from every window and every alleyway. I remembered the hot strength in her body.

We stopped when Mister de Corvis' house came into sight.

"Is that Mister de Corvis' house, Cal?" whispered Ty, and I realised that he had chosen this way home on purpose.

I nodded. A curious expression filled his face; a rabbit

watching a serpent. He drew a long wobbly breath. Sighed it out.

"So my father leaves his craft to work for a man like that. In a place like this."

I shrugged. "Your father is not God. What he does, he does for you."

Ty turned on me, his face angry now. "I know that! I know it well! And that is his great folly, to abandon his own right spirit for what he thinks is best for others. *Malédiction!*"

He shouted his French curse at the sky. Quickly, I covered his mouth again, but not a soul had heard him. We slipped into the shadow of the doorway opposite the de Corvis house and waited, listening. Our long night in the open air had left us nervous as a pair of field mice on harvest day, and the gin churned unquietly in my guts.

Creeeeak.

Ty clutched at my arm. He put a mocking smile on his thin yellow face, but his fear was real. So was mine.

Thumpthump. Creeeeeeeeeeak.

Above us, in the eaves, we caught the faintest sound of soft footsteps and the murmuring of men. Pale yellow light dripped down, forcing its way between the tight rafters.

I had not been mistaken when I had thought I heard those noises all those weeks before. Some secret work was afoot above us, some enterprise that dared not make a sound in daylight.

"What do they do up there?" whispered Ty.

I frowned. Emilia's room was just below the eaves. For sure, she could hear those creaks and whispers as loud as thunder. She knew what it was, but I wondered if I dared ask her.

"This is no place for us," said Ty firmly, though his face was pale from drink and puking. "If they see us here, we risk your employment, and my father's too. And though I may not wish it for him, it is his choice and not mine."

I followed him up Bear Street towards the Fleet Bridge, marvelling at his sure way with right and wrong. For Ty's sake, I did not speak again of the secret works in Mister de Corvis' house. But I felt in the devil-red roots of my hair, in the cold French core of my heart, that there was some profit for me in what I had heard. Whether it was in aiding my patron or betraying him, I cared not in that moment. I would have my money and my freedom. God forgive me, I swore it on my mother's dead eyes.

Shouting stirred me from nauseous sleep.

I pushed the shutters open with my foot, gagging, for it seemed that a crow had shat in my mouth during the night. The sky loomed storm-grey with clouds, their undersides churned by a fast wind that rattled the shutters against the outside wall. Below me, Peter thudded away at the loom.

Garric's voice was raised in anger.

"What do you promise from me, eh, idiot? You are like the mother, blooding fool English!"

I sat up and leaned my elbows on the sill to watch. Garric was stood in the street, his arms open wide and his head thrown back as if he asked God for judgement. Ty sat bare-sleeved on his porch, Abigail two steps below him with her arms folded.

Ty said something quietly.

"You think you are better than your Frenchy father, eh? You make a promise to some woman, you talk *patati patata* of shillings and pence and sudden you are rich, eh? Maledict English!"

Garric took off his jerkin and flung it on the roadway at Abigail's feet. She shook her head at him, but he ignored her, unlacing his shirt and pulling it over his head. Again, he threw it down, though I saw he took care that it land on top of the jerkin, and not on the rain-damp ground.

Ty spoke again, still too faintly for me to hear.

Garric turned his face away, his big bare chest heaving as he planted his hands on his waist. Up and down the street, weavers and mercers came out of their doors, a crowd for the great play-actor.

Ty leaned towards his father, making shapes and stories with his narrow fingers. He was speaking French, his mouth shaping itself into the round pout of his father's language, not the flat-mouthed babble of the English tongue. As he told the story, he proudly put on his jerkin, turning this way and that to show Mistress Fintry's artful tailoring. Abigail cocked her head and arched her back a little, as a cat will do when a dog looms by.

Garric still did not look at his son, but his shoulders dropped and he absent-mindedly took up his shirt again. Abigail covered her smile.

"*Cinq livres, tu m'as dit?*" growled Garric at last.

Ty splayed out the fingers of his right hand to say, *Yes, it was five pounds of profit.*

Below me, the loom stopped. Peter limped out onto the street, letting the door bang behind him in the wind. It sent a shaft of pain through my head, and I swore never to try the gin again.

He walked up to Garric and asked him quietly why he made such a fuss on the street while honest men worked. Garric pretended not to hear the insult. Instead, he seized Peter's hand in greeting and told him that Ty had sold more silk than three men could make in a month, shaking his fist mockingly at his son.

Peter asked piously, "And is it not well that your son seeks an honest living for himself and his guild brothers? How many fires must you set for that same profit?"

Garric lifted his hand as if he would strike. Abigail took a step towards the two men. My father moved his weight onto his back foot, the strong one. He clenched his left fist behind his back, and I saw that his fingers had healed at last. I blinked back the thoughts of Salstead. Of my mother.

"Will you help us, Master Spinks?" asked Ty boldly, getting to his feet. "We need your brother weavers to trust us with their cloth before we can make payment, and we are but boys."

Garric quietly dropped his arms while Peter was looking at Ty.

"We, do you say?" snapped Peter. "Who is 'we'?"

Ty, seeing his mistake, closed his mouth but could not help looking up at my window. Swift as an adder, Peter turned on his good foot and saw me before I could drop back on my bed, out of sight.

"You and the great man up there, is it? Well, it *seems* I have given life to an apprentice brigand," said Peter coldly, looking me straight in the face. "It *seems* that Calumny Spinks is now a mercer without licence, as well as a merchant's errand boy. For sure, he is too good to stay under a poor weaver's roof."

He turned his back on me again. "Well, Tyburn, I will not stand in your way if you seek to turn an honest penny. But mark you this…"

He clamped his thumb and first two fingers together, priest-like.

"…Calumny's share is to be paid to me," he demanded. "He has no proper trade, and so he has no rights to any coin of his own without that I give it to him. It is the guild law."

Garric nodded reluctantly.

"And if you are wise," my father scolded Ty, "you will pay your half to your mother so that it is spent on food and land-rent. Not on drinking and fighting."

He turned his back and returned to his work.

Abigail caught my eye and pointed at her house. I was to come to her straightaway.

Well, I was not about to face the old bastard when he was in such vicious temper. Nor would I risk him taking the coin that I had earned fair with my own sweat and wit. So I took out my guineas and my shillings, nestled them in my waistcoat pocket and clambered out on to my sill. I dropped on the canvas awning, slid down and rolled over the edge, swinging my legs over my head and letting them come slowly down in front of me so I could drop onto the porch.

Abigail shooed Garric away as I crossed the street.

"Begone, Frenchy fool, to Auchan! This house is still barred to you."

Her husband laughed for the crowd, then stalked sulkily away down the street. All the world knew he was forbidden his own bed, but still he kept his shaggy head high.

Abigail, showing no remorse, shoved us indoors. Once we were inside, she gave us both a warm grin and kissed us on our foreheads.

"It was well done, you brave boys. Now tell me the story, the true story. What were they like, these tailor-women?"

We sat at the table with a honey-cake in front of us. She twirled her hair like a maid as we told her the story. She made Ty give her every detail, every colour and cloth in the seamstresses' room, and sighed happily to hear of it. I realised then that Abigail spent all her days among men. All of the other women stayed indoors, or went to the market together. None of them had the cares and business of Abigail, who had become a master mercer in all but name while Garric was serving Mister de Corvis.

Ty stared at her while we talked. I had not seen how he loved Abigail before – it was always the way that she cared for him, tended to his weak health, but now the glove was on the other hand. It was good.

"When will you return there, Cal?" she asked.

"Why, today," I replied. The more Abigail drew the story from me, the more I missed Violet, and my feet were twitching to go.

"Bless you, lad," she laughed. "I do not think you will be off so soon. It is no small matter to get your mucky young hands on the best silk in Christendom, without paying a penny deposit. It will take my husband a good while to work his charms on the guild brothers, and then there is the small matter of carting a hundred and five yards of silk across this city of thieves."

"How long, then?" asked Ty anxiously. I shot him a sideways look. Why was he so eager? I was afraid that Abigail would go cold towards our whole enterprise. But he ignored me, planting his elbows on the table and leaning across to his mother.

Abigail carefully put a chunk of honey-cake in her mouth, closing her eyes. She did not chew, but clamped her mouth shut, waiting for her spit to soak and soften the cake until it drizzled like molten butter into her throat. She took so long that Ty and I grew unquiet, shifting in our seats.

At last she spoke.

"Perhaps three weeks," she murmured, and licked her lips. "But there is work enough for you both here in the meantime."

We looked at each other. Though three weeks was an age, we had no choice but to wait. I could not tell if Abigail had already smelled the scent of my desire for Violet, but there was a dancing flicker in her eyes as she set us to measuring and cutting cloth.

I did not let myself think that three weeks was half my time left on earth – if I could not find Anthony's eighty pounds. I would work, and wait, and dream of Violet.

*

Abigail kept us busy, serving customers by day and tidying up her storeroom by night.

Garric was out of the house all day, wheedling and haggling with weavers, both Silk Street Huguenots and Middlem's Englishmen, pushing them to fill our order.

On the third day, Garric's voice came from the street. There was laughter and backslapping, and then he came in, a smiling light in his eyes.

"I have made a bargain with Auchan. Twenty-five is agreed, Calumny. Twenty-five yards!"

"Leaves eighty yards," grumbled Ty from behind him.

Garric rolled his eyes. "Child ingrate," he complained. "Let him do better with his *patati* and *patata* and mathematic."

I tried to thank Garric with a smile, though it came out more as a grimace. "How long?" I asked in a small voice.

"Twenty-five yards," he said again, as though I were a dolt.

"How long till you have it all, you French fool!" shouted Abigail, throwing a velvet offcut at her husband's head. He laid it over his big greasy head like a wig, making a pompous judge-face.

"Well… ehhh… How may I respond?" he teased her.

"How long?" we all yelled.

"Perhaps two… three weeks."

Ty groaned. Abigail whistled a little song as she folded up the two shawls we had made and put them on a chair near the fire. She took a wooden bowl and ladled a calf's foot into it for Garric, who had already sat at the table. She pulled two roasted parsnips from the coals and wiped them clean of ash on her apron, then took the food over to her husband.

"It is well," she said. "I have much to teach these two apprentices. Now, eat this and be gone again. I have not forgiven you, wild-boar Frenchy liar."

Garric winked at her.

Three more weeks. For sure, Violet would have forgotten me by then.

There was no work for me the next day, Friday. Well, it irked me enough even to sleep under Peter's roof, without spending my days with the old ghost too. I thought I would seek out Garric and ask if Mister de Corvis had more work for me, since I was due my next ten shillings on Saturday.

Garric was sitting on Auchan's front step, looking up at the sunless sky. Before him was one of his covered baskets, a corner of brocaded silk peeking out.

"*Le patron* –" I began.

Garric shushed me with a flick of his hand.

"Think you that he will rain?" he asked in English, still looking skywards.

I tasted the air as my mother had taught me, and shook my head. There was none of the sweetness of rain, only the salty tang of woodsmoke and the thousand foul brews of the city.

"Then let you learn how to trade with a Genoese," he said, handing me a sausage. "Make ware, for an Italian can slice your purse while he shakes your hand."

We passed through the tanner-stink of Wapping, where the shops were smaller and meaner, and every man wore a watchful look. Little bands of dock-men walked the streets armed with cudgels, for there was no Watch here. Garric made me put on the mercer-guild-badge, a bust of a flax-haired princess in a red robe, so that we would be left in peace.

The clouds hung dull and close over the unpainted houses. It was a blessing to leave the narrow streets behind and see the river. Dozens of tall ships rocked gently at anchor in the broad Pool of London.

We walked slowly through the dock-warehouses. Ships rumbled with the cries of sailors and the orders of their captains while the shore rang with sullen hammering. Clerks flanked by burly guards sat behind their desks, writing down lists of what the porters carried past them. It was like Sunday worship at Salstead, every man staring at us like we carried the mark of Cain.

"You must make dissemblant to speak only the French," Garric said, putting the basket down. "Ask for Pinetti, but do not say why you know him. And try to win twelve pounds for these brocades. They are worth the double anyway."

"My pay?" I demanded.

"You are the little commerce-fellow!" he said, pretending to kick me in the backside. "For twelve pounds, nothing. But… if by hazard you make the price above the twelve… I will give you ten *per centum* of what you have gained additional."

He smiled at me slyly, but ten *per centum* I knew now from Ty. It meant one thumb for me, all the other fingers for Garric.

"Why do you not sell the brocade at the market, master mercer?" I asked with an innocent voice. I knew he had some secret.

He tapped his nose with a finger, still blackened under the nail from his midnight works. "It is commerce. One day you will have more wisdom. Twenty *per centum*."

Both thumbs.

"Why do you not sell the wares to Mister Pinetti yourself, master mercer?" I mocked, backing away so he could not seize me without spilling his brocades.

"Make a good price and I will tell you, maledict boy. Now listen me well!"

His neck and face were reddening with a rising fury, and I decided I would not demand thirty. He soon calmed himself, taking the weight of the basket off my shoulders and placing it gently between us.

Garric quickly explained how I could gull the Genoese trader. I could not hold back a smile as he play-acted the character of the Italian, showing his shrewd instinct for another man's desires. Again I saw how light he was on his feet, how quick with his words, and without thinking I mimicked him, pursing my lips the way he did, making mock-surprise with my eyebrows, teasing with the shimmer of the brocade.

He chuckled as I stuttered over my part, folding my arms for me to show how to pretend aloofness.

"*Elle t'a enseigné alors, ta mère?*" he asked after a while. My mother, had she taught me?

I tidied the brocades back into their basket.

"Nothing of the world," I said sullenly. "Nothing but stories."

"Ah," he sighed. "Then she taught you everything you need."

I trudged towards Pinetti's new-built warehouse at the end of the dock. I carried the basket awkwardly, leaning backwards against its weight, as a herdsman bears a sick sheep.

I tapped softly at the warehouse door. The knock echoed inside, but at first no one came. I tapped again, and this time a man opened the door wide.

"What?" he demanded.

Shorter than me, his eyes were glassy, like a dog's. He wore a soft purple velvet cap, folded over to one side of his close-cropped head, and a gold chain around his neck bore a cross with a tiny writhing Jesus clamped to it. His shoes were square-buckled, and there was no garter for his stocking. A strange stew of plain and gaudy, this fellow.

"*Je cherche Monsieur Pinetti, le seigneur d'entrepôt, très important...*"

"Speak English, idiot," the doorman said rudely, in a throaty Italian accent.

"*Erhhh, jenelebarbelezvous...*"

"I speak French. Better than you. Speak the English."

"Erhhh... Monsieur Pinetti?" I burbled again.

He seized the basket off my shoulder and dropped it on its side, spilling several brocades on the ground.

"I am myself Pinetti, you deficient of the mental!" he said angrily, lifting up the top cloth with his polished toecap to look at the one below. "You dare to make mock of me…"

"Three," I said.

"Eh? Three pounds for all of these?"

"I will sell you no more than three," I said quickly, packing up the basket and leaving only the red-gold one on show. Pinetti reached out for the cloths, but I grabbed his wrist boldly. "No more than three."

"Insult! Insult!" spat the Genoese, rising to his feet. He darted inside the little door and slammed it. There was no echo of footsteps, so I carefully covered the basket with the damask and waited with my hands on my hips, looking out at the huddled ships wallowing in the river's swell. Out of the corner of my eye, I saw Garric peeking out from the corner of the warehouse where I'd left him. I waved him back, smirking to myself.

After I had counted thirty-four ships, proud of my growing mathematic, Pinetti came out again.

"How many you have?"

I pulled down my lips to show him I was too great to count mere brocades, and pointed a lazy finger at the basket. He knelt on the dry dock-boards and laid the damask to one side, piling the folded brocades one by one upon it. I knew from Garric that he was from an old silk-trading family, and there was love in his hands as he felt the delicate overstitching.

"*Otto*," he said at last, showing me the number on his fingers, and stood up as if he cared nothing for the rich wares.

"Eight," I agreed coldly, "but no more than three shall you buy."

"Twelve pounds," grumbled the Genoese. "For all of them."

"Twelve pounds for three," I said.

"Fourteen for all."

"Twelve for three."

"Eighteen for all," he said angrily, spitting on his palm and holding it out to me. "Eighteen for all, or I tell the dock-men that you have come here without guild-badge."

I spat on my hand and gave it to him, and in a breath Garric was at our side.

"Monsieur Pinetti," he said with a dainty bow.

Pinetti grinned through gritted teeth and bowed back. "It was well done, Signor Pettit. Your play-actor here is a good servant, though it is shame on you for sending a boy to pay when the account is short. I give you eighteen pounds for him."

"Not for him," replied Garric softly, "but for these fine brocades, against my account with your house. It rests but forty-two of debts, praise God."

"Forty-eight," said Pinetti sharply, clicking his fingers to show that I should pack up the rich cloths in their basket. I had to play the boy again now, though I had bargained with this fine merchant but a moment before.

"Forty-two," sniffed Garric, resting his hand on the handle of his cudgel.

"It is October now, friend. Interest due, interest added. Forty-eight."

Garric pinched the bridge of his nose between thumb and forefinger, but did not argue further. Interest due, I thought. Interest means loan.

When I had finished packing the basket, I lifted it as if to take it inside the Pinetti warehouse, but the Genoese took it from me, barring my way.

"Good day," he said firmly, looking above my head. I stared at the lines on his face, for a man's wrinkles show whether he has more smiled or frowned in his life. Pinetti's skin spoke of snarling.

As we turned to go, the Italian called after us.

"At least these brocades will be safe from fire in my building. You should have paid for your Indian wares to be stored here too."

"*Salaud*," whispered Garric.

"Master Pettit of Silk Street!" came a cheery voice as we walked back down the row of warehouses. "Will you not drink a cup with a guild brother?"

The speaker, nearly as short as Ty but twice as broad, was bare-armed under a sleeveless leather jerkin, his cropped silver hair poking out from the wool cap he wore despite the heat. His skin was flecked with little scars, and there was danger in his broad jaw and wide-spaced eyes, like a fighting dog.

"Master Barcus," said Garric grudgingly.

"Master Dock-man Kit Barcus at your service, brothers," said the other, giving us each a mocking bow. Two more dock-men kept pace with us as we walked down the wharf. Barcus steered Garric into the second row of warehouses. Carpenters and joiners were building a tall frame for a new warehouse over foundations that had been blackened by fire.

"The calico warehouse that burned, Master Pettit," said Barcus, pointing.

Garric pursed his lips.

"Calico is a curse on our weaver brothers. That cheap stuff will kill their trade," the dock-man said, making us pause in the roadway. "Though we are paid by the merchants to guard it, there are some nights when such a warehouse may catch fire. All of its own will."

He gave a dry chuckle, miming the falling of the warehouse. "For sure, Master Pettit, I do not say that you know who fired the storehouse. You are the last man in London to burn calico, I am sure of it!"

He laughed out loud, joined by his two friends, now stood close behind us. Garric gave a "Ha!" and clapped me on the back, but I saw that it was a way to make me move again. We were off before the dock-men had finished laughing.

"Greet my kin for me," called out Barcus.

I held my tongue until we had passed through Wapping. Garric's frown deepened, pulling his gentle eyes into his skull until they grew dark and menacing. At last he puffed out his cheeks and smiled at me.

I understood now. It was Garric's own calico that the weavers' guild had burned in the warehouse. He had broken the guild law and sold a cheaper cloth that undercut their trade. He had borrowed from the Genoese to buy the calico, and he had some feud with the dock-men besides. He should be dead, and yet here he was, grinning at me as if he was not forbidden his own wife's bed.

"Let me see," he said in French. "Thirty *per centum* of six pounds profit –"

"Twenty," I said in the same language, cursing myself for an honest fool.

"Thirty. One pound and sixteen shillings," he said, digging the coins out of a leather purse, but I did not take them. I saw how his elbow twitched, as if it longed to snatch the gold sovereign and silver shillings back, and I needed to know why.

"Well," he said cheerfully, tucking the coins back into his purse. "It will serve towards Ty's schooling."

"At the guild-house? Does it cost so much?"

"Bah! The guild-house – a few pennies, that is. No, I mean for the college."

"College?" I asked in English, not sure I had understood him. "But Ty is not a gentleman – he may not study in such places –"

"The College Secular is the third part of the House of Three Mysteries, Calonnie," he replied quietly, his heavy accent drawing out the words like a cat stretching. "You have been in the *cave*, the foundations of the College where the guild brothers and noblemen meet with the scholars. It is a place where a guild son may study, if his family have fifty pounds a year."

"And if his mother permits it. If she does not stand in his way," I said, leading the way home. Garric bought a pair of oranges from a hawker and ran to catch me up.

"A woman," he whispered, "will agree to anything. If it is already done and paid for!"

He laughed deep in his chest, passed me one of the fruit and dug his thumbs into the knobbled flesh of the other. Juice squirted out, striking his eye, and now it was my turn to laugh. He dabbed at his eyelid with the corner of his cloak.

"You were a brave fellow today, Calonnie. This Pinetti, he is cunning, but you made a bargain perfect with him."

We walked on, peeling the oranges and flinging the peel into the sides of the streets, careless of the apothecaries and barber-surgeons standing in their doorways. Though the fruit was too young and sour, its juice made my eyes see sharper and my heels land lighter on the roadway.

I was not alone. Garric, too, dragged debts and secrets behind him. Forty-eight pounds to the Genoese, fifty a year for Ty's hopes – and if the guild should find out he had traded in calico, it would be death for sure. Little wonder he'd risked his life to bring Peter to London: without my father, Mister de Corvis would have had less use for him, and the Genoese would not forgive such a debt. Yet here he was, eating oranges and making great plans as if he were the king's own nephew.

I glanced at the mercer, and saw that he was watching me, a small smile on his lips, holding his breath.

"I did not like that fellow from Genoa," I said loudly. "I do not think I will shame myself by telling Ty or the guild brothers about him."

Which was to say, *I would hold a flame to the story of the calico and let it burn away from my memory.*

Garric put an arm around my shoulders.

"I know what it cost you to leave me that coin…" he began. "I promise–"

He shook his head. We were drawing close to Auchan's home, and it was time to part. I nodded at him and carried on up the street, knowing he watched me. Like a real father.

Peter was not in the workshop, praise Jesus, so I could go into my home without bearing the weight of his sullen judgement. He had left the front door unlocked, trusting in the watchfulness of his guild brothers. I climbed up to my room and took off my jerkin. From the front pocket fell a gold coin. It bounced on the floorboards, skipped towards the bed and spun around in a circle before falling dead on its back. I lifted it to the meagre daylight, looking at Cromwell's ghastly face, his fat lips clamped together in mimicry of my father's God-fearing anger.

Garric must have slipped it in my pocket when he bid me farewell. And so he knew that my need was even greater than his. What Peter and I faced when the eighty pounds fell due. I clasped my fist around the coin. The smell of burning puffed out between my fingers and stung my eyes.

CHAPTER TWENTY-TWO

The Healing

In which Calumny falls foul of contract law

The next morning, Ty and I were left to tend the mercery, but a chill October wind kept away the passing trade. Ty cut down some of the white-flowered weeds that grew from under the porch, and put them neatly in a pair of old jars to make the shopfront look pretty. Then we went inside to wait for custom.

We had less than six weeks to find the eighty pounds, and nothing to do but wait for three of them, unless Mister de Corvis sent for me. To escape my thoughts, I climbed up the wall and lay down on a rafter, out of sight of the door. Ty sat below, carving his patterns and numbers into the surface of the counting-desk. The air was still, for all the buzzing and crawling bugs had died with the coming of the fall.

A knock at the door, and an open-faced gentleman walked in. White curls burst out of his wide skull and poured down his cloaked back. His head twitched doglike left and right as he looked around the workshop, holding his hands behind his back as if afraid to touch the cloths.

"Boy," he said to Ty, "how much for the sheeny silk here, by the door?"

He had not seen me stretched out on the rafter above him.

"Eightpence a yard," said Ty without looking up. "Seven and eight for that bolt. But the one next to it is shorter. From the look of it I should say, six shillings tuppence ha'penny."

"And this one?" asked the gentleman, pointing left of himself. He had a habit of dabbing his lips each time he asked a question.

"Sixpence farthing a yard," replied Ty. "Four and ten the bolt. Four and ten and three farthings, but there's a colouration halfway through, so I will grant you the three farthings."

"And what do you carve there, boy?" asked the gentleman. "Is it a star in a circle? Why have you carved it with five points?"

"See here," answered Ty, at last looking into the man's face, "how the circle's rim makes eight-fifths of the side of the star."

The man shook his head, and I wondered to myself if perhaps Ty had not counted properly.

"Have you taken the measure of the circle?" he asked.

"No need, for I see it," laughed Ty. The man joined in, shaking his head again as if to tell if he had been dreaming. It was the first time I had seen Ty answer questions, instead of asking them.

"Can you read and write?" he asked.

"I can, but I do prefer the numbers to the letters," said Ty, turning his face down to his carving again. He drew a spiralling snake with the circled star as its head, and the man knelt down to see closer.

"What is your name, boy?"

"Tyburn. Tree. Pettit," replied Ty, for once without blushing.

"Why do you ask so many questions, eh?" I shouted from above. The gentleman looked up. Smiling, he took a small stone from his pocket and tossed it up for me to catch. His pale ox's face sat awkwardly on his slim body; his lips were red and swollen as if he bit them every time he had a thought. He released me from his gaze.

"Now we will conduct an experiment, concerning the speeds and accelerations of objects, using the very latest natural-philosophical and scientific methods. You, rafter-dweller, shall be the subject," he said solemnly, and Ty chuckled.

I began to protest, but the man ignored me.

"How shall we proceed, young mathematicker?" he asked Ty.

Ty looked up at me with a big smile on his face. "Cal, you are to hold the pebble down by your feet," he ordered. "And when you jump down, you are to let go of the pebble at the same time. Now which do you think will land first?"

I shook my head at his stupidity and pointed at my chest. Of course I would land before the tiny pebble, I thought, this is but a trick to make me jump around like a monkey on a chain.

"You will land at the same time," said Ty, and the gentleman smiled again.

"Your friend is a miracle, rafter-boy. He has the right of it."

I did not want to play my part in this tumbling-act. I pointed at Ty spitefully. "They are no miracle, those great boils on his neck."

Ty blushed, but the gentleman stepped closer and gently tugged down the kerchief round his neck. He nodded and cocked his head to look at the red lumps better.

"Very well!" I called out, and leapt, dropping the pebble from close by my feet. Time slowed its pace enough for me to watch the stone fall with me, inch by inch. It seemed that we were still and that the floor was flying up to meet us, side by side.

Just in time I bent my legs, and rolled, and cracked my skull on the counting-desk. Then all I heard was Ty laughing, and I had to laugh too, for I had thought myself dead.

When I caught my breath again, the gentleman had gone. My head hurt. Ty was crouched next to me, staring amazed around the shop as if he had at last forgotten all the prices and lengths and measures.

"I am to go to the College Secular on Thursday next," he said proudly. "There, a surgeon will examine my neck. Perhaps there is a cure for it."

I wondered who had sent the gentleman philosopher.

The days wore on. Saturday had passed without word or coin from Mister de Corvis. I did not miss his ten shillings. It would not make the noose any less tight around my throat, and I feared the grim-faced merchant and where his tasks might lead me. Besides, I knew that the harder I worked, the sooner I would return to Violet;

and perhaps find Anthony's master and free myself altogether from debt.

It seemed that every day Peter would limp past with some excuse to call on Abigail. Could she mend his woollen stockings? Did she wish for anything from the market? Each time he would find a way to peek at Ty and me at our work, though he never caught my eye.

The next Thursday morning, Ty had to confess to his mother that he was expected at the College Secular. He waited until she was halfway through taking in a petticoat-waist, her mouth full of pins, but she spat them out furiously.

"This is your father's doing," she said. "You could be the youngest master craftsman in the city, but instead you must play at being the gentleman. Tall poppies will ever be cut down, Ty, mark it."

"But –" I protested.

"Hold your tongue, Calumny Spinks," she burst out, laying the petticoat on the table. "I'll take no fool's wisdom from you in my own house. I will not let you lead Ty into a godless life. That college is a nest of atheists and law-breakers. It is no place for my son."

Flushed, I turned away. Those were the first unkind words she had spoken in all the many weeks I had spent in Silk Street, and her accusing words cut me to the quick.

"Good day, Abigail," called my father, tapping at the workshop door.

"Will you let us be a while, Master Spinks?" replied Abigail calmly, though her chest heaved up and down. Peter did not reply, but pushed open the door and limped cheerfully in, tucking his old high-crowned hat under his arm. He wore his best boots, and his faded leather uniform.

"Peter Spinks, why do you dress so odd? Do you go before the judge?" asked Mistress Pettit sharply, crossing her arms.

"Before a gentleman of a more accurate profession, Abigail," he said, glancing at Ty. "A man should always wear his best coat to face a man who cuts for a living."

A jest! The ancient ghost grew more witty the closer he stumbled to the scaffold.

"A surgeon, you mean?" pressed Abigail, fiddling with the keys she wore at her belt.

"Has Ty not told you that he is to be cured of the King's Evil?"

She frowned and tightened her lips.

"Well," said my father, patting his chest as if he had the wind, "that is a marvel, that Tyburn Tree Pettit should forget such a thing. Shame on you, Ty."

"I – forgive me, Master Spinks –"

Peter waved him into confused silence. "It is of no matter. When you have taken sword-thrusts to your carcass, as I have, the wounds of pride sting but little."

I huffed to myself.

"Who is to pay this surgeon you speak of?" demanded Abigail.

"There is a bursary from the House... You know the House that Garric and I belong to –"

"Where is this surgeon?"

"Close by the House," replied Peter smugly, stepping back out of the door. We all followed him into the street.

"You mean the College Secular," hissed the tailoress, grabbing at Ty's collar to stop him following my father. "He is forbidden to step into that place."

"Is he forbidden to be healed?" asked my father in a voice as tough as Spanish steel, and carefully placed his hat on his head. He had tied a turquoise ribbon around it, jauntily adorned with a blackbird-feather. Moony madness, I thought.

Abigail shook her head but did not let go of Ty, stroking the kerchief that covered his boils.

"It is well, then," said Peter, his voice locking the door on her arguments.

"It is well," she echoed, dropping her hands helplessly. Ty turned and kissed her cheek.

"You too, if you please, Calumny," ordered my father without looking back. His shoulders lifted a touch under his old coat, though whether it was from the cold breeze or from laughter, I could not tell.

"Cal, it was well done indeed!" exclaimed Ty when we were out of Abigail's sight. "You are a true friend, to tell your father –"

"I did not," I said shortly. "This is *his* scheme."

Peter, hiding his limp as best he could, still wore a possessed smile.

We had to jump back as a carter drove too fast down the middle of the street, cooped chickens screeching and fluttering in the wagon behind him. Goodwives scolded, and a pot-hawker dropped his wares with a curse and a coppery clash.

"But that white-haired gentleman was no surgeon, so why should he look at Ty's boils? It is a nonsense," I complained, and spat on the roadway.

"If nonsense is purveyed here," said Peter to the sky, "it is not by me or young Apprentice Pettit."

I fell behind, kicking my heels in the dirt. So full of clever words, the pair of them. I did not keep a watch on where we walked, for a sulking fellow must pay heed only to his own suffering; and we were soon in a place I did not know at all. We squeezed through narrow winding lanes bounded by storehouses that thrummed to the beat of hidden engines. A door swung open near to my side, spitting out a squint-eyed urchin in a red cap and a smutty overcoat that was too big for his stunted frame. He carried a bound parcel of papers, so large that they flopped down both front and back, giving him the look of a wild turkey. He could not pass me by.

"Dutch Fleet Sets Sail!" cried the news-hawker full in my face, spattering my cheeks with snuff-stinking spittle. "Broadside One Penny!"

"I Cannot Read!" I yelled back, putting my mouth as close to his waxy ear as I could bear. "Devil Take You!"

He pushed past me. Ty and my father were waiting for me further up the alley, shaking their heads.

"It is the College Secular," whispered Ty when I had caught up with them.

"That is no college – it is a news-printing place," I scoffed.

"There," said Peter in a patient voice, turning my shoulders so I could see the doorway behind me. A pair of ribbed pillars were set deep into the wall, bounding a solid oak door that was wedged open by a scarred cannonball. In the gloom of the alleyway, a man could walk past the doorway and never know it was there.

I followed my father and Ty into a long corridor, feeling watched. Mullioned windows set into its stone roof lit up a line of gentlemen's portraits. Each held something different – a knife, a glass vial, a dead butterfly. The other wall bore a strip of marble, inscribed in gold leaf.

"It is Latin," said Ty. "*Deus...*"

"Read me no *Deus*," I cut him off. "I have had enough of *Deus*."

He fell silent. I pointed at the last portrait in the corridor, which was of the white-haired gentleman we knew, holding up a small-cogged engine of pale steel.

We came out into a square courtyard. Three sides were of the same polished grey stone as the entryway, and the fourth was old and half-timbered, its plasterwork freshly painted in creamy white, sunlight flickering on the sagging old windows. A strange music came from within. I knew that it was the back of the house I'd seen gentlefolk go into before dawn on a Sunday; I had spied and lied in its foundations, hot with steam and conspiracy. The College Secular was the third way into the House of Three Mysteries, as Garric had said.

"Come," snapped Peter, clapping his hands. I could see that he had no love for the gentlefolk who met in the fine house.

We passed through a door in the opposite wall of the courtyard.

"Why are we allowed to walk freely here?" I whispered to Ty.

"It is a college," he replied, like a man at prayer. "Learning cannot be bounded."

"But trinkets can be sold," I muttered, stroking a solid bronze gargoyle that served as a doorknob. Ty tutted, and we followed Peter through an arched hall and down a flight of steps, our footsteps ringing loudly.

"Provost," called Peter as he reached the bottom of the stairs. He led us into a round room with a table in the middle, its leather top stained in patches. Next to it were two smaller tables, porcelain-topped. A fire burned in a small brazier hanging down on a chain. Though we were now underground, the room was brightly lit, its shiny marble walls reflecting the glow of oil lamps.

The white-haired gentleman came through a door to our right, seeming to sail across the brindled marble floor, his soft slippers poking under the hem of a long russet robe. He finished wiping tarry grease from his fingers with a kidskin cloth, and clasped Peter's hands.

"Mister Cole," said the Provost solemnly. The hairs on my arms stood on end as I heard my father's true name spoken aloud. Peter flashed a warning look as a stocky, level-gazed fellow entered. With his chubby face, he could have been any age from five-and-twenty to five-and-forty.

"The Respected Surgeon-Principal," the Provost said, and the surgeon bowed slightly, touching his stubby fingers to his breast. The Provost nodded his head at each of us as he gave our names, though this time he called Peter by the name of Spinks, and we bowed back.

"Which of these is the subject?" asked the Surgeon-Principal coldly, snapping his fingers towards the door.

"The *patient*," replied the Provost warmly, "is a scholar-inductand to this college, Tyburn Pettit here."

I did not know what "inductand" meant, but if Ty was called "scholar" already, then Peter and Garric had tricked Abigail. I began to feel sick: curing him at the College meant she would accept him studying there.

Two younger, black-gowned men came in, their heads shaved and their hands gloved. One carried a basin of water, the other a tray of devices made from steel and bone. I shivered.

"Very well, Master Inductand," said the surgeon crisply. "Do lay yourself upon the table there, and let us examine your scrofula."

"He means the King's Evil, Ty," said Peter gently. The surgeon gave a dry cough, as if he scorned kings and evil alike. When Ty had lain himself on the table, we were bid to stand near his feet, the Provost gently taking away the kerchief so the surgeon could see the boils.

He pressed against the lumps, making Ty wince, and jerked his head to show the younger men that they should do so too. "You will feel the hard edge of the scrofula, which is a good fortune for this inductand. It may be treated by curettage, as the Provost has intimated."

The Provost smiled, and laid his hand on Ty's other shoulder. "Not every scrofula may be so easily cured, though you must bear some pain now. Are you willing?"

Ty licked his lips and swallowed. He looked at Peter and me as if to ask us what he should do, and I could not help but shrug at him. What did I know of disease and cure? My mother's tisick had been cured only by her murder, and Peter's wounded leg would never heal. This was beyond my knowing.

Peter nodded at Ty, and Ty said, "Aye," as boldly as he could.

The Surgeon-Principal took a sharpened steel rod from the silver tray. One of his students bathed Ty's neck. Water ran down onto the table-top, making a new stain, and I realised that the other patches were of dried blood. I wheezed. Spinning wheels of light hid the sight of Ty's face for a while until Peter squeezed my arm.

"The curette," said the surgeon, holding the pointed end in the flames that crackled from the hanging brazier. "What is the principal purpose of this device?"

The first student ceased sponging Ty's neck and busied himself with squeezing out the cloth above the basin. He does not know, I told myself, for I knew all the tricks of hiding ignorance.

"*Aborior,*" said the other, crossing himself.

"Such symbols are for the church, Grasset," the Provost scolded him. "Here, science must prevail."

"*Aborior* is correct," said the surgeon, holding the curette aloft to let it cool. "You, boy –"

"I, sir?" I asked, wondering if his sight was so poor that he would address the wrong fellow from so close by.

"You, do you know the meaning of *aborior?*"

I shook my head. Peter tapped his foot next to me, a sure sign of anger, though I doubted he would act upon it.

"It is when a man's lust makes a whore of a woman, and gets her with sickly child. Sometimes the baby must die so that the woman can live. And sometimes the woman desires that the baby should die."

"We do not make a surgery for such a case," said the Provost hastily, catching Peter's eye.

"Indeed not," replied the surgeon, nodding to tell his students to hold Ty down by the ankles and shoulders. "But it is well to know that an unwanted child may only be removed in safety with such a knife as this."

Satan's cold breath clamped my belly. Peter had not wanted me; he had said it in Salstead. If my mother had not kept me, a knife would have taken me, unborn.

Ty cried out as the point of the curette burst open the smaller boil, and the surgeon twisted it in the wound to scrape away the yellow-pink mass inside. My friend shrieked again as the greater boil was lanced, kicking frantically at the hands that restrained him. This time blood as well as lumpy pus came out, pouring over the table's leather rim.

"Cauter," snapped the surgeon, and the student holding Ty's feet let them go. Peter seized them quickly. Taking a rod topped with an eye-shaped lump of iron, the student thrust it into the hottest part of the brazier, then handed it carefully to his master, who laid it three times on Ty's bleeding wounds. At the first touch Ty gasped and fell silent, his clenched fists flopping open, and the smell of burning flesh leapt up at us like scattering pigeons. I turned away to puke, stumbling to the bottom of the stairs to keep my foulness away.

When I looked around again, Peter let go of Ty's legs and went to touch his neck, but the Provost gently tapped him on the elbow.

"It is unwise to touch an undressed wound, old friend. Let the boy be bandaged cleanly. Take your son into the air until we call for you."

Peter glared at the surgeon, who ignored him as he bent down to look at Ty's wounds. The goblin boy's eyes had rolled upwards into his narrow skull, a lock of black hair stuck down across his forehead with fearful sweat, and one of his boots had near come off from kicking against the student's grip.

My father obeyed the Provost and came to fetch me, roughly pushing me up the stairs and out into the courtyard, where he pointed to a small water-pump in the corner. I was to clean the speckles of puke from my boots. As if that small shame were worse than Ty being branded like a beast.

I pumped at the handle and put my boots under the stream, not caring that my feet inside were growing wet. Then I held my face in it, washing out my mouth and cleansing the memory of Ty's pain.

I dried my face on my sleeve while my father talked.

"Science is a marvel of God, but that fellow is an atheistical butcher who would as soon slice a man's liver as care for his morals. If that is the medicine of this age, then I do not care for it."

I stared at him, speechless at his hypocrisy.

"I know right well that I brought Ty here. The Provost is a good man – I know him from the days of the Commonwealth, when Cromwell was our Protector and we had no king. But in those days, doctor and surgeon were right-thinking men, who prayed before they healed. Now –"

"But Ty is healed, is he not?" I asked, unquietly.

"God willing, he is. God willing."

Now it was Peter's turn to take a drink from the pump.

I see no God here, I thought. I see one man who prays and one man with a knife, and it is the cutting-man who has brought salvation to my friend.

CHAPTER TWENTY-THREE

Catamite

In which Calumny learns of a new craft

After his return that night, bandaged and pale, Ty was kept in his room for a week. Garric was allowed back into his house, and his wife's bed. Abigail nursed her son, boiling up soup at every hour of the day and night, putting damp cloths on his head, bringing him books from the College Secular.

Since he had been cured, Abigail had forgotten her anger towards the college. Garric told me how she fawned on the Provost, drinking in his praise of Ty.

"Your father has made a miracle," the mercer told me.

Though I was grateful that Peter had found a cure for Ty, I raged at him for letting the days slip by without earning a penny towards the eighty pounds. All he seemed to wish for was a place in heaven, and he cared little that I would end my days so young.

I worked away at Abigail's tailoring, finding that I had a touch for stitching and cutting after all. I would bring up my work to show her and Ty, and each time there was a little more praise. Ty had his pale face buried in a book most of the time, but he always raised it to give me a smile. *The barracks*, his eyes said. *We shall go back to the barracks.*

*

Slowly, slowly, Garric brought together the rest of our order. By the next Tuesday he had sixty yards promised, by that Saturday it was one hundred, and he went down to the river to hire a boatman for the next Monday.

"Do we not need the full hundred and five yards?" I protested to Ty as he left. He had been up and about for a few days now, and he looked better than he had before the cutting. His skin had lost its yellow hue, and his voice was stronger. The bandages had come off his neck, leaving a pair of pink-edged burns that he did not bother to cover with a kerchief.

"The last five are for you alone to find," replied my friend teasingly, and ran to catch his father up. Angry that the order was not complete, I watched them stroll down Silk Street with the noonday sun in their faces. Garric put his arm around Ty's shoulders and greeted the other weavers loudly, like a king showing the crown prince to his people. I could tell he boasted of Ty's great dealings with the army, and of his miraculous healing. Men came close to gawk at the scars on Ty's neck.

I turned to go back inside, but Abigail was in my way, her hand outstretched to keep me back.

"There is no more work for you here, Calumny Spinks."

"But I – but Abigail, I do not ask for coin –"

"And short shrift would you get if you did! Your mending is done, Cal. Go you about your business, now. I have my counting to do and I cannot have you buzzing about the place. Go home!"

She pushed me off her porch. A dry cough came from across the street. Peter leaned against the porch-post, his hand gripping his hip. He beckoned me over and went inside, leaving the door open. The shutters were shut tight even though the sun shone and the air was October-mild.

I dallied in the roadway, kicking the dusty stones. Where else had I to go?

Feeling Abigail's eyes on my back, I walked slowly back to Peter's house, fearing his words as much as his blows.

My father was at the loom, his feet on the treadles but his arms idle, watching the door.

"Leave it open, if you please, Calumny," he said quietly. It was the first time he had ever If-you-pleased me, and I did not know what to say. He had put a second stool by the loom.

As I drew closer, I began to see better in the dimness. He was halfway through a length of silk. Ghostly strands clung tightly to the loom's frame in a shimmering waterfall of thread. He had made near three yards, piled untidily in the wicker basket behind the engine.

I did not sit on the stool, but knelt by the pile of woven silk and began to fold it neatly. It was the finest white, so dense that you could have stretched it over a leaky boat and kept it dry inside forever.

Peter did not weave, watching my folding until it was done. When I stood at last, I saw that his eyes were shining. Quickly, he wiped them with his sleeve and cleared his throat.

"We shall make five yards of this," he said, looking at the rafters.

I spoke not.

"It is for… it is for Ty Pettit," he said.

I sat on the stool at the loom's side.

"And you," whispered Peter.

I folded my lips inwards and stared at my feet.

"Will you… work the loom?" asked my father.

I backed away, shaking my head. The loom's mended frame and skewed treadles reproached me. It had never been the same since I had broken it.

He stood too, yielding his seat.

"Two yards more," he said. "You will be finished by midnight. And then… And then you will deliver this parcel of beauty, which you have made with your own hands. There is no better thing in life."

I can think of one better, I thought, remembering Violet's face as she came to kiss me farewell. But I kept my mouth shut and let the old man speak.

"Sit," he said.

I sat.

"Now get your stool closer to the treadles," he instructed me. "Your knees should be almost touching the weft so. Your back straight, not hunched like a toad."

I clenched my teeth. He touched my shoulder to show he meant no insult.

"Now take the shuttle out. With care, Cal – that was well done – and let it rest in your palm like a sleeping mouse. Do not wake it. When you are perfectly still, we may begin."

I took a deep, deep breath, settled myself on the stool.

"One foot at a time, put them gently on the treadles…"

Left foot, right foot.

"Now look you up and down the loom. Is the heddle

still and clear? Do the threads hang straight down? Is your chest full face to the warp?"

I made a little "yes", without a sound.

"And now –"

From the street came the crackling of iron-rimmed wheels on loose stones. A horse blew out its nostrils loud enough to frighten a whale, coming closer and closer until it stopped hard by our porch. Cucullan.

"First the treadles, then the shuttle," murmured Peter, as if we had not heard the commotion from outside.

Frazier huffed his way down from the coach and clumped up our stairs.

"The treadles," said Peter again, with ice in his voice.

"Master Spinks, saving your pardon," said Frazier from the doorway, his shadow turning the pure white sheen of Peter's silk into a frozen blue.

Peter did not stand or turn, but addressed Frazier while looking at me.

"What is your business here, fellow?"

"It is Calumny Spinks, your son. His master calls for him."

"His master, do you say? Is he apprenticed, then?" asked Peter. He reached over and took the shuttle from my hands.

"He has made his mark on a contract letter, Master Spinks," said Frazier, giving me a sad look.

"I wonder that he did not ask his father first," said Peter. He rose and took my elbow in a hard grip, lifting me to my feet. "Well, if he is already apprenticed, then I have no call to teach him my craft. Tell your master this boy is clever enough for any trade, but that he is better at keeping secrets than at earning a man's trust. God speed."

With a little wince at the pain in his hips and fingers, Peter sat again and put his feet on the treadles. He held the shuttle ready beside the weft, stroking its smooth skin with the ball of his thumb, but did not begin to weave.

Frazier coughed. It was time for us to go.

Not until I had closed the door behind me, leaving Peter in the near dark, did the *chumpa chumpa* strike up again. Cucullan's iron-bound hooves skipped to its echoing beat as we left Silk Street.

Mister de Corvis was waiting for me in the coach, rubbing at his left wrist. Cucullan pulled away swiftly, throwing me onto the seat next to my patron. The windows were opened, the curtains pulled apart, and my master sat up straight, allowing the breeze to ruffle his short wiry hair. He seemed different, not so taut and closed.

At last he spoke.

"The ships are launched, Calumny, and we are waiting for the wind to fill their sails."

"What do you mean, sir? Is it the Dutch navy, come to attack England? Is it war, as they say?"

"No, no. Though I should say that it may well be that the Dutch are coming, but that is not my object. I mean that a great enterprise is afoot."

He pointed out of the window. A shattered building, its charred timbers sagging uselessly into its empty heart, was being pulled down by workers while a crowd gawped, drinking and throwing dice.

"That house has been empty for more than twenty years, since the Great Fire. But now, someone has had the courage, the dream, to pull it down and build something better in its place. It is such an enterprise we are about!"

"To build houses?"

"No," he said sternly. "To build a new England."

This was the second time he had spoken treason to me. He was so cold and clear in commerce, yet so passionate, mad almost, when he spoke of this. I cleared my throat.

"And what is my part to be, sir?"

He pulled out a purse and handed me a sovereign and a ten-shilling angel, which made three weeks' pay in all.

"You are to play the part of my ward, Calumny Spinks."

"What is a ward, sir?"

"It is a young person of good birth who is in a protector's keeping. Although I must tell you that many a patron has… a certain weakness… How should I say it? Do you know what is a catamite?"

I shook my head.

"Do you know that many men have lusts outside their marriage?"

"Well, yes, sir –"

"And outside the fair gender? I mean, not for women?"

I swallowed and looked at my hands, twisting them around each other in shame. I thought of the men in the steamy rooms under the House of Three Mysteries, touching each other and whispering, beckoning to me. I did not answer.

"Then you must understand that certain patrons will… use… their male wards in such a way. And such a boy is called a catamite."

"Ah."

"Yes."

I shifted my backside further away from his, until I was crammed red-faced up against the door of the coach. Mister de Corvis stared at me. The silence tightened until at last he blinked and gave a little dry laugh.

"Ah – you mistake me! I did not mean that I was such a patron, or you a catamite! Dear God!"

"Then what –"

"I mean that you must *play* the catamite in our enterprise. You do have some skill with the mimicry, do you not?"

"I have skill enough to make a blind mother forswear her own son," I said loudly. Frazier choked off a snort of laughter overhead.

"Thus is it settled," said Mister de Corvis. He pulled his cuffs lower over his wrists and looked unquietly out of his own window.

I watched London drift away behind us, tucking the coins in my waistcoat pocket with the others. Our debt fell due in three weeks' time.

After passing through Holborn's elegant streets, we entered shadowy twisting roads, where voices called out in a dozen strange tongues. Flat-faced Tartars in their strange furs idled on steps, picking at their teeth with curved daggers, while small Chinese ancients hefted sacks of rice into hidden basements. There was scarce an English face to be seen here.

"These are the most powerful men in England," murmured Mister de Corvis.

I did not know what he meant by it.

"They bring the wealth and goods of far nations to London. They fill the city with commerce and hard work and ancient knowledge, while the lazy English grow fat on them. And if ever they should leave, all England will mourn their passing."

I looked at them again, the brown-faced Indians and the arguing Norweyan traders. I felt whole among them, not a half-breed.

"Soon we will come to Dover Street," he said, "the home of Lord Montalbion, the king's Secretary of Commerce. Tomorrow you will play the catamite here, but I will chiefly call on your mimicry and natural strength."

He pulled off his glove and tapped his forefinger scratchily on the window. Again, he tugged his cuff into place with his other hand.

"Lord Montalbion," he continued softly, "is a man of great import. He too is part of this enterprise. But –"

He pulled his black leather glove on.

"It is vital that you are not discovered, Calumny. Though Lord Montalbion and I are allied, you cannot be caught in your task. It would go ill for all of us."

"Well, I have little enough to lose," I muttered, before I could stop up my foolish mouth.

"Then I must tell you that I have plenty to lose, my daughter above all. And I cannot permit any harm to come to her, do you understand? I will kill… well…"

It made my head spin, how he flew from secrets to threats.

"John – Frazier, stop the coach!" he called out. Across the street, behind high iron railings, was a garden, packed with pine trees, spreading silver birches and curious shrubs.

Behind was a yellow mansion, its sheer walls adorned by richly carved spiralling columns.

"Is Lord Montalbion English, sir?" I asked.

"His house has a very foreign air, does it not? I suppose he is English, because of his accent and schooling. But he is the bastard son of the king's brother, King Charles the Second as was. And bastardy can be made on a woman of any nation."

"Is he not from the Indies, sir?" I blurted out, thinking of my mother's stories. Emeralds like robins' eggs, gold statues bigger than horses, sorcery sung on tar-black rivers...

"I doubt that he is, Calumny. Why do you say so?"

I pointed at the roof of the house. Under the point of the eaves was a sandstone sculpture of wild cats fighting while long-haired men – or fighting women, I could not tell – brandished curved knives at each other.

Mister de Corvis remained silent, watching and waiting.

After a while, a pair of blackamoors in puffed blue uniforms, frogged with ruby lace, pranced down the street like horses, pulling an open carriage. Half a dozen boy-men with painted lips sprawled on the leather seats. Mister de Corvis pulled back from the window and motioned for me to look at the catamites.

They were not soft and secret like the molly-men in the steamy room. Instead, cheeks powdered and eyelids stained, they preened themselves, giggling loudly. Behind them walked a couple of flour-faced lawyers in black robes, pretending to make legal chit-chat to hide their lust for the painted boys.

A bearded doorman opened the gates, and the catamites fell silent as they passed out of our sight.

My master tapped at the roof, and Frazier moved the carriage a little further on. Mister de Corvis pointed.

"On this side are seven windows on three floors. Each window lies behind a different door, coloured for the colours of the rainbow. You do know the colours of the rainbow, do you not?"

"Why, yes –"

"Good," he said.

What are those colours, I asked myself. Red, yellow, white, blue, purple. Or is there orange? Satan take my foolish pride!

"When we enter that house tomorrow, you will enter the indigo door, go onto the balcony and climb unseen to the second balcony below it, do you see?"

He showed me where an elegant balcony sprang from the stonework.

"And when the talking is finished, you will climb to the third balcony below it and come back inside as if you have been taking the air. That is the room where the catamites are made to wait."

I swallowed my spit and moved back across to my old seat.

"Repeat it to me, I tell you," ordered Mister de Corvis testily.

"The indigo room, climb down, listen, climb to third balcony, play the catamite…"

"Good. Good," he muttered.

"… and come back with my master to the carriage to receive my reward. Of twenty pounds," I said daringly.

Whack. His cane struck at me before I could see it coming, hitting me on the temple. My ears rang like they did the day I was trapped in the Salstead bell tower at evensong.

Mister de Corvis, as if he had never hit me at all, leaned over and closed the window.

So it was with my grim patron. Do his will, and you would be rewarded more than was right. But cross him, and you were nothing in his eyes once again. Up, down, up, down, until the world fell to ruin.

CHAPTER TWENTY-FOUR

Le Comte de Calonnie

In which Calumny becomes a gentleman of breeding

We drove back to the house on Bear Street. I followed my master into the main hall. Emilia, hands clasped virtuously in front of her, was now wearing a high-waisted gown of shimmering witch-elm green that swaggered loosely across her bare shoulders. She gave me a little curtsey, planting one cloudy slipper in front of her body, and I began to dream of being Mister Calumny Spinks again.

"Bow to me," ordered Emilia.

I frowned. Was this another of her games?

"You'll be needing to bow to the lady," said Frazier from the doorway to his master's study. I had not noticed him lurking there, my eye drawn magpie-like to the sparkling girl.

"Begging your pardon, my lord," he added with a little smile when I looked back at him. Mister de Corvis brushed past him and into his study, closing the door behind him.

Emilia sighed angrily. "You are to play the gentleman, do you not see? And a gentleman must always bow to a lady, or another gentleman."

"But not to a lower person," I said in Cowans' snotty voice, clicking my fingers at Frazier. He smiled again and bowed his head to me.

Emilia turned and walked to the far side of the hall.

"Proceed," she ordered.

"Like a strutting pigeon," said Emilia once I had reached her and bowed. "Bouncing to the tips of your toes, rushing along like a vulgar hawker… It is a desperate walk. Again."

Frazier chuckled as I went back to the servants' door, shamefaced. "A true gentleman, he must seem tired of life," he said. "Tread the floor as if it sullies you, go slowly as if you have never broken sweat, do not look another person in the eye."

Emilia narrowed her eyes, but Frazier's face was open, as if he had not spoken harshly of the gentry.

I placed each heel down with care, gazing dully past Emilia and pulling back my shoulders, as I had seen gentlemen do.

"Better," said Frazier, "but you'll be needing to bow to the mistress still."

Emilia rolled her eyes. It was to be a long lesson.

When the light had begun to fade, we went into the study. Mister de Corvis had disappeared through the far door. Emilia sat down behind her father's desk, arranging the quills and inkpot while Frazier seated me at a small table near the fireplace.

"Do not lean on your elbows!" demanded Emilia, striking the desk with her palm. "You are not on a pig farm now!"

Frazier's eyebrows twitched at the mention of a farm, but still he kept his face plain. "Sit back in your seat, thusly," he told me. "Now push one foot under your chair, and the other out to one side."

I remembered the gentlemen in the Moor's Head coffeehouse, and made myself as cocky-like as I could.

"It is well done," said Emilia, surprised. Frazier patted my shoulder as he left.

"Emilia –" I began.

"Miss de Corvis," she said coldly, flicking her eyes at the closed door. I understood – we were overheard.

"Miss de Corvis, I do not know what I am to do for your father –"

"You may begin by obeying my commands, without fail," said Mister de Corvis, opening the far door and stepping back into the study. The last warm wisps of dusk-light flickered across his sallow face.

"Now, let us test this mimicry of yours," said Mister de Corvis. "Let me see… The Scots accent is the hardest. Perhaps the Duke of Firth?"

Desperately I stood, making my chair squeak. Mister de Corvis frowned and opened his mouth to speak, but I drew myself up into the duke's tall, weary frame and pointed a crooked finger at him.

"When will you make the first delivery?" I demanded in the dry voice I had heard in the House of Three Mysteries.

"Father, why does he –?" asked Emilia.

"You will address me as Your Grace," I said with menace, delicately lacing my words with Scots tones.

"You play him well enough," said Mister de Corvis flatly.

He was silent for a long time, looking out of the window until the last glimmer of daylight had vanished. I had guessed right. It was indeed the duke that my master had sent me to spy on.

"Mark it, Emilia. Prize-money to be paid on completion, a further ten shillings."

He was not a man for full praise when there was coin to be saved. Emilia smiled a little as she wrote down the numbers, and I was glad to see she had a care for me still.

"And you speak the French tongue, boy?" asked Mister de Corvis, rubbing his left wrist against the edge of the desk.

"It was my mother's language, sir," I replied. Emilia cleared her throat and looked at her father. It seemed they knew my story already. Garric, I thought.

"I did not ask that, Calumny Spinks. I asked if you had the knowledge of it."

I did not want to confess that I had enough French to ask my mother to feed me or tell me a tale, but not nearly enough to pass for a gentleman. Instead, I puffed out my lips as Garric would have done, shrugged one shoulder and spread out my hands honestly, the way a butcher will when he is about to tip his scales against a goodwife.

Emilia snorted. Walking towards the door, her father said, "I see he has neither the King's English nor the Devil's French. Then he must play the part of a rich but witless foreign fool. God knows that there are enough such people in London today."

The door snickered shut behind him, leaving me with Emilia. She wet her lips quickly, a mouse's tongue-dab.

"We must find you a title then," she murmured, casting a glance at me. I leaned back in my chair again so she could picture me as a lord. "*Le baron de… le comte de…*"

"Calonnie," I said warmly, thinking of my mother.

She stood and came around the desk towards me. "*Le comte de Calonnie*," she answered, and bobbed her head. "It is good."

I waited for her to come to me, to try to touch me again, but this was a different Emilia. With her father close by, she was stern in her words, cold-eyed, all the mischief and madness choked down below her mantua's tight waist.

"Up," she ordered.

I stood and bowed to her. "Madame," I said.

Emilia folded her arms, cocked her head to one side and looked at me.

"Always stand on one leg. Let the other be work-shy," she said, and I let my right hip slouch. Straightaway, I felt more foppish.

"Never say a whole thing, not in French or English. Nor should you reply to a question," Emilia went on, pacing towards the bookshelves with her arms still folded.

I followed her.

"*Euhhhh... madame...* In England you..." I burbled.

"Good," said Emilia, her back still to me. "It is gentlemanly to be foolish and nonsensical. Now – *monsieur le comte*, does your family have a residence at Paris?"

"*Pfff*," I giggled. "*Quelle question*, you English!"

She looked back over her shoulder at me, her wiry curls drifting over her face.

"I must draw the balconies of Lord Montalbion's house for you," she said, leaning over the polished desk to pull a sheet of paper towards her. Her hair fell forward over her shoulders, showing the slender chain of her spine. The spicy scent of her was caught up in a heady spirit, as tangy as gin, which left a bitter tingle on the back of my tongue. I thought of Violet, and swallowed.

"Charcoal…" she said dreamily, and I could not help glancing up at the top of the bookshelf before I remembered that I had Ty's quiver of coals in my waistcoat. As I took it out, she seized my wrist.

"Thief!" she hissed, too quietly for anyone listening at the door.

"These are my friend's coals –" I began in a whisper.

"My drawing, you viper! It was you who stole my drawing of…"

She pushed me away, her nails catching my hand as she let go. Of a sudden, her eyes were glistening in the candlelight.

"I will give it you back. I only… I only wanted to keep something of you."

Now the tears began to flow, silently and without sobs, and the bailiff-woman was gone. Here was the child again, her chin crumpled into little ripples.

"It was all I had of my mother's home… in Jamaica."

I wanted to ask why her mother was not in London, but she pressed her hand to my mouth. With the other, she reached inside the billowy sleeve of her mantua and took out a small corked vial, a brown juice swirling inside it.

"A woman need not feel pain," she said in a different voice, deeper and with a faint accent that was more like song than speech. She took her hand away from my face, unstoppered the vial and drank it down.

"Miss Emilia –" I whispered.

She turned and went to close the velvet curtains. When she came back, her face was calm but her eyes swam with colours, the way they had that first time I went into her bedroom.

"Charcoal," she said in a stronger voice.

I opened Ty's box and gave her a stick.

"Here," she said, the coal skittering quickly over the paper, "is the wall of Lord Montalbion's house, hidden from Dover Street. Here, on the first floor, is the balcony of the orange room, where the catamites wait for their patrons. Here, on the right…"

She pointed at a double window without a balcony, and then made some quick strokes with the coal-stick, as if drawing curtains across them.

"Do not look in the red room," she said in a dull voice. "It is for women only. And they are not used as well as the molly-boys."

Sitting at the desk again, she drew two more windows above the red and orange rooms, then three more small ones above those. Each of the three floors had only one balcony, poised one above the other. I came round the desk to look as she pointed to them in turn.

"Indigo," she said. "Green. Orange."

I waited.

"You will go to the indigo room on the highest floor. My father will show you where to go once you are in the house. From the indigo room you climb down to the green room. You will listen to all that is said, marking the voices and the words of each man so you may play them for Mister de Corvis afterwards. When the talking is done, you will climb down again to the orange room, and come in from the balcony as if you have always been there."

"But why –" I began.

"Do not be impertinent, Calumny Spinks," she chided me. "You are bound by contract, and my father has been generous indeed in forgiving your breach of Monday. Do not waste your thoughts on why this and why that – there is much to do before you can pass for even the shadow of a gentleman. Frazier!"

The coachman stamped across the hall and came into the room. He frowned, as if it was not the first time he had seen his mistress' eyes stolen by the faeries.

"Take *le comte de Calonnie* upstairs. It is time he dressed according to his station."

At the top of the stairs were three doors. The little one to the side led to the servants' staircase. Frazier pointed at the door before us, its varnished panels proud with carved vines.

"You'll not be trying that way, young fellow," he said softly. "The master's room is forbidden to all but me."

"Then how does his maidservant dress him?" I asked as he led me into the room on the right.

Frazier shushed me, closed the door and took his oil lamp to the empty mantel. This room was almost bare, its floorboards painted the watery blue of April skies. In the corner was a pair of bulky chairs, covered over with calico drapes, and against the opposite wall was a trestle-table piled high with fine clothes. The moon outside was swollen and fiery, like a lantern glowing behind a lace curtain, and the broken surface of the far-off Thames glittered with a thousand splinters of light.

"How does his servant dress him if she cannot go into his chamber?" I asked again, curious now.

Frazier ruffled the clothes into two piles. "Have you ever seen servant or maid in this house, Calumny Spinks? Any but Mistress Frazier or my own self?"

In truth, there were so many floors and staircases in this great house that I had filled them with imagined servants: a scullery maid and housemaid for Mistress Frazier, a handmaid for the master and his daughter. But now I realised I had heard nought more than echoes and silences there, like a church on Mondays. Confused, I stood.

"But does the master dress himself?" I asked. I could not credit it.

"Blessing you, no," laughed Frazier, waving me to my feet. "He is too much of a gentleman for that, never mind. I have skill enough for such things. Now take you off that waistcoat and those breeches."

I stood and obeyed, still wondering how I had never noticed that this household was but four people: the Fraziers, my master and his daughter.

"Now, let us see that shirt," he murmured, beckoning me closer to the window. The moon's waxy rays lit his face, and the wrinkled corners of his cracked lips lifted as he pinched the front of my shirt.

"Soft weave indeed," he said to himself, "and well-stitched besides."

He cocked his head.

"You carry more weight than when first we met," he said, squeezing my shoulders. "My master's shillings have been spent on good meat, I see."

It was true. Weeks of eating well, of work both honest and secret, had given me another covering of flesh, harder than the first. I broadened myself under his touch. He let go and went to the table, offering me a choice of breeches.

"A good coat will suit any man, but the wrong breeches will make a fool of him."

I tried a pair of old-fashioned rhinegraves, but they were more like petticoats on my long legs, and Frazier chuckled with delight at the picture. Then he gave me a pair in the modern fashion, the way Mister de Corvis wore them, as close-fitting as craftsmen's breeches except that they were gathered at the knee.

He brought the oil lamp to the window so I could see myself in pale reflection, floating like a ghost over the wharf's reflection. This pair was more seemly, but it showed how scrawny I was.

"I shall be asking the master if you may keep these breeches," said Frazier kindly, "for they would serve you well. But a gentlemen may not seem so ill-fed."

He put back the lamp and handed me a pair of coffee-brown velvet breeches, trimmed with raspberry-pink satin. I knew before I put them on that they were right for me, broad enough to call out the width of my shoulders, and long enough to show my height. I tucked in my shirt-tails, and Frazier knelt at my feet.

"What do you do there, Master Frazier?" I asked,

peering down at his thinning iron-grey hair. I could see little beyond his lumpy shoulders.

"Portcannon, my lord," he replied in a muffled voice, tightening something around the tops of each of my calves.

At last he leaned back. Lace vallances hung down my calves like willows shading water.

"Bide a while," said Frazier, handing me a waistcoat that matched my breeches. A London gentleman's coat would have as many buttons as could fit on its edges and pockets, each one stitched over with silk thread, but this one was simple, the soft velvet glistening in the oil-light. As I took off my own waistcoat, I felt the shape of Ty's quiver of coals. I slipped it into my new coat for good luck.

Standing in the buckled shoes, I was taller than Frazier. I walked, feeling like a lord already, but after two paces, my left ankle gave way. I yelped, and Frazier caught me before I could rip the fine clothes.

"Let you stand before you walk," he said, holding his arms out to either side of me as a mother does with an infant.

I stood there, wobbling on my toes until I could trust the heels of the shoes. My calves began to ache.

"Now look you ahead," murmured Frazier, taking a step back. "Now come towards me."

I bent my knees and slid one foot after another across the floor, wobbling. When I reached the table I leaned against it, resting my calves. "Master Frazier, will you take these demons from my feet?"

"No, my lord," he said. "Indeed, your costume is not finished."

I groaned as he tied a lace bib at my throat, and set a periwig on my prickling head.

"One more thing a gentleman must bear with him always," Frazier said, handing me a gold-leafed watch. It fluttered like a spider as he tucked it into my waistcoat pocket, leaving a little chain dangling. Time, like a fresh-hanged man, kicked its doomed legs against my belly.

"You must play the French count now. It is your test," whispered Frazier. I went downstairs cautiously, his lamp making the banisters cast flickering cage-shadows. A puddle of candlelight spilled under the closed door of the study.

I shivered. Always, a little breeze would blow through Mister de Corvis' house, carrying with it the smell of cleaning-lye. Beneath it was a fouler scent, the memory of night-soil and corrupt rain, as if the Fleet itself ran under the chequered floor-tiles.

We clacked across the hall and paused in front of the study door so that Frazier could tug my wig into place. He pressed a firm hand into the small of my back, using the other to tilt my shoulders. Feeling strong and whole for a breath, I prayed that I would pass muster.

"Now you are a French gentleman," he breathed.

"Come," called out Emilia.

She was closest to the door, but I knew now that a French nobleman does not greet a lady until all gentlemen have first been acknowledged. I strode past her towards her father, one hand behind my back and the other raised before my chest clutching a lace handkerchief, like a mummer at Colchester fair. Five or six wax candles were burning in the room, and my master's dark complexion seemed to glow as he awaited me.

I stood two paces before him, still with my kerchief raised, and waited. Since Mister de Corvis' rank was less than that of a count, he should bow first. At last he made a little bob of his head. I swept the kerchief down, clasped my hands together behind my back, and slid my left foot forward into a deep and mocking bow.

"*Monsieur le comte* –" he began, but I was already prancing towards his daughter.

I bowed before Emilia could curtsey, sweeping back her cuff to kiss the inside of her wrist.

Frazier coughed, and I could feel his master frown at me.

"Monsieur, you do insult me," said Emilia, taking her hand away, though her curtsey was enough to tell me it was an insult she had enjoyed.

"*Impossible*," I giggled in French. I strutted over to the round table and sat down, stretching out my legs with one foot crossed over the other. I felt a silver buckle scratch the polished leather boot.

Mister de Corvis joined me, nodding to ask permission before he sat down primly. I took a pinch of air from a pocket and sniffed it like snuff.

"*Monsieur le comte*, of what family?"

"Oh, *vous savez...*" You know, I meant.

"The Edict of Nantes, are you in favour?" he asked.

I pursed my lips, dabbed at my chin with my handkerchief and then looked at my watch, yawning. Catching Emilia's eye across the room, I blew her a kiss.

"You English," I said to Mister de Corvis in an accent even stronger than Bouleau's. "The religion, she is your mistress. The *argent*, the silver, he is your master. *Pfff*..."

I rose to my feet.

"Enough!" he rapped out. "Sit. And do not carry this comedy further."

I obeyed, taking off the sweltering wig.

"Emilia, write."

She went to the desk for her paper and quill, bending her head to work.

"*Primo*," her father went on, "no French gentleman walks so eagerly. *Secondo*: insolence towards a lady is tolerable in a man of his rank, but he must mask it better. This is still London. *Tertio*: you must instruct *le comte* to hide his wit. Religion may be an Englishman's mistress, but to tell him so is folly. *Quarto*: his skin is unpowdered and unshaven, and the filth of the street clings to it. Frazier, you must see to that in the morning."

Frazier clicked his heels together.

"*Quinto*," said Mister de Corvis to Emilia, "you must tell this young ingrate that his part was well played. But should he ever turn his back on me again, I will crack his skull forthwith."

He rose and walked slowly to the door. As Frazier opened it, his master told him, "You shall begin again at nine o'clock. Calumny Spinks shall sleep in your room. And lock the door well."

I looked at Emilia, but she had busied herself with blowing sand across the instructions she had just written, to dry the ink. Frazier tilted his head, and I followed him into the empty servants' quarters.

"Has Mistress Frazier gone to bed already?" I asked, trying to hide the disappointment in my voice.

"Blessing you, no," said Frazier. He began taking out onions, carrots and turnips from a row of covered earthen pots, chopping them up with a heavy-bladed cleaver. He saw me staring at him and smiled. "A seaman learns to cook with the tools at hand. Stoke the fire, will you?"

The embers in the hearth were glowing feebly. I took a few cords of wood from the stack, piled them up on fresh kindling, and blew. Once the flame had taken, I took the poker from its hook on the mantel and stirred until the fire came to life. I thought of how my father ended each day like this, kneeling at the fireplace.

Frazier hefted a cast-iron pot onto the hook above the fire. I helped him to fill it with the chopped vegetables and with water from the jug, to which he added a handful of bones.

"Where does Mistress Frazier sleep?" I asked, sitting at the table while Frazier cut two hunks of bread for us.

"Tonight, she is with her family, over east in the city," he said mildly, not meeting my eye.

"Are they craftsmen, then?" I asked.

He shrugged. "She does not like me to speak of them. It is not her way."

Elbows planted firmly on the table, he held the bread to his mouth, tearing each mouthful away with a sideways yank of his bulky grey head. His front teeth are rotten, I thought, and so he cannot bite.

The oil-light caressed the steam as it burst from the pot. The cords of wood were aflame now, the sweet smell of simmering mixed with burning. As I chewed on my bread, fear sent its worry-spies to the corners of my mind. What was to be my task tomorrow? What would happen if I were caught spying in Lord Montalbion's home?

The coachman put his bread down and laid a heavy hand on my arm.

"Never fear, Calumny Spinks. I have been in many a dangerous place with the master, and he has never made a poor plan yet."

For if he had, you would not be sat here telling me, I thought.

When the soup was finished, he led me to the little room overlooking the Fleet.

"Good night to you, young fellow," he said.

"But Master Frazier – where will you sleep?"

"God save you, in a house with so many rooms and no servants, I am sure to find a place," he said cheerily, and locked the door behind him. I was a prisoner for the night. The air was stale, and the bedsheets smelled as if they had not been touched since I had last stayed there, weeks before.

Neither Frazier nor his mistress had ever slept in this room. The whole house was as hollow as a priest's promise.

CHAPTER TWENTY-FIVE

Dutch Gold and Murder

In which Calumny conspires in high treason

Mister de Corvis strode along the moist cobbles of Dover Street. I had to use my little silver-topped cane to keep from twisting my ankle as I followed. The misty afternoon air cooled my face under the wig's stifling curls. I knew that I was as good as hanged if I failed, and did not understand why I had to run such dangers simply to listen at a window.

It was the next day. My master had been calm that morning, testing me once more in his chilly study. As I watched him, he glanced up at the foggy sky, blowing a puff of steam-breath towards the heavens. A man who knew his own mind, and the mind of the world.

Though I was nobly dressed, I was still Calumny Spinks, my satin-kissed calves trembling from holding their own against the slippery roadway. My throat stung: Frazier had made me swill brandy and mint to cover my rat's-turd breath.

When we came to Lord Montalbion's tree-shrouded gate, Mister de Corvis began to tap his cane cheerfully. Inside it, the blade that had bruised and cut Anthony Anthony sang faintly. Fresh powder floated off his wig, and the higher the breeze took it, the deeper my misery sank. His lightness made me sure that if there were a price to pay today, it would be paid by me and not him.

"Sir!" I hissed, though I knew it was too late to ask him more of my mission.

"Serve me with your silence," he replied without looking back. "You know your part."

Rap rap. My master banged the door with his cane, clicking his tongue to tell me to join him on the top step. The doorman appeared, but we turned our backs as if we surveyed the people of Dover Street.

"They keep us waiting, do they not?" demanded Mister de Corvis of me in lordly fashion.

The doorman coughed behind our backs.

My master turned and pretended surprise to see the servant, a grey-and-red uniformed man-wolf with trimmed beard and shaggy eyebrows who was trying to hide his anger.

"My good... man, I did you wrong," said Mister de Corvis penitently.

He waited so long to say "man" that we all heard the unspoken "beast" in the still air, and I choked back a laugh. My master dumped his gloves in the man-wolf's hairy hands as we swished past him.

"Sir, sir," insisted the doorman, "whom shall I... Sir!"

"De Corvis and his ward."

He tossed his words over his shoulder, crossing a perfectly smooth floor of rat-grey flags. The hall was egg-shaped, with a sweeping staircase at the pointed end. Two mighty portraits adorned its columnless walls, and the domed ceiling was entirely painted with a scene of warring angels. Bear Street seemed a pauper's home next to this great mansion.

To one side of the staircase, clerks in fussy midnight-blue coats scuttled down a corridor, bearing sheafs of papers. Like ants, they could not pass each other without a touch on the arm, a whisper in the ear, a smug shake of the head.

Lawyers, I thought, for I had seen such men before, skulking in their jackdaw-winged cloaks in the cloisters of Colchester market. Men who would rather take a ball in the eye than a contract unsigned. The man-wolf clapped his hands. A clerk raised his head and bustled over to the door, hiding the corridor from my curious gaze. Mister de Corvis, halfway up the marble stairs, turned and put a hand on the banister.

"*Monsieur le comte, je vous prie...*"

I pray you, his words said. I will cut your throat, Calumny Spinks, his eyes said.

I made a play of consulting my pocket watch, yawned, and lazily followed him up. Mister de Corvis knew his way around this house. The landing at the top of the stairs faced a pair of double doors, with heavy gold-leaf curls sitting proud on shining white paintwork. The doors were slightly open so we could hear the babble within, but my master held me back with a hand on my neck. I felt the fast heartbeat through his thumb as he pointed down a hallway at a pair of coloured doors.

"Red and orange on this floor, yellow and green above, then blue, indigo and violet on the top floor. Those are the colours of the doors," he whispered. "You will be asked to join the other young men in the orange room, but I wish for you to run on to the indigo door. Go out onto the balcony, climb down to the balcony of the green room below, and listen without fail to what is spoken. Last of all, come down to the balcony of the orange room and make pretence that you have been there all along."

"And so I bid you wait for me in that room, *monsieur le comte*," he continued in a loud voice, pointing again at the orange door.

"Indeed, Monsieur de Corvis," I replied haughtily in my Frenchy voice. "And I put in you confidence, that this door conceals no men of ill-breeding."

Out of the red door came a shimmering blue cloud, bringing with it a waft of curious perfume, a bastard cross-breed of horse's sweat and womanly scent.

A wig, so large it could have been sired by a Portugee hunting dog, sat atop a square-jawed face, which in its turn floated in an old-fashioned cream ruff. He wore a narrow-waisted foppish coat, its blue satin billowing out at the shoulders and in the matching petticoat-breeches, but drawn tightly together at its narrow waist. The lamps in their sconces around us shone brilliantly off glossy papist-purple shoes, laced with silver-threaded ribbons.

"Benjamin de Corvis," the man said softly, "you do us wrong to snub our little gathering,"

There was tempered steel in his voice. Under the powder and paint, he had a powerful face: hazel eyes that bulged intensely as they looked me up and down, a wide mouth set in a determined line, a thrusting chin. He scraped at his stained fingernails with a delicate little stiletto before slyly slipping it between the folds of his costume, and I saw then why Mister de Corvis had outrun the doorman's announcing of us. This was a dangerous man.

"*Milord, je vous présente le comte de Calonnie*," he introduced me. I gave a little sniffy bow, to show that I had not the habit of being polite to Englishmen.

"*Enchanté, enchanté*," replied the creature, and asked me a long question that I did not understand. He tested me, to see if I was truly a French count, but I was unmoved by his trick. I simply sulked my lips together and shrugged, until both the gentlemen laughed.

"My honoured friend here is sharp as that blade you carry in your breast, Lord Montalbion," said Mister de Corvis.

Montalbion gave a tiny amused sniff. "And how is the… *sugar* trade, de Corvis?" he asked delicately.

"It is the sweetest life, my lord, as you know," replied Mister de Corvis.

"Sweet indeed, since a merchant like you does not need an exclusivity to trade in sugar. My natural father… I speak of the late king, you understand…"

Montalbion crossed himself in a mockery of the popish gesture.

"…was generous with his exclusivities, but also exclusive with his generosities."

He waited, but my master did not smile at his wit.

"Which is to say," said Montalbion dryly, "that he was happy to acknowledge his bastards provided we did not ask for favour."

"And so you must labour for England, my lord," said Mister de Corvis, kindly.

"And so I must labour," sighed Montalbion, throwing out a hand towards the stairs as if sowing corn on the regiment of lawyers below.

He tapped his cane on the floor, and the double doors were opened from within. Montalbion and Mister de Corvis entered the drawing room of His Majesty's Secretary of Commerce.

I had thought it would be a bright ballroom, full of the gay chatter of sparkly stupid ladies, not this parlour of sunset-red where hard-faced gentlemen in wigs frowned and conspired at tiny tables, butting elbows like stags jousting. The sun struggled to make its way in through the miserly gaps in the curtains.

I caught sight of a fellow who looked out of place in the room. Without wig, without frown, he sat a little apart from his table, a balding ugly man in the dress of an ancient Puritan. Martin van Stijn.

"The orange room, *monsieur le comte*," breathed Mister de Corvis before I could raise a hand in foolish greeting. Lord Montalbion swept before us as my master shut me out on the landing.

Hot with the fear of being caught, I looked over the railings at the hall below. Master Man-wolf sat with his back to the staircase, neck hairs thrusting through his tight collar. I took off my high shoes and went quietly to the orange door, pausing to listen outside. The room bubbled with the high-pitched giggles of catamites. Swiftly, I pushed down on the handle, slipped an arm inside and pushed my shoes and cane into the corner, then closed the door as softly as I could.

I ran to the curving stairway at the end of the hallway and scaled it, my stockinged feet warm on the carpeted treads. On the next floor, I peeked into the corridor. A man coughed deep in his chest from behind the nearer door, the green one, and I dashed up the next flight of stairs to hide from him.

The highest hallway was narrower, uncarpeted, with the three doors Mister de Corvis had promised – but they were all blue, one light and two dark.

So which of the dark doors was indigo? Which should I take? Laughter spiralled up from the floors below. I had to find the indigo balcony before I was surprised.

I opened the first door, guessing that this was above the green room. It was a simple bedroom, with a cot to one side and an unpainted chest of drawers on the other. A long-stemmed pipe and a book lay upon the chest of drawers, and a travelling-bag was stowed under the bed. I knew the pipe to be Martin van Stijn's, and I picked up the book and spelled out the letters aloud as Ty had shown me. "Deh, eh… Buh, ih, juh, buh, eh, luh. *Bijbel. De bijbel.*"

A Dutch Bible, I had little doubt. Why did van Stijn sleep under Montalbion's roof?

I listened carefully at the door, but the hallway was still silent, so I knelt and pulled out the travelling-bag instead of going onto the balcony. The bag was filled with printed sheets, all identical, though it weighed far more than paper should. There was some other cargo inside it.

I passed my fingers over the harsh calico lining of the case. Here and there it was tough and flat, unyielding. I felt along the lining until I found where the stitches had been undone. I bent my knuckles inside the cloth, and grasped at a bar of metal. Carefully, I took out a cold tongue of hardness, weighty as a traitor's soul, and held it to the cloudy light that bulged sullenly into the room.

Gold. A sliver of pure gold nested in my hand, the four eyes of the window reflecting on its oily skin. Feeling a carved pattern on the underside, I turned it over. A roaring lion was stamped upon it, its curious tail tufted twice, once in the middle and once at the end. Tiny symbols were carved in a row below its feet.

Holding the treasure against my chest, I knelt and fumbled inside the travelling-bag's lining with my other hand, counting the hidden shapes. Another bar, and then another – ten in all.

Dusty air settled in my chest. Calumny Spinks the apprentice spy, trapped alone at the end of the hallway in the dead-eyed lord's house, holding the gold he should not have seen.

Was this my chance; could I take this gold and make my escape? I could hardly guess at its value, but I was sure it was many times more that the eighty pounds I needed.

Leather-shod feet trod softly on carpeted stairs.

A madness took me. Though I dared not steal such a lump of gold, I would take its secret with me. I seized one of the pamphlets from the bag and held it flat over the carving of the lion, pushing the paper into the holes to make the beast's shape. But it was not enough – I needed to make the lion-pattern more clear, and so I took one of Ty's little sticks of charcoal from my coat pocket and rubbed it back and forth until the stamp stood out bold white amid the dark coal strokes. Quickly, wheezing now, I tucked the gold bar back into its hiding place, tidied the papers and pushed the bag back under the bed. Just as the door handle rattled, I jumped out of the window.

There was no balcony here. Toppling forwards, I seized the outside windowsill just in time to break my fall. I swung around below the ledge until I was able to push my toes into a crack between the stones. The wind was cold on my knuckles. My eyes stung as I clung to the sill, looking down. No tree to catch my fall; below was nothing but hard stone flags. Five men standing on each other's shoulders could not have reached me. To my right, a yard out of my reach, was the balcony I was meant to come out upon, and below it the balcony of the green room. It was a man's height below my chilly stockinged feet, and an armspan to one side. Letting go of the sill with my left hand, I pushed the window closed and then felt the bricks around me as fast as I could, pressing my fingers in, looking for handholds, but the masons had mortared the wall as smooth as a priest's lie.

From inside I heard a voice. It was Martin van Stijn, inviting Mister de Corvis into his room. Hugging the wall tight, my fingers aching on the sill, I looked down and across at the balcony of the green room again. A leap and I might die, or else I could lift my head above the sill, and forfeit every trust I had gained from Mister de Corvis. Perhaps my life too.

Now Mister de Corvis spoke, his back to the window.

"I will bring you the strongest of the guilds, the saddlers and the lightermen and the rest. You have seen what they can do, and those ten ingots in your bag will suffice to buy all the guildmasters," said Mister de Corvis. "But I must know that the licences will be mine if I do."

Rumble rumble, came van Stijn's voice, too far from the glass for me to hear.

"And when all is done, and your man is king, will a man like me be welcome at court?" replied my patron in a bitter tone, turning towards the glass. I was terrified of his rage if he caught me there. Without waiting to think, I turned and leapt into the void.

I was able to break my fall with my hands, but my elbows gave way and I caught the middle balcony's rail in my gut. I could not breathe. I had the rail under my arm but my limbs failed me. I dragged and drew and strained the air into my chest, clutching at the rail until I was over, crouching and crying in the corner of the green room's balcony.

I looked up. Mister de Corvis was turning to look out of the window, and there I was, in the place he had commanded me. His left eyelid fluttered, and he turned back to the Hollander. I had made good my disobedience before he caught me.

Wheezing, I crawled below the window of the green room, shivering as the autumn wind dug its fingernails into my stockinged feet. A door opened, and three voices came inside, talking politely of the king, the court and the weather. One was Lord Montalbion's, for sure. The second spoke in unquiet, stabbing tones; and the third was the Duke of Firth's, dry and full of tired experience.

Again, this duke: my master had set me to spy on the most powerful man in England after the king. I could feel the hemp closing around my neck.

Close to where I knelt was a shadow hidden among the gathered curtains, a looming wraith that neither spoke nor moved. I did not dare to lift my head and look, but stayed down, nursing the fiery ache that was spreading across my belly and chest.

The door closed inside, and the pleasant chatter stopped, as if a play had finished and the masks had come off. The Duke of Firth spoke first.

"We have given all you asked of us," he said angrily. "Even you, the heret… the Dissenters, may have your peace. Let us make an end of it!"

"Empty words," spat the unquiet man, and coughed violently. Peeping above the window's lintel, I watched a man in Puritan garb spit into a bloodstained kerchief. "Empty words, when every time I cough, my spittle smells of the smoke of my burning brothers. Firth, you are a popish knave."

"Your tongue, Wilton," ordered Montalbion with calm menace. "The Duke of Firth is here in peace, and since you will not respect his high rank then I dismiss you."

The Puritan left, his silent rage bursting out in a racking cough that shook him from head to foot. The noise of his leaving allowed me to scuttle to the other side of the window, far from the man who lurked in the curtains. I raised my head and peered through a gap between the curtains and the window frame.

"And what of the Crown's power?" asked Montalbion. He was sat upright on a low-backed chair, leaning towards the duke, who was slumped to one side of an armchair with a weary look on his old face. "Does Parliament command the army now or no? Your regiment – let us speak of that – does it answer to the king or Parliament?"

Firth did not answer the question. He gazed steadily at the other lord.

"Why do you have a Dutch spy in your parlour, Montalbion? I little knew that your fondness for trade could overwhelm your duty to your king–"

"My duty is to England," replied Montalbion.

Firth did not reply, and Montalbion shifted in his seat under the older man's glare. I shrank down again.

"I do not want a Dutch king!" he insisted, his voice higher-pitched now.

"Indeed not," said the older man slowly. "You think that Parliament would rather have Charles' bastard son on the throne than the king himself? You, mayhap? And you are prepared to risk invasion to dethrone His Majesty."

"Be silent!" demanded Montalbion. The shadow stirred within the other curtain, out of sight of the Scots duke.

Lord Montalbion spoke again, more quietly, and I pressed my face against the cold window-glass to hear him better.

"I know full well what is duty here," he said, "and *I* will say who is traitor and who is not. I have not forgot your embassy to France, nor your dealings with French spice traders –"

"And I will not forgive your welcoming of Holland," cried the duke, but then he choked strangely on his words, as if he had been plunged into water.

I dared to lift my eyes above the sill again. A bulky soldier in scarlet uniform was bent over the Duke of Firth, whose wig was sliding gently off his thin white hair. The dying man tried to rise, his eyes open wide, but his movement only pushed his chest further onto the blade. Montalbion was sat up heartily, his body tipped towards the murder.

"Alcott," said Montalbion, as the duke's struggles faded and his eyes fluttered shut, "a most impious murder has taken place."

"*Grrmm*," said the assassin's broad back.

"It was commendable that you would find and capture the Duke of Firth's assassin, since he was commander of your regiment, and yet I know it was with heavy heart that you arrested Mister Wilton."

"*Hrr hrr*," shrugged the red-coated murderer as he pulled his blade back out of Firth's chest and thrust it unwiped into its sheath. He turned towards Montalbion, and I ducked, too cowardly to look on his face.

"Good. Now please tell that Scottish ruffian that his master is detained here."

There was no reply, but the door clicked open and shut. All was silent inside the room. I closed my eyes and waited for Montalbion to leave.

Instead, the balcony doors were pulled open, and the lord himself was stood above me. His powdered face was wiped clean, and he glared at me like a judge passing sentence.

"You," he said to me in a hellish voice, pulling me up by the scruff of my neck. He wiped his hand on a little lace kerchief and thrust it back into his billowing blue waistcoat, the jewelled rings on his fingers clinking against the stiletto's handle.

"*Milord, je suis, je veux, je proteste...*"

Without warning, he whipped out his little dagger and held its point to my eye.

"Enough of your masquery, villain! You played the Frenchman well enough for those fools out there, but I know you for a penniless whore-boy. If you call out, I will kill you. If you disobey me, I will kill you. If you show fear, I will kill you. You are the mimic, are you not?"

"My lord –"

He scratched the tip of the dagger over the soft skin at the corner of my eye.

"Yes," I gasped.

"And you heard the voice of His Grace here..." – Montalbion waved his gloved hand at Firth's body on the shiny varnished floor, the square white collar blossoming with crimson petals – "...while he yet lived?"

"I did –"

"Then you will be the Duke of Firth when his Scots dog comes calling. Make Campbell leave, do you hear me?"

I made a tiny nod, careful to jerk my eye away from his stiletto. All pride, all hope were driven from my spirit. Mister de Corvis had told this devil everything of Calumny Spinks. I let him push me inside, where three armchairs were gathered in a circle around a little table that carried a decanter of golden liquid. I saw how Montalbion had used Wilton to distract the duke from the waiting assassin.

Montalbion shoved me again, and I had to step over the pool of blood that was spreading out from Firth's body. Trembling, my hands clamped at my sides, I waited at the door. To one side of it was a portrait of a sickly woman leaning on soft cushions with her child standing behind her. She bore Montalbion's dead eyes, and I knew the painted child to be him. His mother's blueish fingers clenched a portrait of King Charles the Second.

My tormentor came close behind me and held his dagger across my throat.

"Your Grace," called a Scots soldier, rattling the door handle.

"Begone," I croaked in Firth's light Scotch tones, closing my eyes against the grisly wound in the duke's chest.

"Your Grace, we must leave –"

Terror overcame my shame, and I knew I must finish this swiftly or perish. My voice came out stronger now.

"Let you go before me, Campbell. My noble cousin and I..." – Montalbion grinned wolfishly – "...have not finished our business. And I have an interview at Mister Wilton's home this afternoon. Attend you to the regiment."

"But my lord –"

"I dismiss you," I said harshly.

The soldier coughed, but he had little choice but to leave when commanded. As he tramped away on the carpeted hallway, I rubbed my face, as if I could wash away what I had seen and done.

"You have conspired in the murder of the king's cousin," said Montalbion quietly. "Let but one word of this cross your lips, and..."

I shook my head. I knew that story well enough. The noose, the breeze, the satin sky.

"Your task is not yet done. You cannot be seen here. Go to the orange room as your master bid you."

As my master bid me. Why had Mister de Corvis not warned me, told me that this lord knew all? Heartsick, terrified, I made as if to pass Montalbion and go to the door. He clicked his tongue, like a shepherd to a wilful hound, and pointed to the balcony.

I went to the rail, one hand on my aching chest, and scrambled over awkwardly. Though my arms and fingers burned from holding on to van Stijn's sill, I was able to let myself down to the lower railing. Because of the cold autumn air, the windows and curtains of the orange room were closed.

A muffled moan broke the silence. It came from the window of the red room. Again a woman cried, and this time there was pain in her voice. Though I wanted nothing more than to be gone from this place, I walked carefully to the side of the balcony and leaned over, my feet chilled in their ripped stockings.

The curtains of the red room were not fully drawn, and at first I could see little more than the backs of two women in low-cut white dresses, kneeling with their heads together in a mess of swirling tresses and golden ribbons. They drew apart, showing a third girl, slumped on a soft couch. Her face was puffed and bruised, her lips smashed like broken berries, and she clutched at her belly. Below her clawing hands was a stain of dried blood, a trail from her groin almost to the hem of her white dress. Her bare arms were marked, too, with half a dozen thundercloud bruises.

To my side, the window-latch of the orange room rattled, and I knew I must play the part of the French fool again. To calm myself, I brushed down my waistcoat, fluffed up the ruffles of my cravat and let a hand drape over the balcony-rail, gazing out at the garden as if longing for Paris.

"She has forgotten to paint her face," giggled a high voice, a jay's rasping call.

"She has forgotten her dancing shoes," replied another, in a soft whisper.

Two catamites pranced out onto the balcony. Their eyes were drawn in the sharp purple-black points of Chinese whores, their wigs piled stiffly on their heads like snow on fence-posts. Their shirts were unlaced to their hairless breastbones, showing off pretty silver-chained lockets.

"Look what a lovely flower has been hiding on our balcony all this time. What is she called?" whispered the taller one, fluttering his lashes at me as he laid a long-nailed hand on my arm.

"*Je suis le comte de Calonnie*," I replied in a bored voice, playing with the chain of my pocket watch. "Your Ongland... she makes cold."

They shrieked and ushered me inside. A man's voice rumbled as he closed the curtains of the red room.

"*Le comte de Calonnie*, a *friend* of our dear lord and master!" announced the jay-voiced little catamite, pinching me jealously with his fingernails as he ushered me to a long couch. Two periwigged gentlemen occupied plush armchairs, a wriggling catamite on each knee, hands probing in each other's breeches.

"*Je ne parle pas...*" I protested, heading towards the door. I had time to slip on the silver-buckled shoes I had left there before the little one caught up with me. Soon I had four or five boys clustered around me, toying with the raspberry ribbons that adorned my arms and calves.

Now that they knew I was no catamite, but a forengie gentleman, they pawed and petted and plied me with questions; but I could play the ignorant as well as any man. I pushed my hands into my waistcoat pocket, clenching the folded paper with the lion's body drawn on it, and listened as the boys talked of who would get which gentleman, and shared rumours of what happened to the girls in the red room.

I did not care. I was a dead man now, and it was the greatest freedom I had ever known.

After a good while, Mister de Corvis let himself into the room. His eyes were empty, but he bowed and invited me in French to return to his house. I nodded my head in superior fashion, casting a final scornful look on the young pieces in the room as I stalked out. The double doors of the drawing room were closed, though the chatter of business still bubbled out onto the landing and followed us down the great staircase.

We took our leave of the man-wolf and departed Dover Street. Mister de Corvis was silent, but he gritted his teeth from time to time as we walked. He tore off his wig and thrust it into his pocket, and it was a relief to do as much with mine. Once or twice I began to speak, to try to say what I had heard, but he ordered me to be silent.

At last we reached the river, not far from Charing Cross. My master led me down to the shingled beach and looked out at the busy river.

"Am I to hail you a boat, Mister de Corvis?"

"No, Calumny. We shall walk."

He sat down on the beach, careless of the wet stones under his clean black clothes. *Tap tap*, he went on the shingle next to him, to show that I must sit down too. Damp soaked up into my breeches.

"Tell me all," he commanded

I did not tell him all. I gave him the murder, I gave him the words that were spoken in that room and my mimicking of the dead Duke of Firth, but I did not give him my knowledge of the lion-faced gold, nor of the words he had said to Mister van Stijn.

As I spoke, I fixed my eye on the moon, hanging nightlorn in the clear evening sky. I knew that my master had whored me to Montalbion. He had told him that I was a pauper, that I could play the duke, and that my troubles were so great that I would have no choice but to hold my peace. What madness, to risk their plot on the voice of a desperate fool like me, I thought, but then I felt again the touch of Montalbion's dagger on my throat as I had spoken to Campbell. I would be next.

We sat for a long while there, watching the river carry its spoils down to the sea. The story of the murder lay like a death warrant on the water-soiled stones between us.

"If Montalbion has the stomach to kill Firth in his own house, then the king's days are numbered. The world is turning my way – this is the proof we needed."

He spoke carelessly, knowing that I could never speak against him now. I was part of Firth's murder, not he.

"Proof, sir?" I would die with as much knowledge in my breast as I could gather.

"The king gave the Duke of Firth command of all troops in London. With him gone, it is a sign to the guilds that their time has come. The guilds, the Dutch, me – we must all play our parts in this great enterprise, now."

"I fear that enterprise will be the death of me soon," I replied.

"Apprentice Spinks, your brave work today may have given me the keys to a little kingdom of my own. And it has earned you not death, but rich reward."

He counted out ten pounds in gold coin and held it out to me in a cupped palm. I was too amazed to take it.

"Do not waste your time in gaping like a fish. Take it."

He got to his feet and crunched his way cheerily along the Thames-bank towards Bear Wharf. Every few paces he lifted his face to the heavens and drank in the air greedily, as he had that same morning. I followed him, many paces behind, stumbling painfully in my heeled shoes on the shifting stones.

Benjamin de Corvis had betrayed me.

I had risked a hanging for ten pounds. That was the price he put on my life, when I needed eighty to live another fortnight.

Well, I had a secret of my own now: of guilds and high treason, and ten bars of buttery Dutch bullion. Though I would pretend meekly to follow my patron's orders, I would enjoy his daughter's body and coin first. And then I would take van Stijn's gold for myself.

CHAPTER TWENTY-SIX

My Father's Wishes

In which Emilia de Corvis makes certain demands

Mister de Corvis left me outside his house, thinking I would make my way back to Silk Street. Instead, I scuttled round to the servants' door, for I had a mind to use Miss Emilia, to drown the memory of murder.

The door opened a crack to let Mistress Frazier's bulgy eye look me up and down.

"You are not expected," she said roughly.

"Miss Emilia has required it," I lied, jamming my foot in the door. Mistress Frazier was strong enough to carry the cast-iron hearth-pot in one hand, but bloody death fed my will, and she grudgingly let me in.

She led me to the bottom of the servants' stairs and called for her mistress. Emilia appeared, met my stare and waved me up. The housekeeper grumbled as she went back to the kitchen.

I kicked off the high shoes and ran up the stairs. My aches still made me gut-sick, but murder had given me a hungry lust. Emilia had gone to sit on her bed. She stared me up and down, then reached under the bed to pull out an empty leather purse, and tossed it over to me like spit.

"Since it is money you want..." she began, but I looked out of the window, ignoring her. Emilia cleared her throat.

"I would like you... it would please me to supplement your wage... there is some coin for you if..."

She is like a young gentleman-officer on his first visit to a camp whore, I thought to myself. Let her beg.

She flew into a rage and flung a pillow at me. It was fringed with little bows and bells, and they stung as they struck my nose and eyes, but I did not move from my place.

"You are to help me tomorrow morning at ten o'clock with... with a matter of commerce. I will pay you half your fee in advance."

I shrugged and knelt down to pick up the limp purse. Her coin would comfort me as well as her bed.

"It is three angels light," whispered Emilia. "I have kept them on my person."

She looked at me with a dangerous light in her eyes, leaned back and loosened her bodice. I spied a little golden flicker between her breasts.

"Crawl over here. And keep both your hands on the moneybag. It is not yours to lose."

To tell true, I did not even think to refuse. I wanted to shame myself. Besides, I knew that both coin and venus awaited me, and what man would say no to such an offer?

I shuffled over on my knees, beetle-like, craning over her breasts with my teeth bared. She leaned out of reach, then back towards me, then out of reach again. Quickly, I lunged and bit her flesh, making her gasp, and the coin was mine. I dropped it into the purse. The red shape of my bite marked her chest.

Who is master now? I thought, nosing at her hair and neck while she squirmed under me. All the time I held carefully onto the moneybag, just as she had bid me, so I kept losing my balance clumsily. My senses filled with her spice, with lust, with red rage.

I nosed out the second angel in her left armpit. It was sweet and sharp, and my tongue tingled long after I spat the coin into the purse. I sat back on my haunches.

She pushed me away with her booted foot. The colour of her eyes had been drowned in inky stains, and I saw that she had emptied the little crystal bottle on her table again. Her voice slurred as she scolded me.

"Shame on you, to give up your quest still ten shillings short."

"If I had shame, I never would have touched you," I said viciously.

I knew full well where the last coin was hid, and she knew that I knew. Well, I wanted to make her father pay for selling me to Montalbion.

Putting the moneybag down, I pushed Emilia onto her back and searched her body again with my fingers, my nose, my tongue and teeth. She pretended to fend me off, like she had not invited me in.

I found the coin in the secret place but left it there, kneeling with my face against her sullied parts. I buried all thought and memory deep inside, long enough for her to speak to God while my jaw ached, my bruised chest burned, and my soul shrivelled with shame. And then, too late, I thought of Violet.

I stood and dropped the last coin on the purse, leaving it on the bed.

"Let Frazier do your commerce. I am no slave of yours."

She sat up and hissed at me.

"You will take this coin or I will tell my father what you have done here."

"Then you must tell him what you have done too. Or does he know you for a whore?"

Emilia flung the bag at me, spilling the angels. One struck me on the chest as she began to weep. I turned to go, but when I reached the door I looked around again. There was a lonely truth in her sobbing.

"Emilia…? Miss Emilia, why do you weep?" Step by step, I crossed the room again.

Madness swam in her eyes.

"I… I must ask you to do hard things for this money. These are my father's wishes, but he makes me his voice. You must come with me to the coffeehouses, and… and I am always writing up my father's accounts, adding money, taking money away… and I am all alone."

Still I could not understand why she wept.

"If you are alone, why do you not marry? You may choose any fool you like, for you are rich."

I tried to keep the bitterness from my voice, but my words only made her turn on her side and curl up, crying again. I sighed and came over, covering up her legs.

"I cannot marry!" she hissed into her pillow. "A married woman is a slave forever. A whore who is never paid."

"Who has told you this?" I demanded. She shook her

head and did not answer. This was Emilia's true self. She made no play now.

I sat beside her on the bed and held her hand gently.

Emilia clenched my fingers and whispered, "I know you want to lie with me, Calumny Spinks. A woman should not use a man so. But I cannot. So long as I do not carry a child, I am at least a little free."

She gave me my hand back and wiped her eyes.

Emilia spoke to her pillow. "I do not have my own money, Calumny Spinks. My father will never let me have such freedom. He says I will inherit all when he is dead, but only if I do not marry…"

"You are your father's slave," I said coldly.

She gave her head a little shake, but I was sure I had the truth of it. Of a sudden, I wanted to be home in Spitalfields. This rich girl's fears were nothing to mine, or my father's.

"I will come back to do this work for you, Miss de Corvis," I said, picking up the three gold coins.

"Calumny, stay–"

But I had closed the door on her.

I walked slowly down the stairs in my ripped stockings, pretending not to see Mistress Frazier looming at the bottom. She had been listening out for the clanking and panting of love, the lusty trout.

"You must leave the master's fine clothes here," she said tartly.

I stalked to the bedroom to take off the coffee-coloured suit. The raspberry ribbons were stained and dusty from clambering on balconies. My feet were scratched and raw, and there was a huge bruise mouldering away on my breastbone, shooting roots of indigo pain through my flesh.

Frazier was looming in the side passage. I expected him to nod at me silently in his usual manner, but he stood his ground. He was solid, Frazier, his spirit rooted heavily to the earth.

"A man should not stay away from his home so long," he said firmly.

I shrugged.

"He should respect his father's wishes," he went on. "He should borrow a horse and go home as quickly as he could."

Behind him stood Cucullan, already saddled. Frazier half-pushed me up onto the horse's back. I had never been on a saddle before, and I slipped over the other side. Frazier grabbed my leg and set me straight, helping me to put my feet in the stirrups and showing me how to hold the reins – not too taut, not too loose. Cucullan snorted, to tell me that he knew where he was going anyway.

"Be quiet, cheeky lubber," growled Frazier. The horse sighed and bowed his head, nearly pulling me forward off the saddle again. The coachman whispered in Cucullan's ear and slapped his backside, and we were away. I swayed from side to side like a carnival fool, clutching at the pommel with my legs rammed straight outwards in the stirrups.

CHAPTER TWENTY-SEVEN
Popish Whores

In which Mistress Fintry shows her contempt for loose words

After an exhausted, dreamless sleep, it was Monday.

I was allowed to sleep until ten o'clock, since we would rely on the incoming tide to take us upstream to the Tyburn. Garric had borrowed a cart to take us and our wares to the Tower Wharf. We rode in silence: Ty had a brooding look about him, and my chest ached within and without from the violences of yesterday. I did not look up at the stern walls; in conscience we should have brought our wares here, not crossed half London so I could track Anthony. Abigail had made Ty and me wear oilskin coats, though I wondered how they would save two boys who could not swim.

A flat-bottomed barge was tethered to the wharf, empty as an Irishman's purse, its planking scrubbed almost white. Garric coughed uncomfortably. Waiting for us on land, leaning his tattooed forearms on a pair of oars stuck upright, was Kit Barcus the bullnecked dock-man.

Barcus bared his teeth at Ty as we began unloading.

"This your boy then, Garric? Takes after his mother, I hope."

Garric ignored the jibe, saying swiftly, "True – Ty Pettit is his name. And this is my friend, young Spinks. Calumny, this is *Christopher* Barcus, dock-master."

He bumped me with a heavy roll of silk; I was to pretend not to have met Barcus before. I gave the dock-man a nod and got down into the barge so Garric and Ty could hand me down the cloth. Barcus did not offer to help.

They passed me down the bolts of silk, each one wrapped in waxy cloth against the spray. When we were nearly done, Barcus passed me the oars and jumped down to help me stow the wares so that the barge was balanced.

Garric said nothing else to us, not one word of advice even. He gave Ty his hand to help my friend climb down, which made the dock-man snort, and then left us alone.

Kit Barcus dropped the oars into their locks, and dug them deep into the gristly grey waters of the Thames. He did not look over his shoulder, rowing unsighted towards the middle of the choppy Thames. Soon, the barge was bucking.

"Christ's name, will you drown us?" I yelled in fury, trying to rise to my feet. Ty grabbed at me, and the boat rocked. The bolts of silk began to slip and roll, so we threw ourselves on top of them. If they fell in the half-salted water, we were ruined beyond hope.

It seemed like an age before the boat was still again. From behind us came the sound of lightermen laughing with Garric on Tower Wharf. Barcus whistled back at them. Slowly, we pushed the bolts of silk back into place.

"You cannot swim," said Barcus.

I shook my head.

"Then sit still on your hairless arses," he said, digging one oar in to turn the barge's nose upstream. Beneath us, the tide had conquered the river's current; slowly at first, the sea's great intent pushed us inland towards the Tyburn.

Ty plucked at a button on his oilskin.

"Master Barcus, you are a dock-man, not a lighterman–"

Barcus cut him off. "This is *my* river. I'll carry cargo if I choose, there's no man dare say otherwise."

"But why would you help a pair of apprentices?" insisted Ty. I gripped his knee to make him give up; sometimes he had little sense when his questions made men angry.

I caught Barcus' eye. He held back for a moment, and then replied, grinding the words out.

"Garric Pettit is... Well, he is a *handy* fellow to me."

Ty frowned and pushed my hand off his leg, but did not persist.

It was a gentle journey now that we went with the tide. For a while, I forgot that I had had a knife to my eye the day before. Had aided in the murder of a duke.

Gulls chattered idly as the river filled with boats. The Thames was a city to itself, packed with grubby sails and laden wherries. To our right, the Strand's fine houses threw their windows open to the fresh breeze, and I watched maids shaking sheets and pillows out, shrieking with laughter as the watermen tilly-tallied at them. On the other side of the river, squat homes wallowed in marshy ground, smoke pouring out from the tanneries behind. It was so like Salstead that I remembered my true purpose: to find Anthony and his master.

*

After the best part of an hour, Barcus pointed at a muddy gap in the riverbank.

"The Tyburn," he said, beckoning me to sit alongside him on the rowing-bench. "We will need to fight our way up it, if young Spinks here has the arms for it. Young Pettit, since you are the weakest, you must push us off from the banks if we come too close."

He nudged a bargepole that lay between his feet. Ty picked it up, and I crawled carefully over our wares to take my place next to Barcus. The boat bumped across the river-waves, jerking as we were slowed by the Tyburn's contrary current. I dug my oar in deep, and we pulled slowly into the woods that edged the Duke of Firth's barracks.

"Push off!" snapped Barcus. Ty had forgotten to look where we sailed, and now we were bound straight for the knotted old roots of a tree that overhung the crumbling riverbank.

Ty shoved at the tree. The pole almost came out of his hands with the force of the collision, and we slid under the roots with barely a thumb's width to spare.

Suddenly we were veering into the path of a little river-barge loaded high with night-soil. The gongfarmer was fast asleep at his tiller, and for a breath I was sure that we would end up at the bottom of the river, our fine silk drowned in London's leavings. But Barcus was at Ty's side now, poling us along so that we squeezed along the gap between the riverbank and the side of the barge.

It was a backbreaking row through the empty woods before Barcus turned the boat into a little channel. Ty and

I took the oars from him and pushed against the banks, as marsh-fishermen do, guiding the boat under low mossy branches.

Through the trees I saw the ghostly streak of the barracks wall. The channel led under it, but our way was blocked by the iron grille of a water-gate. I strode to the front of the boat and rattled the bars with my oar.

No man replied.

I leaned out and pushed my face up against the bars to look through. The stream led through a short lightless tunnel to another water-gate, also closed. Now I could see why our cries had been unanswered.

"We must go in by the whores' gate," I told the other two as I shuffled back, careful not to fall in the murky water between the boat and the banks.

"I will go," offered Ty, but I shook my head and leapt out of the boat, leaving it rocking behind me. Barcus steadied the craft.

It was a short but muddy walk to the narrow whores' gate. Mindful of my foolish fall last time, I reached through the gate and unhooked the strip of green cloth that held it. At the far side of the yard, soldiers milled around between their barracks, and I darted over to the ladder that led to the seamstresses' workshop before I could be seen. I banged on the hatch, and it was only a breath or two before Mistress Fintry opened it.

In the light of day, her eyes were more crinkly and her skin more faded, and she hid an angry look under her neat brows.

"You cannot make such a racket in the barracks, Master Mercer. Here, the soldier-laws govern, and you must keep yourself better hid than that. Besides, where is my cloth?" she asked. "You are later than your promise."

"I have it all, good lady," I replied, mimicking Mister de Corvis to give myself courage. "It waits for you at the water-gate."

"The water-gate? You did not come by cart?"

"We are busy men," I said foolishly.

"Well, you do not do much by the laws of trade, do you now? You shall have to ask the porter to unlock it," she grumbled, bustling me back down the ladder and round the corner of the building. The path that ran back along the inside of the wall skirted row after row of grubby white tents, pegged loosely in sandy soil. Blackened pots lay on their sides next to fire-holes, their rims caked with white ash. Here and there, a soldier moved among the tents, every one of them with a limp or hacking cough or some other ailment.

"This is where the sick and wounded stay. Tell Cormac I sent you – his hut is near the water-gate," said Mistress Fintry. "Now be swift, for the muster is in the yard at noon."

I thanked her and walked to the moss-stained tunnel at the end of the path. A way beyond it was a little windowless hut. I knocked on the door.

The porter grumbled and came out, scowling. He was a short, youngish fellow with a worm-child's face, deathly pale with pink lips and crimson-shot eyes. His hair and brows were white as snow, the eyelashes too long, blinking, blinking, like a caterpillar's legs.

"It is no devilry," he said sternly, angered by my unashamed staring. "I am albino, that is all."

"I am Calumny," I replied with unmoving face. "And I have little to reproach you for." I tugged at my clumsy mop of red hair to show him how I, too, was ugly and devilish. He gave me a little clap on the back, one abomination to another.

"Albino is not my name, it is my affliction," he said in a softer voice, leaning towards me and squinting at my features like a half-blind crone. "Call me Cormac."

An Irishman. A popish rat.

He leaned towards the water-gate, turned a long iron key in the green-edged lock, and tugged the grille into its berth above. I helped him to lift it upwards; it squealed in its damp wooden tracks.

Inside the tunnel was a narrow towpath. Cormac hunched over and shuffled his way along the ledge, balancing with his left hand trailing on the wall. The waterway gave off a rotten smell.

I did not follow, but called to Ty and Barcus to make themselves ready. Voices rumbled, and then with another squeak, the second water-gate was shifted upwards.

Cormac climbed into the boat and guided it back towards me, tugging at a row of small hoops that were sunk into the stone roof of the tunnel. Behind him, Ty leaned out to one side to grin and wave. I could not see why the goblin boy should be so excited. I had Violet to look forward to, but he was only here for commerce, the maggot. Though I prayed we could make good coin from the barracks: to work for Mister de Corvis seemed too great a risk.

Screwing his pink eyes against the cloud-dimmed daylight, Cormac steadied the boat next to me, and Barcus waved me into the craft. We were to punt a little further along the stream. It ran around the other edge of the encampment, in a low-lying channel, so that we could not see the wounded soldiers, nor they us. The stream's banks were strewn with empty flasks, and those vile goat-bladders men put on their pimmies to keep the whore's pox at bay. Now I knew why the back gate was never locked. Soldiers and their doxies cannot be kept apart for long.

We neared the building where the Fintrys lived. From the kitchens' barred windows below came woodsmoke, and the smell of mutton roasting. I picked up an oar and helped Cormac push the boat forward.

The albino porter whistled sharply. Mistress Fintry appeared at a double doorway in the upper floor of the building, above which were fixed a little gantry and pulley. We were to use it to pass the silk up, which would need one man above and three below. I leaned forward to get out, but Ty had already leapt over me and scrambled up the channel's sandy bank. Laughing, Mistress Fintry shook her head and went to let Ty in.

After a good while, Ty and Mistress Fintry appeared at the doorway and hooked a long line of hemp rope over the pulley. I climbed up to the bank and passed the looped end down to Barcus and Cormac. One at a time, they secured the bolts with the rope, then swung it over to me to catch and steady before the other two pulled it up to the seamstresses' workshop. I watched unquietly, careful that the silk did not swing into the dirty stream-bank, or catch on a splinter in the wall.

Though the sky was cold with clouds, I was sweating by the time we finished unloading. Kit Barcus took his leave of us, punting down the channel with Cormac at his side. They made a strange pairing, the straw-haired English Catholic and the Irishman with his wintry features. A man could make good coin by showing them at the fair, I thought, smiling to myself.

I made my way around the building alone, shaking out the ache in my neck. Around the corner I saw Violet taking her leave of a husky-voiced man in cloak and hood, but I was too late to spy the other's face.

"Violet –" I blurted out.

She turned to me and smiled, such a sunburst that I forgot in half a breath to ask her who she had been speaking to.

"You have kept me waiting more than twenty nights, Calumny Spinks," she grumbled, though her eyes still shone. I tried to speak but I could only look at her. In the daylight she was still beautiful, though now I saw the sad blue tendrils that fringed her glossy brown eyes. Her hair peeped out in wisps from under a servant's lace cap. The hard curves of her body pressed through the soft petticoat and leaf-green shawl.

"D'you greet me, or what lies beneath these clothes?" she demanded, poking a strong finger into my chest.

I smiled at her sharpness. "You have a nose for cloth. The wool of your shawl is as fine as baby's hair, and this green shows the forest sparkle in your eyes."

"Does it, now?" she asked, but the lowering of her gaze showed how pleased she was. My chin tickled from her long-faded kiss.

"Well, I..."

I searched my dusty throat for a witty word, but none came.

"Well, I will not leave it so long again, for my heart has ached sorely for you," I said in the end, stumbling over the words like a blind man.

"I'll trust your words when they match your deeds," she said sharply, and I followed her into the courtyard. It was already beginning to fill with soldiers, their boots and breastplates dusty. Three or four of them oohed and jeered at me.

Violet whispered, "You must not be seen by the officers, Master Spinks. There is a curfew now – none may come in or out without permission, unless they be whores, God forgive them – and so you must keep hidden when you are here."

She took my hand and led me up the ladder to her mother's quarters, where Ty was showing Mistress Fintry the silk.

"It is good, Master Pettit," she said admiringly. "It is very well done. With those Genoese thieves at the docks, there is always a roll or two of rough among the finer stuff, and there is little we can say. Lucky for me, the quarter-master here is not afraid of them, and I believe he will willingly pay for what you have brought."

"You do not have the coin?" I blurted, fearing the worst. Ty glared at me while Violet came up behind and stroked me secretly on the neck.

"Why, for sure I do not!" laughed Mistress Fintry. "You speak as though you have never made trade with the army before..."

"But how will we –"

"D'you look for me to revoke your welcome?" demanded the seamstress.

"Do not fear. Quartermaster Baines will take your goods, I am sure of it. Mother spoke to him of it not half an hour ago," said Violet calmly, ignoring her mother's clenched jaw. "Now, will you eat?"

She sat us down at the table, now cleared of tailorings, and began to slice a boiled ham. My eyes flickered from Violet to the scented meat and back again, and I clutched at my knife and wooden plate impatiently. Mistress Fintry finished tallying up the bolts and wrote down the reckoning on the back of a yellow-leaved pamphlet.

"Eat," she commanded, and sat at the head of the table. Violet joined in, opening up a little clay pot and smearing yellow paste thickly on her ham. She closed her eyes in ecstasy, and so I put the paste on my meat and shoved it in my mouth, only to find that it carried with it a sting more vicious than a wasp's. I choked and tried not to spit it out on the table.

"Mustard," said Mistress Fintry dryly.

Violet stroked my leg under the table. My pimmy twitched, and stretched, and blew up like a pig's bladder at Michaelmas. The mustard's sting faded swiftly.

"How was your journey? Was the river safe on such a windy day?" asked Violet.

"We fear no danger from the elements," I boasted. "But we had to be on our guard today, for it seems that your water-gate guard is a servant of the great whore of Rome."

"How do you mean?" asked Mistress Fintry, in a cold voice.

"Well, I mean that it is not right to have a popish rat within these walls," I replied cockily. Ty tried to make a signal with his eyes, but I ignored him.

There was a long and nasty silence after my last words. Violet took her hand away from my leg and shoved the rest of her ham in her mouth. I chewed on merrily, sucking the woody flavour from the ham.

Mistress Fintry took away my still-full plate and got to her feet.

"We do not speak of religion at my table, Master Spinks," she hissed. "Now I must finish my business with young Master Pettit here. Hide yourself in the sicklings' quarters, and do not come again unless you are bid."

"Violet –" I began, thinking of the tents by the water-gate, and how we might go and lie there together.

"Violet has many tasks to do," interrupted her mother, going over to the hatchway and unbolting it. "Now go."

I could not fathom why she was so cold with me, but I had no choice. As I descended the ladder alone, the worm of doubt shuffled its coils in my belly.

CHAPTER TWENTY-EIGHT

The Water-gate

In which revenge brings only despair

Well, I was not a man to be scolded by a shrewish seamstress.

I had come to the barracks to trade my cloth, and I did not intend to leave without my coin. Climbing down the ladder into the still-empty yard, I looked over at the quartermaster's storehouse.

Flat-roofed, it matched the seamstresses' gable for height. Its windows were caged in iron, the steel-bound doors so heavy that I had to push with my legs and both arms to get one side open. It banged shut behind me.

Hooded lanterns were placed in the four corners of the storeroom, a cat's-eye slit in each one spitting out a sliver of light. Fat oaken shelves were laden with flour sacks, sealed wooden boxes, and neatly piled uniforms. The rafters were lost in the darkness far above, and the whole room smelled corrupt, a barn-stench of dead rats and rotted straw.

Behind the counter in the middle was a long row of ledgers, their spines stained with fingerprints, sides pinched from countless grabbings.

The stores were empty. No sign of the quartermaster.

Well, I thought, I must not stand against the door like a homesick shadow. Let us see what we have here.

On the shelves high above me loomed a dark pile of Bibles, breathing down judgement; and below them were half a dozen tobacco-pouches, blazed with the Duke of Firth's emblem. The same pouch that Anthony wore. Shuddering, I stepped back and wiped my sweaty hands on my thighs.

A dark bulk loomed out of the corner, unhooded a lantern and shone its blinding white light in my face.

"You're late, lad. Should have been here last night already," it growled, stepping closer. "Wait now – who are you?"

"I… I have business with the quarterman…"

"Here is no quarterman, lad, but quartermaster have you found," said the man, pushing me towards the counter. "Now then. Why do you fear the Bible?"

His features were still in shadow behind the lantern's rays. The voice was Yorkish, blunt, like the sound of Ramage hammering at a coffin.

"The Bible was written by men, not God," I said in Peter's voice, "and a man will hide under it to muffle the voice of his own conscience." The light jerked as I mimicked my father.

"What do you call yourself, boy?"

"Master Spinks of Spitalfields –"

"Do you dare to come before me then?" roared the quartermaster, thumping his fist on the counter. I backed away.

"But Mistress Fintry spoke to you, sir, did she not?" I stammered. "The price for our silk was agreed at seven pounds –"

"Hmm," he grunted, pushing past me to throw open the doors. "Baines does not recall it so well. I will speak to the seamstress of it again."

Sunlight poured in. Quartermaster Baines' patchy hair was cropped, his forehead pushing so far out above his nose that it left the bristle-browed eyes in shadow. Thin-lipped, heavy-jawed, he leaned forward with his back hunched, like a Norfolk boar ready to charge.

"So you're the *brussen* as beds the Fintry girl," he said.

I felt my freckled skin blush raw.

"You may keep your counsel if you wish, ferret, but I see everything in these barracks. Now get gone before I have you beaten for curfew-break."

I swallowed my fear and replied quietly, "Seven pounds for the silk..."

He punched the hardwood doorframe.

"I'll not hand you a penny!" he bellowed furiously. "Break the dock price, will you?"

It was as I had feared – he was making good profit from the dock-men.

"Then I must return for my wares," I said, "as guild law demands."

"Christ's dead body, he talks of guild law," he scoffed, pulling me out into the daylight. "Very well, I'll pay your seven pounds. But not to you – I'll have it sent to Spitalfields. Now get yourself gone. If I see you in these barracks again, you'll feel the lash till it bares your bones."

I could little afford to make an enemy of him, not with so much money at stake. I bowed my head and turned to leave. Baines held me back by the shoulder.

"It is nought to me whether I buy from the dock-men or from you, for I will make the same profit whichever way. I will make a bargain with any man if there be but gold in it. So do not think you have outwitted me."

He pushed me so hard that I had to leap the six storehouse steps to keep from falling, and skidded foolishly across the yard. I hid behind a pillar under the Fintrys' workshop as Baines slammed the doors. I was free, but I had not a penny to show for a hundred and five yards of finest silk.

Dust spiralled viciously in the courtyard. Soldiers bunched close together, heads hunched, eyes slitted against the sharp grains. The blockhouse leaned its bulky shoulders into the wind. From behind it came the sound of men marching on gravel, for the regiment's muster had ended. Grooms in their white-frogged scarlet uniforms led harnessed horses around the side of the blockhouse, through the courtyard and into the stables opposite me.

No one saw me, hiding behind a wooden pillar in my dusty clothes. Small mobs of soldiers stamped their feet. They stared suspiciously at each other until an insult was shouted by a horse-groom near the stables, his Londonish accent like a magpie's cackle. Two or three pikemen threw their weapons down, ran over and wrestled the groom to the ground. Others came to join in the fight, but two officers stepped out of the stables with swords drawn and struck the wrestlers hard over the heads with the flats of their blades.

"To quarters, you lowland hogs," commanded the shorter officer, addressing the whole courtyard.

The second officer, shaven-headed and as old as my father, saw me behind the pillar. Crimson sleeves billowed out from his polished cuirass as he strode over. His glaring eyes were almost hidden by sagging lids.

"Good day, sir," I said pleasantly. "Spinks of the mercers' guild, at your service. Lieutenant…?"

"*Captain* Marks. There is no business for rag-merchants here, Master Spinks. Begone before I have you flogged."

He put on his steel helmet and looked away, as if to dismiss me.

"I do not trade," I lied boldly. "I seek a gentleman. Well, a half-gentleman, for he is not a soldier, but he has the badge of your regiment on his tobacco-pouch. One Anthony Anthony."

Marks spat in the dust at his feet. He scuffed a little pile of dirt over the spittle, as if to bury my words, not meeting my eye.

"There are no… *gentlemen*… who may wear His Grace's badge. Now get you gone."

He reached out to grab me. I ducked and backed away.

"I came by the water-gate, good captain… I leave forthwith!"

I had dashed around the building and into the sicklings' quarters before Captain Marks could reply, regretting my words. If he was a friend to Anthony, then I was in greater trouble yet.

The soldiers had all gone in to eat, leaving me alone in the courtyard. I looked across at the barred storehouse and wondered if it had been foolish to accost the quarter-master without Mistress Fintry's goodwill..

"Cal," called Ty from above me. He had taken his jacket off, and was leaning out of the back window with his shirt so far unbuttoned that I could see his nipples, clinging on like ancient limpets.

I waited.

"You spoke too harshly, Cal," he said. "Mistress Fintry is still boiling with anger."

"Well, I thank you for your loyalty," I whispered back sulkily, and walked under the building's overhang so that he could not see me.

"Cal!" he called after me in a loud whisper. "Come back when it is dark – all will be well."

I did not give him the comfort of a reply. Treacherous goblin bastard boy, eating and drinking in my lover's home while I stood hungry in the wind.

Cold. I had left the oilskin and my long-sleeved waistcoat in the workshop. I thought that I would seek out my fellow abomination, Cormac, and stay warm in his dark hut.

I walked quickly towards the stream that ran through the camp. Now and then, little groans came from the sicklings. A hundred-throated roar came from the eating-house, far behind me. I could not tell if it was laughter or anger, but it carried on for a while, and I did not hear the man climbing up the hidden banks of the stream until he stood not six paces from me.

"Do you theek me, boy?" asked a cutting voice.

I knew before I turned that it was Anthony. Again I cursed my folly, not to bring my father's pistol.

"How am I to pay you if I cannot find you?" I asked as I met his eyes.

"I thaid that I would find you. And then your viciouth friend beat me. And now here you are. In my home."

I took a step back, almost tripping on a tent-rope. He took two steps forward so I could see how badly bruised his face had been. Though more than a month had passed, the flesh was still orange and puffed, and he held his ribs on the left side. The other hand was out of sight inside his long coat. Spreading my hands out wide, I gave him a simpleton's smile.

"I must ask you to forgive me for that gentleman's attack on you. It was not… not what I expected."

"Of no matter. I thay it ith you who did thith to me," he hissed, pushing his chin towards me.

"Well, you can see that I wish to pay you –"

"You wish to kill me! And I care not if I am forbidden, I will kill you mythelf!"

Anthony pulled out a sword with his good right hand. He pointed the blade at me, its sharp point an arm's length from my heart.

"How can I pay you if I am dead?" I asked in a peaceful voice, though my whole body trembled like a hunted fawn's. I stared into Anthony's eyes, willing help to appear from within the tents, from the eating-house, from anywhere.

"Your father shall pay," he growled, and lunged at me. Lifting my foot above the tent-rope, I spun on my other heel and raced away between the tents, weaving back and forth to make it harder for him to chase with his injured ribs. He did not follow me directly, but flanked me this way and that, always with a tent or two between us. He was sheepdogging me into the corner where the stream met the outer wall: the water-gate.

"Cormac!" I called, but there was no reply from the porter's hut. Anthony laughed and drew closer. I could not run between him and the outer wall, there was no time, and so I backed up against the water-gate. It was open. Perhaps Cormac had left both gates unlocked. Perhaps Barcus was still there.

I did not call out Barcus' name, for I did not want Anthony to raise the alarm. Instead, I slipped inside the gate and shuffled along the tow-ledge, bending over in the darkness of the tunnel.

Anthony's shadow fell across the stream, blocking my way back out.

"Your father will pay," he said again, "to thave his own neck. Even if you are dead. Now I will pay you out for that beating. And for your inthulth, God damn you."

I backed further away from him, but my way was blocked by the outer water-gate.

"Barcus," I whispered, turning my face to look out through the iron grille, but the dock-man was gone. All that remained were the damp black trees, the corrupt water, and the gate that imprisoned me.

Anthony stepped onto the towpath, his sword held out to one side over the stream. It was near dark now, and he leaned forward, looking for me in the gloom. I was trapped; but clothed in strange peace.

"Pursue you the boy?" asked another voice from outside the tunnel. Its northern tones burred soft and high, slow as a barber-surgeon telling a man he will cut off his leg.

Anthony turned impatiently, hiding the sword behind his back.

"Us said, pursue you the boy?" asked the slow voice again.

"What boy do you thpeak of, fellow?" demanded Anthony, edging towards the light.

"Intent to wound him, is a?" insisted the other.

"To kill him, and you too if you perthitht –"

Anthony swung his sword towards the voice and charged out of my sight.

Swords hissed and clashed, and the two men grunted as they struggled. Their shadows mingled on the water, blades grinding against each other.

I had to escape the water-gate while they fought. I edged back along the towpath but the struggle was not two paces from the tunnel's end. I watched as Anthony drove a slimmer fellow back onto his haunches and raised his sword to strike. He will kill that northerner, I thought, and now he comes for me. Desperate, I looked at the water. Could I swim away from him? Even if I did not drown, how could I get past his sword, against the stream's current?

The other man ducked, spun round under Anthony's blade, and thrust upwards. With a vile sucking sound, his sword burrowed through the cocky's guts and up into his chest. Anthony staggered back onto the towpath, his swordtip wavering close to my face.

"A should teach them fops to fight better, see," laughed the slow voice from beyond the tunnel. Anthony drew a last bubbling breath and fell face forward into the stream, his sword clattering off the walls. He floated slowly down towards me, his body crumpling as it struck the water-gate. I stayed where I was, watching to make sure it was no trick, but his nose and mouth stayed underwater. He was dead.

"Out," called the voice.

I held my breath.

"Out, us say. Know art there. Or should us fetch thee?"

Out I came, one shuffling step at a time, looking back at Anthony's corpse butting softly up against the outer gate, too frightened to look at the killer.

"Turn."

I turned.

The man's face was in shadow, a tunic hood pulled down over his brow. He was slim of shoulder, hardly taller than Ty, but still he had been powerful enough to beat Anthony. His sword was sheathed. The air sagged loosely around us, stained with violence.

"Us killed a man for thee, braggart fool," he said, strangely without anger. "And now must make it look as though this fellow has been robbed. A been stabbed by camp whore."

He pointed at the ground a few paces away to show me I should wait there. I squatted and retched, spitting a mouthful of bile onto the crushed grass. Stooping, he shuffled his way down the tunnel towards Anthony's body. He knelt carefully on the towpath and turned the carcass over, searching for the man's purse. When he had found it, he tugged at the dead man's breeches until the limp pimmy showed, a faded firefly in the darkness of the tunnel. Now it looked like he had been cut and robbed by a whore, just as the killer wanted.

As he came back towards me, I was sure that I was next to be laid to rest in the dirty stream. I gathered strength in my thighs, ready to spring at him.

The killer walked with a curious step. His feet went one in front of the other in a straight line, like a child playing Hop the Pope. His face, still shadowed under his hood, was clean-shaven, with full unsmiling lips and a narrow neck. Under his tunic he wore the belt and boots of a soldier, and the pommel of his sword peeped out at his waist.

"Art horny dog who were sniffing around Miss Fintry, are not?" he said quietly.

"Better a living dog than a dead man," I replied, still waiting for him to strike.

The soldier gave a short high laugh.

"Thank thee for thy wit, and us will take it in part payment of thy life," he said.

"And for the other part?" I asked, too timorously.

"A will collect. Would find a cunny-hunting, carrot-headed braggart like thee, no matter where a hid in London. Besides, thou'll be sniffing around barracks until Miss Violet sends thee away."

Swish splat. He lunged and smacked me hard across the thighs with his scabbarded blade. I tripped on the tent-ropes and fell on my backside.

Shaking his head, the soldier held out his hand and helped me up. He squeezed my knuckles a little. His hands were strong, slim and soft on the outside but tough around the pads and fingers where he held his blade.

"Robbie Cartwright is us name... Sign of trust, this handshaking," he said, thinking that I did not understand. "Says that us will not stab thee with fighting hand, see?"

"And what about the dagger in your left?" I asked quietly.

He showed me his other hand with a half-smile. It was as I had said: a blade peeked out from the cuff, its tip nestling like a snake's tongue in his palm.

"Why would you let me live when I have seen you kill–"

He put a finger to his lips.

"That's for us to know, not thee. And now must get key to water-gate from Cormac. Thee and thy friend must be gone before dawn."

He turned on his heel, leaving me alone with the sick and the dead.

CHAPTER TWENTY-NINE

Sanctuary

In which sleep evades Calumny Spinks

It was settled. I could not stay out in the open after Marks' warning: I would have to face Mistress Fintry's anger.

I scrambled along the channel's crumbling banks towards the eating-house. The courtyard beyond it echoed to the sound of sparring and grumbling, and I did not want to risk being arrested. Instead, I climbed the pulley rope to the upper doorway, hand over hand, trying to keep my ragged breath quiet.

Halfway up, I heard footsteps coming around the corner of the house closest to the whores' gate. Three women, their painted faces shining in the moonlight, picked their way across the muddy camp. They called out softly for custom, their sweet voices given the lie by sluggish tread and slumping shoulders. The wounded will pay more for a woman's touch, I thought.

I waited until they had all been swallowed up by the tents, and swung myself through the half-closed doors, high above the ground.

Swiftly I turned and closed the doors behind me, crouching in the dark corner. The sound of the soldier's blade entering Anthony's flesh echoed inside my skull. I clenched my fists to stop my fingers from trembling and readied myself to beg Mistress Fintry's forgiveness.

Though no candles were lit, the room was awake with little creaks and puffs of breath. I made my way towards Violet's rope ladder, crouching, but a little groan made me look round.

The seamstress was sitting upright in her bed. At first I thought she was watching me, but then I saw that her eyes were shut, panting as she straddled the elder of two men in her bed, her hands gripping his shoulders. His head lolled off the end of the bed facing me, his eyes glazed with sleep. Mistress Fintry's hand roamed over the bare chest of a young man who lay next to her. He seemed spent, but I could tell from his shallow breathing that he only pretended to sleep. He opened his eyes and fixed me with a stare.

It was Ty.

The goblin had been tupping Violet's mother.

As if he felt my gaze, Ty opened one eye to give me a look. Then he shut his eye again, his head bouncing up and down in time with Mistress Fintry's backside as she reached blindly under the blankets for his groin.

She began to groan loudly as she entered the wild place. I had no wish to see Ty join her there, so I scuttled up the ladder to Violet's room. Anthony was dead, and I was alive, and I did not care to think beyond tonight.

Violet was cross-legged on the floor, a single candle casting a warm light from behind her. She shrank away at first when I pushed my head through the hatch, holding up her hand to keep me at bay. I prayed that I had not mistaken her feelings for me as I kissed her bare knee.

Still she held up her hand, pressing my head away, but I felt her fingers twine themselves in my hair, and I pressed my lips further up her thigh.

"Be in with you then," she whispered roughly, pulling my head closer and kissing my eyes, my nose, my chin, filling my chest with a whirl of wild nature. I was still clinging to the swinging ropes below, and so I surrendered to her kisses, letting her wash away the terrors of the last two days. At last I forgot the sight of Anthony's wrinkled pimmy, lying lifeless in the pissy stream, and I climbed into the room.

"What I said –" I whispered.

Violet, her hair falling over her linen nightshift, pressed a finger to her lips and helped me up. I stepped over the row of candle stubs and laid myself on her bed while she gently closed the hatch.

"I –"

This time she pressed her whole hand to my mouth, lavender and lemon and woman's sweat, and I kissed her palm, hard. She pushed me back onto the bed and pulled off my boots and breeches. I blinked away the memory of Emilia, pushing me on the bed, mounting me.

Violet laid herself next to me, her shift crumpling against the cold threads of my shirt, her skin warming mine. Her hair had fallen across her eyes, and I tucked it away behind her ear. Sliding my fingertips round to the place where her spine met her head, I felt the soft flicker of her heart.

We wriggled closer, her breath sweeping over me, apple-and-wheat, sun falling on warm soil, and I pulled the blankets over us. Slowly slowly, we opened buttons, we lifted linen, we touched and kissed each lip's width of skin. Still I had not kissed her face, her eyes, her mouth. Still she had not spoken.

Violet. She circled me with her arms, her legs, and I held her head more precious than a baby, all her dreams singing out through my hands, the candle-flame glowing from her eyes. All was silent but for the calling of gulls high above our window.

I did not know where Calumny ended or where Violet took her beginning. I did not know if I felt what was in her or what was in me. We wept, both of us; we were still as death; it was enough, it was too much. She cried harder now, songless, pulling me in, and I was lost.

She laughed a little through her tears, both of us breathing like horses raced too hard.

"You will leave again," whispered Violet, though whether it was command or accusation I did not know.

"I will always come to you," I replied, a spark of truth in the words.

This woman's bed was the one place where the hangman's noose could never follow me. In Violet's arms I was already dead – sweetly, lovingly dead – and life held no fears for me.

I wanted to see her fully before the last candles guttered. Warm now, I drew down the blankets, pulling her up until we were kneeling before each other, naked. Her nipples spread darkly across her breasts, tightening under my gaze, and she rested a hand on the curve of her belly, her little finger's nail pointing at the shadowy secrets below. She reached out her other hand and traced the line of my cheekbones, drew close and kissed me again. Tenderness gave way to need, and her teeth crushed my lips as we opened our mouths. I rocked back on my knees the way the field-girl had shown me, lifting Violet by her buttocks until we had slipped together again, leaning apart so we could caress and squeeze each other's chests and arms.

Now she was fierce and quick, her fingers hard as she held on to my neck. She kept her cries inside to hide them from the sleeper below, but I could hear them as loud as screams. Then she stilled herself, and we pulled close so that our tongues could meet again, exploring each other's skin with our fingers.

We began to move once more, pressing the sweat between our wrestling bodies, until she prisoned me with her thighs, screwing her eyes tight against the unbearable.

I was ready to sleep, but Violet wanted me to hold her. To lie on our sides with me behind, watching the night lighten, sometimes talking and sometimes not. A third time we came together, her legs wrapped around my hips, swallowing me. I had never known a woman to start again when the loving was done, nor to say such tender things of my eyes, my lips, my shoulders.

Later, we held each other, our sideways heads facing on her pillow, our fingers laced between us.

"Cal, why does Ty not have a girl?"

I shook my head.

"My mother has found him a place to stay," she whispered, letting me nuzzle her neck. "What will your own mother say of you staying here all night?"

"Little enough, for she is dead," I said harshly.

"Oh, Cal..."

Violet turned and laid her head on my chest, scalding it with tears.

"Why do you cry for a woman you have never met?" I asked, as gently as I could.

"My father is gone, too. These men..." – she waved to show she meant the soldiers – "...are my fathers now. But they will all die by a blade as he did."

Now it was my turn to hold her, to stroke her hair, to kiss the tears away from her flickering eyelashes. She told me how the army was her true father now, in law as well as in life.

"Many a soldier lives long," I muttered foolishly.

"They do not! I have seen it!" she whispered fiercely. "We had to follow them as they roved about this year, hanging men they thought to be rebels. Killing in every town. And now they fight each other, English against Scots. And then the Dutch will come... It will never end."

I had no words to gainsay her.

"I cannot stay," said Violet tightly. "Yet I cannot go without my mother's word, and the regiment's besides..."

"How can a woman belong to the army?" I demanded. She fell silent, trouble wrinkling her forehead.

"But your own father… Does he have no other woman yet?" she asked, making her voice lighter.

I could not speak of Peter in this precious place. Nor could I speak of how little time had passed since Mirella's body was broken in the cold waters of the Salstead sheep pond.

I smoothed the little curling strands of hair that edged her face so sweetly. *Prrrr prrr*, she went, and wrapped her leg a little tighter round mine.

"Why do your people trust you and Ty with seven pounds' worth of their finest silk, since neither of you is a master mercer?" she asked, quickly kissing my chest. "What is Spitalfields? Are not they all heretics and Frenchmen?"

"We are," I said proudly. "Every man of us."

She leaned her head up on one elbow so she could look me in the eye, stars reflecting dimly on her pupils.

"Tell me," she demanded.

Violet wanted to know the name and trade of every man and woman on Silk Street. How they stood, how they clothed themselves, if they worshipped of a Sunday or no, did they speak French or English on the street, were there tailors as well as mercers and weavers, was the trade better or worse with the tidings of war?

Most of all, she made me speak of Peter and Garric and Abigail – all the little stories of Sunday meals and arguments and laughter. I was glad that she did not guess at Garric's work for Mister de Corvis, for I doubted I could have hidden my own secrets from her then. But it was bad enough that I had burdened Ty with them. I wanted Violet to stay like this, cheerily asking for Silk

Street gossip, weaving our families around her until she was one of us.

"And you have not married yet?" she asked suddenly.

"I am but seventeen years in this world, and I have not a penny of my own. Married – are you moony?"

She lay down on her side again, closing her eyes.

"A woman must ask. Adultery is the road to Hell," she said. Within three breaths she was asleep, leaving me staring at the garret window.

Despair poured in through my skin and filled my bones. To have escaped a stabbing seemed like no mercy at all. Now, I owed some new debt to this killer, who seemed to know me already. I still had but two weeks to find most of the eighty pounds, but no idea of who to pay, since Anthony was now dead. Would the blackmailer now come to kill me, since his messenger had been murdered? Or would he give up, betray Peter's secret and leave us both to be hanged?

At last I quit torturing myself and turned on my side. Violet was lying on her front, her head turned away from me. I slipped further under the covers and held her tight.

I dreamed of hanged men, their feet twitching, coins dropping from their groins like gouts of blood.

CHAPTER THIRTY

Seven-and-Twenty Pounds

In which Peter Spinks weeps

Sweet air wafted me awake. Violet knelt at the foot of the bed to pull on a dress, faint dawn light caressing the curve of her belly.

"Violet, do you know a soldier named Robbie Cartwright?" I asked.

"Why do you ask of him?" she answered, muffled.

I did not speak, filled with a sudden jealousy. Her head popped out of the dress.

"He is a good man, Cal. True to you if you are but true to him."

"So it is with many soldiers, I will be bound," I said jealously, reaching for my breeches.

"What do you know of soldiering, Cal?" she asked angrily, her chin trembling.

"Leave this place with me," I said, pulling her onto the bed so that I could hug her.

"I cannot. My mother will not let me go. Besides, since I was born in the regiment, it has right of possession over me… so even if I could slip past the guards, there is no one who would take me."

I pressed my fingernail into my thumb to keep myself silent. It would not bring Mirella back; it would not save my father; it was a fool's idea.

Violet lifted her face and kissed me softly. I held her tight, but she broke away, handing me my shirt.

"I did not give myself to you for that reason, Cal. This is not your fight. Begone with you."

I opened my mouth to protest, but she turned her shoulder, refusing to talk further. Well, I thought, it will be easy enough for me to come back when you are less moony. I was well used to the moods of women.

I put on my coat and boots and climbed down to Mistress Fintry's workshop, closing the hatch after me. Violet's mother was sewing, a stern look on her face, while Ty slept soundly on her bed. The older soldier had gone.

"You have fornicated with my daughter," she accused quietly.

"Fornicator yourself," I replied. "I hope you gave my friend a ride after you finished with the grizzly ancient."

"I have not forgiven your intolerant words, Master Spinks," she growled. "But I care not if Violet chose to use you so. I gave myself to her father too young – God rest his soul – and I had no life of my own until he was taken from us. And do not wait for her to fall in love with you. She is too young to marry."

Ty stirred in the bed.

"Why did you not marry again?" I asked, not wanting to hear more cruel words.

Mistress Fintry scratched the corner of her lips. "An army wife is pensioned sixpence a day, but a seamstress is paid a shilling or more. Was ever so – the wages of marriage are but half the cost of freedom lost!"

The rumble of soldiers eating rose up through the floorboards. I had little time; I sat next to Mistress Fintry and touched her arm.

"Mistress… by what law does Violet belong to the regiment?"

Her face darkened. "By no law of man. Only the sacred duty of daughter to mother, and…"

"And?" I pressed her.

"And you may put her out of your mind. Bed-play is one thing, but you will not give Violet fancy ideas, d'you hear? Else I will take back the kind words I spoke to Quartermaster Baines for you."

"The quartermaster –"

"The soldiers leave the eating-room at eight o'clock," she said firmly, "so you'd best be about your business with him. And do not come back up. I shall send Tyburn home when it pleases me."

I did not know if I should tell her I'd already seen Baines.

"Mistress –"

"Seven pounds is agreed. But it will be five if you linger a moment longer," she said harshly. Ty twitched in his sleep behind her. I did not want to leave him alone in the barracks, but she had given me little choice. I put on my oilskin and left.

*

I ran for the whores' gate, counting my misfortunes. Banished by Violet, her mother, and the quartermaster too.

As I closed the gate behind me, I though of how we had broken the ties between the quartermaster, the dock-men and the fearsome Genoese traders. If the guild of mercers knew what we had done, we would be named great heroes of the trade – but the dock-men would have our guts for sure, and so it was to stay secret. And even if the quartermaster kept his word and paid Ty, that five pounds of profit was far short of the eighty I needed.

The thought settled in my mouth like ash.

"Word with thee," said a voice from behind, making me start and look round. It was the killer Robbie Cartwright, who'd slipped through the whores' gate behind me. He took my arm and led me into the black woods. Once out of sight of the barracks wall, he stopped and stared me full in the face, as if he could read my secret thoughts in the blackness of my eyes.

"Owe me nought for killing that villain," he said scratchily. "But thou's made a promise to that Violet now. Expects thee to return, see?"

"She did not say so." I tugged my sleeve out of his grip.

"Stay alive, Calumny Spinks. No foolish dangers for thee now, thou must stay alive for Violet Fintry. No more gin-supping on riverfront. And if thou dies, us will kill thee."

Robbie grinned briefly at his witty threat, but his eyes were unsmiling.

"Do you mean… that Violet asked you to protect me?" I stammered. "But why?"

It must have been he who trailed in our footsteps as we drank and chattered along the river shore that night.

"Is a bad time for an Irish girl in London, hear me? Even of a Sunday evening, us and Baines must escort her to church. If those bastard Dutchies invade then she will need thee, Calumny Spinks, trouble-maker though thou art."

"But you killed that man," I said, hearing again his low laugh as Anthony fell into the stream. He shrugged.

"Us made a promise to Violet, and will need thee alive to keep thine.

He turned and slipped back through the gate. I left as quickly as I could, troubled in my soul by this man who would kill a stranger for a promise. I was deep into the woods before I heard his words again, echoing from the yellowing leaves.

An Irish girl, he had said.

Now at last I heard how Mistress Fintry's English voice hid an Irish way of speaking. Of course she had thrown me out when I had cursed the Catholics!

I had loved a murderous papist, one of the people who had killed my own mother's family. And she had wanted more from me – to marry her perhaps. I choked back bile and ran further away from the barracks, brushing my arms and sides as I ran, as if cleaning myself of dusty spiderwebs. In love with a popish whore. Protected by her murderous friend. Aching to go back and see her; sick with the thought that I had been in her bed.

I ran and ran, desperate to cross the Tyburn bridge and leave my shame behind. The sinews of my arms and legs groaned, tender from the strain of climbing down

Montalbion's balconies and a night spent tupping Violet. I had half-forgotten in that long night that I was now accomplice to a Duke's murder, as well as to the killing of Anthony Anthony.

My mind was so full of plans and fears that the streets blurred before my eyes. Though it must have been an hour or two, it felt like only moments before I was in Spitalfields'. It was less than a day since I had seen Anthony killed, not two days since the murder at Montalbion's house, and now Silk Street felt like a strange dream to me.

I tied Cucullan outside Garric's house, where Abigail sat vinegar-faced and alone on her porch, knitting furiously.

"So my whoremaster son is staying at that bleeding barracks now," she complained, giving me the evil eye. "A fallen woman has snared him, I knew it.

"And now my fat fool of a husband has gone over there on some pretence that he helps your father. To tup the same whore as his son, no doubt."

"Ty has not –"

"No lies, Calumny Spinks!" Abigail flung her knitting down. "Only a woman's wiles could keep my... my boy away for so long –"

She stopped and buried her face in her hands, not able to speak Ty's name. I did not know if I should comfort her or not. Ty, the maggot, had best give me my profit back good and proper, I thought, fearful for a moment that he and Garric had double-crossed me.

"Your father told me he was out looking for you. At that Mister de C... At that man's house."

I thanked her and went to my father's workshop. I took out the gun and lay on my bed, still as a corpse, thinking.

Martin van Stijn kept his gold bars safe in Lord Montalbion's house, but he would have to take them out into London to pay the guilds. And when he did, Mister de Corvis would know about it, so I needed to stay close to my treacherous master. I would be ready.

I ran my thumbtip over the pistol's butt, tracing the staghorn swirls. I did not want to kill van Stijn, but his gold would give me all: freedom for myself and Peter, and the name of Mister for us both. And when I had those, I would take a ship for the Indies.

I could not rob the Dutchman on my own. I needed a strong man's help. Garric? Well, the mercer had told Mister de Corvis every secret he knew of me and Peter, and so I dared not trust him with such a task. Ty was neither fighter nor thief, and my father would rather have died an honest fool than steal and live.

I turned it round and round in my mind, listening to the Watch call the hour-halves until night fell.

Though my limbs trembled with tiredness, I did not sleep, for I feared that the dead faces of Mirella, Anthony and Firth would curse me in my dreams. I was guilty in all their murders – guilty of not stopping them, guilty of provoking them with my angry haste.

Deep in the dead time, Peter limped softly home. Water splashed as he washed himself in the workshop below. Damp logs thumped dully as he piled them up in the hearth. For a breath I was back in Salstead, back in my tiny coffin-room, a blind fool begging to leave the safety of his true home.

The pistol's handle weighed down on my empty stomach, making it gurgle.

"Cal?" rasped my father from below.

Like a sleepwalker, I rose and went down to the workshop. Peter was stripped to the waist, kneeling by the fire. His clothes, dropped in a little heap by the door, were black with smuts, and his knuckles were cut up again.

"I thought you would not return," he said to the blue flames that licked at the damp bark.

"Is that what you wished?" I asked him, cruelly. I had untucked my shirt so that its tails hid the pistol-butt.

He pushed the poker tiredly at the kindling, blowing. His breath caught a little, and it made me take a step towards him, hold out my hands.

"You should not see me like this," he whispered, a whiff of gin on his breath.

"I have seen you drink before," I replied, folding my arms. The first firefly sparks warmed my face.

He shook his head and snorted. "Not drinking. Like… like this."

Peter held out his bleeding knuckles to me. Pointed at his smoky clothes.

"Like every other brutish villain in this God-forsaken town," he said viciously, clenching his fists. "Selling my soul to a devil who cares only for coin."

Now I saw it. He was just like Garric, with the beatings and the burnings. Peter worked for Mister de Corvis like the rest of us, but he was the only one to deny it.

"Jesus Christ, you are a poxy liar," I whispered savagely. "To make me feel the sinner in all this. All along, you were no better than me."

"I do it *for* you!" he protested, desperately. "I break my vows, I give up my soul, to keep *you* alive!"

"Then why are you shamed by it? Why is it secret? Why is everything you do a secret?" I cried back. I took a stride towards him, wrested the poker away and hurled it at the floor, cracking a splinter from a flagstone.

"I thought if you did not know I worked for de C… for *him* – that I could make you stop going to him. I wanted you to be… to be clean –"

I spat on the fire, my spittle foaming in its growing heat.

"You will never *make* me do anything again. And we will never be clean, neither of us. We are going to Hell, Peter Spinks. You have sent us both there!"

I turned my back on my father, breathing heavily.

After a long while, he said, "I have nearly eight pounds already –"

"Then you need two-and-seventy more," I shot back, harshly.

He breathed out noisily as he rose to his feet.

"Enough, you God-damned ingrate! Whatever I have done, I have done it for you. I will not allow this bitter talk in my own home. I have done more than find the money, we have nearly found the villain –"

"Who is *we*?" I demanded, facing him. "Who have you brought into this? Who have you told our secret to?"

"Garric," he whispered. "Garric helps us. Because I cannot, he has been finding out where this Anthony lives, who he speaks to –"

"He will not speak more," I interrupted. "He will not threaten more. He is gone."

"Did you –"

I shook my head. "Another man, a soldier –"

"God, God... We sink deeper all the time."

Peter covered his eyes, and I had no choice but to put my arm around him, hold the old man close. He pressed his gnarly fingers to my skull, and we embraced like two men about to climb the scaffold. It is the tiniest of comforts, to know that you will not die alone.

Peter drew back. "Cal, I only –"

"I know it," I said, and kissed him on the side of his head, and then our embrace was finished.

"Garric must not drop further into our pit," I told him. "Let us finish this alone. He faces dangers enough already."

My father dipped his head to show he agreed with me. "How much do you have now?" he asked, sitting down at the eating-table.

At first I was silent, remembering his angry vow to take any coin I made for myself. But there was honesty between us now. I counted out my treasure on my fingers.

"Two golden guineas from the House of Three Mysteries I gave to you already."

"You went to the House?"

I ignored him. "A pound or so from Pinetti... Five pounds' profit from the Duke of Firth's... from the army.

More than a pound from Anthony's body… Three angels from Emilia."

Peter tried to keep his face calm, though I could see how surprised he was. "Seventeen," he murmured, his eyes glassy as he thought of the eighty we owed.

"And ten sovereigns more from Mister de Corvis yesterday," I whispered, staring down at my hands as I folded the fingers and thumbs over. I waited for my father to ask me how I had earned it, and I knew I would tell him if he did.

"That is seven-and-twenty," he coughed. "And we still have two weeks to find the rest: less than three-and-fifty pounds. If the villain who threatens us does not find out who killed Anthony –"

"And if we are not imprisoned for helping Mister de Corvis –"

"And if the Irishmen do not take their revenge –"

"And if war does not break out and stop our enterprise –"

I stopped and laughed. We needed more good fortune than a thousand black cats. Peter made a little barking chuckle. For a golden moment, it all seemed light enough to bear.

"Well," I said.

"Well," replied my father. "I will take my sleep now, and so should you. Tomorrow I have more… more *work* among the coffeehouses of London."

"As do I," I whispered to myself as he climbed the ladder.

CHAPTER THIRTY-ONE

The Bitter Trade

In which Calumny must learn the harsh ways of commerce

Chumpa chumpa. Chumpa chumpa.

The loom beat out its battered song. Still drunk with sleep, I sat up to dress. In my heart I knew what it had cost my father, in pride and soul, to do the violent work of Mister de Corvis. And I knew he did it for me. For himself, Peter would rather have taken the noose than the shilling.

I was not so honourable. I had signed the contract-paper to save my own neck, and my father be damned.

Well, I thought, choking my shame back down, I can only be what I am. I will protect the old ghost as best I can now, and risk my own neck instead of his.

I took a handful of my shirt and breathed in the apple-and-wheat of Violet's skin. It seemed like a madness now, to turn my back on her because of a couple of rosaries and a ball of flaming incense. But it was no good to think of Violet. There was violent work to do, for coin and freedom – though my conscience was besmirched with the memory of Firth's agonising death, unshielded by his wealth and title.

I tucked the pistol under my waistcoat. Licking my palms, I tried to tame my wild red hair, but there was no winning that battle. Last, I wrapped all the gold coins in the executioner's mask, leaving a handful of silver shillings that I slipped into my breeches pocket, and went down the ladder into the workshop. I dropped my backside on the little stool near the loom, and watched Peter for a little while as he worked.

"Old fool, eh?" he muttered, his eyes flicking up and down the waterfall of threads, trying to protect the engine that I had wrecked. "To sit here, spinning out a few shillings' worth of cloth when the hangman awaits me... So be it. At least I have the daylight hours to pretend to be an honest man, before I must beat and burn for your master."

I shrugged, though it cut me to the bone to hear him call Mister de Corvis my master. "Honest work is rewarded in Heaven."

"Ha!" he barked. "Well, I hope I was right to tell you so. But I feel..."

He stopped weaving, carefully tucking the shuttle away.

"...I feel in my heart that it is true. If I give myself to work, here, then money may come from somewhere over there. Shake one tree, and the apple falls from its neighbour."

I nodded. I did not believe him, but what else did we have?

"You are dressed very fine for a Wednesday, Cal."

"I must work today, Father."

He pursed his lips, knowing full well that I was going to Bear Street. We sat there in silence, watching dust flutter in the morn-light. I took out the pistol and the coins in their black silk, and put them gently next to the shuttle.

"This is all I have, Pe... Father. We have five pounds more coming from Ty and Garric, just as I told you. I want... I want you to keep it safe. For us."

Peter's eyes shone. He did not open the hood to look at the coins, but his fingers brushed it lightly on their way to the pistol.

He laid the muzzle on his left hand so that the two cogged steel wheels were uppermost, reflecting the watery light on his face. In his right hand was a three-sided wooden powder horn and a half-dozen round shot.

"I bought these for you, Calumny," he said.

Carefully, he showed me how to prime the pan and load the muzzle, how to span the wheels with a little wrench, how to pull back the doglock ready for firing.

He sighed.

"I do not know why I did not ask you for this gun before. I must have known that you carried it since you fired on Cowans."

I held out my hand for the gun, but he shook his head.

"I cannot let you wield this in ignorance. You will harm yourself for sure. Close the windows fully and light all the candles."

"All, Father?"

He grumbled in his throat, fiddling with the pan-cover, and I obeyed him.

By the time I finished, Peter was standing in his fighting-pose. He held the pistol before him, the doglock made safe so it could not go off, and hefted the gun to feel its balance.

"Your pistol must be a part of your arm," he murmured. "You must grow accustomed to its weight and power, or it will betray you. Come."

I came closer, going to his left side to be as far from the muzzle as possible.

"Hold."

He took me by the wrist, uncurled my fingers and let me grasp the gun.

"This is a wheel lock," he said.

Carefully hefting the pistol as he had, I let it settle against the pad of my hand, its weight tugging at my shoulders. Fire licked at the edges of my chest-bruise.

"It is the truest of pistols. A flintlock sometimes will not spark. A matchlock is worse, for it must be lit, so that its light gives you away by night and its flame may be snuffed out by rain. But a wheel lock keeps its flint and flare inside. And you may even keep it hidden under your clothes."

I cleared my throat as my father spoke on.

"But mind that you fire the pistol on its side, as you did in Salstead. If you hold it like a matchlock, the spark may not land in the powder-pan, and then you are a dead man. Now..."

He stood back a pace and showed me how to brace my shoulders against the pistol's kick, with my eyes narrowed against its flare.

"You have two triggers and two barrels," he warned me. "Do not use them both at once. Better still, never fire the gun at all. It is more powerful when it is not used."

Barely listening, I squinted along the barrel's spike-sight. Could I fire it at van Stijn if I needed to?

"It is enough to show the pistol, Calumny," repeated Peter, with more fire in his voice. "A wise man never shoots unless his life is at stake."

"I must go, Father," I said carelessly, tucking the pistol into my waistband again. "I must be there at ten o'clock, and I heard the half-hour from Spitalfields bells already."

He passed the back of his hand over his forehead and stared at me, as if he would hold me back, but the moment passed.

"It is well that you can count the time now, my buck," he said softly, opening the door for me.

I touched him on the shoulder as I left. Though ghostly pale, his flesh was solid. I carried the warmth of him in my palm, all the way to Bear Street.

As Mister de Corvis' carriage bore us to Covent Garden, Emilia gave me a stiff speech.

"Today we aid the coffee-men of London, Master Spinks," she said. "Every house in London has been taking expensive, tasteless beans from holders of the royal licences for far too long."

Calm words indeed, from the wildcat who'd held a knife to my throat while she straddled me half-naked.

"You will give them our coffee to taste. Then you ask them to sign the paper. It is a contract to give us an exclusivity..."

Exclusivity, I thought. That is what Firth spoke to the two Frenchmen of. And now he is dead.

"And if they will not sign..."

She touched the butt of my pistol.

"And if they are not afraid of pistols?"

"Then we will burn their coffeehouse to the ground, and give them a beating besides. Not you," she said quickly, "but we have some... some fellows who do this work."

Fellows be damned, I thought furiously. That is my father you speak of.

"Emilia..."

"Since you are serving my father, you should call me by Mistress, or Miss de Corvis."

"If they buy coffee with no royal licence, will they not be punished?"

Emilia's breath tickled my ear. "Tell them to come to Bear Wharf at noon on Friday week. We will show the new licences then. But they must sign first."

She thought to play me, to be cold one moment and teasing the next, but she was mistaken. She was mine to use now.

We rode on in silence, and my fears for Peter and Garric grew. If I failed in my task, a brutal task would fall on them. Calumny Wig-thief, I thought. Lottie the serving-girl had told me to go somewhere else for a warmer welcome. If we went somewhere I was known, it would be easier to do my business, and keep my father safe.

Emilia read from a list. "The first place is Walter Feeney's coffeehouse. Do you know it?"

"I do," I lied, "but why do we not begin with John Hollow's? It will be richer pickings than Feeney's."

Emilia stared at me suspiciously. When her gaze slipped to my mouth, I knew I had won. She shrugged and pulled down her window. "Frazier! John Hollow's, if you please."

"Feeney's would be better, miss," said Frazier, stopping the carriage.

"I said Hollow's coffeehouse, man, and be about it!"

"Craving your forgiveness, miss," replied Frazier cheerfully, and the coach lurched, jerking my face close to Emilia's. I pulled away and looked out of my window.

We turned off the Strand and up into the narrow streets of Covent Garden. The crowds were thinner and faster today, men greeting each other with a curt tip of the hat instead of stopping to talk at length, and I saw many a shopman waiting in his doorway for custom.

They waited for war, I realised; and I had conspired in the murder that would start it all off.

It came back to me like a flare of lightning. The red-coated assassin standing over the Duke of Firth. The look of recognition in the dying man's eyes. It had been a soldier from his own regiment. Montalbion had called him Alcott, but now I realised that it had been Quartermaster Baines, with his hunching bull-back and his deep growling voice.

Baines, I thought. A man who said he would make any bargain if there were but gold in it for him. A man whose high treason I had witnessed. My perfect ally.

The coach stopped in a little three-sided yard. The streets were clean here, and the houses well-kept. Little fruit trees, half-bare by now, lined the yard.

"It is around that corner," said Emilia. "I will follow you by and by, but we cannot be seen together."

The plaster bubbled between the wet-black timbers of John Hollow's house – a sure sign that a cheat had mixed too much water in it. I did not knock, but pushed the door open and walked quickly to the back of the coffee-house, keeping the pistol hidden under my long-sleeved waistcoat. I snapped my fingers at the maid behind the counter as I crossed, holding up a finger to ask for a pot of coffee.

In John Hollow's, the men did not wear their wigs, but hooked them on the backs of their chairs. There was less caution here than at the Moor's Head: the laughter and loud voices made me feel welcome. Two fires warmed the room, and faces were flushed in the half-light. I recognised two men from the House of Three Mysteries, and settled myself at a table that was screened by wooden panels that stretched from floor to ceiling. Words floated on streams of pipesmoke.

"But is the House of Orange from the Stuart line or no?"

"A man should be able to sell his stocks with ease, not have to tramp the coffeehouses like a whore with a portfolio..."

"War with France would be no bad thing..."

"I do not hold with voting..."

"At the Guildhall they propose to make a bust of Cromwell, the lunatics..."

"I have asked the Secretary of State to withdraw trade-licences from the Scots, to make the bastards squeal for Union..."

Every concern of these men filled me with unease. Licences, Cromwell, the Dutch king – all of these were straps in my harness.

The serving-girl brought my coffee, and I lifted it to my nose as I had seen van Stijn do in the Moor's Head. The smell was of dark earth, its spicy sting mixed with the soft womanly strength of soup on a cold day. It was as good as a lover's first kiss. Its tendrils climbed under the skin of my face and smoothed out my frowns and aches.

I blew across the foamy brown surface and took a sip. My tongue burst into life. Stars sparkled in my eyes, and I could hear every throat-clearing and chair-scraping in the room.

I took a bigger sip. I beckoned the maid with my crooked finger, proudly avoiding her eye, and asked her how much I should pay.

"One shilling," she said, holding out her hand. I counted out two sixpences and two pennies, but she kept her hand open, to say that tuppence tip was unworthy of her house. So I dropped another of Emilia's sixpences in her hand.

One shilling for a teaspoonful of black dust? Well, I could not make the numbers like Ty, but I knew it was good commerce. One shilling a cup, when you could drown yourself in gin for as much. I saw why Mister de Corvis risked a hanging to play in this game.

"You are rising up in the world, wig-thief," said the serving-girl tartly.

It was Lottie, the coffee-maid from the Moor's Head, and I smiled at her in relief. Now, perhaps, I had a chance to make good commerce. Her hazel eyes were laughing at me. A thin, green velvet band circled her neck, making the freckles of her chest look prettier.

Wig-thief, I thought. That is no bad name for my apprenticeship.

"It seems you are too, Miss Lottie No-name," I teased her. "From the Moor's Head to John Hollow's you rise."

She tucked my coins into the pocket of her blue-and-white striped petticoat and picked up my cup. As she stretched, her sleeve withdrew slowly along her slim forearm, showing a delicate pattern of apricot-coloured freckles under the downy hairs. Her serving clothes were freshly washed and pressed, and I had to catch my breath to stop from drinking her in. Jesus Satan, had I not enough women's scents already swirling through my poor body?

"I have not finished –" I protested hoarsely.

"But I have not started," she replied with a grin. As she lifted my cup, her wrist brushed on mine, and the fine red hairs of our arms sparked once again. Steam from the coffee rose in front of her face like a shimmering veil. She closed her eyes and breathed in slowly, taking care not to burn her nostrils on the hot steam. Breathed out, smelled it again. And one more time, like a dying woman watching her last dawn.

Lottie sipped the coffee and made a face, to say, *It is not so bad, and not so good neither.*

"Master John Hollow?" I asked her, and she frowned.

"You promised me a warm welcome here, Miss Lottie," I chided her. "Will you not say a kind word of introduction to Master Hollow for me?"

Still grimacing, she went back behind her counter, pointing briefly at a door. I wound my way between the tables, sucking in the coffee smells.

Behind the door was a little passageway leading to a counting-room. Through its open door I spied walls decked with shelves of papers and boxes, and a Chinese counting machine such as I had seen at the Spitalfields market. It had rows of black and white beads, strung on little metal poles, the whole held in a polished dark wood frame.

"*Monsieur Jean Ollow*?" I called out.

Once again I would play the Frenchy. If things went ill, Mister de Corvis wished for all suspicion to fall on the shoulders of forengies. It was as my mother always said. In the city, they will hang you for another man's crime if you cannot claim the English blood.

"Who asks?" demanded a woman's voice.

"I wish to speak with Monsieur Jean Ollow," I said in Garric's bold voice, poking my head in. A wiry-haired old woman of perhaps fifty years sat at her book of accounts, clutching a quill awkwardly between swollen ink-stained fingers. Her eyeglasses were swallowed up in the wrinkly lumps of her cheeks. She warmed a steel pot at a fire.

"What business with him?" she rattled, still scratching at her ledger.

I took a small twist of paper from my pocket, pulling open my coat a hand's breadth so that the pistol bared its teeth at the starchy old woman.

She was no coward, the dame. For sure she had seen my gun, but she did not blink as she reached over for the twist of paper.

"Strange to see a Frenchman with the red hair," she murmured, opening up the little package.

I blurted out, "It is from my father's side, he is…"

She raised an eyebrow.

"Norweyan you might be, or Yorkshireman, it's all one to me. Now what is this?"

The woman fumbled the twist of paper open and ran her little finger through the small pile of fresh ground coffee. Its rich ripe scent filled the room, making spit pour out under my greedy tongue.

"There is no John Hollow, Monsieur Frenchy. Or at least, I am he. For what is a woman but a hollow man, a man without all the guts and bile and sentiment?"

She gave a little yowl of laughter. I wondered what kind of a woman would bother to play with words while an armed man stood in her coin-room.

"Now, let us see what this fine-smelling bean may make for us," she mused, opening up the steel pot and pressing the coffee dust into a little basket with her thumbs. There was a horrid hiss and a smell of burning flesh. The pot was red hot from being in the fireplace, yet she had pressed the soft flesh of her fingers into the scalding metal. She poured in water from a little kettle on her desk and put the pot back on the grate.

"But, madame, your hands…"

"Every affliction is a benediction," replied Mistress John Hollow.

She showed me her hands. Red rings were burned into her fingers and thumbs. I leaned in closer and saw that the flesh of her hands was scarred and lumpy, the grey skin gathering in wrinkly folds at her knuckles.

"I feel no pain, pistol-monkey."

A leper.

Bile rose in my throat. I took a step back but dared not leave, not with Emilia behind me in the coffeehouse, and Mister de Corvis waiting for news of my success. I clasped my pistol through my coat as if it could protect me from the flesh-rot.

Mistress John Hollow sighed.

"I do not think it goes so easily from one body to another, redhead, or else my daughter should have it too. And if she does, then you would too, if you have drunk her coffee already this morning."

Lottie was this leper's daughter?

Mistress Hollow fussed over the hissing pot, her nose twitching with coffee-love. I looked away, trying not to think about her rotting hands. How could I threaten a woman who was already mortal sick? A yellowy brass statue was on the mantel: a fat man with a strange beast's head. It had a hound's long droopy ears and a vile snake for a nose, and sharp spears in its chewing mouth.

"Is that from Africa?" I asked.

"It is an Indian elephant god," she replied softly.

"All my life…" I began, forgetting to speak in the Frenchy way.

"Yes, for sure," she snapped. "All your life you have wanted to be on a ship to the Indies, to seek adventure and coin and other such foolishness. So it was with my husband."

Angrily, she poured us each a draught of coffee. My fingers trembled as I took my cup from her, and I scalded my palm in trying not to touch where she had touched. As I blew on the coffee, a face appeared in the froth, stretched into a silent scream, and was gone.

"Master Hollow was just such a one as you. 'Give me two pistols and a fair wind, and I will return with gold,' he would say, with his chest puffed up," muttered Mistress Hollow.

We sipped and sighed. This was far richer than the coffee Lottie had served me. It was buttery and golden, yet it had a peaty flame in its depths.

"Well, he did return," she went on. "With a brass elephant god and less than three pounds of sailor's wages. And leprosy, that he did not confess to me until after he had had me on my back again. It was too late for me then, but I threatened to tell the world he was diseased if he stayed near Lottie. And so he sailed away once more to the Indies. That was fourteen years ago."

She showed me her hands again, twisted with scars and cuts and burns.

"A body that cannot feel pain is a body that will die by a thousand cuts. Well, so be it. At least I can smell and taste. And I must tell you, pistol-monkey, that this coffee is worth losing a hand for."

I cleared my throat. Now I must make my offer.

"I –"

"Let me see if I can say your part," said Mistress Hollow curtly. "'Sign here, madame, or else we will burn your place as we did the Moor's Head in Southwark.' Then I will say my part. 'But pistol-monkey, even though I am afeared of you, I must buy from the lawful licence-holders or else my customers in there, the excise-men and the judges, they will see me clapped.' And then you say –"

"And then I ask you," I replied passionately, "what is a licence but a way for the king's family to steal more money from the hard-working souls of London? Why should men drink poor coffee, sawdust and tar, when they could have a drink of such beauty, for half the price, from an honest Frenchman?"

"And then I say," she smiled, "you may shoot me if you will, but I cannot buy your coffee without that you have a royal licence."

"And then I say," I whispered, "a new king may grant new licences."

Now, at last, I had spoken treason myself. At last, I was guilty of the crime they would hang me for. All the weight of the world fell from my shoulders, for it is worse to be accused of a sin you have not committed, than to commit the sin and be justly condemned.

Mistress Hollow sipped the dregs of her coffee; her faded brown-grey eyes stared through me as if I were but an autumn leaf-skeleton. At last she put down the cup and turned to her desk, dipping the pen and scratching again at her ledger.

What now? I thought.

"What price?" she asked, not looking up.

"Four pounds the sack, madame," I replied.

"Three," she said, writing the number large in her ledger. With a pang, I wished that Ty were there with me, to speak of numbers. But I had to trust my own self now.

"Four," said I, stern as a bishop, "and you shall see the licences before you buy. But first you must make your mark here."

I laid out the papers I carried in my coat, and she read the words that Emilia had put down there.

"Come you to Bear Wharf at noon Friday after next,

madame," I said, waiting while she made her mark on both papers. I took one, but she held on to the other end.

"A kiss first, pistol-monkey," she demanded.

I stroked my face with trembling fingers.

"Is all well, Mother?" called Lottie from the hallway.

Mistress Hollow laughed, her face wrinkling.

"Well, missy, you have saved this boy from a love he would never have forgot – but we must not regret its passing!"

She gave me the paper and waved me out. Lottie was waiting, and closed the counting-room door behind me.

"Miss Hollow," I whispered.

Wordlessly, she showed me the blunderbuss that she had hidden behind her back.

"I am glad you were kind to my mother," she said gently, leading me into the main room.

"I too," I replied in a low voice, pushing the gun's muzzle away. "Though I cannot tell why you would have served at the Moor's Head when your own mother has a coffeehouse."

"She sent me away for my own good," she said grimly, "but I could not leave her unguarded. Not when coffee-houses are menaced at gunpoint."

By men like me, she meant. I nodded, and left.

Outside, Emilia seized the paper from me and rushed around the corner to the carriage. In she climbed, while Frazier looked away from us both with a face of stone. I did not follow, but closed the door gently behind her.

"Come back with me," she whispered, "and you will not have to sleep in that hovel again tonight."

"I must go to my father," I said with a grave face.

"Do not lie to me, Calumny! I know full well that he is engaged this night."

To tell true, I did want to stay in her bed, but I could no longer do this to-and-fro of women. It was making my red hair fall out, for me to find strewn across my pillow every morning.

"And my father will be at home tonight," wheedled Emilia with a sad little hope in her eyes.

If I stayed close to Mister de Corvis, I would find a way to steal the Dutchman's gold.

Pretending reluctance, I opened the carriage door and stepped inside. Emilia took off her gloves and clasped my hand.

Emilia undressed and lay on the bed. I took off my boots but kept my clothes on as I looked at her. It was the first time I had seen her naked. Her limbs were thin, her breasts as small as a girl's. I thought of Violet's full body, the swell of soft brown skin, the sway of her thigh, the gentle flesh under her arms. Violet was not ashamed of her body like Emilia was. She had let me gaze at her gently curving belly and her dark wide nipples by candlelight, but this girl, her dense black hair covering her face, was curled up to hide her venus, tugging the covers down to stop me staring.

"Lie with me," she whispered, her face turned into the pillow.

I held back. Was she no longer afraid I would get her with child? Why had she changed towards me? I had still thought to marry her, long after I'd bedded Violet, but I did not want her now she was offering herself.

"Lie with me, Calumny Spinks," she said, her eyes pleading now. "I care not for my father's warnings and commands. I give myself to you."

With a harsh ache, I knew that I could not have Violet, and loneliness drew me towards Emilia. She tried to kiss me, to stroke my face, but I spread her arms wide while I rolled on top of her. She whispered my name as I pressed my dead eyes deep into her pillow. I tried not to hear her say she loved me, tried not to feel her caresses through my clothes, tried to lose myself in the fire that sprang up between our bodies, but there was a dark cold place in the middle of my head that thought bitterly of Violet even while we thrashed around. Emilia kissed me in the corner of my eye. I took her love and gave nothing back.

Emilia clutched my back, keeping me inside her while she fell asleep. Now I could see how plain she was, when her eyes were not flashing, when her teasing commands had ceased. Her jaw was square and wide like a man's, her hair coarse, and the spicy smell was too strong on her neck. It was not her true scent, but a perfume that stung my tongue where I had licked her.

Violet's smell came from her skin, from her hair, from her heart. Too late, I knew for sure what was true and what was false. Now I had betrayed them both.

I slowly rolled off Emilia, letting the covers settle to keep her from waking. I had not forgotten how her father had abandoned me to Montalbion's plot. That was my true purpose in lying with the girl; her bedroom was under the attic. I wanted to see why he had men working there secretly in the middle of the night. Since he had so much power over me, over my father and Garric's family too, I needed to know his secret. I needed my own power now. And with barely a fortnight to live, what had I to fear?

I slipped out onto the little landing and looked up. Above me was a scratched and splintered hatch, bearing a brass ring. Taking the hooked pole that leaned in the corner, I quietly pulled down the hatch. I leapt, caught hold of the edge, and scrambled up swiftly.

It was dark and curious warm up there, but enough light seeped through the hatchway for me to see. Chalk squares were marked out in neat rows on the attic floor, and it smelled of black loamy earth, rich as sin. Coffee, the same as the little twist I had taken to Mistress John Hollow's.

I tippytoed into the darkness at the other end of the attic. Hemp sacks were carefully stacked in four neat rows. I pinched into the closest one, making it leak. Out came a little stream of black shells. These were the coffee beans, kept warm and dry and far from the eyes of the street. But how had Mister de Corvis got them up here without people seeing the sacks go in and out of his house?

I walked slowly between the high rows of sacks towards the chimney breast at the end of the attic. A large oaken box was bolted to the bricks, its lid secured by a sturdy hasp. From inside came a creaking. I sniffed at the burned coffee smell that came strongly out from between its uneven timbers. I tried but could not open the padlock.

"Indeed, Apprentice Spinks," said Mister de Corvis, "I do not recall writing in the contract that you should bed my daughter and steal my stock."

CHAPTER THIRTY-TWO

Conspiracy

In which Benjamin de Corvis allows Calumny into his grand plan

Mister de Corvis had been devilish quiet as he followed me up the ladder and through the attic. A match flared, and he showed me a coarse red hair in its sulphurous light.

"You must know that there is only one person who would leave such a gift for me. Outside my only daughter's room. Under the hatchway that hides my most precious secret."

He held the hair to the flame.

"Ergo, I must choose whether to trust you."

Or kill you for bedding my daughter, he did not say. Usually his clothes were buttoned up neat around him, but now he wore his collar open so that I could see the tight little curls of black hair that peppered his chest.

Lighting a lantern, he stepped up to the oaken box that was bolted to the wall, took out a key and freed the hasp. He lifted the lid and beckoned me over to look. The box covered a deep hole with a pulley inside it, a rope leading far down into the dark. A little breeze blew upwards, washing my face with the strong scent of roasted coffee, and something fouler besides.

"First you must tell me," he said.

"Tell you, sir?"

My own secret, he meant, though I was stone-sure he knew it already. Making him wait, I pulled four sacks from the top of a row and made them into two seats, one against each wall of coffee, so that we could sit facing each other. Mister de Corvis hung the lantern on a hook and sat down.

I drew a long breath, and told him the story of my life. Peter's crime. How he had saved Mirella and her brother, and how they were both dead now. How we came to London, where Anthony and his unknown master had demanded the eighty pounds, and why I chose to work for him. I gave him the power of life and death over me – but what did I have to fear, in truth? I was twice doomed already, by Peter's crime and Montalbion's murder.

"Then we are bound together, Calumny Spinks," he said. "My enterprise will give you back your freedom, if you will but honour your contract to me."

I did not reply.

"I will help you buy your freedom," he said quietly, "on two provisos."

Still I waited.

"*Primo*: if you betray or disobey me, I will kill you, and your father, and Garric Pettit, and his family too."

I picked at a sack with my thumbnail.

"*Secondo*: if you enter my daughter's bed again, or if she is with child, I will do the same."

I could not speak, but I knuckled my forehead to show him that I understood. God help me, we had lain together, and for all I knew she could be with child already!

"All this is my fortune," said Mister de Corvis, like a shriven man. "My coffee, Calumny. Grown in Jamaica, shipped and roasted by me alone. And not a bean of it may I sell on the streets of England."

The pulley creaked as it swung back and forth in the darkling breeze. He stood and closed the box, speaking as he moved.

"My father was a slave-trader out of Bristol. He took his cargo from the east side of Africa, where no other slaver would go, because the long voyage would kill so many more in the hold. But he reckoned that he could buy the slaves so cheap that the losses would be worth the sea miles."

Mister de Corvis took a little knife from inside his coat and sliced open a sack at my shoulder. Black shells poured out, and he held a fat handful out for me to sniff at.

"This is a fine roast," he whispered. "She'll take a pretty price in the coffeehouses of the Strand."

He sat down again and poured the beans into two piles.

"If a hundred slaves were bought for a shilling each including expenses, and fifty died, they would be worth the same as fifty slaves bought for two shillings each, would they not?"

I nodded. I did not need Ty for this kind of mathematic.

"Well, Master Spinks, so it is with coffee, but not with men. For each slave must be fed and watered on the long voyage, which means that a hundred slaves would cost you plenty more. And so my father thought to himself, 'Why not let the fifty who are to die, die first, and then my costs will be the same as the others?'

He swept aside half the beans on the floor.

"My father sailed all the way to Ile-de-France near Madagascar, and bought men there, much cheaper than in the Yorubaland. And for the first six days he gave no food to the slaves, only water, and all who died were thrown overboard. The ones who lived were strong, they had no sickness, and so he fed them happily all the way to Kingston in Jamaica, where they fetched a good price. And all along he only took enough food for half the slaves. It was his plan and his desire that half should die."

He was silent for a long breath.

"My mother died when I was younger than you are now, and so my father had taken me with him to the Indian Ocean. I was to be a slaver too, though my father treated me as little better than a blackamoor myself."

He sighed, rubbing at his ankles.

"It happened that a Frenchman spoke to me at the slave market, wanting an English ship to take him away. I sensed an opportunity, and agreed a price with him. My father was furious when we arrived at the docks, for he shunned passengers to protect his secret, but he took the man's coin none the less.

"He was an officer of the French army, and he had but one large crate to take on board with us. Inside was a bush, an ugly little thing with red berries, but he tended it like it was the Christ-child, watering it three times a day and scouring its limbs for insects and mould."

"It was a coffee bush," I croaked, thinking of the drawing that Emilia had made, and that I stole.

"Yes, Calumny. Come – since we hold each other's lives in our hands, I will show you something else."

As we stumbled blindly out of the attic, the coffee pressed me tight, whispering of the chained hands that had dug and planted and picked. Down we went, out of the tomblike attic and past Emilia's room. I saw as we passed that her keyhole was black, blocked by her watching eye.

"Bathe yourself before you sleep," Mister de Corvis called out to his daughter as we went down the servants' staircase, and I blushed raw with shame.

"Mistress Frazier," said Mister de Corvis, coming into the kitchen.

"Mister de Corvis," she replied curtly, not bothering to curtsey.

"Is your husband below?"

"He is."

"And is the soup ready, Cassie?"

"It will not spoil," she said insolently, leading the way out of the servants' quarters and into the side alley. We sucked the fresh air deep into our chests.

"To the river, Master Spinks," said Mister de Corvis without mockery, and at last there was a kind of joy in his voice. What madness, to threaten my life one moment and salute me the next!

Mistress Frazier turned right instead of going onto Bear Street, taking us to the river-gate. She tucked up her skirts, swung over the side and shimmied down the rungs that led to the Fleet.

"Come," she ordered me, already out of sight.

"Where did the Frenchman want to go?" I asked breathlessly on the way down.

"To Martinique," answered Mister de Corvis when he had joined me on the mudbank, "for he had a family there, and it is in the same seas as Jamaica. But he did not get so far."

"Did your father kill him?"

"The typhus took him, as it took most of our slaves and half the crew," he replied.

Mistress Frazier was making her way down the stinking Fleet-bank towards Bear Wharf. We kept close to the high-bricked sides, treading carefully; God only knew what rusty blades and splintered bones hid under the sewer-river's grimy surface.

"Before the Frenchman died," said Mister de Corvis behind me, "he told me what his plant was. And how he had stolen it from the French king's own plantation in the Indies. France in those days grew much of the coffee, and sold precious little to their poor English neighbours. He had hoped to make a fortune from desperate London merchants with his own crop. But he had seen how my father treated me, and in his dying days he took pity on me and gave me the secrets of growing the red berries. In here!"

Mistress Frazier had stopped at a low arch, well hidden behind a broken cart. Looking around first, Mister de Corvis unlocked an iron gate and led us into a barrel-curved tunnel. The housekeeper pulled the gate back down and locked it. The air hummed with the rustling of distant rats and the ache of forgotten days. Down the middle flowed an open drain, so rank that we both covered our faces to keep from puking. Mistress Frazier pushed on ahead.

"*Blehblehbleh…*" mumbled Mister de Corvis into his glove.

"I cannot hear you, sir," I said, taking my hand off my face for a breath.

"I said, if you want to keep a secret, hide it behind another man's shit," replied Mister de Corvis dryly.

Ahead of us, a turning glowed with golden light.

"My roasting-room," he said as we came into an oil-lit cave. An iron engine stood in the middle, its belly turning round over a fire on a deep-set tray. The engine's handle was turned by Frazier, his back to us. At the back of the cave was a basket with two or three full sacks piled in it, its handles tied to two long ropes that led high into the roof.

"Well, young fellow," said Frazier with a sly smile.

"Give here," said his mistress sharply, taking the handle from him and bending her back to the task. She no longer carried herself like a servant, but like a man who is his own master, strong-necked and hard-eyed.

"Let us not have discord. Our story is not yet done," said Mister de Corvis.

I looked at him, and I looked at the Fraziers, with my mouth open wide.

"Oh, you wonder that I will tell it in front of John and Cassie here? No need to conceal, for they are in the story too. Frazier, I have told Master Spinks how we took the Frenchman from Ile-de-France, and how he died."

The engine rattled with the sound of coffee beans roasting.

"Coffee," said Frazier softly. "We brought the sacks in at night and stored them in the master's attic above. Now we bring them down here to roast."

"The smell of night-soil hides the scent of roasting," Mister de Corvis interrupted.

"Aye," Frazier went on. "Then we grind them and put them in the sacks, and then they go back up to Mister de Corvis' attic. We have been roasting since July, and now we have but a month to sell them before the taste is all gone."

My master pointed at the ropes disappearing into the roof.

"There is two thousand guineas' worth in here and in the attic," he said, the sum echoing fatly in the cave.

"We are below your house, Mister de Corvis?"

"Oh yes," growled Frazier. "This is how we get the beans in without that anybody sees the master's hand in it. But growing the beans… that has been our great labour."

He looked at his master and fell silent.

"It is harder than you might think," Mister de Corvis went on, "so what the Frenchman told me was pure gold. The science of planting and tending coffee bushes. But…"

Looking at my master warmly, Frazier took up the story.

"Old Frederick de Corvis heard the Frenchman talking, and told me to bring his son to him."

"You were on the ship?"

"First mate," replied Frazier, proudly. "The captain said to me, 'Bring that Benjamin up on deck, manacled.' And he cried at the boy – begging your pardon, sir – 'Tell me what the Frenchy said to you!' But the master stood there with his wrists held forward and said only, 'Take off my cuffs.' And the captain struck him so hard that he fell to the deck, but still he said only, 'Take off my cuffs.' And then…"

Mistress Frazier tipped up the engine to pour a bucketful of black steaming beans into a tin tray, her face as clear as an August night. She had heard this story before.

"And then," said Mister de Corvis in a tight voice, "my father took the sabre from his waistband and raised it above my left wrist. 'You can work with one hand,' he said, 'and so that is how I will take off your cuff, if you do not tell me what that French pig told you.'"

"How did you keep your hand?" I burst out.

"Do you know what is a marlinspike?" asked Frazier.

I shook my head, staring at Mister de Corvis' empty eyes, drifting under his cropped black fringe of hair.

"It is a spear with a vicious point and a hook behind it, crafted to pull big fish out of the sea. When I saw that man raise a blade to his own son, I took my marlinspike and I struck it through old Frederick de Corvis' back, and out through his sour belly. And then I pulled his guts clean through his ribs."

Hrrrr hrrrr. The engine turned and the beans burned. I knew full well why they risked confessing their murder to me. We were all dead men down there in the grinding-cave.

"Calumny,' said Mister de Corvis quietly, taking me out of the Fraziers' hearing, "if you knew the man who held the noose over your head, the one who takes your eighty pounds a year for his silence, would you not spike him through? Even if he were your own father?"

I fell silent then, for I had thought often enough of spiking Peter for his stubborn-headed silence, and it shamed me to own it.

"It does you credit that you cannot answer such a question," said Mister de Corvis, putting his left hand on my back. The hand his father would have cut off without Frazier's boldness, though I could not understand why he had taken such a risk for a boy.

"And it may yet come to it. Not that you should strike your father, but it may be that I can free you from your debt if you are ready to refuse the blackmailer."

"You would give me the eighty pounds, Mister de Corvis?"

"No, Calumny, not the eighty pounds. For if you pay this time, you will pay forever. No, I mean a royal pardon."

"But why would the king pardon my father for killing his uncle, the old King Charles?"

"This king will not, Calumny. The next one might."

Treason again. Treason was in my blood before I was born, and treason would put the noose around my neck, and drop the hatch from under my feet.

"The next king?" I asked.

"The Dutch king, William the Stadhouder of Orange, will land his forces in this country within three weeks. If I raise the guilds to his banner, then my friend Martin van Stijn will give me what I want. My own coffee licences, Calumny, my fortune – and my family to have a good name at last. And for you, if you serve me, a royal pardon. I will speak to van Stijn about it directly."

"So when will you see him next?" I asked, trying to draw him out, but he was silent. I folded my arms. Was I now to believe this man, who had betrayed me, who was ready to turn traitor on his own king?

"I see you do not trust me," said Mister de Corvis.

"Why should you not kill me now?" I demanded loudly, stepping away from him. "Why tell all to a tradeless boy, when you do not truly need me?"

Mistress Frazier stopped turning the engine, and all three of them watched me in silence.

"My father," I said. "Your bargain is with Peter Spinks, not with me. I am only the ink on your contract-paper."

"Enough," commanded Mister de Corvis. "Master Spinks, my daughter will give you your tasks tomorrow. There is a fortnight's work, of fire and fury I'll be bound, and you must play your part well. Else there will be no pardon and no coin besides."

His face was cold and harsh again. When he ordered me about, Master Spinks this and Master Spinks that, I was but an ant without the courage to naysay him. This was a man who could tell you a darkmost secret, and still have a thousand more hidden away.

"Bolt him in his room, Cassie," said Mister de Corvis. "I will not have him blabbing about the city."

Mistress Frazier led me back, and we did not speak again until we had closed the river-gate behind us.

"Mistress Frazier –" I began.

"Barcus," she said, striding along the side passage. "Cassie is my given name, Barcus my guild name, and I will thank you to use it now."

"Kit Barcus," I breathed, waiting for her to unlock the servants' door. Now I remembered her embracing a silver-haired dock-man at that very river-gate. "Your husband?"

"My brother," she said. "But I am his master, and of all the dock-men besides."

She led me to the kitchen, where soup still bubbled lazily over the dying coals. She poured me out a bowl, handed it to me and jerked her head to show that I should go to the little room I had slept in before.

"Barcus," I asked carefully, for I wanted to know this secret too, "why do you give me your room?"

"Ha!" she bellowed. "This ain't my room. I sleep on a lighter downriver, same as I have done all my days."

"Then Master Frazier –"

"Warms another's bed. See?"

Sitting on the bed with the bowl of soup, I sniffed, "But you are married..."

"In law only," said Cassie Barcus from the doorway. "Master Frazier and Mister de Corvis are my partners in commerce, is all. Thought they could smuggle their coffee past the dock-men without licence, they did. Well, not a rat sneaks through my docks without I get an inch of its tail. So I will take a third part of that two thousand guineas..."

"And in return you have let them bring their whole cargo upriver," I finished, through a mouthful of soup. "Though your brother showed little friendliness towards Master Pettit, for all that."

"Garric Pettit," she growled, rattling the metal hoop that hung on the door, "is a fool who owes the Genoese a good deal of coin. If it were not for Kit and me, his carcass would have been nibbled to pieces by Thames-crabs months ago. Kit made Pinetti give him time, and I asked de Corvis to give him work. Now take your nose out of dock-business, or it will be *your* legs that are weighted with chains on the quayside."

She stepped into the room, took the empty bowl away from me, and ruffled my hair.

"Two more weeks, weaver-brat. And then Cassie will have time to show you a thing or two in this here room."

"Barcus," I said stiffly, as one man to another.

"Spinks," she mocked me, wiggling her hips.

The key turned in the lock, and I was alone.

CHAPTER THIRTY-THREE

Lawless

In which London descends into darkness

Those were my loneliest days, trapped at night and watched by day, while the hours of my life withered on the vine. There were close to two hundred coffeehouses in the city. Frazier drove us remorselessly, a dozen houses in different parishes between dawn and dusk. By the end of each day, even Cucullan dragged his hooves.

Since Mister de Corvis had made his bloody threat, I had not touched Emilia, and in truth my lust had died. Exhausted, she scratched endlessly at lists of coffeehouses, her accounting of stocks and orders. Her petticoats grew blotchy with ink, and those fiery eyes grew widow-dim.

It was a blessing to step out of the miserable coach and go about my business, more sure of myself by the day. I learned how to make a coffee-man sign without that I even show him the pistol, how to make a pantomime of letting him smell and taste the coffee, how to make the pot myself.

If he would not sign, I would tell him what violences awaited. I began to forget that it was my father and Garric who would be coming by, with cudgels and fire, and thought of myself as the man who saved the poor merchants from their menaces. Most times the coffee-men would change their minds and sign the contract.

I did not see any of my Spitalfields family for near two weeks, since Cassie Barcus locked me up each night. I did not even know if Ty had come back from the barracks with the profit, nor if Garric had found the name of my enemy. It was strange to know that Peter walked in my footsteps a full day behind, cudgel in hand.

No more wages came. Perhaps Mister de Corvis thought it was enough to spin me a tale of royal pardons. Well, I would find a way to steal the Dutchman's gold, and perdition to all of them. I'd take a ship for the Indies if I had to. All I had to do was wait, and spy, and strike.

I carried my tracing of the Dutch treasury-mark everywhere, like a talisman. With van Stijn's bullion in my hands I could choose whatever woman I wanted: Violet, or Lottie from John Hollow's – or another. Though if it was Violet, I'd need to find a way to get her away from the regiment.

Rattling through the streets of London, I made my plan. The last time I saw him, Robbie had told me that he and Baines escorted Violet and her mother to church every Sunday night, in the papist fashion. And so I did not need to risk breaking the barracks curfew.

That Saturday evening, we were driving back to Bear Street, Frazier singing a mournful sea-hymn.

"My father thinks that a pile of coin is a better guardian than any man can be," said Emilia bitterly to the window. Her breath spread wetly on the cold glass.

"Wise," I said.

She uncurled my fingers from around the pistol's handle.

"Could you not love me?" she demanded, and pressed her mouth against mine. I did not pull away, but nor did I kiss her back. She ran her dry tongue over my lips, then drew back to look at me.

"You have given yourself to another woman. I knew it."

I shrugged.

"Do you care for me at all?"

I hesitated, then gave a little jerk of my head to say that I did. And it was the truth, for once.

"I am afraid to be alone. My father –"

"I will protect you, Emilia."

I squeezed her hands, not caring whether I meant my words or not. Carefully, holding Violet's face in my mind, I slipped along the seat and held Emilia in my arms. She pressed her face into my chest and fell asleep.

Mister de Corvis himself was waiting for us at his front door. He looked up and down the street as we went in, and I felt the power of his intention. Something was afoot.

I followed Emilia into her father's study while he remained at the front door. The bookshelves and paintings flickered dreamlike in the waxlight. Seven chairs surrounded a table in the middle of the room, one of them already filled by Garric. I rushed over to greet him.

Garric embraced me.

"I have made inquests to find that demon who threatens you," said Garric urgently. "The Captain Marks –"

"Garric, you should not have risked yourself," I said, cutting him off.

"Family is the beginning and the end," he replied. "You and your good father would do equal for Ty."

I will share my gold with you when I have it, I swore to myself. Then I realised what he had said.

"Captain Marks?" I hissed. I had my enemy's name at last. Marks was old enough to have fought for Cromwell; he had known Anthony; and even Robbie had told me he was a dangerous man. Well, I would settle his account before I left England.

Garric opened his mouth to reply but Mister de Corvis had come in, followed by my father, Frazier and Martin van Stijn.

Peter came and put his arms around me. He had never done such a thing before, and he was quick to break away. "Too long, Cal," he said, his voice cracking.

Van Stijn, in his hooded cloak, nodded at me. I tried not to stare, but I could not help but imagine the Dutchman's resistance as I tried to seize his treasure.

We all waited for Mister de Corvis to sit down first, even Peter.

"It seems there is one more person to come," said van Stijn, pointing at the empty chair next to Frazier.

"She is here," replied Cassie Barcus, plopping her backside down.

"Must we invite every woman in London?" demanded Peter, tapping his fingers on the table.

"Barcus here is every bit your equal," replied Mister de Corvis firmly. "Her brother is the guildmaster of the dock-men, and it is her word that will keep the English navy in its moorings on Friday next."

"Why does everyone speak of Friday this, Friday that?" I demanded, filling the silence out of fear that my father and Mister de Corvis would come to harsh words.

"Can you not see it, Master Spinks?" asked Martin van Stijn gently. Under his cloak, he wore a crisp black jacket and a yellow porcelain badge adorned with a flame-red lion, the same sign that was stamped on the gold bars I had seen in his travelling-bag – the image that I had traced, now folded up small in my breeches pocket. It would give me my freedom.

"I must ask you who you are, citizen," interrupted Peter. "You speak to my son as a friend, yet you wear the uniform of a Netherlandish general. We are here to conspire in commerce, not war."

"It is both," I whispered, looking down at my hands. I blushed to feel the eyes of the other seven on me. I forced my chin up.

"The Dutch king will land on Friday," I said, in a stronger voice now. "Mistress Frazier's brother will keep the docks closed so that the English warships cannot launch. The guildsmen will come out onto the streets this week to frighten the king and make the people demand him to leave. Lord Montalbion will change his loyalty at the last moment. And we… and Mister de Corvis will have royal licences from the new king, to let him trade his coffee. Half the coffeehouses in London have already signed to take it. It is commerce, and war, in one."

"War," spat Peter, pushing his chair away from the table and raising his fist to van Stijn. "To replace one tyrant with another, paid for in the blood of ordinary men, while the merchants profit. I will have no part in it!"

"A royal pardon," said van Stijn calmly.

"What do you say?" demanded Peter.

"A royal pardon, for you and your son. In the name of King William the Third, as he will become on Friday next."

Next to me, Garric held his breath.

"I do not know what my foolish son has told you, but it is not enough," said Peter. "I will not trade my life, nor even Cal's, for the horror of –"

"No bloodshed," interrupted Mister de Corvis. "There is only one regiment in London now, and our ally Lord Montalbion has been its commander since the death of the Duke of Firth. At ten o'clock on Friday, the Hyde barracks will empty and the whole company will be barged down the river to the Tower, leaving London free of soldiers. With the streets full of guildsmen, the king will be forced to flee without a sword being drawn."

"My master has forty thousand men, already at sea," finished van Stijn. "You know that the Catholic king has not enough loyal commanders to make a stand against such a force. It is over."

"But to do such a thing… for trade…" protested Peter, defeated.

"For a king who will give power back to Parliament. Who will sign laws tolerating all religions. A king who will pardon you, and give your son his life back."

Martin van Stijn had stood up stiffly to give his little speech, fierce belief pouring out through his frowning eyes.

"Let us plan," said Mister de Corvis sharply, motioning to Peter and van Stijn to sit back at the table. I leaned forward in my chair. Where the gold went, there would I be.

Mister de Corvis was marvellous bold. He spoke of high treason and war as if they were goods to be traded at the market. Unrolling a map of London, he showed us where the soldiers would be stationed, which streets the guilds would block, where the Dutch soldiers would land. My father's face filled with colour as he asked questions of de Corvis and van Stijn, pointing here and there.

Cassie Barcus leaned over and pointed. "Dock-men at the Pool to blockade the English navy. Lightermen to the Tower Wharf to block the streets with cargo so the army cannot ride out."

"There will be a gathering on the Strand on Wednesday next," Mister de Corvis told us, though I could scarcely hear him through the roaring in my ears. "Montalbion is pretending to reassure all the Catholics that the Crown will protect them, but in truth it is a wonderful reason to make a protest against the king. Master Spinks..." – he pointed at Peter so it was clear he did not mean me – "...will, I am sure, find a way to incite riot that day."

Peter's face glowed, and he tapped the table to show that he would.

"And under cover of the protest –" began Emilia.

Her father ignored her. "We have some commercial scores to settle along the Strand that day too. Master

Pettit, will you make sure that Feeney's and the others who have not signed… well, that they are encouraged in the normal manner."

Garric nodded, not meeting anyone's eye.

"Now to Friday's plans. Who is to accompany me to the House of Three Mysteries?" asked Martin van Stijn.

"Why do you need a companion?" demanded Peter, still suspicious of the Hollander.

"He is our new king's ambassador plenipotentiary," replied Mister de Corvis lightly. "Which is to say, he carries a fortune in gold bars. Master Pettit, will you guard him with your life?"

Garric shrugged and touched his forelock. I narrowed my eyes, wondering again if he would steal the Dutchman's ingots with me. But I knew in my heart that he would not betray the guilds. Well, I would not have him harmed. I must find a way to keep him away from van Stijn on Friday.

"Very well," said the Dutchman to Garric. "You must be in Dover Street, outside the house of Lord Montalbion, at half past ten precisely. I will not wait for you. At a quarter past eleven, I shall meet Peter Spinks at the House, and then we will meet with the guildmasters at the Clerkenwell."

"Why must it be precise?" asked Peter. "The weavers and mercers can wait if I tell them so."

"Lord Montalbion is commander of Firth's regiment in name only," replied Mister de Corvis. "We cannot be sure they will obey him if they know a foreign army has landed in London. So everything must be done between ten and twelve o'clock, while they are on the river."

"But the guilds will control the city –" Peter began.

"If Mister van Stijn does not bring certain... *treaties...* to the Clerkenwell by quarter past eleven, then we will lift our blockade of the docks," said Cassie Barcus, her words spattering like winter hail.

"I tell you straight," said Peter, "I will declare a republic at the Clerkenwell if I do not see proof of the laws you have told me of."

"Which will mean war on the streets of London," said van Stijn.

"Better to fight for freedom than to trade one tyrant for another," said Peter.

There was a long silence. Van Stijn cleared his throat.

"All promises will be kept. And I shall be at Bear Wharf at half past eleven with your licences, and Master Spinks' royal pardon," he said, reaching across to shake Mister de Corvis by the hand. "Let you all play your parts to perfection before then, and I will deliver my side of the bargain. For now, I must take a boat and meet my king at sea, and then he will sign all your papers and licences."

"The pardon is not yet signed?" I asked.

"I am not a king, citizen," replied van Stijn, shrugging.

So be it, I thought. I will take your gold before I wager your word against my life.

Frazier ushered the Dutchman out, and we all sat in silence for a while. "Master..." I said at last. Peter bit his lip.

"I am no man's master," snapped Mister de Corvis. "What is it, Calumny?"

"The gathering on the Strand... will many Catholics be there?"

"Every popish whore in London," growled Peter, and I realised then that he had already spoken to Mister de Corvis of the whole plan. He had known full well of the invasion when he challenged van Stijn, the old bastard. He had done it to show me that he had a conscience.

Then I had no choice: I had to go to Violet that Sunday, the next night, and stop her going to the assembly on the Strand. Catholic or no Catholic, I'd not risk her life; and besides, it would fit well enough with my plans.

And I would need lodgings of my own. John Hollow's, I thought; if I choose Lottie, then it will not harm to have a bed close by.

"Calumny, I must bid you to wait in the hall now," said Mister de Corvis. "What follows is not for your ears."

I left willingly, thinking I might enjoy a little freedom at his expense. But the front door was open. A man in black robes leaned against the jamb, reading a slender book by moonlight. A slip of hair escaped the fur trim of his cap.

Ty looked up.

"I thought you'd still be taking bed-lessons from Mistress Fintry," I said sourly, hiding my surprise.

He shrugged. Lifted one arm to show me the student's robe he wore.

"Better things to be learned at the College Secular. If you're leaving, then you should join me there... There's good work to be done –"

"My name is on a contract-paper."

The words came out bluntly. I did not want to argue – Ty would sniff out my plans for van Stijn's gold if I did.

"But was your father not offered a pardon? You'll have no need of employment. When there is a republic, the College will have right-thinking work –"

"You're worse than my father!" I hissed. Ty looked over my shoulder and swallowed uncomfortably.

"Will you not come home now, Calumny?" said Peter from behind me. I turned, hiding my shame with a frown.

"He ain't permitted," rasped Cassie Barcus, pushing past him and clamping her fingers on my neck. I lifted my hands helplessly towards my father, though in truth I was glad the dock-mistress had come between us. I could not look him in the eyes when I had larceny in my head, and a Catholic girl in my heart. Garric came out, nodded to Ty, and they led my father down the steps to Bear Street. Ty turned and looked up at me. He opened his mouth to speak, but I closed the door.

As Barcus led me to my room, I let triumph sing out in my breast. By eleven o'clock on Friday I would have Peter's pardon. And I would be a man of property and title at last.

CHAPTER THIRTY-FOUR

Confession

In which Calumny kneels before the Cross of Rome

On Sunday, we sped down the empty streets, coffeehouse after coffeehouse, until Emilia's quill grew blunt from writing orders on her paper of accounts. Something different was in the air. The coffee-men seemed almost eager to sign the contract-papers, and one fellow even invited me to stay and drink a cup together.

"A rat is never caught in a house fire," said Emilia sourly as we counted up the day's takings. Frazier had halted the carriage to buy walnuts from a Charing Cross hawker. "Merchants know if war is coming long before kings or labourers, and these coffee-men have smelled the smoke of revolution. The popinjays who hold those royal exclusivities will be headless by Saint Sylvester's Day, and so they have no choice but to take our stock."

Dusk was coming, and it was time to slip away from Emilia and Frazier.

"Feeney's is close by..." I said, as if to myself alone.

Emilia ran her fingernail down the margin of her paper.

"For burning," she said flatly. "On Thursday he threatened you with the Watch."

"He is a rat like all the rest," I said. "I will try him again. There is more profit for your father in a house that is still standing than in a needless burning."

"Do as you will," replied Emilia, pressing her fingertips to her brows. "But do not think you can spare your father his duties if you fail."

Your father does not have to forbid you to marry, I thought. There's not a man in London would let his wife's tongue flay him as yours does me.

"Miss," I said, getting out from the carriage. Feeney's was a hundred paces across the straw-strewn cobbles of the Strand. A small crowd was gathering round a crier at the old king's statue. He was calling out the news of a flogging on Wednesday as his apprentice nailed posters to the timbers of the watch-post.

I had chosen Feeney's with good reason. I needed a Catholic who would tell me what I needed to know, and keep it to himself. Knocking on the splintered door, its cheap timbers weathered to watery grey, I thought about the Irish: the weavers, risking their skins to bring their own thread across the grasping seas; Violet and her mother, unmarried in a nest of uniformed whoremasters and killers. Crossing themselves, clicking their heretics' beads in a land that wished them dead. Was it courage, to walk their own stony path away from the world's wishes?

"Begone," came Feeney's croak from behind the door. "We break no Sabbath here. Come back the morrow. Away with ye."

"Do you have no warm drink for a countryman?" I growled, making the Irish as best I could.

"Tenpence a cup," he snapped, opening the door a pinch. I turned my face away, hoping that my red hair would show him I was Irish indeed. "Ha'penny for your seat, penny against the midden-charge, farthing each for spoon and saucer. Shilling to come inside, that is."

Keeping my face turned, I passed a silver coin through the gap in the door. "They told me your coffee was the cheapest in Westminster, so they did," I mocked, "but with your fees for this, and fees for that, your house is as dear as any in England, though not so well-kempt."

Feeney snorted, sneeze-pus gurgling in his throat, but opened the door. I stepped inside quickly, closing the door behind me, and took out the pistol as the old man shuffled towards his counter. Tables and chairs were scattered across the empty room, half of them thick with dust that reeked of gin and piss. It was true that he served no one of a Sunday, as I had hoped. His bald crown was covered with sprawling fleshy freckles that sucked in the light of the two tallow candles on the counter. He was clad in a nightshirt, the stains of armpit-sweat reaching almost to his waist, and his heels spilled out of tattered sheepskin slippers.

"You have forgotten me so soon, Walter Feeney?" I asked, tapping him on the shoulder with the pistol. He turned slowly and pushed the barrel away.

"Told you no and be damned, so I did," he replied fiercely. He wrinkled up his blotchy freckled nose and spat. A startle-eyed rat halted its run across the boards and darted back under the counter.

"On Wednesday this place will burn, and you in it," I said quietly, lowering the pistol.

"Will I, so? Then burning it is, before I will give an English thief a penny of what is mine. So you may keep your contract-paper. And may Lucifer take your soul."

"You may keep your house, and sign nothing, if you choose," I said, picking the dark rings of dirt from under my fingernails.

He put his hands under his arms, hugging himself, and raised his brows.

"Exemption," he said. His throat rasped over the words like a cutler sharpening a cleaver.

I did not know what he meant, but I nodded none the less. "If you will but tell me one thing."

"Tenpence," he barked. "Tenpence if you want to know what Feeney knows."

I lifted the pistol again and aimed it at his head. His mouth lolled open and he thrust his tongue at me, but he could not argue with a ball. Grunting, he threw my shilling back to me.

"What, then?" he demanded.

"Where is the Catholic church?"

"What d'you mean by that?"

"Where do you worship of a Sunday night? You: the Irish, the papists?"

"Ignorant devil you are! Have you ever heard tell of a Roman church in London?"

I shook my head. "Else I should not have to ask a stinking weasel like you, should I?"

Feeney threw back his head, a damp cough breaking through his laughter.

"I'll tell you, robbing English. There's no church built for us yet, though the king has permitted it, and so we worship as we always have. Crawling and bowing to the English lords who have kept the true faith, we are given leave to use their own chapels when they are done. I will not go, myself, not to a rich man's house like a common beggar. The Virgin will see me saved," he said, and crossed himself.

My heart sank. "And so there is more than one chapel?" I muttered. How would I find Violet and Baines in all of London?

"Ah, there are not more than a handful. Wycombe, Firth, Derry, and a pair of others, is all."

"So a soldier of Firth's regiment..." I said, cursing my tongue as soon as it had finished its wagging.

"Aye. Would go to Firth's home to worship. Is it such a one you seek?"

I stood and tapped the pistol's muzzle on the table. It would not be long before Emilia would come knocking. "You have a way out of the back. I remember it."

"The Duke of Firth's home is at Sutherland Row, though he himself is with the Virgin in heaven already," said Feeney slyly. "Will you not sign for my exemption?"

"You have my word," I said, remembering how van Stijn had shrugged off talk of a royal pardon. "I am not a king."

"Well, cutpurse, I will not forget you. If your men pay me another visit, you can be sure the Watch will know of the stork-legged redhair who took a pistol to poor Lord Firth's chapel."

He pointed at the back door. I did not blink at his threats, for he was the least of my enemies. "They will pass you by," I said, and opened the door.

The back alley was overshadowed by leaning houses, closing in the smell of rotting food and night-soil. A squat boy made the pokey with a heifer-hipped whore, holding onto her bare udders with both hands while he battered frantically away. All the while she took huge crunching bites from an apple, chewing noisily with her open mouth barely a hand's breath from the lad's panting face.

"He'll be done quick enough, gentleman," the doxy sputtered through her food. "Day is yet young, and so a sixpence turn is only fourpence ha'penny."

"I thank you, mistress," I said, cuffing the boy over the head, though it did not slow him as he squeaked towards the dying-place. "But I cannot sell you myself for a sixpence, for it would offend the ladies who pay ten guineas at Whitehall for my services."

She choked on her apple, and I walked on, bending low to keep from grazing my head on the overhanging walls. The soiled ground slipped uneasily beneath my feet, a slow tide that shifted from side to rotting side and never reached the daylight.

When I had almost reached the end of the alley, I was stopped in my tracks by Emilia's voice, echoing down the passageway. She made a sound of outrage, opening out into a scream that was choked off.

I hesitated, half-turning. The boy had finished his rut, and was collapsed over the whore's breasts, nibbling like a newborn. She winked at me, thinking I was coming back for her, but I shook my head, listening out. I hoped that Frazier would have heard Emilia's shriek, but there was no sound of banging.

Time was pressing on me. The sky was shrugging off the sad day, and I did not know how long I had before the worship began at the Duke of Firth's home, but still I could not leave Emilia. I should have known she would be forcing her way into Feeney's when I did not come out.

"Jesus' wounds, but this girl is a torment to me," I muttered as I passed the doxy. She snorted, pulling the lad's hair to get him off her. I took out my pistol and carefully pushed open Feeney's back door.

He was waiting for me just inside. He held Emilia before him, a bony elbow crooked around her throat. In his other hand he held an ancient pistol, as long as a child's arm, its frayed old match glowing in the darkened coffee-room. Its barrel was but a spit from my forehead.

"You said they would pass me by, liar," he said bleakly.

"And so they will, Walter Feeney," I replied, letting a gentle Irishness glide through my tones. "Did this girl bring fire or club with her, or no?"

Feeney tightened his hold on Emilia's neck. Though she wriggled and whimpered under his grip, her eyes showed little fear, glaring at me as if to say, *This is your doing. Now undo it.*

"Liar," he said, backing away from the back door. "Come inside and close that damned door behind you, and we'll see what price you pay for breaking an oath."

"*Saute*," I hissed in French, ordering Emilia to jump.

Without a blink, she kicked her heels against the floor and pushed back against the old Irishman. I grabbed his left arm to free her neck, ducking under the flare of his shot. The explosion hit me like a fist, but I did not stop. I let go of his arm and fell upon Emilia where she lay upon him on the floor. Horsehair and plaster-dust fell down on us, blinding me for an instant as I rolled off the girl.

He had already dropped his weapon, since it had but one barrel, and he threw Emilia off. Then he was upon me, clutching at my face with one hand as he fumbled in his stocking with the other. The dust cleared in time for me to see the stubby blade before he could plunge it into my neck. I seized his wrist with my left hand, pulling his strike sideways so that he lost his balance, and clasped him to my chest.

"Be still, Feeney!" I hissed. He tried to bite my face, but I was stronger than he, and he could not free his blade hand from my grip. We struggled for a breath or two, and then Emilia was kneeling next to us, my pistol in her hand with its barrel against Feeney's straggling hair.

"Hold, miss," I said loudly, for there was a loose look in her eyes, and I knew she would pull the trigger without remorse. "I have made this man a promise. I am to blame, not he."

Still she held the gun to the old man's skull. I could not look at the misery in his faded eyes, not even in the dusty dimness of the room. His fingers loosened around his little knife, and it fell on the floor as softly as the first frost of winter.

"He will not sign, miss," I murmured. "We shall leave him be. It is agreed."

Emilia leaned back far enough for me to push Feeney up, though she still pointed my gun at him.

"You are a contract-breaker, born and bred, Calumny Spinks," she said, her shoulders tightening with contempt as she rose to her feet. I took the pistol back, making sure I kept my foot on Feeney's blade for now. The coffee-man slumped on his knees.

"Where do you go?" she demanded.

"I have business," I said harshly. "Contract be damned, I am no slave of yours."

"What am I to say?" she asked.

"I will return tonight, as late as I please. And you may tell Frazier and your father what you will, but be sure to take this house off the list. Now go."

Emilia walked slowly across the darkened room and picked up her cloak from the dirty floor. She left without a backwards glance.

"Fool you are, Calumny Spinks," scoffed Feeney.

I kicked his pistol and blade into a corner, but did not reply.

"Fool to come back for such a mistress, who gives your true name to a stranger. Fool to keep your word to a drunkard who would have cut your throat."

"Would you cut it still?" I asked, meeting his gaze.

"If you broke your word," he said, grudgingly.

"As I would cut yours if you used my name again, Walter Feeney."

I left him kneeling there, his gnarled fingers trembling in his lap. The alley was almost dark now, and the whore and boy had left. My ragged breath echoed weakly against the sagging walls.

The Covent Garden was a grinding mess of hawkers and doxies, play-actors and idlers, clicking and whistling to catch the eyes of the Sunday walkers. As I pushed my way through the square there was a fever in the air, like the last hour of the harvest dance when men's eyes burn brightly as the women's backsides swirl faster. Dusk draped its veil over the faces of the crowd, making their voices bold and their bargaining furious.

A family of sad-eyed Tartars in furs and pointed deerhide boots sang mournfully to the chattering mob that circled them. One daughter, in a sheeny dress of scarlet and blue, walked before her kin, holding out her upturned hat for coins, but her smiling chestnut eyes were a mere distraction. Her elder brother, clad English-fashion in a dull knee-long coat and broad-brimmed hat, passed around the outside of the crowd, cheerily slitting the moneybags that the watchers hid from his sister. Grimly I smiled as I passed on. I did not need reminding that my place in the world was to be the cutpurse, to show my pistol and witness murder while others played the honest craftsman.

Garric Pettit, Cassie Barcus, Calumny Spinks: ours was the bitterest trade of all. Hiding in other people's clothes, tricking and beating our thorny way through the world, and for little more than another day's bread and water.

"Band of orange!" growled an ancient spike-chinned hawker at my side, pressing a faded garter into my chest.

His wares were tied to the inside of his coat. A ribbon-tip poked out from between two buttons at his belly.

"Sutherland Row?" I asked, showing him a penny. He bit the copper coin with his last two teeth, dropped it in his coat pocket and told me which way to go.

The streets were empty again the other side of the Covent Garden, and I could hear the Watchman calling five o'clock. I hoped I was in time for Violet.

The Sutherland Row gate was guarded by a soldier in the scarlet and white of the Duke of Firth's regiment. I made an awkward cross between my nose and chin.

"Walter Feeney, servant to His Grace, God rest his soul," I croaked.

"Worship is not till six o'clock. You may not wait," replied the soldier in a whining Scots accent, blocking my passage.

"Can not a man pray for his lord's soul?" I asked, hoping that he was as popish as his dead master. "Can not he ask the Almighty that soldiers of the true faith will triumph against the heathen invasion?"

"Ach," grumbled the guard, stepping aside. "You Irish could talk a badger from his den."

Ahead of me, a maid in frilled cap and black petticoats came out of a cottage and dashed across the roadway, cursing at herself. Night had fallen, and the air was so crisp that the hum of the Covent Garden crowd came tumbling over the roofs and followed me along the roadway.

A line of yellowing sycamore trees fringed the row of houses, their frill-fingered leaves catching the moonlight as they dropped. I had not thought of Salstead for a long while, for there were precious few trees and fields in this vast midden of a city, but now the season's melancholy fall sent pangs of longing through my limbs. It was on a November night that my mother had first told me her family's story, sitting me on her lap before the hearth and stroking my hair to show me that I was safe, that the Catholics were not coming to choke me like my uncle.

The bruise on my breast began to ache as I walked on into a half-moon yard that fronted a red stone building, twice as broad as the others, its pillared gate carved with the Duke of Firth's snake emblem. At its left was a chapel, light pouring out through its slitted stained-glass windows.

A heathen smell mingled with the cool London air. It was a heady incense, and I prayed to the English Jesus to protect me from popish witchery. But my prayer sounded empty, a whispered nonsense that would serve to nought against the blood-drinking Antichrists who preached in the temple before me.

I crinkled the tracing in my pocket. Gold, I thought. Gold is real, and it is proof against any witch or soldier that ever lived. Baines will help me to get my gold, and Baines will be here soon. It gave me a curious comfort to think of the rough Yorkshireman as my ally.

The pathway was strewn with crunching pebbles. One, I said to myself. Two, three, counting each pace with false courage to keep myself from fleeing. The varnished chapel door was a little open, and incense smoke seeped shyly through the gold-lit gap. Boldly, I went inside, taking care to close the door behind me with a soft click.

The chapel sweltered with riches: jewelled goblets, delicate crosses of gold filigree, relic chests dressed with silver-threaded brocade. Paintings of gilt-haloed Virgins stood in sconces, each lit by a pair of beeswax candles. Behind the altar loomed a painted Jesus on a cross, lifelike with his bloodstained robes and tortured arms.

This was a worship of gold and graven idols, a false faith that made a horror of the Saviour. I stilled my breath and stepped into the aisle. I had not thought the chapel would be so small, and now I did not know how I could speak to each of Baines and Violet without the other one knowing. It would not be long before the congregation came in.

To my left was an alcove with a box in it, taller than a man, two curtains masking it.

Confession, I thought. A papist sits in one side and listens to the sinners who go in the other, but he cannot see their faces, and he gives them penance. Well, it will serve as a hiding place for now.

There was a burst of cold air as the main door opened. From far outside I heard the church bells tolling six. Perhaps seven or eight people had come into the chapel, whispering and shuffling down the aisle. Each in turn knelt before Christ and crossed themselves. The last was Violet, and I twitched the curtain aside a little further to stare at the popish girl whose memory had brought me to this place. I knew her so well already: how the tender lower lip cushioned its twin, and the slow way she blinked, and the curious crooking of her little finger as she crossed herself.

A priest strutted up to the altar, spread his arms like a conjuror and began to speak in Latin. The heathen chant dulled my mind until at last the prayer ended, and the priest beckoned the people to stand. As they began to sing a hymn together, I slipped out of the box and went to stand next to Violet on the back pew.

"Violet," I murmured. "On Wednesday you must stay away –"

She took a sharp breath. The hymn droned on.

"Get you gone, Calumny," she whispered, and turned to look me in the face, her eyes huge in the candlelight. "I carry another man's child in my belly, do you not see? Get you gone before there is trouble, for the babe is property of the regiment."

At last I understood. The swell of her stomach. Why she could not leave the barracks.

"Did you give yourself to me," I wheezed, "to make me believe that I had fathered your baby?"

Violet seized my hand.

"At first I would have trapped you, but I did not!" she hissed fiercely. "I would have confessed it to you. But my mother has charged the captains of the regiment with keeping me close, now that she knows I am with child. The babe will be given to the army, and its life will be nothing better than brawling, whoring and an early grave, like my own father's. Unless I can destroy it first. Or take my own life."

Aborior, I thought, the air scraping at my throat. I saw again the cruel hollowed point of the curette that had cured Ty, but this time it sliced into Violet's tender sacred flesh, and it was she who screamed and bled.

"You shall not kill the child. Promise me," I said quietly, squeezing her fingers.

Two Catholic soldiers in the next pew turned and frowned at us.

"But what can we do?" she whispered, the sweet autumn smell of her breath caressing my face.

"Stay away from the assembly on the Strand this Wednesday, you and your mother both," I said swiftly, hearing the hymn draw to a close. "Seek me out at Hollow's coffeehouse."

"They will not let me leave," said Violet.

"We'll find a way," I told her. It was against my own intentions; it was time to come to my true purpose. "I must leave. Did Baines bring you here?"

She nodded, letting go of my hand.

The singing ended, and the worshippers had to go and kneel before the priest for a sip of wine. I watched Violet walk carefully up the aisle, holding onto the pews. With child, I thought. Little wonder that she did not fear to lie with me, for the worst had already happened to her. Though my guts churned at the thought of her lying with another man, I felt no disgust that she was carrying a baby. I could see it now, in the pure whiteness of her eyes and the glow of her cheeks, and lost myself for a moment in the memory of her curving belly.

Bastard or no bastard, I thought, with ten bars of Hollandish gold I can buy her freedom. I've no need to care for her beyond that, by God – now let me make my bargain with the quartermaster!

I slipped out of the main door. Quartermaster Baines crunched up and down the pathway, hunched like an angry bull. I closed the door, half-raised my pistol and spoke out.

"Alcott Baines," I said. He paused, his back to me, his shoulders working under his scarlet uniform.

"I pray you, do not take out your weapon," I said.

"Now then," replied Baines, turning so I could see that his hand was away from the butt of his own gun. He lifted his chest, as if he waited for a killing blow, and then breathed out slowly. "Why does a young ferret follow Baines here?"

"To bargain," I replied, resting my pistol on my forearm.

He crossed his arms. "Not contented to trick me once, eh? Had gold off me once already, you have, and best for you that it ends so."

"Alcott," I said in Montalbion's mocking voice, "a most impious assassination has taken place. And now that murderer mocks his victim by taking Communion in his own chapel."

Baines tilted his head gently up at the moonlight, revealing lashless round eyes under his jutting brow.

"Mayhap you think that Baines did not know you saw him kill the old man," he said grimly. "That there is coin for you in this knowledge. Not a penny is there, weaver-brat. If you live, it is because I have chosen not to kill you already. Though Montalbion wishes you dead, that's for sure."

I took a deep breath. I could see he was near-ready to charge me, ready to take a ball to the chest if he needed to.

"I pray that Lord Montalbion rewards you as well as my guild brothers, for you have been bold in his service," I said softly, taking out the crinkled charcoal-rubbing of van Stijn's gold and holding it out to the quartermaster, still with my other hand on the pistol's handle.

Baines slowly stepped towards me and took the paper. I held the pistol closer to my body, so he could not grab at it. He bent over the pamphlet, casting his eyes into deep shadow.

"Do not jest with Baines, ferret," he snarled. "What reward is this? It is but a broadsheet speaking of that bastard Dutch king's virtues. I swear –"

"Turn it over, Mister Baines."

I lowered the pistol slowly to show him I meant no violence. Baines turned the paper so that the rough drawing was uppermost, and pushed his broad fingers into the hollows of the paper where I had traced the outline of the lion. He ran their tips round and round the beast's shape, slitting his eyes.

"Tell me true, lad, or I will break your cursed face on that papist altar. Was it a gold bar you traced this from?"

I bobbed my head, locking a smile away.

"This lion is Netherlandish. How have you come by it?"

I shrugged. "There is a Dutchman who sleeps under Montalbion's roof. There are ten ingots like this in his travelling-bag, to pay the guilds for their part this Friday next. You know what is to happen, do you not?"

Baines wagged a finger at me. "Baines knows all, ferret. Baines will have his reward when the new king comes..."

His voice trailed into nothingness and he gave me a curious look, as if he would have sucked my spirit into the drowning depths of his eye-sockets.

"Reward," he growled. "A pension that I may never taste, and for that I have risked my neck. And a Hollander will hand a fortune to a band of guild-vermin while I must carry a pike to war again, with not a shaving of gold for poor Baines. By God, I will choke him on his own cheese!"

Baines thumped his fist on the dead duke's wall.

"A bargain," I said, looking down at the staghorn whorls that danced across the pistol's handle. Baines snorted. Grey hairs speckled his head and stubbled chin, and the skin of his face had begun to loosen with age. I had not seen it in the darkness of his storeroom, where he had loomed and threatened me like a bull in its prime, but he might have been fifty years of age or more. Younger than Marks, too young to have fought in the old war, but death's lonely shadow was upon him already.

"Ferret knows where the Dutchman may be taken, but has not the belly to do it alone, nor has he trust enough in his friends. Do I have the right of it?"

"It may be," I shrugged.

"And the spy will have a guard or two with him, will he not?"

"Only Garric," I said, not thinking to hide his name, "and I will make good and sure he is not there. The Dutchman will be on his own, though I warn you that he has fought a battle or two in his time."

"Baines will prevail, ferret. Now who is this Garric you speak of? Is it the runt-boy's father, that Frenchy softbelly who has been nosing about the barracks?"

I shrugged. "He is a partner in my enterprise, is all."

"I will believe it. But he should not ask questions about one Captain Marks. That man is the very devil. Once cut out a man's eye for looking at him askance. Well, what is to be my share if I make this compact with you, ragman?"

"Half for you, half for me," I replied, and spat on my palm. I held it out, leaving the pistol at my side. Baines stared at the weapon for a breath, then spat in his hand and shook mine.

"Bargain it is," he growled. "Now where and when shall we meet?"

"On Friday, at eleven o'clock..." I began. He leaned forward eagerly, still gripping my fingers, and I shook my head.

"I will show you the place then. It is not far from the Clerkenwell. Meet me there at eleven. Be neither late nor early."

"Well, lad. It seems you know what you are about. I will not press you further," he said brightly, letting go of my hand so he could stand. "Five gold bars apiece, or a noose apiece, our road is the same now, ferret. Now begone."

"Till Friday," I said, leaving.

Baines raised his eyebrows and grinned as I left. His front teeth were chipped and uneven.

I tapped my pistol's barrel to my forehead in farewell, and left him there. Gold or the noose. But what of Violet?

As I walked down Sutherland Row, fine rain began to fall, plastering my hair down in cool strands. Stone-jawed words marched across my mind. Violet had lied to me. She had plotted to make me her husband, and father of her bastard brat. She had given herself to another before me, and for all I knew she still lay with that soldier. Was it Robbie Cartwright? But why should he have saved my life, and bidden me return to her?

Well, I had time to decide. If on Wednesday I did not want the girl, then I would leave her and her child to the army's care. Violet or no Violet, Martin van Stijn was bringing my life, my freedom, and my fortune to the House of Three Mysteries on Friday morning.

I would return to Mister de Corvis' house. But first I must take up my lodgings at John Hollow's.

CHAPTER THIRTY-FIVE

Trust

In which new alliances are formed

I was soaked by the time I came to John Hollow's. The place was full, with gentlemen standing three deep around the two biggest tables, each one seeking to bargain with the men who were sat down. Papers spilled all over the tables.

"Buy VOC," said an axe-faced gentleman whose tight-curled wig did little to hide his flaky scalp, leaning over a clerk whose spectacles were half-misted with sweat.

"Credit?" asked the clerk, without looking up. The gentleman next to him, leathery of skin, snatched a spoon out of a little china sugar bowl and struck the clerk on the knuckles with it.

"Say, 'What is your credit, Mister Sharples?', do you hear me?"

The clerk cleared his throat and dipped his quill in a pot the shape of a small onion. Writing, he muttered, "What is your credit, Mister Sharples? Since you have already bought a hundred VOC today and lodged no more cash with my master's banker today..."

The knuckle-rapping gentleman hid a smile under his white-flecked beard. I saw how he had used his clerk to hide his distrust of Sharples.

Lottie had seen me, and came to lead me through the thronged room.

"What do they do here?" I whispered.

"The buying and selling of stocks," she muttered back. "It is the safest way to profit from war."

"Lodgings?" I asked Lottie crisply, pretending I did not know her as we went towards her mother's counting-room.

"Fourpence a night," she answered, without looking back at me.

"And for a wide bed?" I said. Lottie put her hand on the door to the passageway and hesitated. No doubt she wondered who might share the bed with me.

"Tenpence," she said in a hard voice, leading me through the passage door.

"Is the bed made of solid gold?" I asked.

"You are not the only jack-of-chance to seek a privy lay-down with his doxy, Master Spinks," she replied. "Eightpence I will give you if my mother agrees. Go ask her now, for I have work to do."

Lottie pressed the heel of her hand to my bruised breastbone to make me give way. The door closed on the tight faces of the stock-sellers in the main room, leaving me in the passageway that ended in a staircase. The only light came from under Mistress John Hollow's counting-room door.

I stood in the dark, listening to the scratch of the leper's quill.

"Come in, pistol-monkey," she called out. "I am not deaf yet."

I obeyed, poking my head through the door with caution. The coffee-woman was huddled up in a woollen shawl, and the single beeswax candle made the elephant god cast a writhing shadow on the chimney breast. Mistress Hollow did not look up from her numbers, but twitched her head to show me I should sit.

"There is wine," she said, and waited for me to pour us each a cup. As I handed her the drink, I saw that she took care not to touch me with her lumpen fingers.

"Health," I saluted her, and drank off half my wine. She sniffed, to show me what a foolish thing it was to say, and sipped at hers. A map was nailed on the other wall, the headless serpent of the Thames crawling crookedly between rows of streets. It was marked with many plague-boil circles, a name scrawled next to each one. I got up and spelled out the letters to myself. Tuh, ah, luh, luh, ih, ss. *Tallis.* Suh, ah, luh, tuh, ah, nuh. *Sultan.*

"These are all coffeehouses," I said, looking at her in surprise. "Why do you have such a map?"

"To save on shoe-leather," she smiled teasingly, pointing at my seat.

"By which you mean that you have been visiting other coffeehouses, several in a day..."

"Much like you," said Mistress Hollow, slurping at her wine. "Though I fancy most men are more afeared of my touch than your weapon."

The pistol's steel barrel pressed uncomfortably into my thigh.

"But why do you tell me this so freely?" I began.

"Did you ever see a woman in a guild?" she interrupted, tugging her fringe over the wrinkle-raw patch on her forehead.

"One or two," I replied, thinking of Abigail and Cassie Barcus.

"*In* a guild?" demanded Mistress Hollow.

I held out my dish for more wine. Since Ty had been taken to the College Secular, I had not had good converse with anyone. It was all, Do this, Sign this, Pistol that.

"Perhaps I should say, *of* their guilds –"

"But without title or right," she finished, pointing as if I were the one who barred the way to women. "Serving, leading, the beating heart that is never seen or given name."

"You have the right of it, I do suppose," I said.

"Indeed I have. And now the coffee-men of London need their own guild. You are not the only brigand with a pistol and a contract-paper to barge your way in here."

I drank my wine, watching her over the dish's edge. She warmed her own wine at the fire, steam wisping upwards.

"Do you mean that you were asked to revoke our contract?" I asked.

She shook her head. "Some hairy villain in a velvet costume came here yesterday. He pretended to be a fellow coffee-man who had signed a fresh contract. And did I know the time and place of delivery, and so on?"

Bear Wharf, I thought. Noon on Friday, less than five days away.

"And did you tell him?"

"You have taken a room from Lottie, I think I heard? Tenpence the night, for how long do you say?" She loved to draw out her story, the dame, to answer a question with another, just like Ty Pettit. I sighed.

"Until Friday at least."

"Which is four shillings and twopence. Three and six, since we are partners in commerce. Master Calumny Spinks."

"Give you a shilling now, the rest when I return," I said, and rubbed my jaw. By Christ, it would not be long before every jabbermouth coffee-man in London knew my true name. "Now tell me how you will form this guild of leper-women."

She showed her teeth as she held out her hand for the shilling. "It is a coffee guild that I am about. And I am glad you have come back here, for we must needs make our bargain before Friday."

"Bargain is made, mistress," I answered softly, laying my hand on the pistol-handle.

"For a handful of sacks, for a few pounds only. But what if I bring two dozen houses with me…" – she waved her scarred fist at the inked map on the wall – "…each one signing for a year?"

"And?"

"And it shall be without exclusivity, which is to say that we may take other supply if we wish. And it shall be at three pounds the sack, not four."

"It is a pretty story, mistress. I will thank you for the keys to my lodgings now," I sniffed, standing. She opened a drawer, clinked through a pile of keys and threw me one.

"Take this list, Master Spinks. You will see names on there who have not yet taken your spice. We will sign as a guild. All or none, and your contract be damned."

I could not help but smile. "Well, I will speak to my master of it."

"Good, so," she replied, and turned to her accounting again. The candle guttered, shadowing her face in a flurry of clutching twilit fingers.

"Mistress John Hollow..."

She grunted.

"Of all the men I have known in London, I think you may be the most alike to me."

"You are not slow to flatter yourself, pistol-monkey. But you have forgotten to ask me something..."

I waited, one hand on the door frame.

"The hairy-faced fellow. I did not tell him of Bear Wharf, for I knew he was no coffee-man. He smelt of lye and wig-powder, and his fingernails were not grimy with the coffee dust. And a velvet costume is not worn in our trade of flame and steam, you see?"

"Well, I thank you for it."

"Tell your master to beware, that is all."

Nodding, I stepped into the unlit passage and felt my way up the staircase, my eyes growing used to the darkness. Three doors led off the landing upstairs, and I used the key to find which was my room.

It was above Mistress Hollow's lair, warmed by the fire that burned in her grate. I opened the small window to allow the moonlight in. The bedclothes were old but clean, and the pallet was thick and freshly stuffed. Next to the bedhead was a stool bearing a stubby tallow candle and three or four sulphur matches. I put my pistol on the stool and lay down.

I will stay here a while, I thought, trying to imagine Violet in that room with me. Where would I take her after

Friday? It seemed so bold and fanciful to believe I could rob a Dutch general, seize a woman from her rightful masters, take a ship to the Indies perhaps… and for what? To raise another man's child. Well, I had made no promise to her. The gold would be enough.

Well, it was better than to pay eighty pounds a year, only for the freedom to sit at a broken loom from Monday to Saturday. I closed my eyes.

Violet lay next to me in the darkness, gently undoing the buttons of my shirt with her leg thrown over mine, venus-warmth pressed to my thigh. Her hair tickled my face as she kissed my neck, finishing with a tiny bite. I felt my way to the laces at her throat, opening up her nightshirt wide enough to slide in my hand, stroking down the side of her neck, her shoulder, around the firm brim of her armpit and then down to her breast, teasing its crest until it swelled beneath my palm. She leaned over to kiss my chest, each press of her lips scalding the tender surface of my bruise. I shifted against her legs, letting the heat build between us, and ran my other hand slowly down her back, feeling each nub of her spine.

Lips pressed against my neck, and she began to stroke, her fingers leaving little trails of fire over my skin, down my arms, around my belly.

"Violet, that burns. Not so hard on my chest, my love, it burns me…"

"Do not call me Violet," whispered the girl who embraced me. "There is no Violet here."

It was Lottie Hollow, her face next to mine, her skin on my skin. I pushed her gently off and rolled to my side so that I could light the candle again.

Lottie leaned on her elbow, her long face and beaky nose given beauty by the softness of the candle-flame behind me.

"Miss Lottie..."

"You are like the rest," she said bitterly. "You will not lie with a leper-woman's girl. There isn't a man in London has the courage to take me."

I asked why she had not left London.

"Where should I go? To the Indies, and break my mother's heart again? To find my father, perhaps, and for that she would never forgive me."

"You are not her husband," I said gently. "It would break her heart for you to stay here till she dies. Did she not tell you to go to the Moor's Head for your own good?"

Lottie nodded, looking at me curiously. She crawled to the end of the bed and sat facing me cross-legged, her head tilted a little to one side.

"Tell me who this Violet is, and why you must rent a room for her. Do you have no home of your own?"

I folded my arms and stared at her. I could not risk speaking of Violet's religion.

"Well then, keep your secrets –" she began.

"Violet carries a bastard," I said quickly. "Another man's child."

"Then you're a fool," she answered, jerking her chin; and without another word, she quit the room.

*

Though the dawn was a long way off when I reached Bear Street, it was chilly, and I knocked loudly at the servants' entrance. There was a long wait before Frazier opened the door, but his eyes were bright and I caught the sweet scent of port wine on his breath.

"Where have you been? The master was waiting for you," he said without rancour, and led me in through the cold kitchen and through the door to the main hall. I followed Frazier upstairs and along the short passage to the master's bedroom door. He knocked softly..

"John?" asked Mister de Corvis as he opened the door from within.

"It is Frazier, sir. With the young fellow."

My patron's eyes did not leave my face as he bid me come inside. Barefoot despite the cold, he wore a soft fur cap and a crow-black satin gown. As Frazier closed the door behind us, Mister de Corvis walked to the window and opened the curtains. Watery moonrays glowed on a white-sheeted bed, no wider than one of Ramage's coffins, marooned in the middle of the floor. The room was bare of wardrobes and night-stands. His clothes hung on a long row of pegs on the far wall, and below them were but two pairs of boots and one of his silver-buckled shoes. There were no candles or lanterns in the room, not even a fireplace.

On the wall at my shoulder was a painting of a woman of around thirty, standing shoeless on the blood-red ground, her long fair hair hanging in loose strands down her back. Behind her a house lurked in a stand of trees, nestling in the foothills of a mountain. She frowned and smiled at the same time, with a sadness that reached inside my belly and twisted it.

I knew it was Emilia's mother. I glanced at Mister de Corvis, but he was no longer watching me. Still at the window, he was turning something weighty over and over in his hands.

"Come here. If you please, Calumny."

If it please me? This was not the de Corvis I knew. I obeyed, trying to see what he held. To spy was in my blood now. A surgeon would have had to cut out my eyes and ears to cure me of it.

He waited for me to join him at the window and gave me a half-rusted ring of iron, near as heavy as a baby's head. It was the manacle that had hung on the back of the Fraziers' bedroom door: mortal cold.

"Why did you risk yourself for Emilia? Why did you come back?" he demanded softly.

"I had not left –" I sputtered.

"She told me," he said, clasping my wrists. "What is it you seek? Do you still hope to marry her, for my fortune?"

So he had known my plan all along. I gave a dry laugh. "I have women enough in my life without your daughter. And you swore you would kill me."

"Then you hope for some reward," he accused, tightening his grip.

"Master, your fortune is but a two thousand guinea hanging-crime," I whispered. "And even if all goes well on Friday, I doubt that you will pay me more than my ten shillings."

"Do not be so bold, Calumny Spinks," he warned me, releasing my hands. The rust on the ring scratched at my palm as I fiddled with it. Silence grew.

Mister de Corvis looked out of his window. It was under Emilia's, overlooking the Fleet, and beyond it the roofs of the plague-streets, Silk Street, Wapping, sheltering all the lonely paupers who loved and fought and died without ever setting foot in a house like this.

"I charge you with another task," he said, the words rasping in his throat like a man dying of the chest-fire. "But first I will show you that you may trust me, more deeply than your own father."

Still I looked out at London – Peter's city of honest work, of guilds and brotherhood.

Mister de Corvis pushed up his cuffs so that I could see the purple scars that circled his wrists. The yellow lantern light slid along the shiny wrinkled cicatrices as he turned his palms over. Then he went and sat on his bed.

His voice crackled and stirred, as though it left his throat against his will. Reaching down, he pulled up his breeches to show the scars that ringed his ankles. These were wider and rougher, as if the skin had been broken over and over again.

"In Jamaica," he said, so quietly I could barely hear him, "a man needs only have a great-grandmother who was an African, to be deemed a negro himself. And I was much darker than this when I was born."

"I did not know that Frederick de Corvis was my father until I was full seven years of age. He had taken my mother for a house-slave, for she was almost white. Then he took his master's rights with her. When she told him I was his son, he denied it blind, and sent her back out into the fields. I was in manacles before I even could walk.

"I tried to run," he murmured, his eyes in shadow. "Once."

I dared not ask him what had happened when he ran. His voice grew harsher.

"My mother died during his third voyage to Ile-de-France, but when he came back he was full of the joys of wealth. He bought himself a house and lands in the Blue Mountains, and took me into his house, and called me Sonny, even sometimes Benjamin. Not 'Boy'. But he kept the manacles upon me, for he said that I was a wild one and could pass for a white man too easily if I escaped. The cuffs were to be my slave-mark. And then one day he told me I was to come with him to Africa. To buy more black-amoors. I should help him to make more men slaves!"

"You met Master Frazier aboard the ship?"

He looked at me sharply.

"I did. Though he had not the kindliness you have seen in him. It was he who wielded the lash and the branding-iron, and his comfort was in drink, not in the company of other men. At first. But I do not wish to speak of the voyage. Time presses."

My master cleared his throat.

"We went to the slave market on Ile-de-France. My father dressed me like a white man, with long sleeves to hide my iron cuffs, my face powdered and my hair cropped short to hide my curls. And I was to choose which slaves we took with us. I had to look in their faces and say, 'Chain this one, Chain him, Chain her.'"

He stood, brushing the scars on his wrists, as I had often seen him do.

Gently, he took the manacle and held it up to the weak moon.

"This was my slave cuff," he whispered. "Frazier struck it off me while my dying father watched. I have never seen him in such a rage, not before or since. He has kept it all these years. Perhaps to remind himself of why he serves such a cold and difficult master."

He smiled sourly to himself, and walked slowly towards the painting of Emilia's mother.

In my master's shuffling shadow I saw the slave Benjamin, the blackamoor bastard boy. I saw how the cuffs rubbed and tore at the scars on his skin, opening them to the stinging air.

As he went by, I squinted, trying to see the true colour of his skin and the shape of his face in the faint moonlight, but he was no different to the first time I saw him, as dark and as light as he ever was. And what difference would it be? Was I not a slave myself, bound to labour for a cruel blackmailing man who would have me killed if I did not pay him to keep my secret?

"It was as well that the crew were afraid of John Frazier," Mister de Corvis said, his back against the wall. "He promised them each a share of the profits when we returned to Jamaica. Even so, he had to kill a pair of mutineers the night of my father's death. But he prevailed, and sold the slaves and the ship at Saint Lucia, far from our home port."

"Why did he..."

I did not finish my question. I did not need to ask my master why John Frazier had saved his life, why he served him still, for his eyes had slid over to the row of boots under his coathooks. A pair of gentlemen's boots of modest size; black, glossy, laced. Two scuffed boots, knee height against the plashing mud of London, made for a man much bigger than Mister de Corvis. And on the bed, two bolsters, each with their own melancholy hollow.

"I could not claim my father's land," he said briskly, avoiding my eye. "Frazier and I found a shack in the mountains and did our best to plant the sickly coffee bush there. Its roots took hold of the dry clayish soil, but it wilted from thirst and from the poverty of the earth. Frazier could not show his face at the docks, and so I left him to tend the bush the way the Frenchman had told me, and signed under a false name to a sugar ship that traded to the Virginia coast and New Amsterdam."

"Martin van Stijn was there," I murmured. My master breathed stiffly through his nostrils, as a brawler will do if his challenger steps away unfought.

"He may have been. But that is not for me to tell."

"The coffee bush?"

"Like a wayward child," he replied. "Many years to grow, and sensitive to the faintest breeze or too much sourness in the soil. I have no God, but still I give thanks that the Frenchman told us the secret of pouring lime upon the soil, and how to split a new shoot from a branch. Let me tell you this: I had learned a good deal of the sugar trade, and saved a healthy portion of my wages, by the time we had half a dozen bushes growing by the shack."

"How did Master Frazier live, all that time?"

Mister de Corvis beckoned me over, showing me the house on Emilia's mother's portrait.

"As foreman to Francesca," he said. "Her father left her a dwindling sugar cane plantation and a rotting home high up in the Blue Mountains, but the income was good. Good enough to keep her, her mother and her sisters alive, and the soil there…"

He trailed off, and then seized me by the shoulders, shaking me as he spoke.

"She was a considerable person then, my wife, do you hear me? Courage she had, and love too, and loyalty. And I warmed her bed because I had affection for her, not for lands or income…"

He let me go, but stayed where he was, our faces close enough for me to see how his cropped hair was dry and wiry, not like an Englishman's at all.

"She died, sir?" I asked, gently.

"Die she did not, divorce her I did not. She is still my wife, still the steward of our plantation, and does say she loves me yet. Though I can scarce credit it, when I have used her so coldly. I am not unknowing of my own actions."

"But Emilia, sir, you brought her here –"

"Laudanum," he whispered harshly. "Francesca caught the yellow fever from a freed slave, not long out of Africa. It cannot be cured, and so to drown the dolours she loses her mind daily. My daughter…"

Laudanum, I thought. Emilia's little flasks, the way the light in her eyes fades and shimmers. He has brought her across the ocean, but he cannot protect her from it.

"Know this, Calumny Spinks: I have always had the shadow of slavery over me. I have not received manumission, and nor can I ever, since my father held my slave-rights. Only true wealth, great wealth, can set me free. It is the law of the world."

The worm of doubt blundered sightlessly through my gut. Why did he tell me such secrets? What price would I pay for this knowledge?

"Calumny Spinks, I make you this promise, that I will have a royal pardon for you and your father. I have given you my life to show I am in earnest. Take my trust."

I clasped his hand.

"But you must keep your side of this bargain," he said.

I let my sigh out as quiet and as slow as I could. I had expected a condition.

"Emilia... Do you understand why she cannot marry?"

"You do not trust other men," I replied, too quickly.

"No, Calumny, it is more than that. Since she is an octoroon... that is to say, an eighth of her blood is African..." He let go of my hand, threw his head back and drew in a shaking breath. On my palm was a scarlet smudge. He had cut himself on the rusty cuff.

"Since she has mixed blood, she is deemed to be a slave unless her deed of enfranchisement is... unless she can be shown to have been freed. And I cannot free her since, in law, I am still a slave myself. Do you see?"

"But can you not buy your freedom, and hers too?"

"I cannot buy my own, Calumny, not without confessing to the murder of my father. And Emilia cannot put herself under another man's protection until... Well, it is very simple, in English society. If you have two hundred pounds and a dark secret, you are a criminal. But if you have twenty thousand pounds and a dark secret, you are the first among equals!"

He forced a sour smile.

"But… Mister de Corvis… all your plans, the coffee and Mister van Stijn, all of it –"

"All of it is to make Emilia safe. Without the security of great wealth, she may be clapped in irons anywhere in the world, as all people of black skin may be."

He looked down at the manacle. I waited for him to speak, but he did not meet my eye. My suspicion grew.

"What is the promise you would have of me, Mister de Corvis?"

"She is all that is mine, wholly mine, do you understand? And it may go ill for me this week, for I have conspired against the king's life, as well as broken the exclusivities."

"But what can I do? I have no coin, no learning –"

"You are a free man, Calumny. A white man. And you will keep your word, I know it."

Oh Jesus. He meant for me to marry Emilia, if he were to fail. Pain flared behind my eyes, as if I had stared too long into the sun.

"Give me your word," he insisted, squeezing my hand. "You owe me your word. And if you do marry her, she and Frazier are the only people in England who know how to find my plantation in Jamaica. It would come to you by right, do you mark it?"

"If the pardon comes on Friday," I told him, my heart missing a beat, "then you have my oath."

For if the pardon comes, I thought, it is because he has succeeded, and so there will be no need for my oath.

"It will come," he answered me. "Now swear."

I knelt before the bed and swore to him that if he could not, then I would protect Emilia, marry her if need be.

Rakers bantered and cursed in the dead silence of the Fleet below.

"Mister de Corvis," I said, still kneeling, "Mistress Hollow wishes to make a bargain with us, to bring a kind of coffee guild to Bear Wharf on Friday…"

He stared at me, his eyes empty. I cleared my throat.

"She says three pounds the sack, not four. I think perhaps three pounds twelve shillings would seal the bargain –"

He held up his hand to silence me.

"Emilia will judge it," he said. "Begone now. You have work to do."

I left him sitting there, one hand resting gently over the manacle, the other covering his eyes.

In those breathless moments, I forgot to tell him that rivals were knocking at coffeehouse doors. And that a wolf-faced man in a velvet uniform had asked questions of Mistress Hollow.

And so we build our own scaffolds, and knot our own nooses.

CHAPTER THIRTY-SIX

Riot and Destruction

In which the tinderbox of London bursts into flame

I walked slowly down the stern staircase. Frazier waited for me, one hand sliding nervously up and down the study's doorframe, his eyes asking if I knew his secret now.

"John Frazier," I said when I reached him, as kindly as I could.

"Calumny Spinks." He tilted his head to thank me for my silence.

Emilia was kneeling before the fireplace, struggling to spark a heap of kindling. Her hair was bound tightly around her head, and smears of coal-dust marked her sandy petticoat. It was the first time I had seen her lift a finger to work.

"Will you not aid me?" she demanded, dropping the flint on the hearthstones.

I did not mock her. I could see a slave girl kneeling there, her blackamoor's skin vivid against white sleeves, so I held my tongue, and went to start the fire.

While we waited for the flames to build, I took out Mistress Hollow's list of coffeehouses and told them of her proposal.

"And you trust this woman?" asked Emilia, squinting.

"What would she have to gain by it?" I replied. "If she does not bring this guild of hers, then she must pay us four pounds the sack."

"Three pounds is too low," said Frazier of a sudden, tapping his knuckles on the desk. Emilia nodded meekly, and I saw that she was used to following Frazier's word. There had never been a servant in this house, and she had never been its mistress. It had all been a mummery-tale, with four players and but one watcher – a country boy who only saw what they wanted him to see.

"She would take three pounds twelve shillings, I am sure of it," I said, helping Emilia to her feet. She looked at Frazier, who held out his hand for Mistress Hollow's list.

"It is well," he said at last. "Seventeen new, three already signed where we must lose eight shillings a sack, and four that we thought lost. And besides, we needed but a dozen more to sell every ounce we have in the attic."

"If she will sign a contract-paper, do you then release me?" I pressed them. "I have not seen my father for more than a week."

"You shall see him at the assembly on the Strand," replied Frazier. "In between times you must stay under our roof."

So be it, I thought. On Wednesday I will steal treasure from the Dutch king's ambassador, then take ship for the Indies.

"Write him a contract for the leper-woman," ordered Frazier, his countryman's tones so gentle that he could have been speaking of newborn lambs, and not of coin or disease.

*

It was daylight by the time Emilia had finished writing the contract-paper. As we waited in the porch for Frazier to harness Cucullan and bring him round the front, she cleared her throat.

"Miss?" I asked, still playing the servant to keep her wildness at bay.

"You think I am weak, Calumny Spinks," she said quietly. She wore a woollen shawl against the November morning chill, and her bare forearms were pocked with goosepimples.

"I know your strength," I replied, "but I think you do not."

"However my father's enterprise goes this Friday," she said calmly, "it will be the last time I answer to him or Frazier. In law I may be my father's property, but he will never force me to it. I shall be free."

I did not tell her the truth – that outside her father's protection, she might be named and shackled as a slave. It was not my secret to tell.

Cucullan's hooves struck the cobbles boldly as the coach rounded the house. Emilia handed me the contract and went inside, without meeting my eyes again.

Now that there was no pretence that Frazier was a servant, I sat and shivered on the driving seat with him. The streets were clotted with farm carts, piled high with roots and beans for the Monday-markets. Lawyers and clerks brushed their cloaks as they squeezed past the slow-trundling wagons, and the farmers chuckled. Merchants were opening their awnings early, and the roadways were filled with scurrying goodwives, their clean white bonnets drifting from side to side like a snow-flurry.

"Forty years without war," muttered Frazier, wrinkling his nose, "and now they do not know if they should hide in their cellars or lift their skirts to the world."

"What do you mean?" I asked.

"I mean that a man who has seen war before knows that it brings but sorrow and pestilence, and that he should take his family as far from the battleground as his coin will allow. But a man who has not, thinks of hoarding his stocks, of barring his gate, and of doubling his prices. All London knows that the Dutch king has boarded his troops, barely a day's sail from here, and every man in the city thinks that he will be the one to escape harm, with a pocketful of gold besides.

"Well, I have fought at sea and I have fought on land, and I would not stay if it were not for Benjamin de Corvis."

"But there will be no war, will there?" I said in a small voice.

"If Montalbion's men are kept to barracks. If the guilds are paid and declare for William. If other lords go over to the Dutch, then there will be no war. If not, then it will be the first time since Christ that men have turned their backs on bloodshed when they have the smell of it in their nostrils."

If the guilds were not paid... Well, it was not my concern. Without that gold, I was a dead man anyway.

Frazier slapped the reins on Cucullan's back, turning his head into the alley behind John Hollow's. It was the longest speech I had heard him make; he'd been almost mute until his secret was shared.

Mistress Hollow herself answered my knock, but did not ask me inside. She had a woollen sailor's coat on over her nightshift. Her eyes glowed with ancient knowing. I showed her the contract-paper, already signed by Emilia in her true name, and the leper-woman had to hold it close to her face to read the tilted scrawl.

"I do not know this name, de Commis," she said at last.

"De Corvis," I said. "Sugar-traders out of Jamaica."

"Mmm. Wait."

She pulled her head back inside and bolted the door, leaving me standing awkwardly on the street to be barged and bumped by half a dozen butcher-boys. They were running against the crowd, quartered calves slung over their rose-stained shoulders.

Wordlessly, Mistress Hollow came back out and gave me the contract-paper, now rolled up, tied with cream ribbon and sealed with a blob of wax.

I slept for most of the day, locked up in the little room. On Tuesday, Frazier took me to the grinding-cave to help him roast the last sacks, and the task was so great that we did not come back out onto the Fleet until long after dark.

I was so tired that I went to bed without eating, but I was awake before dawn. To gain freedom and fortune on Friday, we had to start a riot that Wednesday.

*

It took me a good while to push my way down the Strand to the assembly at Charing Cross. The road was clogged with people. Dull-clothed craftsmen mingled with be-ribboned merchants and their silk-shawled wives, while gaggles of children stared wide-eyed at tousled urchins selling orange bands for a ha'penny each.

Outside the Tallis coffeehouse, I saw Gorton Bouleau and half a dozen men I knew from the night of the cutting-party. There was no sign of Garric or my father, and I cleared my throat to catch the saddler's attention. "Feeney's is not to be touched today. The master has said."

Bouleau grinned and shoved me on my way.

"Make you the cries, make we the blows," he growled, and the others chuckled.

Good, I thought, squeezing through the crowd towards the Charing Cross. Let me be alone.

I scrambled onto Feeney's windowsill to look out over the mob. Near to the old king's statue they had built a platform, royal banners flying from its corners. On one side of the platform a troop of soldiers had lined up, their rifle-butts planted firmly next to their feet. On the other side was a stocks, guarded by a burly man in a sleeveless jerkin. Behind it all, a rich purple tent had been raised on the roadway.

To my right, a Catholic priest stood at a wooden pulpit, waving his hands over the crowd and chanting. Thousands of brightly clothed papists filled the Strand before him.

To my left, the other end of the Strand was sparrow-speckled with the dull brown and black clothes of

Protestants, twice as many as the Catholics. The two crowds were kept apart by a double line of soldiers, running from the Charing Cross to the wall of Saint Martin's churchyard.

Peter stood grim-faced at a brazier with Gorton Bouleau and his saddlers, all of them holding unlit torches. Garric had just left them, and was pushing through the crowd towards the stage.

There was a deep sigh from the waiting mob as Lord Montalbion emerged from the purple tent and climbed to the stage. He'd stripped off his powder and paint; his head was bare, his long dark-brown hair bound tightly back, and he walked tall with a jewelled sword at his belt and a star on a chain around his neck. His bright silver gorget shone in the crisp sunlight. The women in the crowd gave a little gasp to see such a fine general.

They loved a good liar, the potrillos. His lips moved in a quiet command. An officer stepped out from behind the troops on the lower platform. It was Captain Marks. I drew in my breath sharply. I had not expected to see my enemy, and I swore he would not escape me today. I slipped off the sill into the crowd. The Catholics chanted, "King James! God save King James!"

Montalbion held his hand high in the air to quiet the crowd.

"We must have toleration in this kingdom," he said gently. "In my life I have seen Englishmen butcher Englishmen, neighbour fight neighbour, and it cannot be borne."

"*Mmmmbrrmmm*," agreed the crowd, Catholics and right-thinkers alike.

"No Catholic may oppress a Protestant," he said, raising his voice, and the voices to my left cried out, "Aye!"

"Nor may a Protestant conjure others to kill a Catholic," shouted Montalbion. Now it was the popish mob's turn to call out, "Never!"

"For how may our king rule a riotous realm?"

Montalbion spoke as if to himself alone, as if he had never had this thought before, and yet his words carried halfway to the Blackfriars. His words were loyal, but his voice was not. Every man among us heard him say, "This king cannot rule," though he did not speak those words aloud.

Bouleau's men lit their torches.

Montalbion looked out at the crowd again, speaking with sadness now. Behind him, Captain Marks lit a slow match from a tinderbox, his lip curling. In his old eyes I saw a man who would not hesitate to send me to the gallows; whose servant Anthony had corrupted my mother and beaten me half to death. I wrapped my fingers around the pistol and began to push through the crowd towards the stage. One shot, and all our troubles would end.

"And yet there are citizens among you who are guilty of murder and treason. Who have said our Catholic king..."

Garric and Peter knew their parts. Their voices were the first to cry out in protest, raising a roar of fury from the Protestant crowd, and the masses seethed back and forth. The double line of soldiers pushed out in both directions to keep the sides apart. On the platform, the glowing taper was passed along the ranks, each in his turn lighting the match of his rifle. Marks rapped out orders under the noise of the crowd. This was my chance. If the soldiers were to fire a warning shot, then I could fire my own weapon amid the noise and smoke.

Montalbion lifted his hand again. By God, but he was a great play-actor.

"Men have said that our king is a Catholic, and that all true Protestants should rise against him and crush the Catholics in the kingdom."

The devil. He pretended only to have heard those words, but they were his. Now they slithered around the crowd, pouring venom into every man's veins. The Protestants heard that they should rise against the king, and the Catholics that they should be crushed.

"And it is such men who murdered our own Duke of Firth. A Catholic perhaps, but a man of honour, and loyal to the Cath… to the king."

Montalbion folded his hands in front of him and bowed his head. I dodged a blow from a fury-faced Puritan as I wriggled towards the stage, trying to get close enough to shoot at Marks.

"The king demands that preachers of intolerance must be punished!" declared Montalbion. One crowd cheered while the other booed. I saw how clever this lord was, to make discord while preaching peace.

"We have caught one!" he said.

"Caught him!" called the crowd.

"Tried him!" Montalbion opened his arms and shook his hands to whip up the frenzy.

"Tried him!" they yelled. Around me, the Protestant crowd began to stamp its feet and surge towards the soldiers. Their Scots captain called out a command, and his men began to retreat in a huddle towards the platform. Now there was no one between the two crowds. I pressed towards the stage, struggling to free my gun-hand.

"And now we shall flog him!" shouted Montalbion, beckoning a guard to bring a bulging-eyed man to the stocks. It was the Puritan from Montalbion's house, Wilton. He was not ten paces from me, and I knew from his blurred cries that they had cut out his tongue. The guard seized the prisoner and closed him into the stocks. All of the crowd, Catholic and Protestant alike, laughed and jeered, cheering the headsman as he took up a long lash. Montalbion watched icily, his hands in their gold-brocaded gloves locked together behind his back.

The headsman wielded the whip. Wilton screamed silently, and the crowd drew a long, shuddering breath. A woman cried out, a child laughed, but the rest was a shivering silence. Every face was turned towards the platform. Men grimaced, stuck out their tongues, clenched their fists, like wolves smelling blood in the depths of winter.

"Death to the Catholic king!" cried out Garric in the silence before the second blow, his French tones hidden by the hoarseness of his voice.

"Long live King William!" I called out, hiding my face from the platform.

Montalbion stared at the sky, as if he awaited orders from God.

"Kill the popish whores!" came an angry roar from the middle of the Protestant crowd. It was my father, making riot, and his words made a vicious smile crawl across Montalbion's face.

I hesitated for a moment; but if I did not play my part, there'd be no gold, no pardon, and Peter's treason would be revealed.

"Kill the papists!" I yelled, and the right-thinking crowd picked up the chant, moving towards the Catholics in a great ripple.

Montalbion crooked a finger at Marks, who shouted at the soldiers as his commander retreated towards the tent behind the stage. The troop lined up, pointing their guns at the Protestant crowd.

"Kill them!" came the cry again, and the Protestant crowd charged. Most of the Catholics broke and ran away westwards. I tried to raise my weapon and aim at Marks, but it was all I could do to keep from being swept away, for now the riot was a war. The fleeing Catholics had to fight their enemies as they ran. Knives and clubs traded blows, hair was pulled bleeding from its roots, throats were cut and women screamed as they fell under running feet.

On the other side of the Strand, flames burst from Feeney's upper windows, and the sound of breaking glass sang out above the roaring of the crowd. I reached the stage, gripped its edge and looked at Marks. He had gathered half a dozen musketeers together, and was pointing out over the Strand.

"That one," he said. "The Frenchman who breaks the windows. Him."

Garric.

The soldiers passed the word along, drawing themselves into a line. I scrambled my way through the blood-frenzied mob, crying out Garric's name.

Gorton Bouleau was in front of Feeney's. In among the mess and terror of the riot, the saddlers had smashed their way in, dragged the old coffee-man out and beaten him half to death. Bedclothes and papers and chairs were strewn across the street, thrown from the windows above the coffeehouse. Feeney lay broken on the street, puking his lifeblood onto the filthy straw.

"Garric!" I yelled at Bouleau, but the saddlers set off again, towards the Tallis house. Of a sudden, Garric appeared out of the smoke, a dozen paces away from me.

"Calonnie?" he said, sadness in his eyes. Around us the crowd was thinning, one half chasing the Catholics towards the river while the other looted its way down the Strand.

I tried to point at the platform, but it was too late. Marks yelled out a command.

The guns all exploded at once. Another man fell against me so that I dropped to the ground, my ears ringing brutally. Gunsmoke billowed across the Strand, filled with the fleeing crowd, and for a while I could see nothing at all. The other man's body lolled heavily on me, his broken skull leaking gore onto my shoulder. I pushed him off and tried to move towards Garric.

I choked on foul smoke as I shredded my palms, crawling over shattered glass. There were more bodies lying wounded and killed, felled by Marks' attack, but I could not see Garric, nor Bouleau and the saddlers. They must have been in Tallis' house, further up the street, for there I could see more tables flying out of the window, more flames… and then I bumped against a lump in the roadway. A big hand pulled me close.

Garric lay on his front in his own blood, his face turned towards me, gore smearing his teeth. His coat was pierced many times with bloody holes. From the biggest of them, pink foam rose and fell, rose and fell with a terrible sigh.

"*O putain*," groaned Garric, calling Fate the whore that she was.

"Why did you not run?" I whispered in French.

"I told them to run when I saw the guns," he coughed, and this time the pink foam burst between his lips and floated down to settle on the pool of blood by his chin. "But I saw you... and I..."

"But why are you hit so many times, you God-damned fool?"

I was weeping as I lay there next to him. He kept his great paw on the side of my head so he could look in my eyes, and his lips twitched as I cursed at him.

"*Ils m'ont ciblé, les salauds.*" The bastards made me their target. "Because... I have made inquests... the captain, Marks..."

"A surgeon!" I shouted, waving my arm blindly in the air.

"*Trop tard*," coughed Garric. Too late.

I put my hand on the hole in his back, but the foam had sunk deep inside his chest and did not rise again. I could not look at his face. This was not the man who whittled and sang, who teased his wife and filled the room with laughter, who would drive his cart into the middle of a crowd stoning a man to death. Who would risk his life to save two strangers.

The matchlocks roared out again. I hid behind Garric's body as windows shattered, and running rioters fell.

Marks called out a command, and I watched the soldiers leave. They swung their guns over their shoulders and hung their heads heavily as they trudged away into the ringing silence.

All for nothing, I thought. The barracks would be full now, and I would have no chance to save Violet.

The soldiers were followed by Montalbion and his guard, mounted on plumed horses who picked their ironshod way delicately through the carcasses. Crows already sipped at Garric's pooled blood. I chased the birds away and knelt down next to the mercer. I closed his eyes and mouth and laid my jerkin over his head.

I got slowly to my feet, my hands leaving bloody prints on my breeches. I staggered into Feeney's and closed the door behind me. My head swam with the din and horror of the day. All the chairs and tables were smashed, thrown into the corners, but there was a bundle of clothes in the middle of the floor.

I knelt down. The old Irishman had crawled inside to die. Face down, his fingers clutched at the floorboards, as if he could take the whole coffeehouse into the next life with him, and his nightshirt was shredded, showing the lumpy blue veins that scarred his scrawny thighs.

The smoky smell of coffee clogged my throat.

CHAPTER THIRTY-SEVEN

The Dice of Hazard

In which Calumny's world ends

Horseshoes tapped on the roadway outside, their iron rims muffled by scattered straw. I roused myself and went to the smeared window. It was Peter, leading Cucullan by the bridle, the horse carefully high-stepping over the bodies in the street. He comes to bring me home, I thought.

"Cal!" he called out, his voice ringing brassily through the mullioned panes. Peter saw my coat on Garric's carcass, let go of Cucullan's bridle and fell to his knees. He lifted the coat and saw that it was his friend who had died, not me. I wanted to call out to him, but I was silent, shamed that Garric had been killed for discovering that Marks was Anthony's master.

Far behind my father, a cloaked woman picked her way down the Strand towards us, every now and then stooping to touch a fallen man. There were dozens of bodies now, many of them stirring and groaning, but others as still as frost.

Peter thrust his arm in the air, catching the woman's eye. I knew already from the ache in my gut that it was Abigail. As she drew close, dragging her feet, my father pulled himself upright. In the wintry silence, the cries of the wounded scarred the air, and from far off came a few distant shouts from the embers of the riot. I shivered as he went to take Abigail's arm.

Her face was chalk-white, her jaw clenched tight, her eyes raised high. Peter spoke quietly in her ear, warning her of what she would see, his spirit wrapping Abigail's pain. As she fell on her husband, I saw Mirella's face again, dead and pale on its broken neck, full of despair and the desire to leave this vicious world. Abigail screamed noiselessly, clutching handfuls of Garric's clothes, pressing her head against his until her face was bloody and her hair soaked.

At last, she rolled off Garric and went to Peter, striking him again and again. He did not resist her, but let her beat him until she had had enough. It was only when Cucullan bent his head to nuzzle at Abigail's bloody hair that she wept at last, great raw sobs that twisted in my guts like a butcher's blade.

Peter reached out to Abigail and drew her close, pressing her face to his neck. Now my father wept for all he had lost: his mother burned alive in the plague-pit, my young uncle choked in the hold by the French soldiers, his wife lying naked in the sheep pond, and his one true friend shot like a beast in the street. I hoped he thought me dead too. For soon enough I would be.

As his face grew blotchy with tears, I felt the weight of all my debts and sins lifting off me. Forget gold, forget title. I'd kill Marks for Peter. Die tradeless.

"We must take him away," said Peter at last.

Abigail held her breath, nodded.

"It was bravely done."

Abigail gave him a wild look, as if she would rise to her feet and stab him, but the wildness faded soon enough and she bobbed her head. She knew what he meant, that Garric's heart was brave and true, and that he had chosen to live and die the way he did.

Peter draped Garric's arm around his shoulder, and lifted him awkwardly until only his legs dragged on the gore-soaked ground. I had not known him to be so strong. Abigail herself had to help my father to lift Garric's body onto Cucullan's back, his quick whittler's hands hanging down below the stirrups.

My father, limping now from the effort of lifting the dead man's bulk, turned Cucullan's head and led him homewards. I pressed my face to the smoke-streaked windows and watched them leave.

Then I waited for the hours to slip away into dusk, watching the scavengers scurry from body to body, pulling off rings, cutting locks of hair for wigs, grubbing in the filth for fallen coins.

Captain Marks would die that night.

I stepped out into the twilit street, took the pistol from my waistband and held it openly before me as I walked towards the Hyde woods. The scavenge-rats shied away from my wild red hair and crimson-stained face.

I should have shot Marks before he killed Garric.

The city was fevered. Watchmen tended fires on every street corner, talking bold, as if they had fought bravely in the riot. Men and women alike stood outside their houses and their shops, gossiping, grave-jawed, of war and revolution. The gutters ran fist-deep with piss, for the taverns were making good custom that night. Every alley I passed was loud with rutting couples. Everyone who had lived through the riot and fighting wanted to fill their empty souls with booze and the hot feel of flesh.

A band of sharply dressed pobjoys stood at the corner of Whitehall Palace, clucking and whistling at women. They beat their orange-sashed chests and swigged from little leather flasks, singing "God save King William!" at the Watchmen.

The *raprap* of marching feet echoed up from the Whitehall Wharf. Swords drawn, a troop of soldiers in Firth's colours was marching back to barracks. The pobjoys turned and ran, throwing off their orange bands.

I darted into the Hyde woods ahead of the troop, hiding behind the first row of night-bark trees. As the soldiers passed me, a dozen or more, I saw that their faces were pinched with weariness and fear. I followed them as closely as I could, keeping off the path and going from tree to tree.

"The palace was empty, did you see?" asked an Englishman.

"The King has left London by barge," said another, a Scot. "Saw the ensign on it. Didnae take well to bloodshed at his doorstep."

"Are we to fight the Dutchmen or no?" asked the English soldier.

"For sure we are," growled a dwarfish fellow whose scabbard scraped on the ground every second step. "On Friday morning we are to ship to the Tower. I heard Baines give the order for the boats. No doubt it is to greet the cheese-men with cannon and powder."

The men around him laughed, seeking bravery from each other.

The first soldier turned towards the others and spoke again. Straight blond hair capped his face, and he carried a little frown on his forehead like a tattoo.

"But if forty thousand Dutchmen sail for Devonshire, why then does the quartermaster send the powder and shot to the docks? Should we sail to fight them on the sea? How can we when we must guard the city?"

The dwarf lowered his voice, pressing a stubby finger into the corner of his eye.

"Montalbion knows his business."

"Well, it was a bloody business that he was about today. I have never seen the like, not since I took the king's shilling." The fair-haired soldier's frown sank deeper into his blemished skin. Rain began to fall, plump drops that wept with secrets.

When they reached the bridge over the Tyburn, I had to hold back. I could not cross it until they were out of sight. I ran down the gravelled road, hoping to follow the troop into the barracks, but the main gate was already closing by the time I reached it.

For a breath I thought I might make mimicry of Baines or Marks, trick my way somehow into the barracks. But I'd had enough of my gift. Mimicry had got me into the service of Mister de Corvis, and it was there that Garric had died. It had served me in the house of Lord Montalbion, but that had made me doubly a traitor, and murder-complice besides. No, I would live and die by my wits and strength alone, however feeble they might be.

I tucked my pistol away and looked up at the wall, blinking away the raindrops. It was too high to scale.

Well, I thought, shivering, I must be patient. Once I've fired this ball, I'll be put in the clay soon enough. No need to hasten the moment.

From the barracks came the faint sounds of men boasting and arguing, their hoarse voices softened by the rain. The air hummed with fear and excitement. Now that shots had been fired, and men killed, unarmed though they were, the battle had begun. I leaned wearily against a tree, sheltering from the rain as best I could under its leafless boughs, and thought of my father, hiding himself in Salstead. Leaving war behind.

After an hour or more, the gate opened wide again. Another small troop of soldiers, dun travelling-cloaks draped over their uniforms, marched reluctantly into the teeming air, their guns' lit matchlocks bobbing like fire-flies in the dark. The door guard had to come out onto the path to pull the gate in again, and I dashed through the gap while his back was turned, hiding myself in the shadowed doorway of the first barrack-house.

The guard bolted the gate and climbed up a flight of stone steps to the parapet. I glanced around. There was no light from the gloomy buildings that flanked the path.

I waited for the guard to begin patrolling the wall and ran further into the barracks, glancing over my shoulder to make sure he had not turned around on the parapet. Coming round a corner, I saw the back of the quartermaster's blockhouse rising up into the teeming air. Leaning against it was the soldiers' tavern, light dribbling under its back door.

Taking out my pistol, I twitched open the door a smidge at a time, until I was sure I could not be seen from inside.

I was screened from the room by a long coloured cloth. Oil-light filled the tavern, shining on the silk curtain. It meant that I could see what was on the other side, but no one could see me in the dark entryway.

Five men sat at a big table, playing with a pair of bone dice. Quartermaster Baines was at the head of the table, side on, while Captain Marks was to his left, facing me. I took out my pistol. Now was my chance. I was well hid, and with good fortune I might escape from there. And if I did not, why then I had little enough to lose now.

With one shot I would rid myself of the debt, and Peter's secret would die with Marks. I held the pistol up to my shoulder, cramped awkwardly in the narrow gap between the flag and the door, but a slovenly lieutenant sat down between me and my enemy, blocking my shot.

I let go my breath, quietly. All around the table, men were gathered in little groups, their eyes bright and their faces flushed, leaning in towards the game with their hands clamped around their tankards of ale.

A man who'd been standing in the shadows made his way to the door. It was Robbie Cartwright, still hooded despite the warmth of the room.

No man spoke out loud of the riot, the shooting, but the low chatter, of women and prizefights and shooting-practice, was rough with pride and violence.

The slovenly officer to Baines' right shrugged heavily. He scratched at the red patches on his neck before he spoke.

"I will bet my eighteen-shillings credit, Baines, and may God forgive me if I do not get my stake back, for I had promised it to my wife."

"Comrade before woman," said Baines briskly, and his words sent frost down my spine. Those were my father's words, said in the same sharp way, as if he had learned them at Peter's own feet.

Robbie opened the far door a crack.

"There goes *Mister Fintry*," called out the quartermaster. Cartwright paused, shook his head, and chuckled as he left.

It could not be. I stepped back, slipped through the door, and darted around the corner. Narrowing my eyes in the heavy rain, I watched Robbie stride across the courtyard, still shaking his head as he scaled the ladder to the Fintrys' hatchway.

Did Robbie warm Mistress Fintry's bed now? I hoped that was Baines' meaning, but dread pressed its gnarly fingertips on my windpipe. I needed to see for myself – I would have to wait for the quartermaster to be alone before I dealt with him. I turned and looked up at where the tavern roof leaned against the blockhouse, and began to climb. It was not so hard, for the joiners had left the ends of the beams sticking out of the plaster, though I had to clamp my fingers hard against the slippery rainwater.

Once I had gained the tavern roof, I squatted carefully on the shingles and looked across at the Fintrys' workshop, the nearest window but a couple of yards from me. Mistress Fintry was sat on her bed alone, brushing out her hair. But where was Robbie Cartwright? If he had not come to tup Mistress Fintry, what was his business?

And then I saw the other rope ladder swinging away beneath the closed hatch at the near end of the room. The way to Violet's room.

My legs trembled with the effort of crouching in the wet, but I trod lightly across the roof-ridge and reached up to the storehouse's parapet. It was made from rough-hewn stones, easy to cling to as I scrambled over and onto the flat roof. At the far corner was a covered stair-head, leading down to my enemy's storeroom, but I had no eyes for it, instead turning around wildly to see my fears come true.

Violet's garret window glowed in the darkness. Her candlelit room swirled and melted with the shape of the rivulets trickling down the window, blurring her features.

Robbie Cartwright, kneeling behind my seamstress-girl on the bed, was talking as he brushed her hair in long slow strokes. Violet tilted her head to one side to listen, though I could hear nothing above the beating of the rain on the slates. She wore only a nightshirt, wide open at the neck so that her shoulders were almost uncovered. The shirt-sleeved soldier's naked blade lay on the bed next to him. She smiled softly. Had she ever smiled at me in such a way?

I had seen Cartwright cheat those officers, not bravely, but whispering in the corners of the room. Taking bets from the ordinary soldiers who might be lashed for their part in the trickery. I wished I had shot the bastard, for sure I would never get close enough with a blade to stop him touching my Violet.

Bolder now, he ran his fingers down the sides of her neck. Violet leaned her head to one side to let him caress her. He broke off for a moment to undo the buttons of his shirt, letting it fall open to his hairless belly. She leaned back against him, letting Robbie kiss her hair, drop his hands slowly down her front.

I would not let this be. I raised the pistol, aiming along its top at Violet's throat. The ball would pierce them both.

As I stared along the barrel, Violet turned and reached behind Robbie to untie his long hair, letting it fall over his shoulders. She pulled apart his shirt, tracing the bruises and cuts of the riot. He shrugged off his shirt, and I gasped. His body was narrow, smooth, and through the swirling rain I saw his swollen breasts, the raised pink nipples as he arched his back.

"A woman..." I whispered.

Violet turned, red-eyed, and pressed her lips to Robbie's chest. Robbie raised her head and kissed her softly on the lips, as they ran their hands through each other's hair. The soldier-woman's hand crept further down my lover's belly, tugging her nightshift upwards, settling her hand in the cleft of her venus. Violet clamped Robbie's wrist, but I knew that it was not the first time they had touched.

Now the girl was the leader, pressing her lips to the older woman's. Laying her fingers over Robbie's to guide them, she lifted up her own nightshirt until she was naked, her child-full belly sitting tenderly in the rain-light as I watched the man-woman's fingers pressing tenderly in that place where I had found my joy.

Violet's cries rose above the lashing of the rain as Robbie laid her gently down, trapping her hand between her thighs as the other girl's hands ran freely over her back and hips. Now Violet reached for Robbie's breeches, fumbling with the drawstring at the waist, and I gasped to see the puffy cloud of the soldier-woman's venus, thrusting and yearning for Violet's touch. Both naked, they pressed their chests together, mouths locking, fingers trapped greedily in each other's secret places.

Alcott Baines chuckled from behind me.

"Move thy bones, lad, there's plenty enough to see for both of us."

Hiding my shock, I kept my back to the quartermaster until I could draw my coat around my pistol. As I turned, his mocking smile faded as he saw that it was me.

"What do you do here?" he demanded. "Curfew breach is a bad business in this regiment. Friday we said. The Clerkenwell."

"True," I said, "half you and half me. But I must tell you more."

Baines looked over my shoulder at the sight of Violet and her woman-lover, their bodies locked in the night-dance, and sighed.

"There's always good sport when Robbie Cartwright climbs to that attic... But coin before cunny," he chuckled, bundling me towards the covered stair-head.

I stumbled and slipped down the dark spiralling steps. A lantern lit a patch of floor at the bottom of the staircase, and Baines told me to take it into the storeroom.

Leaving me next to the counter, he shook himself like a dog, muddy water flying from his rough whiskers. He walked puffing around the great room, lighting the lanterns and counting off the stores under his breath, as if he were afraid that some of them had got up and escaped him while he had been playing the dice next door.

"That Miss Fintry, eh?"

He winked at me like we were two old lechers in a tavern. I saw now how well he'd played his part at Firth's chapel, when he must have thought I had come to kill him. I did not answer, but touched the pistol's handle. Dare I fire on him? Was the powder wet in my pistol? And would a single ball be enough to drop this beast?

"She is a fine piece, to be sure."

He licked the corners of his mouth, watching me slyly from under his black caterpillar brows. I cursed my pale skin and blushing freckles.

"I would tup her myself, but for that young Robbie Cartwright. It's a good wench, that one..." He sighed and made a pious face, then roared with laughter. "Let her have her delights, for all the throats she's cut for me!"

Still I kept my peace. Baines spoke into his chest.

"And I would not risk my life against Robbie's blade. She is as strong as a viper, as young Violet knows full well."

Blushing with rage now, I walked widdershins round the room, keeping the counter always between us. I freed my pistol from the waistband.

"I'll give you my news and be on my way then, Master Baines," I said quietly, with a faint echo of Firth's dry voice.

"Brave words you squeak, young ferret. But why should I let you out when you have broken curfew, eh?"

I backed away towards the door as he bore down on me. I snatched out my pistol and pointed it at his head, and he stopped in his tracks, steam rising from his balding crown. With my other hand, I tugged the door-bolt open. Baines stared at me, hate in his eyes.

"Garric," I said, and pulled the trigger. The firing-wheel clicked wetly, but there was no explosion.

Baines roared and threw himself at me, seized the barrel of the pistol and wrenched it away from me.

"I thank thee for the weapon, but not the manner of its giving," he said grimly, and struck me hard on the collar-bone, making me fall against the door. His iron hands were around my throat before I could wriggle away.

I have not had half a life, I thought. I have had no life at all, and now it is gone.

But Baines did not kill me. He lifted me up against the door, pinning my legs with his great bulk. His furry arm was pressed against my neck so that my breath wheezed in and out, and the sparkling stars flew across my sight.

"Be still, or I will send thee to Hell," he growled, his accent thickening.

"Then kill me now," I choked.

"You are Calumny Spinks," he answered, in a voice like a coffin lid closing.

"I will... I will..."

"You are Calumny Spinks, spawned by Peter Cole, the greatest traitor in England. And if I say a word to any man in London, you and he will both hang."

"I..."

"I have known you since before you were whelped. Always, every breath of your life has been mine to give or take, do you hear me?"

He stood back a pace, letting me go. I slumped against the door, my hands hanging uselessly at my sides. He threw my pistol into a corner.

"So let that be the last time you take arms against Alcott Baines. If Baines dies, you die. Did you think I'd keep your secret alone?"

"But who would–"

"Who else would know? Can you not think of such a one? Why, she has had to risk her life to save yours, for I would not lose your eighty pounds a year so easy. Even had to kill Anthony, the poor lad."

"Robbie," I said quietly, the gallows trap opening under my feet. So it had been Baines who had ordered him to follow me, not Violet at all. Well, it was but a small deceit of hers, for I had seen a greater betrayal that night.

"Robbie Cartwright. Kill me if you will, and then you'll find out if she will tell or no."

Baines went behind the counter and pulled a ledger off a shelf. From the gap behind it he pulled out a squat baked-earth bottle and a pair of little glass goblets.

"All is not lost, young ferret."

He poured out a milky grey fluid, one swallow for each of us.

"Drink," he commanded, pushing my drink towards me.

I took it with my left hand and sniffed it while he threw his down.

"It is no poison, ferret. Your life means gold to me, every year of mine. So drink."

I drank, choking on the strong spirits, but Baines did not laugh.

"You should not have sent the Frenchy after Anthony and Marks, ferret – besides, Marks knows nothing of your father. I would have kept our bargain for the Dutchman's gold."

"Would you, now?"

I laughed bitterly as Baines poured out a second glass for me.

"Aye, though old Peter Spinks would owe me yet."

"All this," I marvelled, "for eighty pounds a year? And still, when you have the Dutchman's gold –"

I broke off.

"Your father owes me a life," hissed Baines. "I was there. My father, Isaac Porter, and Peter Cole, as they called him then. They stood under the gallows in their black masks and talked of who should kill the king, while I hid behind a stanchion. I was only a lad of twelve, but already had I killed three men for Cromwell. Cutting throats in the night, see?"

He reached again into the place he had taken the bottle from, and pulled out a scrap of black silk, the twin of Peter's mask.

"We had all fought long enough to want the king dead. But my father was afraid. And Peter Cole, bastard that he was, ordered Isaac to be part of it, to lead the king to the block. He said that men could never become angels if they let other men between them and God."

My skin crawled to hear it. My father had said those words to me often.

"Well, my father played his part, all right."

Baines spread the mask out on the counter so that I could see the Dee Em Ee in its faded gold. His eyes were red, his bull chin trembling.

"Isaac lived his last days in terror, the coward. Drinking and gambling his wages away until your father had him whipped and drummed out of the regiment. Hanged himself when Cromwell died, and I had to watch my mother become a whore to a every chancer with a smile and a story to tell. But I still took her name of Baines. Better a whore's son than a coward's. All because of Peter Christ-cursed Cole."

"Our bargain," I whispered, backing towards the door. Baines dug in his pockets, took out a key and threw it to me.

"Bargain has changed, ferret. All for me, none for you, and I will let thee live. But your father's full eighty pounds is now due on Friday. Let him come to the Clerkenwell too, at eleven. Get you gone. Whores' gate is thy path."

I fled into the sticky mud of the yard. Baines laughed and slammed the iron-bound doors behind me as I stood there, rain pouring down my neck and onto my shivering skin.

I was the traitor. Not Peter, not Baines. Calumny Spinks, coward and traitor.

A stable door banged, and I jerked my head around. The Master of the Horse was stood before his stalls, his hair plastered thinly over his scalp. He stared at me wordlessly, looked up at Violet's garret window, and then at me again. Shaking his head, he went back inside.

Voices came from the soldiers' tavern. Fearing to be caught and beaten for curfew-break, I ran clumsily across the yard for the whores' gate and struggled with the key until I had wrenched the gate open.

I threw myself into the woods, tripping over the bracken. The moon was hidden above the knotted black clouds, and I could not see my way. At last I came to a long clearing, but I had hardly taken two steps inside it before I was sliding down the steep bank of the Tyburn, scrabbling at the slippery mud for a handhold.

It was too late to catch myself, and I fell feet-first into the icy water, which swept me along in its swollen current. Again and again it covered my face, and each time I came up to gulp for breath, it took me under again. I could barely move my toes and fingers as icy shards of pain plunged through my flesh.

Once more I struggled above the surface, seeing that I was almost at the Tyburn-mouth, where the waters clashed whitely with the great river. Far downstream was a cluster of barges. I tried to yell for help but choked in the swirling current.

I knew full well what happened to a man alone in the Thames. Its current was so strong that it would wash you halfway to the sea, leaving your body on a stinking mudflat for crows to pick at in the morning.

I quit my struggles, closed my eyes, and the water covered me over in perfect darkness.

CHAPTER THIRTY-EIGHT

The Glorious Revolution

In which Calumny finds life after death to be little different to what went before

"Empty his pockets," murmured a singsong voice, deep in my death-sleep.

I have died and gone to the wrong heaven, I thought. I am among Wapping thieves, not with right-thinking Christians.

I opened one of my dead eyes. It seemed I had brought the chill Tyburn to the next world with me, for I was borne down by the weight of soaking clothes, and my throat was raw from retching. A ghoul stared at me, its oily hair as curly as a gypsy's.

"Leave it," he said, spittle flicking from the gaps in his crooked white teeth. His tawny eyes crinkled.

I shivered like an ash in a January gale. Sunrise reddened the gypsy's teary eyes as he pressed a blanket over me. From its weight on my sodden shirt I knew that I was not in any kind of heaven. I was still alive, aching and burdened with memory and debt. My belly grumbled hotly until I puked out the melancholic Tyburn waters. Too weak to move my head, I choked on bile until the heathen lifted me onto my side. I was lying in the stinking Thames mud, with rough stones for a pillow.

"That's two shillings you owe me," said the gypsy, pressing his knuckles in my back as I retched. "One for your life, and one for risking my own to drag you out."

Behind me, another man chuckled.

I spat and tried to lift my head, but I lacked the strength. "Give you three," I said, "if you take me to John Hollow's coffee-house."

"Take the three shillings and throw him back in," said the second man from behind me.

I forced a little bold laugh.

"The money's at my lodgings," I lied, "and I'll forget your unkind words this once."

I closed my eyes as shivers wracked my body.

"Damn it," said the first gypsy, "if he dies of cold there's no coin at all for me. Grab his legs."

He put his hands under my armpits and lifted me up. The other fellow took my legs. Trembling, pain gripping my scalp, I squeezed the light from my eyes.

I woke in a bed. It was mercifully dry and warm. Dim daylight struggled through closed shutters, making a shadow of the woman who wiped the hot dream-sweat off my face.

"Hush," she said, putting a hand behind my head to lift it. "You have a fever. Drink this."

I sipped at a cup of water, spilling it on the sheets. It was Lottie Hollow whose fingertips gently stroked the damp hair at the back of my head. Hot, I tried to throw off the sheet and blankets.

"You must sweat," she said, holding me down. "We must burn the demon out. Rest now."

"Jesus, but I am too hot –"

"Sssshhh. We must send for your family. Where is your mother?"

"In the ground."

"Your father, then?"

Through the window came shouts, the rumbling of wagons.

"What is that noise outside?" I demanded feebly.

"They say that the Dutch king has landed forty thousand troops in England, and that there will be war, though not a soldier have I seen. It is always like this in London; the men are as light-headed as little girls. Now sleep."

I lay still as she washed my temples.

"There is a good deal of custom today," she murmured as I closed my eyes. "My mother will see to you."

Horrid visions seized me, of burning and hanging and the torments of the damned. Red-haired devils led my mother Mirella towards the burning cave, and she looked back at me with eyes as wide and terrible as the sea. And then I was screaming until the door burst open.

"Well, pistol-monkey, you have a curious way about you," said Mistress Hollow in a sweet voice. "At first you threaten me if I do not sign. And then when I sign, you arrive sickly, borne by a gypsy who demands three shillings of me. I think perhaps you are a madman."

She wrapped her lumpy leper-hands carefully in a clean cloth from the washstand, sat against the bedpost and lifted my head into her lap. Then she sang me children's rhymes until I had fallen deep into the dreamless place.

It was still morning when I woke again, the blue-white day pressing at the shutters. A woman leaned over me, hair falling over her face.

My fever had broken. I was naked but dry under the sheets. Thoughts swam freely in the clear waters of my mind. Baines. My father. Violet –

"Lottie..." I began, thinking to ask her for my clothes.

"Knowst me not?" demanded Robbie Cartwright, her harsh northern tones like fist-blows. I bucked under the sheets, trying to shake her off, but I was swaddled up tightly. Robbie took her dagger from where it lay on the washstand and held its tip to my throat.

"Whore!" I cursed her.

"Call us whore?" she demanded. "And that Lottie, what is she to thee? Art whoremaster thyself."

"Satan will take you," I said viciously. "I saw you! I saw it..."

Shameful tears pricked my eyes. Robbie lifted the blade from my neck and went to throw open the shutters so I could see her clearly. I tore the sheets away from my arms and chest, keeping my nakedness hidden.

The she-soldier's lank black hair hid the manly corners of her jaw, framing her long lashes and little snub nose. She wore her scarlet-and-white uniform under a travelling-cloak. My clothes lay on a chest of drawers behind her. I marvelled that Mistress Hollow could have washed and dried them in half a morning.

"Thought to steal our Violet from us, did a?" she asked, pointing the knife.

"She is no man's to steal," I said sourly, "and no woman's neither."

Robbie put the weapon back in her sleeve.

"Why did a come to barracks? What compact hast with Baines?"

"To kill him," I replied defiantly, offering her my neck. "Now strike, Cartwright. Do your master's bidding."

She knelt at the bedside, her fingers resting lightly on my throat.

"Why did a want Violet? With another's babe in belly?"

I looked out at the cloudless sky.

"Was love?" she asked quietly, letting go of my throat. I closed my eyes and waited for the blade to fall.

Breath on my cheeks, lips grazing my eyelashes, hair tickling my forehead.

"Cal..." whispered Violet.

I kept my eyes closed. This was but another fever-dream.

"Cal, I know you came for me," she said, kissing my nose. Robbie coughed.

"I saw you," I said coldly. I did not deny that I'd come for Violet.

"Thought thou was dead in riot, did this lass," said Robbie, kicking the foot of the bed.

"But was it the first time... the first time between you...?"

Violet twitched her head to tell me that it was not, and then laid her face on my chest. I put my arms around her weakly, feeling her heart jerk without rhythm.

"Woman and woman are made to love, is all," said Robbie gruffly, laying her cloak on top of my clothes. "Born to it us was, and right it is for me, see?"

"You are married?" I asked, running my hand down Violet's hair.

"Was," replied Robbie, looking away with a twisted smile as she tied her hair back up. "But king's shilling is a prettier wage than husband's groats."

Pulling up her kerchief, she became a man again, her chest out, her jaw tight. She untied one of the two swords at her belt, putting it down on top of the cloak.

"You have broken the curfew," I said in amazement. "Were you not charged with guarding Violet? They will beat you for this."

"Have no officer to command us, see? Only Alcott Baines. And Baines left camp without word this morning. As long as us gets to Tower Wharf by eleven, can join regiment without quartermaster knowing."

"But he is your master –"

"Master have us none," she spat, sinking her fingers into the wormy windowsill. "That Baines kept our secret long, but a used us sorely for it. Be damned to him."

"Did he not tell you to follow me, to kill Anthony –?"

Robbie laughed without joy and shook her head. Her eyes crinkled, showing the weariness of long years hiding her true self. I saw that she was perhaps over thirty years of age, though as a man she had seemed younger.

"I did so," said Violet, lifting herself up, her eyes catching the sunlight. Breeze from the open window raised goosebumps on my chest, and Robbie tossed my clothes over, giving Violet a glinting look.

"Sword is for thee, weaver," said Robbie. "Violet will not stay with regiment, and so art charged with her safekeep. And baby's. Else a will answer to Robbie Cartwright."

"Cannot you –" I began, regretting that I had ever told Violet about John Hollow's.

"Must be at Tower by eleven latest," she cut me off. "Promise to keep, thou does."

"But the Tower," I protested, confused, "the regiment should not sail there until Friday –"

"It *is* Friday morning," Violet said, getting up off the bed and going to open the door. "Mistress!" she called.

"No need to cry out," replied Mistress John Hollow, who was earwigging on the landing.

"What o'clock?" demanded Robbie.

"A quarter of eleven... sir," said the leper, peering curiously.

"Quarter of an hour to reach Tower Wharf," hissed the soldier-woman. Ignoring Mistress Hollow's stare, she went to Violet and kissed her full on the lips.

"Will keep an eye for thee, Violet Fintry," she said firmly. Striding for the door, she pointed at me. "Keep her safe, lad!"

She pulled Mistress Hollow out with her, and closed the door behind them. I got out of bed and began to dress. Baines would be at the Clerkenwell by eleven – if I did not stop him, he'd take the guilds' gold. The blockades would be abandoned, and the Dutch would bring war to the streets of London.

"Violet, I must go. Stay you here –"

"No!" she protested, seizing my breeches before I could put them on. "No more going away. No more war –"

I snatched at the breeches, and then she was upon me, grappling me to the bed, trying to crush my arms to my sides, but I was too strong for her. I pushed her on her back and held her wrists down, trying to keep my weight from her pregnant belly as she wriggled under me, tears of fury in her eyes.

"Why do you fight me?" I demanded.

"Why must you go?" she shot back. "I have given up my mother for your promise, and my only true friend besides –"

"Friend!" I choked, letting her hands go so that I could pluck at her dress. "Friend, that you lay with, like a hell-bound forengie…"

She brushed away my hands. Her stare withered me, as if she had seen into my little treacherous soul.

"Better to share a kiss with a trusted friend, than lie with whore or whoremaster," she said. "There is nor hell nor harm in love between women. Or should I have given myself to every man in the regiment, as my mother does?"

There was no time. "Stay!" I commanded, taking up the sword. I left her there and stumbled downstairs. Mistress Hollow's door was open. She was packing a small sack with a purse and some papers.

"Bear Wharf at noon, Master Spinks!" she called out as I went past.

Bear Wharf at noon, I thought. First, I must fight a demon who bested me but a day since.

*

I ran through a thin stream of Catholics in their bright colours, Irishmen and forengies, all trying to make their way to the protection of the Tower. I heard fearful talk of the Protestant army that was said to have landed in the west, and of the king's flight from London.

Merchants stood before their shops, wearing their guild-badges proudly on their breasts, waiting for the Dutch army. As the Holborn churches chimed the eleventh hour, a tailor shouted that Montalbion's regiment were rowing downriver for safety.

Just before the Fleet Bridge, the crowd turned left, making their way to the wharves upstream. As I ran over the stinking river, I saw frowning boatmen pole downriver, packed in close with Catholic families clutching at bundles of clothes, spinning wheels and cookpots. Their heads were bowed, but the small children did not cry out despite their parents' fear. This was not the first time they had fled like this.

A mob of orange-sashed men were marching up the other side of the Fleet. I had to pass the Clerkenwell before they reached it.

From the crest of the Fleet Bridge, I could see two men heading up the alley towards the House of Three Mysteries. Van Stijn's cropped white hair glared, a fiery mirror to the sun, and I could not make out who the other fellow was. Well, I could forget larceny at least: I'd not be fighting two men.

I glanced down Bear Street towards Mister de Corvis' house. He stood at the top of his steps, a tiny figure dwarfed by his house's long shadow. Emilia came out on the steps behind him, her arms folded. There was no sign of Frazier, who should already have been at Bear Wharf, stacking the coffee sacks. Mister de Corvis spoke to his daughter, and she followed him meekly down the stairs, turning left towards his treasure and her freedom.

I reached the eastern bank. Not thirty paces away, just beyond the Clerkenwell itself, was Alcott Baines in his scarlet uniform. He was following van Stijn and the other man, sword drawn.

Before I could give chase, Violet cried my name from the bridge behind me. Shiny beads of sweat nestled among the baby-curls on her temples. She had followed me.

Though I had but moments to stop Baines, I ran back for Violet, letting the scabbard bump on my legs. The mob of orange-men, barely two hundred paces away, had seen us. Their leader called out a challenge, and without thinking, Violet crossed herself. Roaring in fury at her popery, they charged.

To slow down the mob, the Catholics threw pots and brooms from their boats. Some of the orange-men threw knives and stones at the boats, and the air was soon full of shouts and screams. One of our pursuers stumbled over a cookpot and fell into the Fleet. As he bobbed about in the water, a pair of Irishmen leaned out of their boats and brained him with their poles.

Violet clutched her belly as we ran, her arm around me. Our only hope now was to cry sanctuary in the church of Saint James beyond it, but I did not believe Violet could get there if I did not turn and fight. Feeling danger at my shoulder, I pushed her onwards, pointing to the church, and turned swiftly.

One of the orange-men had run ahead of his fellows to catch us. He was one of Bouleau's saddlers, a rough bush-headed villain with bulging forearms and tiny vicious eyes. I wedged my back foot against the well-head and slashed at the air to keep him at bay. He struck at my blade with his club, and it was all I could do to keep hold of its pommel. I kept it high, waiting for him to strike again, but he waited patiently for the rest of the band to catch him. Violet had stayed at my side, arming herself with two loose cobblestones.

Soon, we were surrounded by the orange-men. They did not attack but parted to allow their leader through. It was the child-killer Gorton Bouleau, hollow eyes burning in his gaunt face.

"*Bestiole,*" he spat, pointing at the bulge of Violet's belly, and his band cawed like hoarse ravens. He took a bradawl from his leather shoulder-belt, stepping closer until his chest was almost on the tip of my sword. I held my breath, feeling the ancient strength of the well-stones at my back. Let him come, I thought.

"Renounce and quit!" bellowed a voice from behind the crowd. "I command you to stand away!"

Peter Spinks stood upon a preaching-block not ten paces off, his head cased in a steel helmet that hid his face's wrinkles and drinking-veins. He wore a shining officer's gorget, an empty scabbard hanging from each baldrick, and his boots were new, folded back at their tops like a cavalry commander's. His two swords were drawn.

"*Va-t'en, vieillard,*" growled Bouleau, pushing his way towards my father. Begone, old man.

"Your guildmaster swore you to come here in peace," said Peter calmly, stepping down from his block. He brought down his second sword, so that both blades faced the slippery ground, and flexed his wrists.

Bouleau nodded his head backwards towards Violet.

"Your son has brought a Catholic whore to this place," he cried out, and his men echoed the word "whore", though they were less brave now.

"And if guild law is not enough for you," continued my father, "then martial law must convince."

He set himself for battle. One foot behind him, sideways for strength, one before. The swords spread like gull's wings. Bouleau took out his own blade, but hesitated.

"God save King William!" I called out into the silence.

"God save King William!" replied a few of the mob, their faces puzzled. Peter took a small step towards the saddler, who in his turn stepped back, bumping against the bush-headed villain.

Voices came from the east and south sides of the green, as bands of guild men marched in: Middlem and the English weavers; a scowling Cassie Barcus and her dock-men. The moment for fighting had passed, and Bouleau put away his blade again, still staring hotly at my father. I made a sign to Peter, and took Violet away from the crowd.

He met us at the mouth of the alley that led to the House of Three Mysteries. Both of us still had swords drawn.

"Who is this girl?" he demanded.

"I am Violet Fintry, seamstress, though my birthname is Catherine," she said boldly. Peter jerked his head back at the sound of the Catholic name.

"Is that your child in her belly?"

"It is not," she replied, standing between us so that he had to look her in the eye.

"Then you must begone, and pray to God for your life," said Peter. "Calumny cannot keep a papist safe, you have seen it, and we have little time to carry out our mission today."

"I will not –" I began, but there was an uproar around the well. Cassie Barcus, clad in a dock-man's jerkin, was making a speech that the other guilds were crying out against. There were scuffles in the crowd as blows were thrown, and Peter left us without a word, limping towards the dock-mistress.

The sound of clashing steel echoed down the winding alley.

"Van Stijn!" I burst out. I had no choice but to pull Violet after me as I ran round the corner. At the end of the lane was the coal-door leading to the House of Three Mysteries. The sounds of swordfighting filled the air, but the alley was empty except for a man lying face down on the roadway.

I knelt at his side. It was Ty, his cheek gashed and swollen, his arm lying limply over Garric's nail-studded cudgel.

CHAPTER THIRTY-NINE

Bear Wharf

In which the trap is sprung

Ty groaned as I shook his shoulder.

"What do you do here?" I hissed in Ty's ear. "Why are you not in the College?"

"Cal?" He winced, opening his bruised eye.

"Where is van Stijn?"

"I went ahead of him… My father's task… De Corvis…"

"Violet, you must take him inside!" I told her, putting my hands under Ty's arms and dragging him towards the House's secret door. As we crossed the alley, I looked into the low passageway. Baines, his back to us, fought at close quarters with Martin van Stijn, driving him back towards the square. And there, on the cobbles between me and the quartermaster, lay the travelling-bag, papers spilling palely out of its sullen mouth.

Ty was able to stand, his arm around Violet's shoulders. "Go inside!" I ordered, and waited for them to stumble down the stairs to the chambers below.

I ran across to the passageway. Crouching so that van Stijn could not see me past Baines' bulk, I picked up the bag and crawled back to the alley. Behind me, the quartermaster cried out as the Dutchman drew blood.

I opened the bag fully, speaking the words aloud as I read each paper. At first I made the shapes in my mouth, but then the words began to pour freely from me.

"P… ar… don… Roy… al…"

I put the pardon on the ground. I would not let it out of my sight.

"Li… cen… ce Royal, Granted this day…"

These I folded up and tucked in the pocket inside my coat. Then I ripped open the bag's lining and took out the first bar of gold, laying it on my royal pardon. Nine were needed for the guilds; one had been for Garric, but he was gone. It was mine.

"Citizen!" shouted van Stijn. Baines was backing away down the passageway towards me. I called out to the Dutchman not to follow, but van Stijn had seen me take his gold, and he fell upon the quartermaster, drawing a dagger as well as his sword.

Baines pretended to slip and fall upon one knee. Van Stijn leaned towards him to cut his throat, but his elbow was hampered by the narrow passage and, swift as a stoat, Baines rose and buried his sword in van Stijn's gut.

The Yorkshireman pulled his sword free, spraying the Dutchman's blood all over the passage. He whirled towards me, roaring a curse as he saw me handling the gold. I rose, sword in hand.

I backed away from Baines's stained blade, and stepped aside from the travelling-bag so that he could attack me without thinking. I had no chance in a fair fight, but I had not forgotten how Robbie Cartwright had felled Anthony Anthony, spinning beneath the strike.

He rushed at me, bubbles of spit at the corners of his mouth, his left sleeve slashed and bloody.

I ducked and twisted under his rising sword, turning fully round, and then I thrust at his wounded thigh, hoping to fell him before he could strike.

But he was no longer there. While I crouched, he had leapt fully over me, and now he held his sword across my neck like a dagger, breaking the skin.

"Drop the blade, ferret."

Clang.

"Clever swordplay for a country lad."

"Peter!" I shouted. A weak echo mocked me.

"Calumny Spinks," grated Baines, "shall not die until *I* say when he is to die. Why should I kill your pension of eighty pounds a year? No, lad, you are to come with me now, and there will be no reckoning until later."

"Release the boy," said Peter, who had come silently up the alley.

"Now then," said Alcott Baines, stilling himself. He angled his sword better against my neck, so that Peter could not have struck him without injuring me.

Peter drew his swords, leaning his head to one side, then the other, and the crack of his old bones was like a pistol-shot in the air.

"D'you have my eighty sovereigns?" asked Baines, cheerily.

"I know you," said my father slowly.

"Alcott Baines at your service," replied the other.

"Porter is your name," Peter went on grimly, circling towards us. Baines edged away towards the travelling-bag.

"I remember you now. Isaac's boy. A murderous little villain you were, and I see that you are little changed."

The quartermaster bent his knees and tried to pick up the travelling-bag, but his injured left arm could not hold its weight. Peter slashed at Baines' hands to make him draw back, then pushed the tip of his sword into the bag's handles and dragged it towards him.

Snarling, Baines leaned over me again, his sword-tip cutting into the soft skin of my chin. He took out the royal pardon and the gold bar, dropping the ingot into his pocket. Then, keeping me always between him and my father's blades, he lifted up the parchment and read it.

When he saw that it was our pardon, freeing us from his blackmail, he put one side of the paper in his mouth and ripped it from side to side. Dropped the pieces on the ground and trod them into the dirt.

"So much for thy royal pardon, Peter Cole."

Peter snarled and lunged at Baines' face, but the big man ducked away, jerking my head so that his blade cut my chin. Warm blood trickled down my neck.

There was a roar from the Clerkenwell. Cassie Barcus yelled wordlessly, and Peter froze in his tracks.

"The dock-men will release the blockade..." he muttered, eyes wild in their sockets.

"You must take the gold, Peter!" I urged him. The quartermaster turned this way and that, keeping my body between my father and him.

"No!" shouted Peter, slashing his sword through the air, unable to attack Baines.

"Take it, Peter Cole," taunted Baines. "I will have my share later, for the rope still dangles above you and your spawn."

He tugged me into the passageway.

"Go," I said. "Baines is a dead man."

Peter waited for a moment longer, leaning towards me, but he knew what he must do. If the dock-guild was not paid, London would burn. He took up the travelling-bag, leaning heavily to one side as he limped away down the alley towards the Clerkenwell.

Baines pulled me backwards through the passage, treading carelessly on van Stijn's body. The Dutchman's lifeless eyes stared dimly up at me. Baines' sword at my back, we marched across the empty square and down to the Fleet wharves, where the dwarfish soldier was waiting, tight-faced, at the oars of a small boat. Baines thrust me into the prow, keeping his sword-tip towards me as he settled heavily in the craft's bowels.

The dwarf rowed strongly down the river, passing the last straggling families poling their way to the Tower.

Inside my coat were Mister de Corvis' coffee licences, signed by the new King William. I knew I had to keep them secret from Baines, or he would rip them up as he had ripped up my pardon. With van Stijn dead, there was no proof they had ever been signed. I sat stiff-backed, as well I might with a bloodied sword pricking my spine, but it was to keep the papers from rustling. The villain spoke not a word, though he puffed with pain. I prayed I might use that arm-wound against him yet.

The sun scorched the soft skin of my cheeks, and briny sweat smeared my eyes. Bear Wharf rose ahead of us, deadly silent even though it was crowded with people. All backs were turned to us as the mob stared at a barge that was docked on the Thames side.

The dwarf swung the boat around, tied its rope to a ladder and climbed up. Baines poked me up after him and came up last. He climbed with his right hand only, one rung at a time.

"Take him," growled Baines as I reached the top, and the dwarf hauled me over, pinning my hands behind me. The crowd murmured and jostled, as if they waited for something to happen.

Baines thrust his sword up under my chin again, wrapped his cloak around me to hide the blade, and pushed into the crowd. The dwarf followed, a few paces behind.

"Bear Wharf at noon," he whispered. A faint roaring filled my head. "Left your contract-paper at Firth's chapel, you did. Bear Wharf at noon today. Montalbion was pleased indeed to learn it."

"But why –" I gasped, stumbling forward through the crowd with each thrust of Baines' elbow.

"Beat my Anthony, de Corvis did," said Baines, viciously. "Gave you gold when your father should have despaired. And now he will pay for it."

We forced our way to the front of the crowd, gathered in a ring around the boarding-plank of a barge that bore Montalbion's crest on its prow. In the crowd I saw Mistress Hollow, her hands gloved, surrounded by coffee-men. Behind them were piled Mister de Corvis' coffee sacks, though there was no sign of Frazier.

On the barge's deck stood Lord Montalbion in a riding coat of soft leather, his general's silver star on a chain around his neck. His wig was black, long, curled, and he looked no more than five and thirty years old as he stood there with his legs apart.

Next to Montalbion stood Mister de Corvis, bare-headed, his hands clasped before him, glancing around the crowd as if he prepared to speak to us all. Emilia was at his shoulder, her teeth pulling at her lower lip. Behind them stood the captains Campbell and Marks, attended by two dozen soldiers in ranks before a big lumpish shape covered in a sail. At either end of the ship, sailors stood to attention at the side-rail. It was as quiet as the moment after they broke my mother's neck. The silence of the condemned.

Montalbion saw the shuffling in the crowd, and glared angrily. Baines, still holding his sword to my neck so that the others could not see, made a little slash in the air with his free hand. He gave his master a little grin, though he groaned under his breath with the pain his arm caused him. Montalbion did not smile back, but he seemed to grow taller as he stepped forward to speak.

"God save the Queen!" he cried.

A few brave souls mumbled back to him, tripping over the name of queen.

"I am Vincent de la Haye, Earl Montalbion, natural son of King Charles the Second, cousin to our new queen, and by Her Majesty's appointment the Governor of the Company of the Caribbean. I speak to you, all loyal servants of the Crown. The so-called king and traitor James has fled London to join his allies in France. Death to the French traitor!"

"Death to the French traitor!" called the soldiers at the back of the crowd, and many others joined in for fear of the guns at their backs. The coffee merchants kept their mouths shut, perhaps wondering if Lord Montalbion was the man who had bullied them into signing the new contracts.

"In the name of the Crown, and of Parliament, the peers have declared a royal republic. We are to be ruled by Mary Stuart, niece to the glorious King Charles the Second. God save the Queen!"

"God save the Queen!" chanted the crowd. Baines grunted as he gripped my arm with his weakened hand, and something bumped against my elbow through the sleeve of his cloak. The sword's tip still pressed against the heartbeat in my neck.

"Queen Mary has required Parliament to recognise her husband and cousin, William of Stuart and Orange. God save King William!"

"God save the King!"

"For too long, the traitor James has ignored the laws of our kingdom, commanded the armies without recourse to Parliament, and made secret treaties with France. No man is above the law!"

The crowd cheered, the coffee-men with them.

"But laws have already been broken in our new kingdom," said Montalbion in a low voice.

"Ohhhhh," moaned the mob. By God, but he could tell a tale well.

"Spices are being smuggled into England without a royal licence. The Royal Excise cheated, our new king betrayed before he has even worn a crown!"

All confusion was now forgotten. The crowd gasped and writhed, making common cause with each other.

"And others will have to pay more to the Excise instead. You, perhaps!"

"No!" cried the crowd. "No!"

I was struck dumb by Montalbion's plan. He had used Mister de Corvis, would take his fortune and his life. Crimson-eyed, Emilia knew full well what was taking shape here. Behind her stood the two Frenchmen, Coste and Collignon – men who'd sought first to trade with Firth, and now with Montalbion.

Mister de Corvis had seen me next to Baines, and was gazing at me. I moved my lips to tell him silently, "I have the licences, I have the licences," but he shook his head and squinted at the sun.

And then I saw that his hands were bound. His fingers twisted and turned making the rough rope rub against the old purple slave-scars; the freed slave boy who had thought he would never wear cuffs again.

Montalbion made a little flick of his fingers, and Captain Marks pulled the sailcloth off the looming frame behind him. It was a gallows, with the noose already strung above a stool. A masked hangman stood next to it.

"This man," roared Montalbion, pointing his ringed forefinger at Mister de Corvis, "is the smuggling traitor. He has brought many honest merchants here today to sell them his wares, but I declare all of them innocent of wrongdoing!"

The coffee-men smiled in their relief and gave a little cheer, for they must have feared punishment themselves.

Montalbion raised his hands for silence. "The penalty for treason is death, and confiscation of all goods," he declared.

The villain would seize Mister de Corvis' coffee, and all the thousands it would bring him.

"What have you to say before you hang, traitor?"

He smiled courteously at Mister de Corvis, as though they conversed in his Dover Street parlour. Mister de Corvis held his hands out to the crowd, and spoke quietly.

"Do you cut my rope, my lord. I will not flee, but I would not die so."

Montalbion did not answer Mister de Corvis. Instead, he lifted an eyebrow to raise a laugh from the crowd. Baines snorted beside me, his rough nostrils flaring. The dwarf peered around him at the scene.

"I have spices to sell, my lord, it is true. But they are under licence. My licences were signed by King William two days ago, and have been *stolen* by a villain here present. I will not name him."

The crowd jeered and mocked him. I opened my mouth to protest, to shout that I held those licences myself, but Baines poked me in the side with his free hand.

"Speak not, or your father dies with you," he murmured. I knew it was true, and I could not trade Peter's life for my master's.

Mister de Corvis waited for the crowd to grow silent before speaking again.

"Since I see I am to die no matter what the law, and whoever the king is, let me make full confession."

Montalbion made a bored face while Emilia stared at her father in amazement. Baines grunted in surprise, and the weight inside his sleeve struck my hip again. I slowly reached around until I could feel its hard outline. He carried a little dagger, just as Robbie had. This time I will kill him, I swore to myself.

"It is true I have offended our new king, for he is the great-nephew of King Charles the First. My dead father fought King Charles, and he has already been condemned out of court, and for all time, for what is called a treason, but what I consider to have been a God-sent duty."

"The Christ-damned fool," muttered Baines. I slipped my fingertips inside his cuff, trying to tease out the blade.

Mister de Corvis spoke on. "My own father executed old King Charles. Praise God, for no man may be close to heaven as long as another man sits on an earthly throne. God save the republic!"

"No!" cried Baines, terrified of losing his hold over me. "I have the traitor here –"

He gasped in pain as I seized his wounded arm with my left hand, plucking the knife from his sleeve with my right. Pulling him towards me, I twisted my neck away from the sword-tip and plunged his own dagger under his ribs.

"That's my debt settled, Alcott Baines," I whispered. His eyes screwed up in his sockets as he collapsed on himself, pulling the dagger away from me. He fell head first onto the hard timbers of the wharf, his cloak covering his scarlet uniform.

My bare forearm was drenched with blood, and I knelt quickly at Baines' side to wipe the gore onto his cloak, holding my other hand to his mouth to be sure he did not breathe. He was still.

"Murder!" I yelled, pointing at the dwarf-soldier. "Stand back!"

The crowd turned on the dwarf, who turned pale and ran for his boat. Half a dozen men gave chase, and in the confusion I pulled out the licences and waved them in the air. "Here are Mister de Corvis' licences! Here is the law of King William! Here I give you your lie, Lord Montalbion!"

Montalbion's dead eyes burned with the fires of hell, his nostrils flaring as wide as a rutting stallion's.

"Take that criminal under arms!" he cried out, and half a dozen soldiers moved to capture me.

"In the name of the Crown, desist!" I cried out in mimicry of the murdered Duke of Firth. The soldiers stopped dead in their tracks, held for a breath by their dead commander's order. "I have seen your justice, thief. Let you come down here to read the law!"

That was enough to save me. Struck by the soldiers' reluctance, the crowd drew close about me. A Scots captain ran down the boarding-plank and took the papers. He read the licences and nodded to Montalbion.

I snatched them back, turned and waved them at the crowd.

"It is the law! It is the law! Let him go!"

"Let him go," they called out, sheeplike.

Montalbion held up his hands, but the crowd roared on. A flick of his gloved hand, and Captain Marks fired his pistol in the air. Silence fell again.

"It is the law," he said, "and the holder of those licences may sell coffee to the merchants here."

The crowd shuffled, confused. The soldiers that had held them at bay crept backwards towards the barge. I held my breath and waited for more treachery.

"But treason is treason," whispered Montalbion hoarsely, pointing again at Mister de Corvis. "This man has confessed his father's regicide. He must die, and all his property is forfeit, and all his male heirs must die too."

"He did not kill the king," I screamed, starting towards the barge. "It was my father, it was *my* father!"

The captain's strong hands seized me.

"Montalbion killed the Duke of Firth," I whispered to the officer as I freed myself from his grip. I ran forward again, but stopped when I saw Mister de Corvis smiling at me and at Emilia. He spoke over the babbling crowd.

"It is my fate to die today," he said. "This boy thinks to offer his life, and even his father's life, for mine. But his duty is to protect my daughter, and not me, as he well knows."

He stepped up onto the gallows. Touching the hangman on the arm, as if to say, *Wait a moment*, he looked down at Montalbion with contempt in his face.

"You say no man is above the law, but do not mean it for yourself, nor for the kings you serve and betray. Creatures like you will always seek to enslave free people, and free thought, but you will never prevail."

He held his scarred wrists high out of his sleeves so the crowd could see them plainly.

"I have worn chains in my life," he called out, silencing the mob. Emilia cried silently.

"I tell you that you wear chains too!" Mister de Corvis cried. "As long as you follow men like Montalbion, this ambitious bastard-son of a dead tyrant, they will cuff men like us. But do not join them in eternal damnation! May you all be free!

"And may you be free," he said quietly to Emilia. "Since you are not my son, you are not condemned with me, and you shall have the licences and the plantations and all. And never bend your knee to a devil like this one."

Montalbion's face was scarlet with rage, but he dared not move for fear of the crowd, who had begun to jeer at him. The hangman took my master by the elbow and made him stand on the stool. Mister de Corvis took the noose and placed it over his own head.

"This girl is not married, Benjamin?" asked Montalbion viciously.

"I am not, thank God," answered Emilia boldly. Montalbion looked to Mister de Corvis, who nodded proudly.

"Then she is her father's property, is she not?"

Mister de Corvis gave Emilia a lightning-struck look.

"She is forfeit to the Crown, Benjamin de Corvis!" cried Montalbion. "And on this ship, by all the laws of man and God, *I* am the Crown! And your life is mine to take."

He flicked his hand one last time. The hangman kicked away the stool, and Mister de Corvis fell, the rope tightening around his neck. His face darkened, and his legs flailed back and forth, but his eyes were still as they watched me. Emilia's knees buckled, and she put her hands over her eyes.

I watched in horror as my master slowly choked.

"Pull his legs! For shame, end it!" cried a voice from the crowd.

A man staggered out from the piles of coffee-sacks at the wharf's edge. It was John Frazier, his wiry grey hair plastered to his head, blood dripping from a wire that was bound round his neck, half-strangling him. No man stood in his way as he limped heavily towards the ship.

Still Mister de Corvis struggled for life, his eyes half-closed now, his guts emptying themselves until his silk stockings were streaked with mess. Frazier himself was half-dead as he struggled up the gangplank, staring at my master.

Montalbion stepped forward to block John Frazier's way. Moving more quickly than I would have credited, he unsheathed his sword and slashed across Frazier's throat. For a breath, there was only the spray of blood in the air, falling towards the soiled waters, and then the weary square head fell forwards.

Mister de Corvis made a choking cry as the older man's body collapsed. It tumbled backwards down the gang-plank, landing in a pitiful heap on the wharf.

"Shame!" cried out Mistress Hollow. "Shame!" called another voice, and soon the whole wharf was booing and jeering at Montalbion. The soldiers stepped over Frazier's body and back up the gangplank as the crowd closed in.

Marks gave the order to lift the gangplank, and in a breath the sailors were pushing the barge away from the wharf. Long oars thrust out from the square locks and dipped gracefully into the oily waters of the Thames. Montalbion seized Emilia by the arm and dragged her away from the scaffold. All the while, she stared at me wildly over his shoulder.

The barge turned away from the wharf, but still I could see the life slipping from Mister de Corvis' face, swollen like an old bruise that will not heal. The noose that had waited so long for me had closed around another's neck.

CHAPTER FORTY

The Reckoning

In which Calumny must make a choice

The barge was borne away from the shore by the soiled flood of the Fleet, the oar-beat like a lament for the man whose body hung twisting in the breeze.

People stepped between me and the wharf's edge, fingering their orange armbands as they leaned out to watch the melancholy corpse all the way to the Tower.

"Cal," said Lottie Hollow urgently, pointing at Baines' carcass. His dagger was buried under his ribs, the crimson of his uniform stained sunset-red.

"What devilry was that?" demanded Mistress Hollow, but I did not answer her as I made for the quartermaster's body. I knew what he carried in his pocket, and it was mine. I knelt at my enemy's side and searched for the hard tablet of stolen gold. To distract the coffee-men, I put my hand on Baines' pale face and opened his clenched eyelids. His eyes were midnight wells, all colour banished by the spreading of their dark hearts.

"No need for that, master," protested one of the men, gently taking my hand away. "That one has gone to Judgement."

God will not judge him, I thought. *I* have judged him.

Faint cheers floated on the windless air, coming from the docks in the east. The orange-banded crowd began to turn and leave the wharf, blind to the murderer's carcass. Mistress Hollow clamped her lumpy hand on my shoulder.

"Whose coffee is that, Master Spinks? Are those licences lawful, or have you put us all in such danger without cause?"

My fingertips touched the edges of the gold bar through Baines' cloak. I pressed them into the carved shape of the Dutch lion.

The other coffee-men had surrounded us, closing out the dregs of the crowd. Chatter turned into protest as their fear of Montalbion drained away. This could go ill, I thought.

"I am *Mister* Calumny Spinks," I said loudly, and rose to my feet, taking the licences out of my waistcoat for all to see. "And these are royal licences for coffee-trade, signed by our new King William!"

"In whose name?" demanded Mistress Hollow. I gave her the papers.

"But…" she said, frowning, and then fell silent as she rustled through the licences. Lottie looked at me like a thrush foraging on frosty soil.

"What is it, mistress?" mumbled a coffee-man.

"Full half of these are in your name, Mister Spinks, and the rest are written out to a Master John Frazier. Who then was that gentleman they hanged?"

"Mister Benjamin de Corvis," I said, my tongue swelling in its seat. He had known that he would die and that his enemies would cheat his daughter of her inheritance. He chose this way so that Peter and I would hold the licences in trust for Emilia; so now I was in his debt again.

"Leave me be a while," I whispered to Lottie, who waited close by, her arms folded. She bustled her mother and the other merchants towards the coffee sacks.

Swiftly, I laid my hand on the dagger handle, twisting and tugging the blade back out. The Yorkshireman's knotted heart had folded itself around the steel, but I prevailed. Not pausing to wipe the blade, I cut away at his cloak until I could pull out the ingot and slip it into my boot. Glancing over my shoulder, I saw alarm on the faces of the coffee-men gathered around the sacks. I laid the dagger on the dead man's breast and went to them, the gold pressing its cold cheek against my skin like a witch-bride.

I pushed my way through the little crowd behind the sacks until I had reached Mistress Hollow, standing back from the horror that lay at the wharf's edge.

John Frazier was curled on his side, his wrinkled eyes closed as gently as a sleeping infant's. Further on, wedged up against the leaning wall of sacks, was the corpse of Dock-master Kit Barcus, pinioned to the coffee beans by a sword that had driven clean through his shoulder. His grappling hook lay at his feet, and his sleeveless leather jerkin was shredded by sword-strokes.

Behind him, her back to us as she looked out over the railings, was Cassie Barcus. The river beyond was as bleak as midwinter cornfields.

"Mistress –" I began.

She turned around, her square jaw twisted with rage, her fists before her like a fighter's. I took the coffee licences from

Mistress Hollow and held them out towards the dock-mistress. She gritted her teeth as she stepped past her brother's body, and then her false husband's, staring at me unblinking.

Cassie Barcus read the papers.

"The leper speaks for you all?" she demanded.

"She does," I answered for Mistress Hollow. "Three pounds twelve shillings the sack is the price agreed. But let us not trade here."

Cassie nodded, keeping her eyes off the two dead men as she handed me back the licences in the name of Mister Spinks. Men cleared a path for her.

"Bring paper, quill and ink," Mistress Hollow told her daughter under her breath as she followed the dock-mistress.

I held on to Lottie's arm to stop her following straight away. "Tell your mother to take my coin for me. I will come for a reckoning by and by."

She looked down at her shawl, where my hand had left a bloody pattern on the wool.

"Who was that man?" she asked, touching my chin where his sword-point had broken the skin.

"He took everything from me," I said, and as I spoke the truth a terrible hollowness filled me. Baines had taken my mother and Garric, but I had given him Martin van Stijn and Mister de Corvis, and Emilia's freedom too. It was the old Calumny Spinks who lay there, pierced to the heart, damned and unmourned.

Lottie put her arms around my neck and hugged me close. "Until we meet again," she whispered.

She broke away and joined her mother, taking out writing tools. The coffee-men watched the leper and the dock-mistress writing their contract. Cassie Barcus cut a hole in one of the coffee sacks and passed a handful of the roasted beans around for each of the merchants to sniff at.

Cheers rang out again, this time much closer. A long procession was marching across the Clerkenwell Bridge, banners flying.

I passed Baines' body, my eyes on the throng. Three people were coming slowly down Bear Street. A woman, one hand on her womb and the other around a slender fellow, his raven head bound with a strip of cloth. An old man walked before them, a steel casque under one arm, his long white hair brushing against an ancient leather uniform.

I waited for them to come, pressing my stained hand to my empty belly. Not the faintest wraith of joy survived in its dry depths.

Once all had been seen, and said; after Violet had wept over Baines' body, for he had been her father as much as any man; after Ty had shown me the bruise that covered half his face; after Peter had taken Baines' sword and flung it in the Fleet, and Mistress Hollow had concluded her commerce; after the dock-men had come and taken Kit Barcus' and Frazier's bodies away for consecration; once it was all done, Cassie Barcus led us back to the house on Bear Wharf, into the cheerless kitchen, where no fire had been laid, where no soup had been simmering. The sun glinted coldly on the dust and cobwebs that had reclaimed the house.

"But why did he have Calumny's name put on the licences?" demanded Peter, with steel in his voice, as Cassie poured herself a pewter mug of brandy. He nodded at her, as if she should draw him one too, but she shoved the flask and another mug towards him.

"It is not Calumny's name," said Ty, poring over the papers. "It says, Mister Peter Spinks of Silk Street. Mister de Corvis has put *your* name upon these deeds."

"What was I to that man, that he should do that?"

Peter drained his mug angrily. He felt the clutch of this new debt, as I did.

Running my fingers over the coarse grain of the table, I told them about Mister de Corvis, and Alcott Baines, and Montalbion's trap. Violet passed her hand around my waist, pressing her fingers into my side.

"But how did Montalbion know of Bear Wharf?" Ty pressed me, knitting his bruised brows together. I kissed Violet on the side of her head to stop from looking at him, feeling the colour rise to my cheeks. Because I dropped a contract-paper in Firth's chapel, I wanted to cry out. Because I made a bargain with Baines to steal the gold; because I risked everything for myself and this girl here.

"Bastard sent spies into near every coffeehouse in London," said Cassie Barcus violently, slamming down her mug. "Calumny here told the master – told de Corvis of it."

She stood up, bulky in her dock-man's jerkin, and fiddled at her waist. She had tied Kit Barcus' hook there, and now she laid it on the table, spikes uppermost.

"Earl or no earl, he shall die," she said icily.

"But this Emilia, must she marry him now?" asked Violet, and I shivered with shame to hear her say the other girl's name.

"He cannot force her so," said Peter. "That is the law. And when she is free, I will give her half my licences."

Even dead, Mister de Corvis had us at his beck. I will give you my life, Calumny Spinks, I heard him say, and you shall see my daughter safe. Here is the contract-paper. Make your mark.

Cassie shrugged. "John Frazier's were half for me, and now they are all mine, since I was his wife. And I am owed blood money for my brother. No more than one-quarter to the girl, if she lives."

There was a long silence. I remembered the girl in Montalbion's red room, wounded and terrified, and I took a sip from my father's second mugful of brandy.

"What does it mean, that Montalbion is Governor of the Caribbean Company?" I asked.

"It means that he is not subject to the laws of England once he has sailed for the West Indies," said Ty slowly. "A governor is his own king, plenipotentiary on his ship and in his colony. He may conduct a wedding, he may make laws, he may kill a man and not be punished."

Cassie rested her hand on the spikes of her dead brother's grappling hook. "Then let us raise the guilds and take him from the Tower!"

I shook my head. "When they have taken gold and sworn to hold the peace for the new king? It cannot be."

Peter met my eye, tapped the table in agreement. The dock-mistress took up the hook again.

"I have need of only one guild," she said in a voice of steel, walking towards the door. "Let you look to the others."

"Garric Pettit's debt –" I said quickly, looking at Ty.

Cassie paused at the door.

"Settled," she said.

"And his gold? For guarding the Dutchman, which I discharged for him?" asked Ty.

"I know nothing of that," she snapped, leaving without another look.

"Baines took it," I said. "He gave it to another soldier to keep…"

The lie scratched and tore at my lips; but I needed that gold, or so I thought. Ty shook his head, but did not ask me more.

"Will the whole regiment sail for the Indies?" asked Violet. Ty bit his lip and looked at her warmly, but did not answer. She thinks of Robbie and her mother, not me, I thought viciously. Or of whoever is the father of that bastard she carries there, nestled safely under Mister de Corvis' table. As if hearing my thoughts, she squeezed me closer and kissed my cheek.

Peter's breath rasped into his raised mug, though he did not sip, and his shoulders lifted as he tried to keep the bitter word inside. *Catholic*. It writhed in the air between our eyes, reaching a tortured hand out towards Violet's bare head.

"I will go back, then," she said. "You cannot keep me in your home, Cal. I have seen your guild brothers. Good men or no, they will not bear the sight of me and my baby. So I will go."

"Did my son make you a promise?" my father asked, holding up his hand.

"I did," I said clearly, though I had not.

"Then it is my word too. You shall stay if you choose. That child shall not be raised by soldiers, but by right-thinking men and women."

I met Peter's eyes, but there was too much to say between us. Too much that I could not tell him, besides. The precious metal pressed against my calf, mockingly calling me Mister. Next to me, Violet arched her back, lifting the weight of her swollen belly, and a sudden sickness twirled in my guts. I knew I could not take her from her own mother now. She was not for the Indies.

"Father, Baines took your pistol from me two nights since," I said to him. "I must see if it is still about him, before the scavengers come."

"I will come," said Ty, though his face was pale in the lowering light, and he had to hold himself against the table as he stood.

"Let him be," my father said, rising to his feet. "I doubt the mob will have left my old pistol alone so long, but let Calumny search if he wills. It was worth a deal of coin when I was young. Now we must meet the Dutch general at the House, Ty. We must call all the guilds together, the dock-men especially."

I turned to Violet and kissed her quick on the lips, but not so long that she could taste my plan.

I slipped away down the passage and out into the dusk. The November breeze reached into my bones, awakening the cold ache of the Fleet-waters, making me cough wretchedly as I walked alone down Bear Street.

The sun was already below the rooftops. I stopped every few paces to stare at the rose-pink light sliding over the unquiet Thames, breathing in the foul rot of the Fleet at my flank. Still the cheers came faintly over the rooftops and echoed round the empty street.

Baines' carcass lay abandoned in the middle of the wharf. His sword, dagger and boots had already been stolen, and his hairy feet looked pitiful against the rutted time-worn planking, the toenails black and splintered from foot-rot.

"I hope you have that *deus me exculpit*," I whispered as I dragged him slowly across the boards, his cloak tearing. He was heavy, but the planks were slippery-smooth, and I managed to push him off the wharf and into the foulness of the darkening Fleet. Face down, he floated swiftly out into the Thames, his arms and legs bobbing up and down as it whisked him away towards the London Bridge, a scrap of jet-black cloth lost in time.

Barges processed slowly upstream, their decks crowded with soldiers in sky-blue uniforms, their triumphant faces glowing in the setting sun. The Dutch army was being carried into the heart of London by the lightermen, who sang and cheered as they rowed their new masters.

The tide was low, and I climbed carefully down to the shingle below Bear Wharf, my bruised breast pulsing and weeping as I took each new rung in my hands. Shivers took hold of me when I reached the shifting shore below, dragging up cough after cough as I stumbled westwards along the shore.

The sun melted and spread behind the city, casting flickering shadows across the wharves and wherries. I could not walk fast. It was near dark by the time I passed Whitehall Palace, its courtyards echoing with shouts and cheers as the Hollanders took possession of their prize. Still the boats came from downstream: I saw Peter and Ty with the College's Provost in a barge crowded with Dutch generals. A nobleman greeted them at the Whitehall Wharf. I knew full well what they planned, those three; and there was no part for me to play.

There was no place for me in that gathering. I stumbled on, past all the empty wharves and loading-engines, watching my father. Cheers still burst out here and there, the wharfside taverns bulging with drinkers toasting the new king.

Peter and Abigail, they would have money to spare now. And Violet – I had kept my word to her, though any pride I felt at it was whelmed by regret.

I took the Dutch gold out of my boot. With it in my hands, I was Mister Calumny Spinks at last. For a sweet moment, I believed that nothing kept me in London now: I could take ship for the Indies and leave my griefs behind.

A wild cheer burst out from the Whitehall gathering, as raw and violent as the Salstead mob when they had murdered my mother. And then I knew I could not leave Violet alone in the city. I was land-bound by a stubborn old man, burdened with a Catholic girl bearing a bastard. I could not go.

I held the gold ingot up to the heavens. Moonlight trickled down the carved furrows, veiling its precious skin with turquoise silk.

Calumny's English

Broadside	Newspaper or poster printed on a large sheet of paper
Brussen	Smart alec; Yorkshire dialect
Cocky	Flashy young gentleman
Claw-finger	Arthritis
Dissenter	Nonconformist Protestant
Draper	Cloth merchant
Fire-chest	Lung cancer
Forengie	Foreign, stranger
Gongfarmer	Collector of excrement
Groat	Fourpence piece
Kersey	Coarse cloth from Suffolk
Mercer	Merchant dealing in textiles
Patati patata	French phrase meaning "blah, blah"
Pobjoy	A surname, probably originating from "King of the Popinjay," a medieval archery prize; Calumny appears to consider it an insult

Pokey-roll	Sex
Popish, papist	Catholic
Portugee	Portuguese
Potrillo	Fool, poltroon
Puritan	Protestant reformers opposed to the Church of England
Right-thinking	Dissenter
Romish	Catholic
Stamboul	Istanbul (Constantinople)
Twitchell	Narrow lane
VOC	Dutch East India Company
Waistcoat	Most seventeenth-century waistcoats had full sleeves and cuffs
Widder-leg	Left or weaker leg
Widdershins	Anti-clockwise

Calumny's Time

Calumny's story is sometimes at odds with the commonly received history and geography of seventeenth-century England.

The identities of Charles I's executioner and his assistant are unknown. Richard Brandon, the official headsman, publicly refused to wield the axe, but is still under suspicion. William Hulet was tried and acquitted for the crime in 1660, and an Irishman named William Gunning has also been named.

There is nothing on the statute books to suggest that the executioner's male heirs would also have been tried for treason, and it is noteworthy that Cromwell's own son Richard was permitted to live out his life peacefully after the Restoration. However, the threat to Calumny was real enough for Peter to hide in Salstead for more than twenty years, so we must give it some credence.

Calumny is contemptuous of his father's decision to join Cowans' congregation in Salstead, but life was made very difficult for Nonconformist believers after the Restoration, especially by the Act of Uniformity. They were excluded from public office, forbidden to worship in groups of more than five, and their ministers prohibited from coming within five miles of their former livings or of major towns (Cal exaggerates when he talks of ten miles). Many churches went through a similar cycle to Salstead's, with their Communion bars and icons taken down during the Civil War, and then put back after the Restoration.

The Declaration of Indulgence was a desperate move by James II, whose Catholicism alienated many of England's power brokers. It rescinded some of the measures against nonconformists, but was resisted by members of the established Church, who had only recently won ground with the Act of Uniformity. As in Salstead, many ministers refused to read the Declaration, making James II issue it twice.

Calumny's account of carpetbaggers arriving in Nonconformist villages is not backed up by the historical record, but there is no reason to doubt his account. Certainly, landlords were enclosing common land all over England by 1688, making it harder for smallholders to graze their livestock, and pushing many of them into the growing cities.

Huguenots had been coming to England since Edward VI's charter of 1547, although for the first half of the seventeenth century they had been protected by the Edict of Nantes, a French royal decree giving them many privileges, including freedom of worship. Since 1661, Louis XIV had gradually begun to chip away at their rights. He revoked the Edict of Nantes in 1685, unleashing repressive measures on the Huguenots including "Dragonnades" – billeting dragoons in Protestant households. By 1688, over 50,000 Huguenots had come to England, only to be accused of low morals, taking work from natives, poor hygiene, and worse diet. The Great Fire of London was blamed on Frenchmen and papists. An innocent Huguenot named Robert Hubert was forced to confess to starting it, then hanged.

It is strange that Mirella's flight from France in the early 1660s led to her brother's death, since there was no official policy of executing Huguenots or preventing them leaving the country until 1685. However, Louis had made a coronation vow to eradicate heresy, and it is entirely possible that customs officers were overzealous in carrying out his wishes.

Frenchmen were not the only foreigners to struggle. During the Civil War, an Irishman bearing arms in England could be summarily hanged.

Calumny's perception of social titles, with a rigid line between Master (for craftsmen and tradesmen) and Mister (for propertied gentlemen), is not commonly referred to in historical sources. The word "Mister" began as an accented version of "Master" in the sixteenth century, but both were abbreviated to "Mr", making it harder to tell if usage was as strict as he suggests. Cowans would have been called "Mister" as a rector, and it may be that Cal has simply extrapolated from his resentment. There certainly was a strict divide between gentlemen and their inferiors, although it had begun to erode by the time of the Glorious Revolution.

His perception of the guilds also seems rather eccentric. He is aware of their history – drapers and mercers did split from the original weavers' guild in the fourteenth century after Edward III allowed Flemish weavers into the country, and there were ongoing tensions between native and immigrant weavers. However, he seems unaware of the idea of a livery company, and the guild-rules he quotes are not part of any official record. Possibly his frequent mentions of guild law are an attempt to justify trespass in the king's woods, not to mention assault and arson in the Irish weavers' workshop.

There is no record of the House of Three Mysteries or College Secular near Clerkenwell, nor of any formal connections between the Guildhall, the merchant class and scientists.

The Glorious Revolution is strangely downplayed in English history, often being presented as a genteel evolution of toleration and democracy, but Calumny's experience of it only scratches the surface. A daughter leading an invasion against her own father; William of Orange seeking the English throne mainly so he could better defend himself against the French; messages passing in invisible ink between Dutch spies and English noblemen until the entire postal system was suspended to halt them; complex legal manoeuvres to justify the coup – the story is extraordinarily dramatic.

William's preparations for invasion, and his progress from the West Country towards London, were deliberately slowed down to give defectors time to leave James II's camp. The whole process took months, and there is no record of Dutch soldiers landing in London on a named day. Certainly, there were plans to re-establish a republic if William did not support the coup. Both the Dutch State and the English conspirators were greatly fearful of waiting longer, since James was consolidating his control over the army.

Charles II did close down London's coffeehouses for a few days in 1675–6, fearing the free exchange of reformist ideas, but he was forced to reopen them. Martin van Stijn was one of many who used coffeehouses for private mail.

It was a Dutch officer who first transplanted coffee trees to the West, having taken them from a Portuguese colony in Kerala in the late seventeenth century. However, there is no record of coffee trees being grown in the Caribbean before 1720, when cultivation began in Martinique and Jamaica.

London seems to buckle and twist in Calumny's memory. There was no Bear Street or Bear Wharf on the western banks of the Fleet, nor was there a Silk Street in Spitalfields. He speaks of the Hyde woods as if they came almost to the walls of Whitehall Palace, but contemporary maps show them to match Hyde Park's current position, without any barracks at their heart. The Tyburn's path is somewhat different to Cal's account of it, and it is highly unlikely that anyone could have sailed a wherry at high speed up it; on one occasion he sees the Tower of London from the other side of London Bridge, which would have been physically impossible, but we must forgive a young man his excesses at such a dangerous point in his life.

*

If anything, Cal's story underplays the challenges of being a woman. Wife sales were commonplace, and scolding was a regular hazard for any woman with an opinion, a vocation or a sexual appetite. Many women tried to join the army, and were turned away laughingly by recruiting sergeants who saw through their poor attempts at disguise. A few were successful, most notably Hannah Snell, who kept her sex a secret from her army comrades for three years in the mid-eighteenth century.

There seems to be no legal basis for Violet's unborn child belonging to the regiment, but it is consistent with the idea of a woman being a man's property.

Thank you

Calumny was born when I was on holiday in Cornwall with Rebecca. I "adapted" her idea for a futuristic story (in which coffee is the new heroin) when Cal popped up in my diary: redheaded and angry, falling through roof tiles into a secret stash. Even if it hadn't been her idea that inspired the story, I couldn't have started or finished it without her love, support, brilliant story-editing skills, wicked sense of humour, and creativity.

Cal has also had a small tribe of supporters from the beginning. I didn't realise just how big a commitment it is to read someone's first novel: how do you tell them what to do with it without bursting their bubble? I was very lucky to have so many honest but supportive readers:

Meg Davis, who first took on the story. Meg also introduced me to the wonderful Sally O-J, mentor, editor and forensically accurate fact-checker, who has been a huge champion of both mine and Calumny's for years.

My mum Anne, who shared her huge love of books with me, and proofread an entire manuscript of *The Bitter Trade*.

I think most men don't get fathers who try to understand their work, who'll risk saying the wrong things in order to say the right things, and I feel very privileged to have had that with my dad Chris.

Stuart Emmerton, creative entrepreneur and representative of the elusive Chester Cordite, who took on the unenviable task of commenting on a very early draft... and turned it into a new form of comedy.

Roland Bearne, who read the wild first draft with kindness and enthusiasm, and who has done an amazing 5D surround sound audiobook with Nick and Cristina at 5a Studios – check it out at thepigeonhole.com.

Lucy and Andrew Darwin for supportive reading, Anna South of TLC for wise words, Richard Sheehan for excellent proofreading, Keith Parker for taking it on holiday and finishing it when it was 250,000 words long.

Rebecca Swift of The Literary Consultancy has been amazing to work with. She has a compelling vision of where the new publishing is going, but is fiercely attached to literary values. Thank you Daniel Pembrey for very helpful insights into the life of an author in the age of e-publishing.

David Eldridge designed the original cover, and piersalexander.com was the work of Kristen Harrison and her Curved House team.

One of the best things about releasing a new edition is that you get to incorporate reader suggestions. A heartfelt thank you to Captain Lieutenant Stephen Ball and Master John Dacombe of Pickering's regiment (weaponry), Katie Kidd (continuity) and Helen Hollick (hanging) for their historical and literary input.

I've had a lot of encouragement and help from all kinds of people, and I'm very grateful. I would particularly like to thank my business partners Alex Williamson and Alex Johnson. Without their courage and skill, I could never have carved out the time to write this book.

Finally, I'm delighted that you're reading this wonderful Pigeonhole edition. I dreamed about serialising this story, and was blown away when the remarkable Anna Jean Hughes got involved. She and my dynamic agent Lucy Luck had some great edits, which I think have improved the story a lot.